Praise
An Indecent F

"Regency fans will thrill to this superbly sensual tale of an icy widow and two decadent rakes.... Balancing deliciously erotic encounters with compelling romantic tension and populating a convincing historical setting with a strong cast of well-developed characters, prolific romance author Wildes provides a spectacular and skillfully handled story that stands head and shoulders above the average historical romance."
—*Publishers Weekly* (starred review)

"Wickedly delicious and daring, Wildes's tale tantalizes with an erotic fantasy that is also a well-crafted Regency romance. She delivers a page-turner that captures the era, the mores, and the scandalous behavior that lurks beneath the surface."
—*Romantic Times* (4½ stars, top pick)

"A luxurious and sensual read. Both deliciously wicked and tenderly romantic.... I didn't want it to end!"
—*New York Times* bestselling author Celeste Bradley

"Emma Wildes has thoroughly enchanted e-book readers with her emotionally charged story lines.... [A] gem of an author ... Ms. Wildes tells this story with plenty of compassion, humor, and even a bit of suspense to keep readers riveted to each scandalous scene—and everything in between."
—Romance Junkies

"A historical gem.... Don't expect a cookie-cutter romance in *An Indecent Proposition*. Ms. Wildes places enough twists and turns in the story as more than one character finds everlasting love."
—TwoLips Reviews

continued ...

ALSO BY EMMA WILDES

An Indecent Proposition

Lessons from a Scarlet Lady

Emma Wildes

Emma Wildes

A SIGNET ECLIPSE BOOK

SIGNET ECLIPSE
Published by New American Library, a division of
Penguin Group (USA) Inc., 375 Hudson Street,
New York, New York 10014, USA
Penguin Group (Canada), 90 Eglinton Avenue East, Suite 700, Toronto,
Ontario M4P 2Y3, Canada (a division of Pearson Penguin Canada Inc.)
Penguin Books Ltd., 80 Strand, London WC2R 0RL, England
Penguin Ireland, 25 St. Stephen's Green, Dublin 2,
Ireland (a division of Penguin Books Ltd.)
Penguin Group (Australia), 250 Camberwell Road, Camberwell, Victoria 3124,
Australia (a division of Pearson Australia Group Pty. Ltd.)
Penguin Books India Pvt. Ltd., 11 Community Centre, Panchsheel Park,
New Delhi - 110 017, India
Penguin Group (NZ), 67 Apollo Drive, Rosedale, North Shore 0632,
New Zealand (a division of Pearson New Zealand Ltd.)
Penguin Books (South Africa) (Pty.) Ltd., 24 Sturdee Avenue,
Rosebank, Johannesburg 2196, South Africa

Penguin Books Ltd., Registered Offices:
80 Strand, London WC2R 0RL, England

First published by Signet Eclipse, an imprint of New American Library,
a division of Penguin Group (USA) Inc.

First Printing, January 2010
10 9 8 7 6 5 4 3 2

*To Aunt Jan and Uncle Mick
with affection and a mischievous wink*

ACKNOWLEDGMENTS

How can I possibly thank Becky Vinter and Barbara Poelle enough? I can't, so let me just tip my proverbial hat to these lovely, talented ladies.

I'd also like to express my appreciation for all the brainstorming moments and support to DL. There's nothing like a good friend with wickedly wonderful suggestions.

My thanks to Jennifer, as well. You know why.

Prologue

If you have not captured his attention in the first place, how can you possibly hold it?

The entire preface to Lady Rothburg's Advice,
published 1802

The vestibule was full of well-dressed people milling like jeweled birds in their finery, just as she'd hoped. Brianna Northfield let her husband slip her velvet cloak from her shoulders and deliberately kept her back toward him, smiling and nodding at several acquaintances in the throng. He handed the garment to a nearby attendant, greeted his old friend Lord Bassford while Brianna waited, still strategically turned away.

This was the first step in her plan and she certainly hoped it worked, for she felt exposed.

Very much so.

Colton finished his conversation and took her arm, his gaze thankfully intent on scanning the crowd for a way to proceed toward their private box. "This way, my dear. I think we can squeeze through over by where the Earl of Farrington is standing."

"That young woman with him is not someone I know," she murmured, noting the beautiful young lady's fiery hair and lush figure. "Good heavens, he must be old enough to be her father."

"His latest mistress, I believe," her husband said

coolly as they edged through the crowd. "I'm sure they are here at the opera together simply to annoy his wife. Discretion has never been Farrington's strong suit."

The note of disapproval in her husband's voice did not escape her, but at least it wasn't directed *at* her. That is, not yet. Colton Northfield, the fifth Duke of Rolthven, did not believe in public displays of one's private life. She had learned that much in three months of marriage.

If he had a mistress, he would certainly not bring her out and flaunt the affair in front of all of fashionable London society. Neither would he purposely hurt or humiliate his wife. Brianna simply prayed he *didn't* have a mistress, nor did she ever want him to feel he required one.

His touch on her arm was light as he guided her toward the carpeted stairs that led up to the elegant box overlooking center stage. Heads turned as they passed, other friends giving greetings, and Brianna noticed more than one gentleman let his gaze linger on her and several raised brows among the ladies.

Fine. After all, she wished to make an impression. If the length of the masculine stares was a good measure, she was certainly succeeding.

She felt the moment when Colton first noticed her gown. They were halfway up the stairs and he faltered, his fingers tightening. One foot on the next step, he stopped cold, his gaze riveted suddenly on her décolletage. "Good God, what are you wearing?"

"Should you really halt on the stairs and stare so pointedly at my bosom?" she asked with a calm she didn't particularly feel, taking another determined step past him. "This is Madame Ellen's latest creation and the neckline is a little daring, yes, but I am assured I have the proper figure to carry it off."

Her husband didn't move for a moment, his glittering gaze still intent on the ivory flesh that swelled above the material of her bodice, the entire upper curves exposed. He bit out in a low tone, "You certainly can carry it off, but perhaps you should have asked yourself if you *should* carry it off. Or better yet, asked me."

Ask him about fashion? As if he normally cared. He dressed impeccably, but he never commented on her clothing at all.

Perhaps that would change. It would be a nice beginning to know he actually looked at her.

Brianna murmured, "People are staring, Colton, wondering if we are actually arguing in public."

"We might be," he muttered. "Have you lost your mind?"

The Duke of Rolthven in an altercation with his wife on the stairs at the opera? Never. She had chosen this venue because she was confident of his ingrained sense of politesse. He would be horrified by the idea of making a scene. Brianna summoned a serene smile—utterly false, for she could feel the warmth in her cheeks and the beat of her pulse in her throat. "Not at all. Shall we take our seats?"

Uttering a low curse, he responded by almost dragging her up the rest of the way, his long fingers locked around her wrist as he ushered her down the gallery and into the balcony with their private box. His expression was hard to read, but his mouth formed a tight line as he seated her and took the next chair.

The theater was packed as always, the huge chandeliers glittering, the gilt boxes holding the buzz of hundreds of conversations. People attended not so much to see the performance as to be seen themselves and to observe others, something her husband knew full well.

"I suppose since we are already here, wrapping you up in your cloak and carrying you outside might be remarked upon," he said sardonically, extending his long legs. "I know our arrival is usually noted, but I wondered why we garnered so much attention as we went through the lobby. Now I understand perfectly. I imagine more opera glasses will be directed toward your breasts on such lavish display this evening than at the stage. Whatever possessed you, madam, to choose such an outrageous gown?"

Because I want to seduce you, she thought, gazing at

him. He looked as devastatingly attractive as ever this
evening, even with a frown on his handsome face and the
sensual line of his mouth compressed in reproof. He was
tall, with thick chestnut hair, and a lean, athletic build,
and on those rare occasions when Colton smiled, every
woman in the room felt a little flushed. High cheekbones
gave his face an arrogant cast, his nose was straight, the
line of jaw and chin nicely chiseled. The first time Brianna had seen him she'd been dazzled by his flagrant
good looks, and when he actually began to show some
interest in her, she had tumbled head over heels in love
like some maiden in a romantic fable.

But there were some aspects to her marriage she
hadn't anticipated. As a mythical prince, Colton had a
few flaws. He was one of the wealthiest men in England,
he had tremendous political power, and his illustrious
background was dazzling to a naïve debutant, but Brianna hadn't anticipated how little of his time he would
deign to give her once she became his wife.

However, he hadn't married the meek little ingénue
she suspected he imagined he'd chosen.

With as much composure as possible, Brianna answered, "There are many ladies in attendance this evening attired in gowns every bit as fashionably low cut as
mine. I thought you would like it."

"*Like* having every man in London ogle my wife's
bare bosom?" His brows lifted, but his gaze strayed
downward again. "Think again, my dear."

"Actually," she answered, a flicker of hope stirring,
because though he sounded annoyed, he couldn't seem
to stop staring, "I thought *you* might like the way I look
in this gown."

For a moment he seemed surprised, his eyes, a vivid
azure shade, narrowing a fraction. "You are stunningly
beautiful, Brianna, and I always admire the way you
look. Why do you think I married you?"

That wasn't what she wanted to hear. It was exactly
what she *didn't* want to hear. Shaking out her fan, Brianna said furiously, "I hope you didn't wed me, Your

Grace, simply to have as an ornament on your arm at functions like this. I am a person, and a woman, and your wife."

Her retort caused an uncharacteristically disconcerted look to cross his face. "Perhaps that wasn't well put. I meant you are always attractive to me. You do not have to be half-naked for me to think so."

"Then prove it."

"I beg your pardon?" His arched brows shot up and he stared at her, obviously mystified.

Good. She truly had his attention. All too often he seemed only absently aware of her presence. He was a busy man, and she understood and accepted that the responsibilities of title and fortune consumed a great deal of his time. But when they were together, she wanted to know her husband at least enjoyed her company. They were both still adjusting to marriage—or at least she was, for she didn't notice him changing much about his routine now that he had a wife. He still worked most of the day, still went to his club, still spent more time in the gaming rooms at balls and soirees than with her. Many society couples lived very separate lives. But it wasn't what she wanted for herself, and to change his attitude about it, she was determined to make him truly *notice* her.

The orchestra began to stir. Raising her voice so he could hear the words, not caring about the inhabitants of the boxes all around them, Brianna said clearly, "Tonight I want you to prove to me that you find me attractive."

"What the devil are you talking about?"

Brianna gazed at her husband and gave a small sigh. "I worried you might say something exactly like that."

Women were such unpredictable, irrational, and emotional creatures, Colton Northfield pondered darkly, only half listening to Herr Mozart's creation, his gaze idly resting on the stage where a brightly clad troupe danced to the same lively melodies he had heard so many times before. Next to him, his lovely wife sat in rapt audience, her fan waving in languid sweeps against the closeness of the huge room. Tendrils of silky, pale gold hair brushed her slender neck, and her delicate face was slightly flushed from the heat.

He hadn't lied. She was one of the most beautiful women he had ever seen, and from the first moment of their introduction nearly a year ago, he had wanted her intensely. Courtship, the necessary engagement, and wedded life had not changed that one bit. Even now, the quiver of her opulent flesh as it swelled above the bodice of an ivory gown that—no matter what she said—bordered on scandalous, made his erection swell uncomfortably against the confinement of his fitted breeches.

What exactly was percolating through her pretty head? If asked before this evening, Colton would have said that Brianna was the last young woman of his acquaintance to wear something so outrageous. Usually she was a proper young lady. Sometimes too proper— but then again, she was innocent and inexperienced still. He had curbed his lust as much as possible and kept lovemaking between them a subdued experience, trying to familiarize her with the intimacy of the act and loosen her understandable inhibitions.

There was certainly nothing inhibited about her tonight, and it affected him in a way that surprised him. He should be irritated by her choice of clothing for such a public appearance. He *was* irritated, actually. But he was also something else.

Intrigued.

She leaned forward and lifted the gold opera glasses in her hand to get a better look at the stage. The mounded flesh barely contained by the bodice of her dress severely tested the material, and he could swear he saw a hint of the edge of one pink, perfect nipple.

Maybe he'd been going about things in the wrong way, he mused, unable to refrain from thinking about her unexpected challenge. Not that he approved in any way of her appearing in public partially naked, but he did admire the view. She certainly had lovely breasts, full and pliant, and the virginal color of the gown offset by the sinfully low neckline did some interesting things to the area below his waist.

Very interesting things.

"The soprano is spectacular, isn't she?" The glasses lowered and his wife smiled, her dark blue eyes, framed by long lashes, still focused on the performance.

Since he wasn't really paying attention, it was hard for him to comment.

You are spectacular.

In a noncommittal tone, he mumbled a less than brilliant response, "Yes. Very talented."

"That last aria was breathtaking."

What was breathtaking was the graceful curve of Brianna's bared shoulders and the flawless perfection of her skin. Not to mention the alluring soft rose of her mouth, the darker color of her brows a contrast to the golden luster of her hair. . . .

Good God, Colton thought with amused self-disgust. What was he doing? Poetic comparisons and lascivious thoughts while sitting in his private box at the opera were not at all in character.

He forced his attention back to the stage. Or at least he tried.

It seemed like forever before the music ended, the applause ceased, and the chaotic exodus from the theater began. Taking advantage of his superior height to spot the appropriate opening, Colton escorted his wife outside as fast as possible to avoid both gossip over her attire and—if he were honest with himself—any other males having the chance to feel similar appreciation for her undeniable charms. The usual after-performance pleasantries to friends they did encounter were administered as expediently as possible, and he waited impatiently to retrieve her cloak. He swirled it around her shoulders with a deep sense of relief.

"My carriage, please," he said in clipped tones to a footman who bowed and apparently caught the urgency in his voice, for the young man practically ran to order it.

"Are you in a hurry?" Brianna asked.

Her question sounded innocent enough, he thought warily as he stood waiting for the vehicle to be brought around, but he wasn't sure it was. There wasn't much question she'd surprised him this evening. "I don't care to wait in an endless queue," he lied.

"It does get tedious," she agreed, slipping the wrap from her shoulders just enough to expose the view he wanted covered. "My, it is a warm evening, isn't it?"

He was certainly sweating, and he wasn't completely sure the temperature was responsible for his discomfort.

Once their carriage arrived, Colton helped Brianna in and followed to settle on the opposite seat, rapping sharply on the roof to signal the driver.

In the shadowed interior of the coach, with her cloak open so the sumptuous flesh that nearly spilled from the front of her gown glimmered pale, Brianna looked more tempting than ever. Clearing his throat, he said, "Did you enjoy the production, my dear?"

"Yes." Her voice was hushed, and she gazed at him from under her long lashes in a provocative way he'd never seen before. With every breath she took, her breasts threatened to burst free from the inadequate confines of her gown. "Did you like it?"

He was riveted. Or still riveted. Oh hell, hadn't she just asked him a question?

It was only polite to answer it.

"The view was glorious," he said dryly, giving up any attempt to hide his salacious interest. "And, yes, I thought the opera itself diverting."

She smiled, looking nothing like the young ingénue he had married, but instead every inch an alluring, sensual woman. "If *I* can divert you in any way, please, feel free to indulge yourself. *Now* would be fine."

"Now?" he repeated, wondering if he understood her meaning correctly.

"Now." Her smile deepened.

Oh yes, she meant it.

In some deep part of his mind it was irksome that she knew how badly she had unsettled him, but that part was not in control at the moment. Another part of his body was now in charge.

He didn't intend to move. After all, engaging in an indiscretion in a carriage was most undignified—but suddenly Colton did not care in the least. He reached over and scooped Brianna into his arms, settling back into his seat with her draped across his lap. Lowering his head, he kissed her hungrily, his tongue exploring her mouth, tasting every sweet corner. She responded with equal abandon, her arms wrapping around his neck, her slender, voluptuous body pressing against him. Not releasing her mouth, he eased the cloth from one shapely shoulder and her bared breast filled his hand with a soft, supple weight.

Perfect.

Everything faded. The clattering of the wheels of the vehicle as it rolled along the cobbled street, the warm evening . . . everything except the hard throbbing of his cock. He could hear her erratic breathing when he finally broke the kiss and slid his mouth down the graceful length of her neck, his lips lingering for a moment at the point where her pulse beat fast and light. Brianna made a small sound as his thumb circled the luscious crest of her pink nipple, her head falling back against his shoulder. "Colton . . . oh, yes."

Her skin was soft, smooth, and infinitely female. His fingers deftly found the fastenings at the back of her gown, and it was around her waist in moments. Licking the enticing valley between her breasts, kissing her mounded flesh, sucking on her nipples until they were erect and tight, he could feel his lovely wife's arousal in the way she clung to him and whispered his name.

The ducal carriage had nice wide seats, something he hadn't particularly appreciated before. "I cannot believe I am doing this but God help me, Brianna, I have to have you," he said raggedly, laying her down on the seat.

"I want you, too." Her hair had loosened, and it framed her face in a silken tumble, her shoulders ivory in the dim light, her naked breasts tight and quivering with the motion of the vehicle. He thought he would cease to breathe when she reached down to pull her skirts up above her waist, baring long, lovely legs in their silk stockings and garters. Her pubic hair was a small golden triangle between her white thighs, and as he discarded his coat, she parted her legs in erotic invitation.

So hot with urgent need he felt like he might combust at any moment, Colton accepted gladly, still jerking at the fastenings on his breeches. Freeing his pulsing erection, he lowered himself over his wife's sprawled, half-dressed body, adjusting himself between her open thighs. One hand braced on the upholstered seat, he guided his rigid cock to her entrance, finding her wet and accommodating to his penetration. Brianna clutched his shoulders as he thrust inside her body, a low moan coming from her throat.

It was so good, he thought in feverish pleasure, not even bothering to caution her to be quiet. The idea of his driver overhearing them make love would normally have appalled him, but at that moment, he just didn't care. Withdrawing, he pushed back inside her tight passage with long strokes, the pumping of his lower body matching the swaying motion of the carriage.

Brianna arched to meet him, her hips lifting for each penetration, her eyes shut, long lashes dark against her flushed cheeks. The sharp bite of her fingernails through the fine lawn of his shirt increased as the rhythm escalated, and Colton was startled to realize she was going to climax so quickly without any other stimulation. A muffled scream rang out as she arched frantically and her inner muscles began to ripple and tighten.

It sent him right over the edge. Pushing deep, he erupted with such intensity his body shook as he held himself still, the rapture taking him prisoner, holding him as he flooded her with his seed and groaned her name.

When he could finally breathe again, he registered two things. The first was that his gorgeous wife smiled up at him in a way that could only be described as triumphant.

The second was that the vehicle they occupied in a state of scandalous near undress was coming to a halt.

"Damnation," Colton muttered in disbelief. Had he actually just ravished his wife in a moving carriage like some randy adolescent?

Chapter One

*Men want to understand us, but only in the most ab-
stract of ways. They believe that our volatile emotions
make us creatures too complicated to fully comprehend. To a certain extent, I have come to agree. Males
deal with life in a very straightforward fashion. It will
work in your favor to remember this. Women, on the
other hand, understand each other very well.*

*From the chapter titled: "Their Reality Versus Our
Illusions"*

The afternoon sun slanted in through the tall windows, laying blocks on the rich patterned rug. French
doors were open to the gardens and the scent of bloom-
ing roses filled the air. Across from Brianna, Rebecca
Marston raised one eyebrow and said suspiciously, "You
look strange, Bri. Are you even listening to the conversation?"

"I agree," Arabella Smythe, the Countess of Bonham, chimed in. Pretty and petite, she perched on the
edge of a delicately embroidered chair, her ebony
hair coiled demurely at her nape, her lovely dark eyes
holding the same hint of question. "You seem very distracted."

"I do?" Feigning innocence was impossible and Brianna laughed. As they sat in Arabella's informal parlor,
sipping tea and chatting, her friends were quite right;

she'd lost track of the chitchat on the latest fashions quite some time ago. The evening before had been a . . . triumph. She might even dub it a revelation. How on earth was it possible to think of it and not smile?

Well, it *wasn't* possible.

"Yes. A cat-who-got-into-the-cream kind of strange." Rebecca sat up a little straighter on the brocade settee. She was a tall, willowy brunette with feminine features and an enviable figure. It was very fashionable for gentlemen to fancy themselves in love with her, but she hadn't yet found one to suit her despite her father's insistence she marry soon. As this was her second season, she now represented a challenge to the young men of the *haut ton*. She demanded, "What has happened?"

The three of them had been fast friends since childhood, and though Brianna tried to look bland, she couldn't succeed. "What makes you think anything has happened?"

The two of them exchanged glances and then looked back at her. Arabella said dryly, "Call it an educated guess. We *know* you. I recognize that expression. It reminds me of the time we explored the abbey ruins at midnight, hoping to see a ghost or two, and when we got caught coming back in, you spun a very improbable tale for my governess that somehow she believed." She added, "We, however, knew the truth, since we were guilty of breaking the rules."

Reaching for her cup of tea, Brianna murmured in amused recollection, "Yes, I did spare us punishment, didn't I?"

"You were very glib," Rebecca commented. "But don't try that technique on us. Now then, what has you staring out the window with that singularly self-satisfied smile?"

Brianna wasn't at all sure she should tell them the truth. It was an awfully scandalous secret. However, she trusted her two friends more than anybody else in the whole world.

Rebecca said, "Bri?"

"I went back and purchased it," she confessed.

Both of them looked puzzled, their teacups suspended in their hands.

She elaborated. "I went back to that tiny little bookshop and bought *Lady Rothburg's Advice*."

Arabella's mouth parted in shock and Rebecca made a choked sound.

Brianna lifted her hand palm upward in supplication. "Before you say anything, just let me tell you that it *worked*. Her advice in the book is invaluable. I read the first chapter and it was very enlightening. You should have seen Colton. I think he gave up on watching the stage halfway through the opera last night and simply stared at me. Well, at a certain part of me anyway."

"What part? Good heavens, Bri, what on earth are you doing?" Arabella came dangerously close to sloshing the rest of her tea out of the cup, she was paying so little attention to it. "Do you have any idea how outraged *my* husband would be if I were in possession of that book? And my apologies for the observation, but I think Andrew is more forgiving than Rolthven."

Her friend's easygoing husband probably *was* more tolerant, but Brianna couldn't help but recall Colton's impetuous passion in the carriage. He couldn't seem to help himself—and that was exactly the effect she wanted.

"He was very startled at first, but then seemed to ... adjust."

"Adjust to what?" Rebecca demanded, her blue-green eyes glimmering. "Stop being so dratted mysterious and just tell us."

Brianna demurely rearranged her skirts. "Well, in the first chapter, it does suggest that if you want to dress to attend church services or a great aunt's social gathering, modest apparel is fine and good, but if you wish to dress to catch the eye of your husband, one should be a bit bolder."

"How bold?" Arabella asked.

"Quite bold." Brianna could feel her blush. "My décolletage was daring, I own it, but while Colton was furious over my scandalous attire, I could tell he was also intrigued, and that was borne out by what happened later. He was outraged at first, but it was too late to drag me home; everyone would have whispered over it, and you know how he hates that sort of thing. I must say, though . . . he rather warmed up to the idea of a garment that afforded such easy *accessibility*."

"You must be joking. The Duke is always so proper and controlled. When people speak of Rolthven—and they do often enough, because we all know your husband is an important man—it is always with the utmost respect for his consequence."

"Well, for once he abandoned it last night." Lowering her voice a notch, Brianna added, "In the carriage on the way home, I was ravished most thoroughly and loved every minute of it. Though I have to say it was a little embarrassing to alight so obviously disheveled." Recalling how her husband barely had time to fasten his trousers and help her jerk her dress back up before one of the footmen opened the door made the heat in her cheeks intensify. Her hair had been loose and his coat still tossed on the floor, so there could have been no doubt about what they'd been doing.

Arabella's cup rattled, she placed it in the saucer so abruptly. Her eyes were wide. "In the carriage? The Duke? Oh, my."

"It was wonderful." Brianna said truthfully. "He comes across stodgy and dignified, but that isn't his true personality. I think Colton thought I would be shocked if he openly exhibited his passionate nature. Furthermore, I know he was raised in the knowledge that he would become a duke and should have a decorum that befits his exalted station. When he courted me, he barely did more than steal a few chaste kisses, though I know he wanted much, much more." Lowering her lashes slightly, she continued. "There are some things a man cannot hide in today's fashion of fitted breeches."

Arabella sighed, sitting back in her chair, adjusting the

sleeve of her light blue day gown. "Andrew would never do such a thing as make love to me in our carriage."

"Neither would Colton unless goaded into it, believe me." Brianna leaned forward. "But it is nice to know he *can* be goaded. I'm finding Lady Rothburg's book quite correct. What women feel is romantic and how men define that same term are truly two different things. Colton is very dutiful in his gifts of jewelry and flowers and the like, but I am sure he would be astounded to know I would appreciate a warm smile or a tender kiss more than some diamond bauble. He simply does not think that way."

"As the unmarried one, I am finding this fascinating. You are going to educate him, I take it?" Rebecca arched a brow. "I don't yet have a husband, but I am beginning to understand how this all works. We are foes living in the same armed camp who are also forced to be allies."

"Close," Brianna confirmed with a light laugh. "Let's just say there is some common ground and I am going to work so Colton and I discover it. If men, like the book says, define romance as sexual interaction, then I'm going to make sure he finds me very romantic. I refuse to let my husband look elsewhere because he finds me dull in bed."

"You are hopelessly idealistic. Men like Rolthven do not fall on their knees and declare themselves madly in love." Arabella shook her head. "They don't have to, Bri."

Her husband's privileged background did present somewhat of a problem, she had found. Hence her covert purchase.

"My sister and her husband are so happily married," Brianna said, hoping she didn't sound wistful. "You should see them together. Sometimes they do little more than exchange a smile, but the affection is obvious. Henry adores her, and Lea married him despite the fact he is nothing more than a solicitor. My parents disapproved to the point where they threatened to disown her over the match, but my sister was in love, and they came around in the end. Quite frankly, their modest home is one of my favorite places to visit. I'd like my house to have the same warmth."

It was rather a stretch to call the London mansion Colton owned a house. A palatial residence perhaps, but a house . . . well, no. Rolthven, the estate in the country, was even larger.

Maybe she *was* idealistic.

"What else does Lady Rothburg say?" Rebecca looked more than a little interested.

"Nothing any of us should probably read, much less repeat. That book," Arabella asserted, eloquently pointing her spoon at Brianna, "is something I doubt your very handsome—but very respectable—husband would want you to have in your possession. I still cannot believe you found it in that dingy little shop, much less bought it."

It was true. Lady Rothburg's work had been publicly banned over a decade before, when it was first published. The worn volume had intrigued Brianna, and once she opened it, she'd known the secret purchase had been a good decision.

Brianna said serenely, "It's most enlightening and to the benefit of our marriage. Why should he mind if I read it?"

"Because it's scandalous and entirely about seduction and licentious behavior, written, no less, by an infamous courtesan," her friend said primly.

A valid point. Colton would be outraged to know she even possessed it. No doubt he would simply order it to be disposed of on the spot.

Unfazed, Brianna reached for a lemon tart on a small plate on the tea trolley. "Maybe so, but he seemed to like her advice in chapter one." Taking a small bite of her pastry, she chewed daintily and swallowed, adding, "And you should see what she suggests in chapter two."

White's was crowded, but then again, it always was. Colton handed his greatcoat to the steward and headed for his favorite table. His youngest brother, Robert, was already there, a brandy in hand, sprawled comfortably in his chair. His paper was neatly folded next to the decanter and he grinned as Colton walked up and tapped it with his finger. Without even a greeting, Robert said, "Your beauteous duchess garnered a paragraph or two in the society pages, I see."

Colton grimaced and pulled out a chair, sitting down to reach for a glass and the decanter. "So I understand."

"In a very prominent place," Robert expounded.

Colton loathed the gossip columns, but he knew Brianna's décolletage could not have gone unremarked upon. "I'm almost afraid to ask, but what does it say?"

Three years younger, as much a friend as he was a brother, Robert had hair just a shade lighter, more dark gold than brown, and the same familial Northfield sky blue eyes. Right now they held open, lively amusement. "It isn't all that bad, Colt. It merely mentions ... er ... her feminine assets were showcased in a manner that caught the eye. That's all. Oh yes, and it speculates on whether or not she might be setting a trend for the younger women of the *ton*."

"She is doing nothing of the kind," Colton muttered, dashing brandy into his glass with a generous hand. "The only reason she wore the gown out in public was because I didn't notice it soon enough. By the time I saw the outrageous garment, we were already at the opera and the damage done."

"How could you *not* notice?" Robert leaned back, his mouth twitching. "Sorry to ask, but quite frankly, her attire sounded infinitely noticeable."

It was a good question. Colton had asked it of himself in retrospect, still astounded he had acted so rashly in the carriage on the way home. He literally had almost been caught bare-assed by a footman, and was sure his entire staff knew what had happened between him and his beautiful, bemusing young wife. He should be grateful that *that* part of the debacle wasn't splattered all across London.

"She was running late and had already donned her wrap when she joined me downstairs before we left," he told his brother. "Otherwise, believe me, I would have noticed."

In short, he was fairly sure she had done that on purpose so he wouldn't order her to change. Her behavior was puzzling, because he could have sworn she wasn't the kind of woman who would try to trick him in any way. The evidence, however, was damning.

"Brianna is young yet," Robert observed, his long fingers playing with the stem of his glass. "I am sure she didn't realize—"

"She realized full well," Colton interrupted in clipped tones, recalling the flushed look on her face when he first truly saw her gown. "But rest assured it won't happen again. After all, I pay her dressmaking bills."

His brother lifted a brow. "I'm hardly an expert on marriage, but I do know women, and playing the despotic husband doesn't seem wise to me."

A table across the room erupted into laughter, but luckily enough it was at a distance where Colton could be sure it wasn't a reaction to Robert's comment. He said in a low, defensive tone, "What am I supposed to do, let her dress that way on a regular basis? I think not. She's the Duchess of Rolthven. I am still not sure what prompted her actions in the first place, but she insists she wore the blasted thing because she thought I would like it."

"Did you?"

Colton sent a sardonic look across the table. "If worn only for me in private, perhaps."

"Perhaps?"

"Well, yes, I thought it was becoming, but from the most primitive male point of view only. As my wife, she shouldn't have worn it."

"Ah."

"What the devil does that mean?"

His brother struggled to hide his smile and failed. "She has thoroughly rattled the prim and proper duke in you, I see. Good for her."

Being called prim was annoying as hell. It brought to mind images of disapproving white-haired old ladies or dour Presbyterian ministers, and he wasn't either one. Yes, Colton believed in at least some measure of decorum, but after all, he was a Peer of the Realm, and his position in society warranted a certain level of behavior. "Not all of us, Robbie, embrace notoriety," he observed, not bothering to hide his irritation. "Nor can we all skip from the bed of one lovely lady to the next, never looking over our shoulders. I do take my responsibilities seriously, and that includes my marriage."

Robert, who had a reputation as a rake of the first order and was infamously opposed to permanence, hardly looked chastened. Instead he chuckled. "I am sure you do. Everything you take on, from estate matters to your seat in the House of Lords, you handle with the same efficiency and expertise. But, let's face it, Colt, you have never taken on a human being before. Not *just* another person, but a woman at that. She isn't going to act as you wish, simply because you wish it. She might not act as you wish even if ordered to do so. Brianna isn't only beautiful, she is intelligent—and, I am sure, confident she can make her own decisions."

Stung, Colton retorted, "I know that. Who better? I had no interest in marrying an empty-headed doll. I admire her spirit and her intellect."

"Then I caution a more subtle approach to this issue than telling her dressmaker you wish to approve her gowns from now on. That is insulting to Brianna, and since you abhor gossip, most ill-advised. It is an indication you disapproved of her attire and will get everyone talking about it again. You cannot count on your instructions to the modiste being kept quiet."

It was galling to think his younger brother might be giving him sage advice—on the subject of marriage, no less, in which Robert had exhibited very little interest. But then again, his brother was right. Robert knew women—or should, for he had certainly sampled the charms of many of them.

Colton finished his brandy and poured another. He rubbed his jaw and sent his brother a narrow-eyed look. "For the sake of argument, let's say I agree with you in principle. I naturally prefer diplomacy over being autocratic, but neither do I wish her name to regularly be on the tongues of the gossipmongers."

Robert's handsome face quirked into a thoughtful frown. "I'd say persuading her to your point of view is preferable to issuing dictates. If she chooses to wear another daring gown, change your mind at the last minute about going out. You just said you would be happy to appreciate it in private. Show her you do. This way, if every time her clothing is too outré for you to want to share her with all of London, you just stay in. She will get the message at once. If she wishes to go out, she will dress more demurely. If you are lucky enough she wants to stay at home, that, I suspect, will be even more pleasant. As I see it, you can't lose."

To Colton's surprise, Robert's advice made sense. At least he would not find himself making rash, uninhibited love to his wife in a moving carriage but could take her properly upstairs and close the bedroom door. Not that the interlude hadn't been gloriously pleasurable, but he really hadn't enjoyed almost being caught in the act. He much preferred to take his time, especially with a woman as alluring as Brianna.

He stared at his brother over the rim of his glass, the fragrance of the fine brandy drifting upward in a tantalizing waft. "That actually sounds like a viable solution."

Robert spread his hands in a self-deprecating gesture, a cheeky grin on his face. "I enjoy discussing this subject much more than the dust-dry politics that usually occupy you, or worse yet, the latest meeting with your solicitors over some financial arrangement. What could be more intriguing than talking about women?"

Spoken like a true rakehell. Colton didn't have the luxury of sitting around and daydreaming about how to placate his latest paramour like his younger brother, but quite frankly, since Robert had just exhibited such educated insight, Colton might have to consult him again.

"I don't suppose I have ever thought of it that way, but I don't have your latitude," he murmured and then drained his glass.

"True enough," Robert agreed cheerfully, reaching for the decanter. "Being the Duke sounds like a dreadful bore. It's infinitely preferable to be third in line. When you get an heir, I won't even be that."

Now and again it *was* a bore to carry the burden of title and responsibility that went with having a great deal of influence, of course, but all of life was that way. His lighthearted younger brother hadn't discovered that reality yet.

"Some day," Colton speculated, his mouth curving as he imagined the event, "the time will come when a young lady brings you to your knees and I will enjoy the moment immensely."

"Perhaps." Robert looked unfazed and more than a little smug. "But until it happens—and I am not convinced it ever will—I'll be around if you want to discuss again how to handle your beautiful bride."

Chapter Two

Intrigue is as essential to the relations between men and women as the air is necessary for us to breathe. Our subtle dance with each other is what makes it all so interesting.

From the chapter titled: "They Are All the
Same and Yet Different"

The image in the mirror wasn't displeasing. Rebecca Marston smoothed one last brown curl into place and studied her appearance with a critical eye. Yes, the pale rose gown was a good choice, for it went well with the ivory of her skin and set off the dark gleam of her hair. There was one advantage to not being fashionably blond: her more dramatic coloring stood out from the other popular debutants vying for the attentions of eligible males. While she did wish she wasn't quite so tall, her height wasn't so pronounced it discouraged many suitors.

No, her real problem was her age, her prominent background, her very marriageable status, *and* her formidable father.

Actually, that was quite a list of problems—but problems that mostly applied to one man.

Rising from her dressing table, she picked up her fan with a sigh and left her bedroom. Downstairs she found both her parents waiting in the foyer. Her mother looked splendid, draped in emerald silk and a fortune in diamonds, a glittering diadem in her intricately coiffed dark hair. Her father was also dressed handsomely in his elegant evening wear, a ruby stickpin in his snowy cravat, his graying hair brushed neatly back. His impatience showed in the way he ran his gloves through his hands, his gaze settling on her with approval as she descended the stairs.

"There you are. I was just going to send up someone to get you, my dear, but it was well worth the wait. You look stunning."

Rebecca smiled, but it was a little forced. She wasn't looking forward to the next few hours. Another ball, another evening of eager men dancing attendance on her while the man she desperately wanted to show even a flicker of interest was laughing, charming, and dazzling *other* women, without even a passing glance in her direction.

It was a depressing thought.

"I'm sorry I'm late," she murmured, turning her back so one of the footmen could settle her cloak over her shoulders. "I couldn't decide what gown to wear."

How frivolous that sounded, though she didn't think of herself as superficial in the slightest. If anything, she was quite the opposite. Music was the true passion of her life, and though her parents discouraged her from mentioning it when out in company, she wasn't just a talented pianist and more than adequate on the harp, flute, and clarinet—her real interest lay in composition. Already, at the age of twenty, she had composed two symphonies and countless other smaller works. It felt as though a tune played continuously in her head. Putting it down on paper seemed only natural.

That, of course, was as unfashionable as the color of her hair.

The carriage was waiting and her father escorted them outside, handing her mother in first and then Rebecca. She settled on the seat and braced herself for the usual lecture.

Her mother lost no time. "Darling, Lord Watts will be at the Hampton's this evening. Please favor him with a dance."

Boring Lord Watts with his staged laugh and wispy mustache. Rebecca didn't care if he was the last man on earth—a potential earldom and fortune aside—she would never enjoy his company. "He's a pompous oaf," she said truthfully. "A philistine with no interest in the arts and—"

"Handsome, wealthy, and the son of a friend of mine," her father interrupted firmly, his gaze holding a flinty look. "Dance with him. He's thoroughly besotted with you and has asked for your hand in marriage twice."

Why she would encourage a man she had no intention of ever marrying was a reasonable question, but she declined to argue. Instead she murmured, "Very well. I can spare a dance."

"You might want to reconsider his suit. I am in favor of the match."

She didn't, couldn't, and never would it be a possibility. Rebecca didn't say a word.

Her mother gave her a reproving look as they clattered along the cobbled street. "You *will* have to choose at some point."

And since many young ladies her age were already engaged or wed—her two closest friends, Arabella and Brianna among them—she needed to make up her mind. She well understood her parents' position on the subject. Rebecca *had* chosen, actually, but it was a wildly impractical, impossible, entirely scandalous selection.

No one knew about her secret infatuation.

The mansion glittered with lights, and the long line of carriages in the circular drive gave an indication of the popularity of the event. They alighted finally and were ushered inside amidst the other arriving guests. Immediately Rebecca scanned the crowd in the well-lit ballroom, unable to help herself. Would *he* make an appearance tonight? He attended most of the prestigious entertainments because his brother was a duke, and . . .

There he was.

So tall, so masculine with his nicely chiseled features and light brown hair that always managed to look well-groomed and yet endearingly tousled at the same time, his face lighting in an animated smile as he greeted a friend. Lord Robert Northfield was a charming rogue, suave, sophisticated, and as uninterested as any man could be in a marriageable young miss. Which, Rebecca thought with a sigh, left her out in the cold. A certain part of her wished she wasn't friends with Brianna so she would never have had the opportunity to meet the Duke of Rolthven's youngest brother, but another part—a treacherous one—was glad she had.

Falling in love could happen in an instant, Rebecca had discovered. One look, one fascinated moment in which he bent over her hand and brushed her with one of those legendary smoldering looks . . . and she was lost.

Her father, at the moment at her side, would be horrified if he could read her thoughts. Robert had, she needed to face it, a wicked reputation. A very wicked reputation for enjoying cards and women, and not in that order. As respectable as Colton might be with his political influence and grandiose fortune, his youngest brother was just the opposite.

Her father disliked him intensely—he'd mentioned the Duke of Rolthven's younger brother with bitter derision more than once—and she had never dared to ask why. Maybe it was merely his notoriety, but she suspected there was more to the story.

Even as she watched from across the crowded room, hoping no one noticed the direction of her stare, Rebecca saw their hostess sidle up and touch Robert's sleeve in a gesture that was both playful and intimate. Rumor had it Lady Hampton had a distinct preference for wild, handsome young men, and the Duke of Rolthven's brother certainly qualified. The two duels he'd fought already didn't enhance his respectability.

When it came to Lord Robert, the only signs of respectability were his family name and his brother's prominent place in society.

Yet here she was, hopelessly fascinated. It *was* hopeless too, because even if by some miracle he ever noticed her, overcame his infamous aversion to marriage, and approached her, Rebecca knew her father would never allow it.

Too bad she didn't write romantic novels instead of composing music. Then she could pen a melancholy tale about a bereft young heroine who pined for a handsome, sinful lover.

"Miss Marston. How delightful to see you. I was hoping you would attend."

The interruption tore her gaze from the sight of Robert Northfield leading Lady Hampton onto the floor for a waltz, his head bent as he listened to whatever the brazen woman had to say, a faint smile on his face over what was undoubtedly clever flirtatious banter.

Were they lovers? Rebecca wished she didn't care, didn't speculate over something that was essentially none of her business, because Robert didn't even know she lived and breathed, and if Lady Hampton wanted to look at him with that particular brand of possessive longing, there was nothing Rebecca could do about it. . . .

"Miss Marston?"

Rebecca jerked her attention away from the striking couple on the dance floor with a dismal sinking feeling. A beaming Lord Watts stood in front of her, wispy mustache and all. "Oh, good evening," she murmured without enthusiasm, earning a frown from her father.

"Dare I assume you will consent to a dance?" The young man looked irritatingly eager, and his pale blue eyes held an imploring light.

If only his eyes were a deeper pure azure, framed by long lashes, his hair not the color of pale straw but instead a vibrant golden brown—if instead of a rather weak chin, he had clean-cut masculine features and a seductive mouth that could curve into a mesmerizing smile.

Even then, if that was all true, he still wouldn't be Robert Northfield.

"Of course she will," her father said smoothly. "Rebecca mentioned earlier she was looking forward to just that. Didn't you, my dear?"

Since she had never been one to tell falsehoods, she simply smiled. Or she tried. It might have come out more as a grimace. It was going to be a long, dismal evening.

"You seem distracted."

The implied intimacy in Maria Hampton's comment grated a little, and focused Robert's attention once again on the woman in his arms as they whirled across the floor in time to the latest popular tune. "I am tired, actually."

"Oh, I see." Maria smiled, a salacious gleam of interest in her green eyes. "Do I know her?"

"There's no 'her.'" Robert replied, irritated. "Or well, I suppose it is due to a woman—but not what you are thinking right now." He swept her into a turn and felt a sardonic twist touch his mouth. "It was my grandmother's birthday today."

Maria, all vibrant red hair and luscious full curves, looked puzzled. "So?"

"So," he explained softly, "I rose at dawn and rode quite a distance to make sure I could be at the family estate for luncheon in her honor."

"You?"

"Is it such a surprise I would make the effort?"

At least Maria didn't patronize him with a simpering denial. She merely said, "Yes, darling, it is."

He didn't suppose he could blame her for her view. Given Robert's reputation, London's gossips would be surprised to learn that he adored his grandmother. Despite the aftereffects of a little too much wine the night before, he'd made the journey gladly. Colton, of course, had already arrived at Rolthven with his lovely wife in tow, and Brianna had looked particularly fetching in a day gown of sprigged muslin adorned with tiny pink rosettes, her flaxen hair caught up simply with a twist of matching pastel ribbon. In direct contrast to the insinuations in the paper and the whispers over her scandalous attire of the other evening, she was dressed in the style of a fresh, innocent schoolgirl. But Robert did notice two interesting things.

The first was Colton seemed to treat her a little differently. Robert wouldn't go so far as to say that he was attentive, but his older brother appeared more *aware* of his wife. Second, she was not quite as shy, as if she was getting a sense of the power of not just her beauty, but her intellect. As Colton had pointed out, he had not selected some vapid chit just to get an heir.

It was hard to put a finger on the cause of her greater aura of confidence and poise, but very interesting just the same.

Jostled by a dancing couple who had evidently imbibed more than their share of wine, Robert broke from his reverie. At the moment, his brother's marriage was not Robert's deepest concern. What he really wanted was to escape the predatory clutches of Maria Hampton. Since politesse wasn't really working to his advantage, he needed to change his tactics. It wasn't that he didn't find the lady attractive—she was striking in an overblown, voluptuous way, with fiery hair, pale skin, and a lush body—but unfortunately he was rather good friends with her husband.

Robert was aware enough of his own reputation, but one thing he did not do was bed the wives of his friends. Even if they were couples who had mutual understandings when it came to infidelity, he wasn't comfortable with the idea. Casual liaisons were fine—he preferred them—but not if they could potentially damage a friendship he valued.

So since he wasn't going to oblige the lovely Maria, no matter how much she pouted, he needed a diplomatic escape route.

He'd waltzed with his hostess two times already this evening, and had no intention of making it three. Fortunately, they were near the French doors open to the terrace when the music ended. Robert bowed and murmured, "Excuse me, my lady. I think a little fresh air is in order. Surely I will see you a bit later."

Maria caught his sleeve. "I'll come with you. It is quite warm in here."

"You have guests," he reminded her, gently removing her clutching fingers. He'd heard that husky tone in a woman's voice many times before. "And while I understand Edmond allows you a great deal of latitude, let's not embarrass him."

Before she could protest further, he turned and walked away, hoping he looked bland and no one had noticed their momentary dissent. In his quest to escape, he collided with someone as he reached the open doors, a young lady who was also seemingly intent on leaving the ballroom with all due haste.

Well, if one had to bump into another person, it was always best (in his opinion) for them to be female, soft, and strategically rounded in all the correct places. The titillating drift of a sweet flowery perfume didn't hurt either, he thought as he caught the young woman by the upper arms and steadied them both.

"I beg your pardon," he murmured, looking down into a pair of wide, blue-green eyes that held a startled look. "Entirely my fault, I'm sure."

"N . . . no," she stammered. "It was probably mine. I was hurrying and not looking."

The air outside smelled fresh and a nearly full moon poured broken light onto the flagstones as thin, ethereal clouds drifted by. Compared to the closeness of the ballroom, it beckoned like paradise. "I think we were both in a rush. After you," he motioned.

"Thank you." She walked out in front of him, her back straight.

He knew her, he realized, following her and admiring the graceful sway of her hips and the gleam of dark, shining hair. She was related to his sister-in-law. No, perhaps not . . . not some distant cousin, but a friend. What was her name?

Since it would be rude to simply walk away, he fell into step beside her as she headed toward the path that led into the vast, ornamental gardens. In the distance, a fountain spilled water in a musical spray of soothing noise.

Rose silk whispered over the stones and the young woman's profile was outlined by the filtered illumination from above. A rather nice profile, Robert noted absently, still searching for her name and coming up blank. Tip-tilted nose, lacy fans for lashes, a smooth forehead, and a slender neck above shapely shoulders. And a nice bosom. A very opulent bosom, in fact. He had quite an appreciation of the female form and couldn't help but notice the rounded fullness under the bodice of her dress. He cleared his throat. "It's much cooler out here, isn't it?"

"Yes," she agreed almost inaudibly, her face still averted.

"The closeness of these affairs always makes me feel a little suffocated," he murmured politely. Since Brianna had been part of the crop of last year's debutants and this young lady was one of her friends, it wasn't all that surprising he had only a passing acquaintance, but usually he was good with faces and names.

The woman continued to avert her face so he couldn't clearly see her features. Her behavior was a little odd. She walked quickly, her hands lightly fisted in her skirts to keep the material out of her way as they reached the descent into the gardens. She nodded. "Suffocated is the *correct* word."

She wasn't referring to the temperature. He caught the implication easily enough from the faintest hint of disgust in her tone. Hence her hurry, hence their dual purpose in escaping the festivities inside. Robert couldn't help it; he laughed. "There are different forms of suffocation, aren't there?"

"Yes, there are."

"Your lack of air is due to a persistent male, I'd venture to guess."

She nodded in answer, sneaking a quick look at him for the first time.

It was fast, just a swift turning of her head, and then she abruptly glanced away. Her betraying gesture made him realize that he made this young woman nervous. There wasn't anything vaguely flirtatious about their exchange—quite the opposite—and there was no doubt she recognized *him* even if he couldn't recall her name.

Was he really painted so black that a young woman couldn't walk ten paces in his company without worrying he'd tarnish her reputation? It was a sobering thought, especially since he was convinced she was one of his sister-in-law's friends. What must Brianna think of him? Automatically he offered his arm at the top of the shallow stairs since the young woman seemed intent on the garden path. She hesitated for a moment and then put her fingers very lightly on his sleeve.

Those slim fingers trembled, and when they reached the bottom, she dropped her hand with unflattering alacrity.

Well, he was no saint, but he never despoiled innocent young ladies, so she was perfectly safe in his company. He bit back the urge to say so, unaccountably irritated. From one extreme to the other, he thought sardonically: first Maria's brazen pursuit and now this trembling little ingénue dodging an ardent suitor and running into him instead.

Shadowed paths snaked in several different directions, box hedges and towering rhododendrons as borders, the early fall evening carrying just a hint of crispness. In light of how his companion seemed to feel about his presence, Robert said coolly, "Perhaps you'd rather walk alone."

That finally brought her head up and she looked at him fully, her eyes wide. "No—no," she stammered. "Not at all."

He relaxed, and then stifled a laugh at his reaction as they began to stroll down the path to the right. Why the hell it mattered what some young—albeit pretty—chit thought of his morals—or lack thereof—was beyond his comprehension. Gossip never bothered him. The opinions of his family and a few close friends were all that counted. He didn't consider himself above scandal or below it—he just didn't consider it at all. Half of what was said about him wasn't true, and the part that was true was no one's business but his own. But if it kept London's elite populace entertained, there was little he could do about it. From the tender age of seventeen, when he'd captured the attention of one of the stage's most famous actresses and she'd made a very public, very risqué comment about his sexual prowess, it seemed like he'd been doomed to notoriety. In those days, he was still young enough to be mortified that his private life was fodder for the gossip mill, not to mention chagrined that his mother would learn about his torrid affair, but it had all worn off in time. At least Elise's comment had been complimentary; nor had he had any complaints since then. Indeed, his popularity with society's reigning belles was very convenient for a man who thoroughly enjoyed women.

Convenient with the exception of small incidents like this evening. Maria Hampton's presumption that he would betray a friend in exchange for a casual tumble annoyed him.

"I just got the impression you might not like my company," he said mildly.

"I'm sorry."

At her timid apology, Robert realized he was frowning. He looked into the lady's upturned face and noted she had bright spots of color in both cheeks, visible even in the wash of moonlight. Consciously shaking off the image of the clinging Lady Hampton, he smiled. "Sorry for what?"

"I . . . don't know, actually," she responded, her blush intensifying.

Whoever she was, she was very attractive, he decided. Not beautiful like Brianna, with her lustrous golden hair and perfect heart-shaped face, but quite striking.

Rebecca Marston. The name came back with sudden clarity. She was one of the Incomparables of last year who had declined to marry, and—for those inclined to court with marriage in mind, which he wasn't—the challenge of this season. Her wealthy father was one of the most influential men in British politics, and there were rumors of the possibility of an appointment as Prime Minister in his future.

The man despised him. Robert knew it full well. That he was innocent of the perceived crime didn't really help the matter much, since Sir Benedict had made it scathingly clear that he believed the worst.

Perhaps he and Miss Marston shouldn't spend time alone in darkened gardens together. Robert opened his mouth to excuse himself, when a voice called out from the terrace, confirming his identification. "Miss Marston?"

Rebecca clutched his arm with unmistakable urgency. "Help me hide."

His brows shot up. "Hide?"

"Please." She glanced around, a clear look of panic on her lovely face. "I can't take another moment of Lord Watts this evening or I fear I will splinter into little tiny pieces."

Robert knew the man and sympathized, recalling her hurry to leave the ballroom. Never one to deny a lady a timely rescue, he glanced around, spotted a smaller path diverting off through the hedge and pointed. "That way."

She responded with alacrity, dashing in front of him, and though it would probably have been more prudent to let her elude the exceedingly dull viscount on her own, Robert followed in amusement. The path led around a small pond filled with fish and lilies but came to a dead end in a tiny niche cut into the hedge. Here a bronze statue of Pan, flute and all, was flanked by two small benches. On a warm summer day it was probably a pleasant place to sit.

Right now, it was shadowed and private.

Miss Marston halted and turned, peering past him. She said in a whisper, "Do you think he saw me?"

Saw *us*, a practical voice in Robert's head corrected. Together in a dark place alone.

Just what the devil was he doing?

"Miss Marston?" The call got a little bolder. And unfortunately, closer. "Rebecca?"

Damnation, it was really too dark for Watts to have identified them clearly, but he must have caught hint of enough movement to see what path they chose.

Robert put his finger to his lips and took her arm, drawing her back into the shadows. He eased her so her back was against the hedge and braced a hand on the sturdy bushes on either side of her slender shoulders, leaning forward to whisper in her ear, "Play along and I'll get rid of him. Whatever you do, don't speak and keep your face hidden."

She nodded, her eyes huge and glimmering.

Robert was quite a bit taller and definitely broader, and with the uncertain lighting, he was fairly certain no one would be able to distinguish her features. Sure enough, he could hear footsteps coming their way and he knew it was just as important for *him* to get rid of Rebecca Marston's importunate suitor as it was for her to evade His Lordship. Why the devil had Robert followed her? His unfathomable impulse would have some alarming consequences if they were caught together alone in this sheltered alcove.

He lowered his head and his mouth just brushed her cheek. Not her lips, though he touched the soft, tempting corner of her mouth and could feel the sweet exhale of her breath. It was an imitation kiss, not the real thing.

Has she had the real thing?

No, not a thought appropriate to the moment.

"Put your hand on my shoulder," he urged.

She did so, the light weight of her fingers settling hesitantly on his jacket.

As predicted, Rebecca's hapless suitor stumbled into the little garden vignette, and Robert sensed it took

Watts a moment to spot the "lovers" in their false embrace.

Well, Robert thought, this was where his reputation actually could do him some good. No one would think he had an innocent young woman backed up to a hedge for a leisurely dalliance. His lovers were always experienced, sophisticated ladies, uninterested in a permanent entanglement. Rebecca Marston didn't fit that description at all, so Watts was unlikely to guess she was the woman in his arms.

He lifted his head, turned just enough so Watts could recognize his features and said in a clear, concise tone, "I would appreciate it if you would bugger off, my lord."

"Oh ... er ... quite. My apologies, Northfield. Looking for someone ... you know. I'll ... well, just move along then." The man sounded both apologetic and embarrassed. "Sorry. Didn't expect to find you here. Looking for someone else."

Robert turned back without answering, ostensibly to resume kissing the young woman whose soft body was pressed just close enough to his chest that he could feel the warm resilience of her breasts through her gown and smell the haunting fragrance of what he registered with an expertise born of much experience to be jasmine.

His very favorite.

She had exquisitely soft skin, he thought as he nuzzled her jaw and listened to that buffoon, Watts, retreat down the path.

To his chagrin, he began to harden, his body reacting to her closeness and that tantalizing scent.

The voice of reason reappeared, thanks to God. *Of course she has lovely skin, a supple body, shining hair that gleams in the moonlight. After all, she is ... what? Nineteen? Twenty at the most? Marriageable? Oh yes. And if her father noticed her departure from the ballroom and decided to follow ...*

Considering how Sir Benedict felt about him, they might be facing each other with pistols at dawn.

Abruptly Robert straightened and stepped back.

"You might want to wait here for a few minutes. I was thinking of leaving the party anyway, and will probably just retreat out the back gate."

Rebecca Marston nodded, staring up at him, her lips just slightly parted. "Thank you. That was . . . inventive."

Her mouth glistened invitingly. And though her gown was demure, it still managed to showcase a figure that was fashioned by nature to make a male take notice. Unlike some of the men of his acquaintance, Robert didn't prefer petite women. Though still too short to look him in the eye, Rebecca was taller than average, and those breasts—well, he had a connoisseur's eye, and naked, he guessed they would be nothing short of spectacular. No wonder Watts was bumbling around the gardens in search of her. She was a delectable young lady.

He might be just as foolish as Watts, standing with her there in the dark—the two of them alone, no less—and fantasizing about touching her tempting person, his growing erection proof of the lascivious direction of his thoughts.

Her undoubtedly untried, innocent person.

It was time to make a quick exit.

Robert essayed a flashing, careless smile. "My pleasure entirely." Though bells of alarm raised a racket in his head, he couldn't help but say, "If you ever need assistance in escaping more unwanted suitors, feel free to call on me."

Then he swung on his heel and wisely walked away.

Chapter Three

The element of surprise is always useful. Keep in mind that men like variety. If you can provide it, then they needn't look elsewhere for diversion.

From the chapter titled: "Understanding Your Quarry"

"Do you mind," Lea asked with one brow lifted askance, "telling me just what you were thinking?"

It was a lovely fall day, the sky cloudless, the air warm, and they were seated in her sister's small garden. One of the children ran in a circle in the grass, dropped down delightedly with a piercing but joyful shriek, and then rolled over without regard to the possibility of stains on her lacy dress. Brianna watched her niece's antics, trying to hide her smile. "Can you be more specific?"

Her sister gave her a quelling glance. Lea was five years older, also blond and slender. They might look alike, but Lea had always been a little on the prim side. "You know perfectly well what I'm talking about. It is all over the society papers—how you wore a gown designed by that French modiste and had everyone whispering at the opera the other evening. By all accounts, it was either the height of fashion or the most provocative attire worn in public in quite some time."

Duchess or not, all at once Brianna felt like the child she used to be, censured by her older sibling. "It was daring," she admitted, "but I had a very good reason for deciding to wear it. It isn't like there weren't other women in attendance with necklines just as low."

"I hope you realize you are one of the most envied women in society." Lea stood up, walked over to lift her daughter gently to her feet and wipe the grass blades from her hem before urging her to resume play with the other two children. Lea returned to the bench in the warm sunshine and sank down in a graceful swirl of skirts. "You can't do something outrageous and assume no one will comment. You are the Duchess of Rolthven."

"I was only trying to get Colton's attention, not everyone else's."

"What on earth are you talking about? It seems to me you have his attention. He is your husband."

"I certainly did catch his notice that evening." Brianna recalled the carriage ride with an inner smile.

"Whatever do you mean?"

Brianna shrugged, hoping it looked like casual dismissal. In truth, her feelings on the subject were anything but casual. "Is it wrong of me to want more from my marriage?"

"I thought you were over the moon with happiness to be marrying Colton, and that you are rather unfashionably in love with your husband." Lea's smooth brow furrowed in a small frown.

That was all true.

It was the problem, really. Had she just wanted to marry a powerful duke, she might have been satisfied with the stature, money, and influence her position now gave her. But Brianna would have married Colton—as Lea had her Henry—if he'd been ordinary in every way.

"I do love Colton—that isn't the issue. Well, it is, I suppose." Brianna idly adjusted her silk skirts with one hand, her gaze focused on the playing children. "I think he is pleased he married me. I know he is attracted to me, and that he even finds my company enjoyable, though we don't see each other nearly often enough in my opinion. But does he love me? Of that, I am not so sure. In our society it is perfectly acceptable for him *not* to love me, for that matter. It is not, however, acceptable to me. Were my own feelings not engaged, I am sure I would be content. But I wish to be more than content. I want to be happy. More than that, I want *Colton* to be happy."

"I doubt it made him happy to have you appear in public wearing only half a gown," Lea pointed out, ever the practical older sister.

"It irritated him very much," Brianna admitted. "But he also—maybe for the first time since we met—got the sense that I am my own person and I may not always act predictably, whether or not it pleases him." She couldn't help a mischievous smile. "Besides, once we were alone, I got the distinct impression he rather admired the gown after all. Which, as I said before, is the only reason I wore it. So far our marriage has been on his terms alone. That is going to change. I want us to share our lives, not just the same address."

Her sister said nothing for a moment, before her mouth twitched and she laughed. "I see. You sound quite determined. You were such a stubborn child when you got a notion into your head. The poor man really doesn't have a chance. Does Colton realize what he is up against?"

Brianna thought of the book and said serenely, "He hasn't the slightest idea."

Something strange was going on—of that there was no doubt.

When the door into his bedroom from the adjoining suite swung open, Colton was a trifle wary. During dinner Brianna had been particularly animated, and if they hadn't had guests, he might have asked her flat out why exactly she was acting so markedly different. He could have sworn she seemed nervous, but for the life of him he couldn't imagine why. Lord and Lady Black were on the dull side and they concentrated more on the food than conversation, so he couldn't believe their company had sparked such a reaction.

"It's late and I dismissed my maid for the night. Will you help me out of my dress?" She'd taken the pins from her hair and it fell to her waist in shining blond curls that caught the low light. Barefoot, she walked slowly toward him, her brows arched slightly in teasing question.

Will I help you out of your dress?

He couldn't think of anything he'd enjoy more.

Colton's fingers fumbled slightly as he complied and slipped free the fastenings on her evening gown. It slid off her slender shoulders and fell to the floor. Her chemise was nothing like the demure undergarments she usually wore, but instead made out of a lace so sheer she might as well have been wearing nothing at all. Colton could not help but take a quick breath. His voice a trifle thick, he said, "I see Madame Ellen has been at her scandalous work again."

Turning around, Brianna smiled at him mischievously. "It was a warm summer, and I wanted something a little cooler to wear under my gowns."

"It's warm, all right," Colton muttered darkly, tugging at his cravat, pulling it loose and discarding it carelessly.

"Shall I go back to my room?"

He almost didn't register her delicately phrased question. Pink, perfect nipples thrust high against the sheer fabric of her shift, and the soft weight of her opulent breasts molded by the fragile material. It fell to midthigh, and Colton could clearly see the intriguing darkness between her legs. "I beg your pardon?"

Her laugh was light and provocative, her soft mouth curving. "I asked if I should go back to my room, but I am going to assume *that*"—she pointed at the sudden prominent bulge in his tight breeches—"is my answer. Here, you helped me. Now it's my turn."

To his utter astonishment, his beautiful, refined young bride dropped to her knees in front of him and began to unfasten his trousers. The brush of her slender fingers through the material as she worked was excruciatingly arousing, and he hardened further, almost holding his breath as she finally tugged open the last button and freed his erection.

"Brianna," he said hoarsely, as she began to stroke his cock, her caressing hands making his entire body quiver. "What are you doing?"

Wiping a bead of semen from the engorged tip, she looked at the substance on her finger with open curiosity, and to his shock, licked it off. "It's salty," she said artlessly, looking up at him like a young nymph, all veiled, lush curves and flowing hair. Her lashes lowered a fraction and Colton felt a rush of molten heat through his veins as she leaned forward with unmistakable intent. Her soft lips slid over the head of his erection, the sensation exquisite.

Never in his life had he been so outraged.

Never in his life had anything felt so good.

Oh, he'd had lovers before his marriage who had pleasured him orally, but they'd been experienced women, not innocent, genteel young ladies who should have no notion of doing any such a thing. His hands went to her hair, and he had every intention of demanding to know just where Brianna had gotten the idea to do something so wanton, but just as his fingers sank into the silky mass to tug her head up, she began to suck gently.

A low sound tore up from his chest and his body shook. Without thought he pushed deeper in her warm mouth. His movement was an unconscious reflex and almost immediately he tried to withdraw, but she cupped his ballocks and instead he groaned again. Sliding up, her tongue licked the crest of his erection and then she repeated the motion with tantalizing slowness over and over. Colton trembled, not able to bring himself to make her stop until he felt his testicles tighten in preparation for ejaculation. He absolutely refused to come in her mouth. It was not something a gentleman did, but he was wild with the need for release.

"Enough," he growled, somehow finding the will to pull free before scooping her off the floor. He crossed the room, practically tossing her on the bed in a flurry of golden curls and long silken limbs. Jerking up the hem of her chemise, he heard the delicate material rip, and a rash part of him he didn't know existed decided that if the garment was already damaged, it would come off faster if he just tore it. Brianna gave a low gasp as he deliberately jerked her bodice apart.

Gloriously exposed, she stared up at him, her body lush and inviting. If he entered her now, Colton knew he'd explode at once and cheat her of any kind of release. He undid two buttons on his linen shirt, decided it would take too long to unfasten it, whipped it off over his head, and then stepped out of his unfastened breeches. "If you wish to play wicked games, madam," he told her, his glittering gaze admiring every inch of her nude form, "it is now my turn."

She licked her lips. "I wish to play any game you choose."

"You'll like this one." Joining her on the bed, he nuzzled her breasts briefly, kissed her stomach, and then buried his face in the sweetness between her legs.

Brianna gasped, as he expected she would, and for a moment her thighs clamped together in protest against such a sinful kiss, but he didn't allow it. Insistently, his hands pushed her slim legs apart, and he pressed his mouth against the sensitive moistness of her sex. Licking and stroking with his tongue, he teased her just as she had teased him, and he could feel her arousal when the small nub between her folds began to swell against the pressure of his mouth. She tasted sweetly female, and as he brought her to climax, her small cries of pleasure inflamed him even more. In moments Brianna convulsed, her hands grasping his arms as she shuddered and moaned. Not giving her time to recover, Colton moved up between her open thighs, and thrust into her still contracting passage.

As predicted, it was over quickly. Her wet heat milking him, release hit him after the first three thrusts, the sensation of carnal pleasure so intense, so good, that he closed his eyes and went rigid. Beneath him, Brianna ran her hands down the damp skin of his back, clutching his buttocks as he flooded her with hot sperm. His muscles shook with the force of his ejaculation.

When he could finally speak again, he stared down at the utterly tempting, disheveled woman in his arms framed in tatters of ruined lace. "Do you mind telling me," he asked unevenly, his chest still lifting in an erratic rhythm as he struggled to regain his breath, "just what has gotten into you, my dear?"

Her fingers traced the small of his back. "It seems to me that *you* are in me, Colton."

A muffled laugh escaped his lips at the erotic joke. "And it is a delightful place to be, but that is not what I meant, as I have a feeling you know full well." The fragrance of flowers drifted from her hair and he couldn't help but kiss the side of her graceful neck, inhaling the sweet scent. "Whatever gave you the idea to . . . well . . ."

How in the hell did a man politely ask a woman why she wanted to suck his cock, Colton thought darkly, discomforted because he could sense Brianna's amusement over his quest for the right words. He wasn't at all used to what seemed to be a sudden shift in power in their relationship. *He* was the experienced one. She had come to their marriage bed a virgin and only knew what he had shown her, and he certainly had never asked her for something he was convinced would shock her to her very core. It was well and good if a light-o'-love wished to use her mouth to bring a man pleasure, but it wasn't something you suggested to your proper young wife of three months.

"I thought you liked it." The husky note in her voice matched the seductive light stroking of her fingers down his bare back.

Liked it? That was putting it mildly.

Colton fought to sound rational and calm while his heart still pounded wildly. "Madam, you know full well I liked it, but you are being evasive."

"Must you be so analytical at this particular moment?" Beneath him, Brianna arched a little, and added breathlessly, "You still feel so big."

Her words sent a jolt of new arousal straight to his groin. It was true; his erection hadn't faded, even with the force of his recent climax. Colton decided she was right—at least for now, the cause of her sudden sexually adventurous spirit wasn't important. Not when he could make love to her again. He kissed her and whispered against her soft lips, "This discussion isn't over. We'll continue it some other time."

Truly the book had been an inspiration.

Sated and a little drowsy, Brianna curled comfortably in her husband's embrace, hours after her uninvited entrance into his bedchamber. After their initial heated, hurried joining, Colton had proceeded to make love to her with restrained tenderness, moving slowly so she savored each slick long glide of their bodies fitting together, caressing her sensitive breasts, teasing the hollow under her ear before taking her mouth in long, searing kisses.

He was so quiet she wondered if he might be asleep, until he murmured, "My apologies for the loss of your shift."

Brianna tilted her head up so she could see his face, trying to read his expression. Without all the formal clothing, his chestnut hair tousled against the pillow slip, he looked different from the refined duke she had married. Not just handsome but devastatingly so, his lean body hard and male, that part of him that had so pleased her now lax between his muscular thighs. It was startling to realize that though they had been married for over three months, she hadn't ever really seen him naked. When he came to her room he wore his dressing gown, and it was always dark before he joined her in bed.

This was much, much better.

Brianna asked playfully, "Are you really sorry? I'm not."

His lashes lowered a fraction. "It seems to me it is a barbaric discourtesy to rip off your wife's clothing."

"Believe me, you are forgiven, Colton." She couldn't be more sincere.

"You caught me rather off guard, my dear."

So had he her, with that wicked intimate kiss between her legs. When she'd read the suggestion she actually put her mouth on his sex she'd been shocked, but true to Lady Rothburg's assertion, he'd obviously enjoyed it immensely. So much he'd ripped off her shift in feverish need.

Progress indeed.

It was a nice balance, she decided in luxurious contentment, between impetuous wild need and the careful gentleness of his later lovemaking. Before the night of the opera, she had experienced only the latter, but both had their merits. It was a little shocking to discover she liked sexual intercourse fast and hard, and that her own level of desire was elevated by her husband's loss of control.

It was exhilarating. From now on, Madame Ellen would make all her underclothing out of sheer lace.

"I hope I wasn't too demanding." His fingers feathered down her arm.

"Did you sense any objection on my part?"

"No." One of his rare smiles surfaced, lighting his fine features. As quickly as it came, it was gone. "But still, I was rather importunate."

That he hadn't been entirely in charge of the situation bothered him. She'd expected it would. He was so very used to making decisions not just for himself, but ones that affected others. In his personal life, there were now two of them; his decision wasn't the only one that mattered. Hopefully he would come to see it that way soon.

"I am rather more than fine, Colton." Brianna yawned. "Deliciously tired, if I may say so, but it is not a bad state to be in."

"No, my dear, I suppose it isn't."

She rubbed her cheek against Colton's damp, hard

chest, hoping he wouldn't suggest she return to her own
room. Usually he came to her bedchamber, following
the pattern set on the night of their wedding. The routine rarely varied, a fact that didn't surprise her since
her husband believed in an ordered life. He would wait
until she was in bed and her maid was dismissed, inquire
politely if she was too tired for his company, and then
proceed to douse the lights. Never before tonight had he
disrobed her completely, choosing instead to touch her
through her nightdress, lifting the hem when he moved
to take her, his entry into her body always careful and
measured. When he was done, he invariably went back
to his own bed. Occasionally he waited until she fell
asleep, but usually he simply excused himself with the
same politesse with which he'd come to her, and left.

It made sense, she supposed when she thought about
it, for all of the *beau monde* considered it fashionable
for husbands and wives to have separate bedrooms, and
Colton was practical to a fault. If he *had* his own bedroom, then why should he not sleep there?

Maybe it made sense, but it was intensely irritating.

It wasn't that she hadn't enjoyed their sexual con-
gress from the very beginning—even that first nervous
night she'd been aroused by her husband—but she had
felt as if she was giving him something and he was taking it. The phrase "conjugal rights" seemed to apply to
those shrouded, restrained encounters. She would never
deny him, but Brianna disliked inherently the idea of
applying the concept of duty to something as beautiful
as what they had just shared.

Before tonight she would not even have really termed
herself his lover. Wife, yes. Lover, no. But now here she
was, finally in his bed, nude and deliciously tired, with
his discharge sticky on her thighs and his arm curled
comfortably around her.

"Brianna." He touched her cheek, his fingers light. "I
have a very early morning and my day is full of appointments."

A feeling of sharp disappointment replaced her languorous well-being. "It sounds similar to most of your days, Your Grace."

"I hardly think you need to address me so formally at a time like this."

She said nothing.

"Rogers will be here at daybreak as per my instructions," her husband said in the same reasonable tone, as if he hadn't just made love to her with consummate passion.

"And heaven forbid your valet should find me in your bed." Brianna sat up, shaking back her long hair, giving her husband a level challenging look. "I take it I am dismissed, now that I've served my purpose."

Relaxed against the crisp white sheets, his skin still holding a sheen of perspiration from their exertions, Colton frowned. "I'd hardly put it that way. I *didn't* put it that way. I just don't want to wake you when I arise."

"How considerate of you."

"Actually, yes, I was trying to be." His brows went up. "But from the sarcasm in your tone, apparently you don't agree."

"Sometimes I think you must be the most obtuse man in all of London." Brianna slid from the bed, trying to remind herself that no one could change quickly, and her handsome but infuriating husband was a particular challenge. She was certain the notion he needed to adjust anything in *his* life to fit *her* romantic sensibilities would startle him.

Love, also, was a word he rarely considered.

"Will you explain to me how allowing my wife an uninterrupted night's sleep makes me obtuse?" He watched her scoop up her discarded clothing, his eyes heavy lidded. Though he remained reclined on the bed, his mouth was tight.

"No." Brianna walked away deliberately so he could watch her nude backside as she headed for the door separating their bedchambers. "Good night, *Your Grace*."

She thought she heard him mutter a low curse before she left the room.

*   *   *

What the hell had just happened?

Colton lay in bed and stared at the ceiling, wondering if he should go into his wife's bedroom and demand an explanation. Well, two explanations.

No, three.

She definitely owed him three.

First there was the dress. He was still befuddled over why she had worn it in the first place, even if Robert had come up with a reasonable way to prevent *that* from happening again. Then she had boldly surprised him by performing an act he would have sworn she could have known nothing about, and now . . . well, he wasn't sure what the devil had just happened.

He had the unsettling knowledge that after the most satisfying sexual experience of his entire life, he'd just committed some kind of marital faux pas and hurt her. It was confounding because he could have sworn that in the blissful postcoital aftermath they had been more in accord than ever before. Certainly Brianna had felt perfect in his arms, warm and flushed from sexual gratification, her slender body fitted to his, the silk of her glorious pale hair spilled across his chest. From the very first time he'd touched her she had been surprisingly responsive, but tonight had been earth-shattering.

Until he'd blundered, apparently.

His moody stare fastened on her door, now firmly shut.

So ripping her clothes off was fine but being solicitous enough to not want to disturb her in the morning wasn't?

. . . and heaven forbid your valet should find me in your bed . . .

If she thought he would be happy about any man, servant or not, seeing her in alluring dishabille, all golden hair and ivory skin, naked underneath only a thin coverlet, she was sorely mistaken. Their private life was just that, private, and her delectable beauty was his alone.

He'd talk to her, he decided, when he wasn't so tired and confused by her erratic behavior.

But despite a full day and lengthy vigorous lovemaking, he found he couldn't sleep right away.

Something odd was going on, he decided as he lay in the darkness, watching the moon send struggling illumination against the draperies. It was disordering his world, and he'd always had such a tidy, predictable existence.

Chapter Four

Avoid men who pose as something they are not. In a lover, character is still important, even if the transient pleasure of his embrace is all you seek. I have a specific affection for young rakehells, for they are genuine and upfront about the fleeting nature of their interest. They are also inevitably charming. If you should be the woman who finally captures the sincere attachment of one, you are lucky indeed.

From the chapter titled:
"Those Darling Wicked Gentlemen"

Their horses walked side by side, both magnificent animals, but like the men who rode them, very different. Robert, of course, chose a Barbary stallion, his favorite breed; the restive animal could prove hard to control, but well worth the effort if you wanted endurance and speed. His oldest brother—no surprise—rode a thoroughbred, all slender legs and massive haunches, with shoulders built for short distances, a sprinter extraordinaire, the toast of the British bloodstock books. After winning a fortune in prizes, Thebes was now retired and in stud, but Colton rode him because the horse was a favorite pet as well as an investment.

They suited each other, aristocratic duke and sleek champion, Robert thought with inner amusement, though at the moment his brother's normally serene, good-looking countenance was wreathed in a severe frown. "I am at a loss over my wife."

"Confounded by a woman?" It was impossible not to laugh. "What a novel concept."

Colton sent him a quelling look. "Your amusement is not helpful."

"Is help what you want?"

After a moment, Colton equivocated, "Maybe. She's behaving erratically."

The park was fairly full on such a lovely autumn morning and they nodded to several acquaintances, falling quiet until they were once again alone on the path. A pure blue sky stretched above, punctuated by eggshell clouds. Robert said mildly, "Brianna seemed perfectly normal at Grandmama's birthday luncheon last week. I wouldn't have used the term 'erratic,' but then again, I don't see her every day."

It was true. Robert had his own townhouse, declining to live in the grandiose family residence in Mayfair. He wasn't the Duke, he wasn't even second in line—his older brother Damien held that distinction for the moment—and Robert liked doing as he pleased without censure.

Again, there was a palpable hesitation. Colton's hands tightened enough on the reins that Thebes tossed his head. He patted the horse's neck in apology. "It isn't something you would notice from the outside, but I sure as the devil am seeing a difference."

It wasn't often his older brother was so obviously discomforted. Robert had to admit it made him curious as hell. He glanced over, wrinkling his brow. "You're going to have to explain, Colt."

"Yes, deuce take it, I realize that."

The irritation in Colton's response was even more curious than his unusual request for a morning ride. Robert waited patiently as their horses walked leisurely along the winding path through the grass and trees, feeling peaceful in the warmth of the unusually fair weather.

"The other night she ... well, let's say it was unexpected."

Now that was hardly enlightening, but Robert at least got a sense of what Colton might be discussing—or *not* discussing as it were—because his normally composed brother had a faint flush on his face. "Do you mean in bed?" Robert asked bluntly.

Colton sent him a quick look and nodded briefly. "Yes."

"Unexpected in a good way or a bad one?" After all, it was Colton who had sent the missive requesting a morning ride and it was Colton who sought his advice. If Robert was going to forego a morning's lie-in for this discussion, they needed to actually *discuss* the matter and stop dancing around it.

"Good." Colton said it shortly. Then he amended. "Very good, if you must know."

"I don't *need* to know anything about the intimacies of your marriage, Colt, but you brought the subject up."

"I realize that." The Duke of Rolthven definitely sounded out of sorts. "Sorry," he added in a more conciliatory tone. "It's one thing to discuss women in a general way, but my wife is something different."

Robert didn't have a comment for that one. There was no precedent in his life for talking about a wife, so how could he know?

"It's private."

"I would imagine." Colton was a private person in general, so the conversation was getting more intriguing by the moment.

Colton stared fixedly at a copse of trees as if it was the most fascinating thing on earth. "Oh hell, well, all right. She ... well, she did something she's never done before."

Oh, that helped. Robert murmured, "Order tea afterwards? Sing a song as she undressed? Dance across the window ledge stark naked? Invite her maid to join you? You are going to have to be blunter. Subtlety is for females as they sit and sip sherry and exchange gossip. I can't read your mind."

"Fine, fine," Colton growled. "Brianna took me in

her mouth. What's more, she did a damn good job of it too."

Though his first thought was that the incident made his brother a lucky man indeed, Robert refrained from mentioning it. With caution, he asked, "And you object to what happened?"

"Good God, of course not." But Colton's laugh was short, and his blue eyes held a troubled look. "I just wonder where she got the idea."

"Not from you?"

"No, not from me. She's a lady. I wouldn't ever ask her to do such a thing."

The light dawned. Sitting at ease in his saddle, Robert fought back a laugh. "You do realize you are fretting over something most men would be toasting and celebrating. Sex is a normal and instinctive process. Brianna has married friends. Maybe there is a husband among them who isn't so polite. Women talk amongst themselves. It is one of their favorite pastimes."

"Not about what happens behind the closed doors of their bedrooms, surely."

"Why not?"

"It's not a delicate subject."

A certain part of Robert wondered in cynical amusement if growing up in the shadow of impending ducal responsibilities sapped so much of a man's attention that he lost focus on the real world. "Colt, think about it. Women are fascinated by romance. By nature they are much more absorbed in the subject than we are. No, I don't think they talk constantly about the mechanics of what happens, but why should they? The act itself is pretty universal. One part into another part. It feels damned good for both parties if done right, and though there are some variations, the basic principles are all the same. Men focus on things like the size of a pair of breasts or how willing or skillful the partner, but women like something else entirely. Tender words, the drift of your fingers through their hair, a poetic phrase about a sunrise when entwined in bed at dawn. None of that is indelicate."

"Which supports my point," Colton said acerbically. "Who would suggest to her I might like such wanton behavior?"

"I thought you just admitted that you did like it."

"That's beside the point, Robbie."

It was his *very* point, but Robert let it go. Instead he patiently explained, "Even if they look at the sexual relationship differently than we do, it seems natural to me that one of her acquaintances might mention how riveted a man becomes when a beautiful woman sucks his cock. Not the way we would talk about it, of course, but in the more delicate way women converse about such things. I imagine them discussing what pleases us. While we tend to think about what *we* like, women are much more selfless. We insist on it."

His older brother shot him a disgruntled look. "Which side are you on, anyway?"

Robert was male through and through, but he did recognize the inequity in the sexes as far as power went, in bed and out of it. "Ours. Very firmly," he asserted. "But let's be honest. The control belongs to us. Intelligent females know this. Keeping us happy makes their lives easier, especially if they are at our mercy, like our wives."

"Brianna is *not* at my mercy." Colton swiveled in his saddle, giving his best display of ducal disdain, eyebrows up, a haughty set to his features. "She's my wife, not a prisoner or slave."

Robert couldn't hide his amusement. "I am sure you give her a generous allowance, but I am just as sure you govern the manner in which she spends it. On the same note, you allow her to accept invitations to various entertainments on the behalf of both of you . . . but I'd wager you reserve the right to approve them and reverse her decisions. She may go out alone, but only if she is accompanied by her maid or some reasonable substitute, so alone is a relative term, correct?"

"I am not some despotic—"

"No," Robert interrupted, "you aren't. You are simply a typical husband. We make females very dependent on us, don't we? What we view as protection could easily be interpreted as smothering dominance."

After a moment, Colton exhaled a long sigh that rang with exasperation. "Let's say I concede all that, though Brianna has never complained even once about any of those small rules. . . ."

Robert gave an inelegant snort at the use of the word "small." For himself, if anyone even attempted to direct him in how he should spend his money or overrode his decision on any matter—even something as trivial as whether to attend a play or go to a soiree—he would be annoyed beyond belief. Then again, he was male, and once he'd reached his majority, he'd had carte blanche in how to live his life. But the status quo among married couples was that husbands always had the last say. Married women had as little autonomy as unmarried women who had to defer to their fathers.

His older brother ignored the derisive sound and went on determinedly, "I still say she is acting strangely."

"And I say she is merely high-spirited and maybe more adventurous than you at first assumed. Why brood over such a delightful thing as an enthusiastic woman in your bed, even if she is your wife?"

Colton rubbed his jaw with a gloved hand, his eyes narrowed against the sun. "I suppose when put that way, it is ridiculous to spend my time worrying over it, but I admit she caught me very off guard. When I queried her about where she got the notion for her behavior, she was evasive."

Robert fought the urge to break into a fit of laughter. "Only you, Colt, would pose an interrogation after a particularly satisfying sexual encounter. You do have a tendency to overthink things. You always have."

"I'm more used to experienced females," his brother murmured. "This is all new to me and, perhaps you're right, could be perfectly natural as she becomes more adjusted to the intimacies of being married. However, her closest two friends are Bonham's new countess and

Rebecca Marston. I can't see Bonham tutoring his wife
in such a way, for they've been married a month less than
Brianna and I. Miss Marston is unmarried, well chaperoned by her protective father, and a very refined young
lady. Neither seems a likely candidate for whispering
scandalous suggestions into my wife's ear, and I can't
think of anyone else with whom Brianna would discuss
something so personal. I suppose my sister-in-law might
have said something, but truly, she's a respectable matron with three children."

The mention of the lovely Rebecca with her sea
green eyes and gleaming dark hair brought back Robert's memories of holding her pressed to that wall of
hedge, his mouth hovering over hers and the quiver of
her shapely body against him. The incident was trivial,
nothing but a few moments of polite speech followed by
the ensuing rush to evade the persistent Lord Watts, but
Robert had found himself thinking back on it more than
once in the past few days. It puzzled him he couldn't just
dismiss it.

That damned jasmine perfume, he told himself wryly.
It evoked fantasies of exotic gardens, soft, smooth skin,
and a singular breathless sigh. . . .

He must truly be jaded to even spare one thought
about the completely off-limits Miss Marston. *Marriageable*, he reminded himself and squelched even the faintest hint of amorous interest. Besides, after *that incident*,
her father, Sir Benedict, had trouble being even mar-
ginally polite to Robert when they occasionally came
face-to-face.

"If you want my opinion, drop the whole matter,
Colt," Robert said succinctly, "or you risk making your
pretty wife self-conscious. While you are at it, I think
I would tell her that as long as she doesn't overspend,
she may handle her pin money as she wishes, and make
any other concessions that won't cause you too much
discomfort. Quite obviously she wants to please you.
Return the favor." He nudged his horse with his heel.
"Now then, shall we gallop? I'm in the mood to try out

Sahir against Thebes. He's in a fine mettle this morning."

The music room was quiet, with long ivory velvet draperies drawn across the windows to improve the acoustics and enhance the aura of privacy. A pot of ink and several lined sheets of paper lay on top of the pianoforte, but just a few unsatisfying notes were written on the bars, and the only sound was the occasional creak of the bench as Rebecca shifted position.

Her muse was elusive this morning, she admitted to herself with a sigh. It had been that way for the past few days. Her new routine was discomforting. She entered the room each morning and began the same set of tasks: readying her pen, arranging the sheets so she could scribble down the notes as they filled her head and flowed to her fingers, settling on the bench with her skirts adjusted demurely, her hands poised over the keyboard.

But nothing came. None of the usual joy. Instead of devoting herself to her passion for music, she found a different kind of passion now absorbed her thoughts and it was infernally distracting.

Chin in her palm, one elbow propped, she pensively played F sharp, holding the single note for a moment before lifting her finger. There. At least she could say she'd done something besides sit there and think about the impossible.

And her dreams *were* impossible.

Now she *knew* what it was like to be close to Robert, to smell the clean, male tang of cologne and fresh linen, to feel the brush of his lips against her skin and the strength of his lean body as he pressed her against him. . . .

Well, it made things much, much worse, and she'd known all along her hopeless infatuation with a seasoned libertine who regarded casual conquest as the order of the day was ridiculous. Not to mention her father's disdain for the man.

A quick knock interrupted her hopeless fantasies of

being held in Robert Northfield's arms. Rebecca prayed
it wasn't the butler or one of the maids come to tell her
Lord Watts was calling. "Yes?"

The door swung open and to her relief Brianna came
into view, just enough to poke her head around the edge
of the door. "I took a chance, Beck, you would be home.
I told Hains not to formally announce me and bother
you. If you're working, I'll call again later if I'm out and
about."

While Rebecca's parents considered composing music
too bluestocking a pastime for her to talk about, of
course Arabella and Brianna knew about her passion
and understood. In fact, they were her best audience
when she had a new piece to share, and they always at
least loyally claimed to be impressed and entranced,
bless them. Rebecca shook her head. "I am trying to
work but failing miserably. Maybe a little visit with a
dear friend will inspire me. Come in."

She should probably take a duchess to the formal
drawing room, but this was Brianna. Sure enough, the
exalted Duchess of Rolthven looked pleased at the in-
formality and settled in one of the embroidered chairs in
a swirl of blue silk skirts. Her pale hair was caught up in
a simple chignon; someone of Brianna's dazzling beauty
didn't need elaborate coiffures. Rebecca often thought
Brianna's modesty made her even more attractive and
was why she had caught the eye of one of England's
most eligible bachelors. The Duchess of Rolthven's air
of self-possession gave her an elegant poise for one so
young.

Last season all three of them had been remarkable
successes. Brianna emerged with her handsome duke,
Arabella with her good-natured earl—and then there
was Rebecca. She'd turned down proposal after proposal
because she had an ill-fated penchant for a reckless rake
who she was fairly sure couldn't even remember her
name the other evening.

Maybe she wasn't much of a success after all.

"I'm going to have a house party."

Rebecca blinked at the bold announcement. "You are? I thought you loathed house parties."

Brianna made a face. "I do, normally. That is, all that archery—which I am horrible at anyway—and musicals, and playacting. But even though I detest them, it doesn't mean everyone does. They are immensely popular, especially in the autumn. I hope Colton will be pleasantly surprised when I explain it is for his birthday, which is in a few weeks. It is deuced hard to find a gift for a man who owns half of Britain, you know. He has everything material anyone could want. I *think* this will please him, though I can't be sure. We can have it at Rolthven Manor and his grandmother can help me organize it. She'll be delighted, and really, that huge house could stand to be used a little more. Except for the staff, she fairly rattles around alone in it most of the time."

"I thought you were just there."

"For her birthday," Brianna confirmed. "The estate is convenient to town and we didn't stay long, just overnight. Robert was there for even a briefer amount of time. He breezed in and then left. Damien couldn't come at all because he was still in Spain, but he will be back in England next week, I'm told. I am really going to only invite close friends and family, so it won't be one of those grand affairs I find so tedious, but hopefully just a pleasant diversion."

Rebecca tried to picture the Duke of Rolthven at a house party, even his own, and failed. It was difficult to imagine him frolicking on the lawn with a bow and arrow or participating in a mock play. He was dignified and reserved and carried his title easily, though once or twice she had seen him smile, usually at his wife, and it lent a warmth to his features that hinted at a different side. Rebecca didn't know him well enough to judge whether he would be pleased at the prospect of having a fete at his ancestral home, but Brianna seemed enthusiastic, and Rebecca said loyally, "I am sure it will be wonderful."

"I truly hope so. It's my aim to make sure Colton

doesn't work so hard all the time." Brianna's feathery brows drew together in a small frown. "I am not at all sure he'll thank me for it, if you want the truth, but I am determined just the same. We have been married for over three months and I still do not know him. I admit things aren't as I expected."

Since one day she was going to have to choose a husband—her parents had made it all too clear they thought they'd been patient long enough—Rebecca asked frankly, "What *did* you expect?"

Brianna fingered the material of her gown, a thoughtful expression on her lovely face. "I think his formality and distance seemed normal as he courted me. He is, after all, a little intimidating on first acquaintance. Unfortunately, nothing much has changed since we wed. Oh, he's generous and polite, almost to a fault. That civility makes my teeth grate at times. I think I envisioned a growing friendship between us, but things aren't much different. We live in the same house, I have his name, and he visits my bed, but otherwise it seems like we are still living separate lives. I know he spends more time at his club than he ever does with me, and he thinks it is perfectly reasonable for his life to continue as it did before we married. Colton has what I think to be some antiquated ideas on the male/female relationship."

"They are hardly antiquated," Rebecca said tartly. "If you mean he believes every woman must act in a certain way, marry by a certain age, and follow the rules set forth by her family and society, then he isn't alone. That's a depressingly conventional view of things."

Brianna straightened her spine and stared at her. "Such vehemence. What's happened? Have your parents been pressuring you again?"

"That's an understatement. I am reminded on a daily basis that this is my second season. It would help considerably if any of the men they approved of even remotely appealed to me." Though she did her best not to sound despondent, Rebecca doubted she pulled it off.

"Is there no one?" Brianna looked sympathetic. "I

understand your father's well-known exactitude over what he deems to be suitable in a potential son-in-law is daunting to some of the men of our acquaintance, but you have had over a dozen offers for your hand, Beck. Hasn't anyone caught your fancy? Not a single handsome young gentleman who has inspired a romantic flutter of the heart?"

Robert's image unfortunately sprang to mind. The way the candlelight glinted off his chestnut hair, the elegant line of his jaw, the roguish curve of his mouth as he smiled, the graceful athletic ease as he waltzed . . .

Always with someone else, of course.

There was a disadvantage to having friends who understood your moods. Rebecca attempted nonchalance. "No."

Brianna's eyes narrowed. "Nonsense. You're blushing."

Well, that was inconvenient. "No, I'm not."

"The red spots on your cheeks support my accusation. Please, don't leave me dangling in suspense. You are never, well, *rattled* like this."

Rebecca longed to tell *someone* about her penchant for Robert Northfield, but Brianna was probably the wrong person. Rebecca trusted her implicitly, but it wasn't a matter of trust. Brianna was also Robert's sister-in-law. Besides, Rebecca wasn't at all sure Brianna wouldn't be as horrified as her father might be at the discovery of Rebecca's unreasonable passion for a known libertine.

The temptation to reveal everything but his name was there, however. She'd been keeping it a secret for well over a year. The other night in the garden hadn't helped to cure her one bit. Robert had been gallant to help her, and so close she could still feel the muscled strength of his body, and their mouths hadn't exactly touched, but . . .

Rebecca cleared her throat and gazed over at one of the shrouded windows. "I'm in love. Or at least I assume so. It must be, for all I do is think of him."

"You are?"

Rebecca nodded.

"How marvelous, Beck! Who is he?"

Rebecca shifted her gaze back to her friend. "It isn't marvelous at all, I'm afraid. Utter misery is more like it. And I am not going to tell you his name, so please do not press me."

The animation on Brianna's delicate features faded, replaced by dismay. "Misery? Why?"

No longer able to sit still, Rebecca got up and walked a few paces toward the window. She sighed and turned back around. "For about one hundred reasons, but the short of it is—it isn't possible. If it *was* possible, it still wouldn't matter because he doesn't share my interest in the least. I think he would be astounded to hear of my infatuation, and worse, even amused."

For a moment there was silence and then Brianna asked hesitantly, "Why isn't it possible? I don't understand."

This was where Rebecca knew she could get into muddy waters if she said too much. Not that there weren't a plethora of rakish gentlemen in English society—touting his reputation as the reason wouldn't narrow the field too much. Robert was more notorious than most, but not unique. She said quietly, "My father wouldn't approve. I am not sure why, but trust me, he would never agree to a courtship, even if our feelings for each other were mutual."

"Why not? Is he a servant?"

"No. His family is a good one." *In fact, you are part of it.*

"Married?"

Thank God Rebecca could deny that one with honesty. "No, of course not. I would never look at another woman's husband."

Brianna's expression held relief. "I know you wouldn't, but I wondered if maybe there was someone from last season who might have married someone else."

"That's not the case." Rebecca whirled and went to

the window to pull the drapery back. Late morning sunshine spilled in. "If it was, I would be hurt, I imagine, but then I would forget him. No, he isn't married. I'd wager the word isn't in his vocabulary. The trouble is, even if it was, even if he did realize I am alive and walk on the same planet, my father would be adamantly against any hint of an association, so it's all moot."

Getting gracefully to her feet, Brianna came across the room and hugged her tightly. "No, it isn't. Not when you look so miserable. You do realize this explains a lot of things, don't you? Bella and I have wondered all along why you seem melancholy sometimes and quite honestly, when you turned down the Marquess of Highton last year, we were both astonished. He was so smitten, not to mention rich, handsome, and most important, *nice*. I thought you liked him. Moreover, I know your parents were very much in favor of a match."

Richard was a nice man. And Rebecca had liked him. Still did. Too much to marry him while she was sitting around dreaming of someone else. "It sounds so stupid," Rebecca said, her voice cracking just a fraction, "but Lord Highton just wasn't *him*. So I turned down a perfectly decent proposal, even while knowing I haven't a chance of getting what I want. I believe that officially makes me a fool."

Brianna let her go and said stoutly, "You are not a fool. Not in the least."

"I must be, to harbor such an infatuation. The very first time I saw him ..." Rebecca trailed off, remembering the first time she'd seen Robert Northfield. She and Brianna had been together as Robert and his older brother had entered the ballroom, both strikingly handsome. Brianna had taken one look at the Duke of Rolthven and no suitor after that moment had a chance.

That had worked out well, for it turned out Colton returned the interest. Unfortunately, Rebecca had been in the same predicament with his wildly attractive but not so reputable brother, and Robert hadn't returned anything.

Not a look. Not a glance. Not a sweet word. They hadn't even been introduced until weeks later, and then only because Rebecca had been with Brianna, not at his request.

It stung. Here she was pining away for a man who even at this moment was probably in some female's bed somewhere. No doubt the woman was gorgeous and sophisticated and . . .

Best not to think about it.

Her head tilted to the side as if she was pondering something, a thoughtful look crossed Brianna's face. "Love at first sight is not just a romantic ideal. It happened to me with Colton, so no one can tell me it isn't possible. And while my husband is imperfect, I am working on changing his attitudes. I wonder if the book could help you too."

Rebecca couldn't help but let out a choked laugh. "What? Are you talking about Lady Rothburg's scandalous writings? You must be joking."

"Indeed I'm not." Brianna turned and went back to her chair in a flurry of blue silk. She folded her hands in her lap. "Contrary to all belief, the volume isn't entirely about sexual matters. Lady R gives a lot of insight into the male mind, and at least one chapter is devoted to how to capture the attention of the man you desire. As mistress to so many, she seems to have gained some very good experience with the opposite sex."

"You must not have been listening to me."

Brianna waved a hand in an airy gesture of dismissal. "There is nothing wrong with my hearing. Your father wouldn't approve and the man in question isn't interested in marriage, right? Neither are insurmountable obstacles."

Rebecca leaned a shoulder on the window frame and stared at her friend. "That is like saying the Alps are mere lumps of rock." She wasn't sure which hurdle would be more formidable.

"Oh please. You're beautiful, Beck, and wonderful in every other way, too. Any man would be interested. As for your father, he loves you, and I'd wager if your happiness is at stake and this young man is from a decent family, even as opposed you think he would be, your father would come around."

To say she had doubts over that was such an understatement Rebecca didn't bother to voice them. "The man we're discussing has clearly no interest in courting anyone, Bri."

"Maybe you could change his mind. If this mystery man asked you to marry him, what would you say?"

The question brought forth every fantasy she'd ever had of Robert Northfield on bended knee, clasping her hand and declaring his undying love. But she'd always known those romantic images were nothing more than unrealistic illusions. Rebecca shook her head. "He *wouldn't* ask."

"But if he did?"

"Bri," she said in exasperation.

"I'll loan you the book at any time, if you want it. I am almost done with it."

"I couldn't." Rebecca said it on a gasp. It was one thing for Brianna to read it—at least she was a married woman.

But the scandalous book did sound intriguing, Rebecca had to admit. Not that she believed it could work a miracle like causing a change of heart in a rake of Robert's stature, but she couldn't deny her curiosity over the forbidden revelations Lady Rothburg had to offer.

"It's very enlightening." Brianna looked mischievous but sincere. "Why does intimacy have to be such a secret, anyway? Men know everything and we know nothing. It isn't fair to keep young women so in the dark over a natural part of life."

Well, that was true enough. Rebecca muttered, "Who said life was fair?"

"The book aside, I hope you'll attend."

Attend. The party. The house party where Robert would no doubt be in attendance, also.

Rebecca felt the traitorous flutter of her pulse, though

it was irrational to want to torture herself by going. "My parents would have to agree. I am not sure they will. You are a married lady and a duchess, but you are still younger than I am by a few months. So is Arabella. They might not consider you reasonable chaperones."

"Colton's grandmother will be there. Can you think of anyone more respectable than the Dowager Duchess of Rolthven? Surely she is suitable enough, and besides, I want you to play some of your pieces."

A chance to play her music for an audience? Rebecca's throat tightened. "You know I can't. My mother would have the vapors if word got out."

Brianna lifted her brows. "I didn't say you had to claim the music as your own. You are a talented pianist. Just play for us. When the audience adores it—as I know they will—and asks the name of the composer, make something up. It will be a chance for you to display your genius without the censure. And you can hear the praise firsthand, as it should be. We'll need some elegant entertainment."

Now she was lost. Robert, and her other passion, her music? There was no way she could resist. "I'd love to come." And while she was being foolish enough to put herself right in the path of possible heartbreak, she might as well extend the madness. "And I'll consider your offer of the book."

Chapter Five

Men and women are not natural companions other than in a physical sense. We do not care for the same entertainments as a rule, nor do we find the same things humorous or interesting, and our everyday lives hold a disparity that makes it sometimes difficult to understand each other. Few men contemplate their wardrobes except with the most casual of attention, and few women wish to discuss horses and hounds. Yet these very differences can be to your advantage. Praise and reward every concession he gives you with his time and purse and watch his generosity grow.

From the chapter titled:
"Turning Reluctance to Eagerness"

The envelope in question was included in a pile of correspondence and had no seal or indication of the sender. Colton's secretary, a thin young man with unprepossessing features and a quiet demeanor, looked puzzled as he handed it over. Mills cleared his throat. "I . . . er . . . believe it is from Her Grace."

Colton took the proffered piece of vellum. "From my wife?"

"Yes, sir."

"Why the devil would she write me a note?" His question was ridiculous. How would his secretary know what Brianna was thinking? Colton certainly didn't understand her most of the time.

"It appears to be an invitation, Your Grace," Mills said helpfully.

"I see that." Colton scanned the script for a second time. "Rather an interesting thing, to be invited to one's own home. It is even more interesting that the Duchess has failed to mention to me her plans. Why on earth is she planning a house party?"

"A surprise, sir?" Mills straightened a stack of papers with his usual efficiency, looking more diffident than ever.

Colton glanced at him and said dryly, "I agree. It's a surprise, but that doesn't help me understand the failure to say one word to me about it."

"Your birthday, Your Grace."

"My birthday?"

"On the fifth. You'll be twenty-nine."

"I do know my own age," he said gruffly, feeling a little foolish. Now that he thought about it, he supposed it was next week. It certainly hadn't crossed his mind his lovely young wife would do something like plan a party to celebrate it. He couldn't decide whether to be touched or slightly irritated. Both, he supposed. While he appreciated the thoughtful gesture, he was also far too busy to drop everything and go lounge in the countryside with a houseful of guests for five days.

Brianna had an infernal knack for complicating things that should be simple.

He sighed and set down the invitation, finding the vague scent of Brianna's perfume that clung to the paper beguiling. "Since she has doubtless sent out other invitations to this event, I suppose I have little choice but to attend. Please check my calendar and rearrange any appointments if possible. I think I am supposed to see Lord Liverpool during this time, and one does not put off the Prime Minister unless he's agreeable to it. If he is, you will accompany me to the country and we can get in some work while at Rolthven. Right now I had better go find my wife and try to discover if she is plotting anything else I am unaware of."

"Yes, Your Grace." Mills moved with his usual unobtrusive efficiency as Colton rose and left his study. In the main hall he found the butler, who informed him that yes, indeed, the Duchess was home, having just returned.

As he went up the graceful sweep of the main stairway to the second floor where their apartments were located, Colton contemplated how to handle the situation. Firm remonstration, at a guess. Though he didn't want to appear ungrateful for a celebration in his honor, she must understand that she couldn't reorder his schedule. He paused to knock on the door of her bedroom, reminded himself she was his wife, this was his house, and opened it instead.

Her maid glanced up, startled at his abrupt and unprecedented entrance into her mistress's bedchamber in the middle of the afternoon. She was in the act of shaking out one of those ridiculously sheer undergarments Brianna had begun to favor, the filmy lace suspended in her hands as she dropped into a deep curtsy. "Your Grace."

A slight splash behind the screen on the dais at the end of the room told him Brianna's location. She was humming as she bathed, a surprisingly melodic tune. He didn't know his beautiful bride could sing.

If she was in her bath, she was naked.

That irrefutable fact held him checked for a moment, for while he'd come to talk to her, he hadn't expected to find her nude. It was probably best for him to turn around and leave, the voice of reason in his head suggested. They could discuss the party over dinner. He could even request her presence beforehand for a glass of sherry and introduce the subject at that time.

There was another faint splash.

The sound was unexpectedly erotic. Odd—before now, he hadn't considered bathing a seductive pastime.

Colton glanced at Brianna's maid. "Please excuse us. She'll ring later if she needs you."

"Yes, Your Grace." The young woman draped the chemise quickly over the dressing table stool and hurried off, discreetly shutting the bedroom door behind her.

"Colton?" Brianna said from behind the screen, obviously registering the sound of his voice.

It was four o'clock in the afternoon, he reminded himself. Besides, he was annoyed with his wife's confounding behavior.

His unruly cock didn't care. Colton hadn't even seen Brianna yet and he could already feel his erection grow, the fragrance of lavender soap reminding him of the softness of her scent. The tantalizing vision his mind created of bare shoulders propped against the edge of the tub evoked a physical response so strong he couldn't quite believe it.

Four o'clock in the afternoon was a fine time to make love to your wife.

He walked over and went around the screen.

A pair of gorgeous dark blue eyes stared up at him as he climbed the two steps and stood at the edge of the tub. Brianna had her pale golden hair caught up in a careless topknot, wayward strands escaping to brush her slender neck. The upper curves of her breasts were completely exposed, the sumptuous flesh wet and glistening, and her smooth cheeks held a pretty flush from the heated water that deepened as he examined what he could see of her with leisurely inspection. "I received your invitation."

There was a double entendre if ever there was one, he thought, his lascivious gaze fastened on the silken mounded flesh visible above the water.

"Did you?" There was a tentative note in her response, the tone of her voice hushed.

God help him, even her knees, just visible above the soapy water, were entrancing.

When a man found himself riveted by a joint, he was in trouble indeed.

"Yes," he said hoarsely.

"Are you angry?"

He had come upstairs with the intention of telling her she couldn't presume to arrange social events without consulting him, but now, looking down into her lovely face, he found he wasn't nearly as exasperated as before. What he was feeling had nothing to do with irritation and everything to do with incipient lust. "I'm not sure. I wouldn't say angry was the right word. Is there some reason you chose to not discuss this with me first?"

"Then it would hardly be a surprise, would it?"

"I suppose not," he agreed, uncertain of how to handle the situation.

Her glimmering smile made blood he didn't know he had left surge to his groin. "I'm so glad you are not upset with me. I wasn't sure you would like the idea."

He didn't particularly, but it was impossible to concentrate on anything except the alluring sight of his breathtaking wife in her bath. Bathing anyone but himself was out of the realm of his experience, but he was willing to give it a try. He shrugged out of his coat and pulled off his cravat, seeing Brianna's eyes widen. With deliberation, he removed the studs at his cuffs and then rolled up his sleeves. The soap sat in a small porcelain dish perched on the edge of the tub, and as he picked it up, he found that even the slick, wet feel of it aroused him. "Allow me to help you finish, madam."

Brianna gave a small gasp as his sudsy hands slid over her exquisite breasts. They felt perfect in the warm water, full, firm, the resilient flesh like satin as he fondled and caressed. Colton took his time, weighing each one in turn, lifting the flesh as if gauging the ripeness. When her nipples hardened against his palms, he smiled, unable to help himself.

"I am ..." Brianna said breathlessly, her eyes half closed, "... perfectly able to bathe myself."

"You are perfect, that is for certain," Colton responded, his cock so hard he feared he would burst from his breeches.

At four in the afternoon.

He washed her slender arms, the nape of her neck,

the mesmerizing smoothness of her thighs. When he found the warm softness between her legs, she parted for him, her breathing shifting to small pants as he slid his fingers into heated tightness. The first moan made him long to elicit the second and he leaned forward to kiss her, his hand beginning a rhythmic motion against her sleek, satiny flesh.

This, he reminded himself, was *not* why he'd come to talk to her.

But a delightful change in plans just the same.

Her inner muscles clenched against his invading fingers and he smiled and deepened the kiss into something more urgent, more carnal.

It was wickedly strange to be touched such a way in broad daylight, but Brianna found she didn't have one single objection.

Not one.

Colton's mouth was warm and insistent, his tongue sweeping deep, and she touched his face lightly, her damp fingers sliding along his lean jaw as his thumb gently rotated between her parted thighs. Involuntarily she quivered, pleasure spiking through her body to settle in the pit of her stomach.

"Delightful," he murmured against her lips. "But I can do even better. I think you are done bathing. Shall we move to the bed?"

Before she could answer he plunged both arms into the water and lifted her from the tub, heedless of his clothes. Brianna gasped at the audacity of the gesture because it was so unexpected and out of character. "Colton! You'll get wet."

"I've an entire wardrobe full of dry clothes in the next room."

That was true, but she was still amazed he would act so impetuously. She clung to his broad shoulders as he strode across the room and deposited her dripping body on her bed. Systematically he began to disrobe, his gaze fastened on her. Boots first, tossed carelessly aside in a very unColton-like way, his fine linen shirt—now soaked—unbuttoned and haphazardly discarded, then his breeches, revealing his rampant erection.

They had never before made love during the day. Naturally the draperies were open, and sunlight fell across his skin, gilding it to gold, defining the sleek, hard muscles of his body, lending highlights to his thick hair. Brianna knew her husband thought she was beautiful, for he had told her so with flattering sincerity, and the evidence of his desire for her was especially obvious at this moment. But she found him beautiful too, in an entirely masculine way, with his lean, hard body and chiseled features. People tended to think of Robert as the handsomest brother because of his roguish charm, but in her not unbiased opinion, Colton was just as attractive if not more so. He didn't smile often enough, it was true, and she wished that would change, but from the very first time she'd seen him, she had just *known*.

He was hers. And she had no intention of sharing him with any other woman.

She *must* be making some progress; the staid, reserved man she'd married three months before wouldn't have hauled her out of her bath in the middle of the afternoon.

"I want you," he said, the declaration unnecessary because the physical evidence stood high against his taut stomach.

"We are in accord then, Your Grace," she murmured, pulling at the ribbon holding her hair and letting the mass tumble free. "I want you."

He climbed on the bed and moved over her, trapping her beneath him, his mouth seeking the sensitive juncture of neck and shoulder. "I don't have time for this."

It was just about the least romantic thing she could think of for a man to say, but from Colton, it was a high compliment. Brianna slid her hands across the muscled hardness of his shoulders with a breathless laugh. "I shall contrive to make every minute worth your while."

"Hmm." He licked her throat, his erection rigid against her thigh.

The noncommittal response didn't bother her because her wayward body was gripped by desire, and as much as she wanted to please and beguile her handsome husband, she also felt an overwhelming need to have him inside her. When his hand cupped her bare breast, she arched into the caress, shameless and uninhibited, and a low moan tore from her throat. Between her legs, she throbbed. She could feel she was wet—and it had nothing to do with her bath.

"So soft," Colton said in a hoarse voice, fondling and gently kneading.

Don't wait. How wanton would it be to ask him to take her as fast and furiously as he had in the carriage and the other night after she practiced the advice in chapter two?

For a man as conservative as her husband, it *would* probably seem wanton, she decided in a haze of need. Brianna bit her lip as his hands continued to roam, but she subtly shifted position, lifting her hips to urge him without words, her heart pounding.

Colton apparently understood, for he used his knees to part her legs and took her mouth in a searing kiss just as he took her body. The long, hard length of his cock sank into her passage and wrung a low cry of pleasure from deep in her throat.

Though she was afraid they had a long way to go in getting to know each other in day-to-day life, Brianna thought as he began to move in long, sure strokes that shot tingles of blissful sensation through every nerve ending, here they were achieving accord. Colton's face was dark with passion, his azure eyes glittering in the afternoon light as he quickened the pace to the sharpening bite of her nails on his shoulders.

Her eyes drifted shut, his scent surrounding her, crisp and clean and male, the power of his body an aphrodisiac, the upward spiral to sexual fulfillment carrying her helplessly to a dizzying, rapturous height before she fell gladly into paradise. Brianna cried out as she climaxed, a short, sharp noise she barely registered, and Colton made a low sound in answer, his tall body going rigid. The pulse of his ejaculation was unmistakable as he surged deep into her trembling body one last time and flooded her with his release.

In the lethargic wash of the aftermath, Brianna didn't protest when he rolled to the side, taking both their entwined bodies. Nestled next to him, she felt the heave of his hard chest with a sense of pure satisfaction.

"I think I've decided bathing oneself is overrated," she murmured teasingly once she could summon the strength to speak. "I might require your assistance from now on."

"I am your servant always, madam." Colton touched her bare hip, just a brush of his fingers and his voice was light, but his expression hard to read. He gave a small sigh. "Though I admit what just happened was not at all my intention when I came up here to speak with you."

Clasped naked in his arms, she recognized her advantage and she pressed it. "Oh yes, the invitation. You said you didn't mind."

"No," he corrected, a hint of the austere duke creeping back into his voice. "I said I wasn't angry. There is a distinct difference. Mills seems to think you are doing this for my birthday."

She hadn't anticipated he would leap for joy, but the thought of tearing him away from his endless dutiful concentration on his ducal responsibilities held too much allure for her to resist. Other than this one aberration—which was heartening—she almost never saw him during the day. When did he ever take time just to enjoy himself? He went hunting now and then, he'd told her absently when she'd posed the question at dinner one evening, and had a box at Newmarket where he occasionally attended the races. To keep fit, he fenced nearly every day and took a morning ride that was penned into his schedule.

She was unlikely to be invited along for any of those

activities, so the house party at least forced him to spend some time with her other than in a solely sexual way. More than half the time he ate dinner at his club or they had guests, and when they did go out together, they were also always surrounded by other people. "I planned it to please you," she explained, not quite telling the truth.

For a moment Colton said nothing. Then he exhaled, his breath stirring her hair. "I realize you had the best of intentions, but in the future, I must insist you consult me first."

The word "insist" was grating. She played her trump card. "Your grandmother is thrilled."

It wasn't a lie. The dowager duchess was enthralled by the idea of a celebration and a horde of guests, not to mention all three of her grandsons visiting at once. Brianna understood that very rarely happened. Damien worked for the Crown and was abroad more than he was home, Robert's notorious interests were legendary and not easily pursued while buried in the countryside, and Colton was so diligent in his responsibilities he had little balance in his life, in her opinion.

"Is she?" There was just a slight edge of irritation in her husband's voice. "Why do I get the feeling I am being manipulated?"

"Colton," Brianna said with as much asperity as she could summon, "I hardly think someone going to a great deal of trouble to honor your birthday is manipulation. I already told you I didn't ask your permission because it was supposed to be a surprise. A pleasant one."

Just wait, her inner voice said. Lady Rothburg had a very outrageous suggestion in the chapter she had just finished reading, and though Brianna blushed every time she thought about it even if she was alone, she was willing to try it if it pleased him.

"Surprises have no real place in my schedule, Brianna."

"It's *our* life, unless I am mistaken, so I should also have some say." She touched his cheek in a tender gesture that was heartfelt.

And maybe, for the first time, he felt it too, for he seemed nonplussed. Those remarkable azure eyes stared into hers.

Maybe it was foolish, but she pressed him. "Shouldn't I?"

No, any man in England might have answered her. But then again, she had married only one.

"I had no idea I had married such a militant female." He rolled her over abruptly, his much larger body pressing hers into the mattress. His mouth lowered until he could whisper against her lips. "I believe you are arguing with me. Am I mistaken, or do you have quite a habit of doing just that?"

"I wouldn't call it a habit." Brianna felt breathless all at once, and needy also, as if they hadn't just made love. He was hardening again. She could feel the pressure of the length of his returning erection along her thigh.

"Hmm, I think I might differ in my opinion." His embrace tightened and firm lips grazed her temple. Then he gave an exhale that echoed with resignation. "But I should go. This has been a very satisfying diversion, but Mills will be wondering what the devil happened to me and I have a dozen—"

Brianna interrupted him by levering up on her elbows and pressing her mouth against his in a deliberately provocative kiss. Her arms slipped around his neck and she clung to him as if she had the power to actually keep him from leaving her bed.

It turned out she did. Despite his self-professed busy schedule, he stayed for another very satisfying hour before he excused himself.

A coup, she thought with elation as she went to wash again in her now tepid bathwater. He hadn't told her that she didn't have any say in their marriage, and the way he kissed and touched her. . . .

Yes, things were going nicely.

Chapter Six

The concept of a "wife" is instantly unexciting. Most males are hunters by nature and, at marriage, the chase is over. Some women prefer the dull role of dutiful spouse, but I have never been able to understand why. Who wants a mere husband when you can have a hot-blooded lover instead? When the bedroom door closes, polite strictures should be abandoned. Remember, one does not have to be a whore to act like one now and then.

From the chapter titled:
"A Little Lust Will Take You a Long Way"

The level of wine in the decanter had lowered significantly and their voices had probably risen in decibel, but this was the most pleasant kind of companionship. Robert lounged back in his chair, his glass dangling from his fingers, his smile genuine. "It is good to have you back. I'm glad you came here first."

Robert and his brother Damien sat comfortably in the room Robert considered his study, without cravats, their jackets discarded amidst the hodgepodge of bachelor furnishings, a mixture of old-world antiques and some pieces from the orient, the eclectic setting of polished lacquer tables and old oak bookcases pleasing to the eye—at least to Robert's. It was no secret he disdained formality whenever possible.

Damien, a year older, currently first in line for the title of Duke of Rolthven but every bit as uninterested in the role as Robert was himself, grinned. Of the three of them, Damien was the quiet one. He had the same coloring and build, but his eyes were dark, not blue. A natural diplomat, he was well suited to the role he played for the British government. None of Colton's assured authority or Robert's more careless approach to life was evident in his unobtrusive demeanor. "I assure you it's nice to be back. I did call at Grosvenor Square, but Colton and his new duchess were out."

"They are in rather high demand when it comes to invitations."

"I'm sure." Damien settled back, eyeing his glass with appreciation. "At least you were home—though I am a bit surprised."

"Contrary to popular opinion, I enjoy a night in alone now and again. And I'm damned glad of it now, since I was here for your arrival. What has it been, over a year since you set foot on English soil?"

"My Lord Wellington can be a ruthless taskmaster at times."

Robert cocked a brow. "I'm sure."

"He wins battles." The simple sentence and slight shrug of the shoulders seemed to sum up his brother's sentiments.

"And hopefully this damned war, with the help of men like you," Robert commented.

"And you." Damien sipped from his glass. "Don't discount your service to the Crown, Robbie. God knows we're grateful for your complicated mind."

Robert did little enough in his own opinion, acting as a consultant from time to time to the War Office. Though no one seemed to mention it, he did have a First in Mathematics from Cambridge. All society whispered about was his dissolute private life and the number of women he took to bed. Although, philosophically speaking, he was indifferent to the narrow view society had of his existence, he still felt a twinge of irritation over the lack of general interest in his intellect. Damien, however, hadn't forgotten Robert's knack for solving impossible little puzzles in record time, and several years before had gently nudged Robert into a position wherein he was sent undecipherable coded French communiqués. The challenge was invigorating, and though Robert had never felt any desire to be a soldier, at least he could help his country in some way. Once he broke the codes, the information was sent back to Spain and used on any captured communications.

"My service," he murmured, "is nominal enough, but thank you. Tell me about Badajoz. I've heard horror stories about the siege."

The next hour was spent in discussion of the Peninsular Campaign and Robert opened a second bottle of claret about halfway through, feeling expansive and relaxed. One of the best things in his life was his relationship with his two brothers, and it was good to have Damien back in London, for however short a time.

"To change the subject from war to something more pleasant, I understand there is to be a party for Colt's birthday." Damien idly swirled the ruby liquid in his glass, and his eyes held a humorous light. "I received an invitation from his new wife when I picked up my personal correspondence. I admit I was surprised he would agree to such an event, but perhaps marriage is having a mellowing effect on our older sibling."

Robert couldn't help it; a grin touched his mouth when he recalled the several different instances when Colton had expressed his confusion over Brianna's behavior. "I don't think it is going quite as he anticipated. His bride has an independent spirit every bit as captivating as her beauty. You know Colton prefers his life be neat and logical; and while Brianna is bright and witty, she isn't at all predictable. So picture our sometimes austere brother dealing with a creature who demands from him spontaneity, and not just that, but also indulgence. This party is an example. From his grumbles on the subject, I understand she just planned it without asking his permission. She sent *him* an invitation and that was the first he learned of it."

Damien laughed in his quiet way. "Maybe she's just what he needs. All that respectability could use a shake now and then."

Robert thought of the low-cut gown that still garnered comments, even though the scandalous moment had been a few weeks before and he hadn't witnessed the event. Since Brianna was his sister-in-law, most males of his acquaintance had the good sense to not say much in front of him, but he'd still overheard a few ribald remarks from those who hoped the beautiful Duchess of Rolthven would appear again in public in a similar mode of dress. "She's doing her best."

"I missed the wedding." Damien sounded truly contrite. "The war does not wait on any of us. Tell me about her. I admit I'm curious."

"Imagine golden hair, dewy skin, and a body Venus would envy." Robert reflected a moment. "But there's substance under those lush curves and behind those entrancing blue eyes. Her looks aside, I like Brianna. She's a good sort. Has a sense of humor and apparently a sense of adventure, too, that our brother is trying his best to comprehend, even if he hasn't quite succeeded yet."

Damien laughed. "She sounds delightful. I can't wait to meet her."

"Though Colton isn't thrilled about it, this celebration will be a good opportunity. At least we will all be together. Grandmama is looking forward to it. You know how she loves the bustle of a celebration. Now that she is too infirm to travel back and forth, she misses London."

"It will be good to see her, and entertaining, I am going to guess, to observe the new Duchess of Rolthven interacting with Colton." There was speculation in Damien's dark eyes. "I admit I was surprised to hear he made a love match. I wouldn't have imagined our older brother doing anything so sentimental."

It was something Robert himself had pondered, and to tell the truth, it made him uneasy. If it could happen to Colton . . . well, it could happen to anyone.

Even him?

He said dryly, "I don't think he looks at his marriage that way quite yet. I imagine he believes he made a practical choice. Brianna is young, beautiful, and of good family. His three essential requirements. And if put that way, it sounds like he indeed did his duty and selected an appropriate duchess to serve his illustrious title. However, as one who observed the relationship from the moment they met, I can say with some authority he reacted to her differently from the first. Much differently than to any of the other simpering ingénues thrust under his exalted nose by all those eager mamas on a constant basis. The interest was immediate and, I am happy to say for him, reciprocated. One of the things I like best about Brianna is I believe the fact that he's a duke is incidental to her."

"As one who is a ducal heir at this moment, that raises her in my estimation." Damien took a solid drink of claret and added, "Young ladies on the hunt for titles and fortunes terrify me in a way no advancing French column could."

"Luckily for us both, when Brianna gives Colton an heir, we will be saved."

"Let's hope it's soon."

Remembering Colton's disquiet over his wife's adventurous sexual spirit, Robert had to let out a low laugh. "I think she is effectively working on it."

Damien raised his brows. "She sounds like a very charming young lady. Tell me, who else might be on the guest list for this affair?"

"I haven't asked, but I got the impression from Colton it only involves the family and a few close friends."

Close friends. Even as he spoke, Robert idly wondered if the delectable, aqua-eyed Miss Marston would be included in the party. According to Colton, the young lady was one of Brianna's trusted companions, along with the Countess of Bonham. Andrew Smythe, the Earl of Bonham, had casually mentioned the other evening he and his new wife would be attending the festivities, so maybe Rebecca Marston would be there also.

Not that it really mattered if she was there or not, Robert thought as he sprawled back comfortably in his chair, legs extended. Whatever interest she'd piqued had been purely because she was attractive in an innocent, doelike way, and maybe he was so used to the practiced sophistication of his usual paramours that her difference struck a chord.

But he'd continued to think about her. Worse, he'd looked for her at the past few parties he'd attended. With her rich sable hair and graceful form she was easy enough to find, and he wondered why he hadn't paid more attention in the past. The night before, after several brandies no doubt, he had even considered asking her for a dance.

Luckily, the insanity had been temporary, though he was halfway across the ballroom before he had realized what he was doing and came to his senses. The gossip sheets columnists would have had a field day if he'd been seen waltzing with an innocent young lady of unquestionable virtue.

"A small party?" Damien broke into his thoughts. "That suits me better than a large affair. I'm so very out of touch with society at this time. Please tell me there won't be eligible young ladies in attendance, though I feel rather doomed you are going to. What is a house party without simpering young misses?"

Rebecca would never simper. It was a startling conviction, since Robert really didn't know her that well. "None I know of," he was able to say honestly.

If he admitted it to himself, he did wish he'd stolen that kiss from her when he'd been tempted. Maybe then his curiosity would have been satisfied and he would be able to put her out of his mind.

He dismissed the off-limits Miss Marston in favor of another glass of wine.

*   *   *

She agonized—agonized like a ninny—over what to wear. Not just for her arrival, but for every single minute of the stay at Rolthven Manor. That, of course, was after she agonized over whether or not her father would agree to her attendance, though in the end, he had acquiesced. Rebecca wasn't even sure she should attend, for that matter.

It was a devil's own dilemma.

"This one, miss?" Her maid held up a silver tissue gown she particularly liked because it was the most daring dress she owned. Not that "daring" meant much in the context of her wardrobe, so carefully selected by her mother, but it was the least conservative.

Why not take it? After all, Brianna had worn that scandalous gown to the opera and reported it drove the Duke to some very unusual behavior. The silver tissue was her best option if she wanted to get noticed. "Yes," Rebecca said with what she hoped was nonchalance. "And the aquamarine silk, too, please. Slippers to match, and my best shawl since the evenings in the country could be cool."

"Yes, miss." Molly carefully folded the silver gown and put it in her trunk.

Five days of being near Robert Northfield. In his childhood home, eating at the same table, exchanging witty banter . . .

Only, Rebecca thought with a twinge, her banter wasn't the least clever in his presence, and if he followed his usual pattern of behavior, he would simply avoid her like she was a plague-ridden rodent.

Cheery thought, that.

Currently, she was fashionably popular. For a second season. Young men fawned over her, but those were gentlemen seeking suitable wives. Heaven deliver her from politically ambitious fools like Lord Watts who valued not just her person, but her father's influence.

The all too handsome, disreputable Robert Northfield wasn't looking for a wife.

But she was going to Essex anyway.

"I'll have the amber lace, the ivory tulle, and the pink muslin. Two of my best riding habits, and traveling attire for the journey back." Rebecca fought a twist of nervousness in her stomach. "I'm sure we'll find Rolthven Manor most formal."

Sally merely nodded and set to work.

Packing done, Rebecca checked her appearance in the mirror, straightened her hair, and headed downstairs to dinner. It was her father's custom for them all to meet in the drawing room for a glass of sherry before they dined, and he hated it when she was late. Inevitably that meant a lecture, and though in many ways she adored him, he could be tedious at times.

She entered the drawing room and said cheerily, "I was packing. Am I late?"

"Almost." In elegant clothing, even for an *en famille* dinner at home, her father was distinguished and imposing. He lifted a small crystal glass and handed it to her with a courtly nod of his head. "Fortunately, that means no. You are just on time, my dear."

"Thank you." She demurely accepted the offering.

"My previous agreement to this outing wasn't made without reservations."

Rebecca stifled an inner groan. That was no surprise. He frequently had reservations. "The Dowager Duchess—" she began.

"Is elderly," he finished. "Though I mean her no disrespect. Your mother and I have decided to accept the invitation to accompany you. It's rather last minute, but I sent word to the Duchess of Rolthven earlier today. She graciously sent a note back that we would be welcome even at such late notice. The matter is settled."

Rebecca's heart sank. Being accompanied by her parents was mortifying. Truly, she was several months older than Brianna, but here she was, coddled like a child, while her friend could throw parties and wear what she wished and ... oh, it was infuriating in so many ways. Rebecca straightened her spine and sank into an embroidered chair, the chilly formality of the room only emphasizing her role as a virtual prisoner.

At that moment, she had a minor revelation. Or maybe even a major one. All she knew was it shook her deeply because it was knowledge she'd been avoiding for months.

Independence was a precious commodity. She craved it, but the only acceptable way for her to leave her parents was to go to a husband. Time was running out, plain and simple.

She stared at her glass. "So I am not to be trusted on my own, I take it? Bri can blithely throw parties and invite whomever she wishes, yet I myself, without the benefit of a male guiding my every move, am not to be trusted for a moment without my hovering parents."

"Your friend is no longer an unmarried maiden," her father said after a brief pause. "Her actions are governed by her husband. You can't say the same. When you can, rest assured we will step aside."

"This is punishment because I haven't married?" She lifted her brows deliberately, the glass of sherry precarious in her hands.

"Your parents' companionship at a country party is punishment?"

Well, her father was a politician, after all, and a neat turning of the tables was his specialty. But Rebecca was *not* looking forward to trying to conceal her awareness of Robert's presence, especially in such a small amount of company. Her parents had just made everything more complicated. "No, of course not."

"Then we are in accord."

Not precisely how she would describe the situation. She chose not to comment.

"What about Damien Northfield?"

Rebecca froze, her glass halfway to her mouth, arrested by her mother's statement. "*Damien* Northfield? What do you mean? What about him?"

"He's returned from Spain."

She stared, speechless at first.

Her mother looked thoughtful. "I hadn't really thought about it before, but he is very suitable. For now, he is even Rolthven's heir—"

The idea was so ludicrous Rebecca cut in, "You must be joking."

Oh dear, she never interrupted her mother. Even as her father's brows knit into a fierce frown, she hastily relented, "What I meant is, I don't know him at all."

Plus he was Robert's brother. But she could hardly use *that* as an argument, so she took an unladylike gulp of sherry instead.

"I was pointing out this might be a chance to make his acquaintance, and who knows? Maybe the two of you will suit." Her mother lifted her brows, her eyes taking on a gleam Rebecca recognized. "It has been a while since he was out in society, but if I recall, he has the Northfield good looks, and a more than respectable fortune. Think of how delighted Brianna would be if you developed a penchant for her brother-in-law—and he for you."

Her penchant was already firmly in place for one of the Northfield brothers whether Rebecca wanted it or not, and if her parents knew about the infatuation, they would never agree to let her go to Rolthven, with or without them. "I'm sure he's a very pleasant man," she said neutrally, "but it seems to me he is quite busy as some sort of aide-de-camp for General Wellington, isn't he? I hardly think he's in the market for a wife at this time."

"There's talk of a knighthood for his service to the Crown," her father commented, not helping matters one bit.

Rebecca shot him a reproachful look that said "traitor."

He raised his brows. "Whether or not you like Northfield, I am sure other young men will be there also to dance attendance upon you and pester me to be allowed to escort you to the various entertainments." His expression changed from slight amusement to a more serious mien. He added, "This might be a nice opportunity for you to get to know some of them better outside the melee of balls and crowded social events."

His implication was clear: further acquaintance might help her make up her mind. This second season hadn't pleased him, but he had endured her adamant refusals of every proposal so far. As her twenty-first birthday loomed, she knew he would soon issue an ultimatum.

What would she do if he did? It wasn't in question: both her parents wanted to see her settled and secure. "I'm sure you're right," she said without any inflection at all, not willing to do battle on the point at the moment. When she really needed to fight—like in the case of Lord Watts as a possible future husband—she would, but she had no desire to depart for this trip already at odds with her watchful parents.

Unfortunately, her father was difficult to fool. He said dryly, "I'm always uneasy when you agree with me so readily."

She summoned an innocent look. "In this case I really do agree. I confess to being tired of all the whirl of London, and this outing sounds like a pleasant break. Just being able to visit with Arabella and Brianna will make it a lovely time, I'm sure."

"And do not forget the Duke's younger brother," her mother said in prim reminder.

As if she could, Rebecca thought with a glimmer of despair, sipping her sherry. She thought all too often about the Duke of Rolthven's younger brother, but not the one her mother meant.

Rebecca had a feeling this might be a grueling five days.

Chapter Seven

Desire is a game. One can play it with subtle nuance, or flagrant flirtation.

From the chapter entitled:
"How to Run and Be Sure You Get Caught"

Brianna grasped the strap to steady herself as they bumped over a particularly rough patch of road. Across from her, Colton barely shifted on the seat, his long legs extended so his booted feet brushed her skirts, his expression abstracted as he read yet another letter from the stack of correspondence he'd brought with him. A lock of chestnut hair had fallen boyishly over his brow at some time during the journey and he was too distracted to notice it, but there was nothing boyish about the width of his shoulders or the clean masculinity of his features.

Finally she yielded to the impulse that had tempted her for the past few miles and leaned across to brush the wayward curl back into place in a familiar gesture.

He glanced up from the piece of vellum in his hand, and then, to her relief, actually set it aside. "I'm ignoring you. My apologies."

"You did tell me you would still have to take care of your affairs during our time at Rolthven, but I admit the silence is wearing on me." Brianna didn't really expect him to understand she was nervous about her first real foray into playing the grand hostess. He was so used to all the pomp and grand affairs she doubted he ever gave them all a second thought. For heaven's sake, Colton greeted the prince regent by his first name.

"What was your childhood like?" The question seemed appropriate to the moment as they neared the estate where he grew up, and she was curious.

Colton's brows went up a fraction. "My childhood?"

"I cannot imagine it is easy, growing up the oldest son of a duke." She pictured her nieces running amuck in the garden the other day and gales of childish laughter. Her own childhood had been wonderful. "Were you allowed to play and ride a pony and learn to swim ... all those typical things children love to do?"

"Actually, yes. To a point, I suppose." Azure eyes regarded her with a look that could only be described as wary. "May I ask why we are having this discussion?"

"It's hardly a discussion," she pointed out. "You've contributed two words. And the reason I asked is because you allow so little time for enjoyment in your day now. I wondered if you were raised to believe life should be lived in such a manner."

"I believe you've met my brother." Colton's tone was dry. "Obviously, we were not raised to disavow frivolity. Not to say Robert is a frivolous man, but he does not deny himself his pleasures."

But neither was Robert an oldest son, Brianna mused, watching her husband from under the fringe of her lashes.

"I attend musicals, the opera, and other entertainments. I have my morning ride unless the weather is foul. I visit my club." Colton extolled the list slowly. His voice deepened. "I especially enjoy my nights since I've married."

Whatever reply she might have made to that suggestive observation was arrested by the swing of the carriage into the long drive. The façade of Rolthven Manor was not precisely medieval, but it somehow managed to convey a sense of that time despite elegant lines and clean, gray stone. Maybe it was the turrets on either side of the grand front, imposing and tall, flanking the structure with the grandiose symbolism of an era when the Northfields had been feudal lords. Colton had explained to her on her first visit that only parts of the original castle remained since the main hall had been torn down and rebuilt several hundred years ago. A grand set of wide steps led to a magnificent terrace and the entrance itself was massive, the double doors sporting stained-glass panels and dark wood. The family coat of arms was carved in the portal so no one could possibly think this country seat of the ducal holdings was anything but theirs, through and through.

On a gloomy day, Brianna found the place a bit daunting from the outside despite the trim grounds and well-tended flower beds. However, on a gloriously sunny day, it managed to look warm and inviting, and she hoped her guests felt the same way.

If she was going to do this for Colton, she wanted to do it well.

The equipage rolled up the drive and the butterflies in her stomach fluttered.

His lack of enthusiasm for the event was obvious enough, she thought with only a measure of resignation. Her resolve to make this enjoyable for a man who had no intention of enjoying it was strengthened by the list of her current successes. To bolster her courage, she mentally counted them. Three so far. She'd actually jotted them down and tucked the piece of vellum into Lady Rothburg's forbidden book.

One wild, erotic carriage ride.

One evening when he . . . well, she felt flushed whenever she thought of it, but when he actually had kissed her in a place she never dreamed any man would kiss and it had felt wickedly wonderful.

One memorable bath and the interlude it had inspired.

On the piece of paper it said: THE OPERA. HIS BEDROOM. MY BATH.

She hardly wanted to take the chance of anyone ever finding the note and interpreting her meaning to both her and Colton's mutual embarrassment. Of one thing she was certain; he would not be happy about it in the least. On the other hand, she needed to chart her progress because at times like this—when he'd ridden with her in a closed carriage for hours and hours and been so preoccupied he barely spoke until these last miles when she'd prodded him into it—she needed to keep a clear idea of her objectives or she was bound to get discouraged.

He enjoyed his nights. Passion was well and good, but not *just* passion. Friendship, too. And then love.

The carriage came to a rocking halt.

She hoped she'd have more triumphs to add to the list after this house party.

"We're here," she said brightly.

"I hope so," her husband replied, a small smile curving his mouth, "otherwise we have stopped moving for no reason."

He well deserved the withering look she sent him, but he was oblivious to it. Colton got out and offered his hand to assist her from the vehicle.

A line of servants had arranged themselves on the steps, Brianna noticed, but he acknowledged their presence only with a brief nod of his head and a wave as he escorted her up to the front door. The flag flying above the house indicated he was in residence, which she knew didn't happen often.

Why would he visit this beautiful house in the country and relax when he could bury himself in his dreary study in London, she thought wryly. Not that he didn't come to Rolthven Manor now and again, but the trips had been fleeting so far, and Brianna had a feeling it was always that way. Certainly his grandmother lamented his absence whenever she had the chance.

"I hope the weather stays fine for our guests," she commented as the butler swept open the door with a flourish.

Colton made a noncommittal sound and turned to the elderly servant, "How are you, Lynley?"

"Very good, Your Grace." The man gave a courtly bow, his silver hair gleaming in the late afternoon sun. "It is nice to see you again so soon."

"Yes, well, you may attribute this repeat trip to my wife." Colton's glance didn't even touch on her. "Tell me, has anyone else arrived?"

"Lords Robert and Damien are here, sir. Perhaps an hour ago." Lynley was impeccably mannered and dressed in elegant clothes that rivaled an aristocrat's. He stepped back to admit them into the enormous main hall.

The impact of the space was powerful even on someone who had been there several times before. There were no fewer than six fireplaces, countless ancient and probably priceless tapestries hanging on the vast walls, and mullioned windows, which let in muted light to give the massive room—if one could call such a large space one room—pleasant illumination. The odd thing was it was actually cozy, though Brianna had no idea how that was possible. It could have been the small, intimate groupings of elegant furniture here and there, designed to encourage conversations between guests, or maybe it was the rich rugs on the polished floor—she wasn't sure. All she knew was she liked Rolthven Manor and wished Colton would deign to spend more time there.

"Shall we go up and change?" her husband asked, clasping her elbow and urging her toward the dual staircases at the end of the hall. If he even noticed their grand surroundings, she couldn't tell. "I, for one, could use a wash and a brandy."

Hot water and a change of clothes did sound appealing, and Brianna nodded and let him lead her up the sweep of the left stairs, toward their suite. It was as magnificent as the rest of the house—maybe a little too much so. She wasn't all that fond of the dark, heavy furniture and abundance of frothy lace in her bedroom. Also, Colton's mother—now remarried to an Italian count and living in the countryside near Florence—obviously loved the color lavender. Brianna wasn't nearly as enamored of it, and though Colton had told her with a careless wave of his hand months ago she could redecorate it as she wished, they never stayed long enough for her to start the project. Maybe if he enjoyed this little trip, she could convince him to leave London more often.

She was quite determined he *was* going to enjoy it.

Her maid and Colton's valet had traveled ahead with their luggage, and Brianna found her trunk already unpacked and her brushes and other necessities sitting on the ornate dressing table. The long windows were open to the warm afternoon and lacy draperies floated on the breeze coming in from the verdant park.

"Your hot water should be here shortly, Your Grace." Her maid, a soft-spoken young Cornish girl, moved to help her undress. "What gown would you prefer for this evening?"

"Nothing lavender," she muttered, looking around. "Maybe the ice blue silk. Tonight is to be just a quiet family meal. The guests won't arrive until tomorrow."

"Very well, Your Grace."

After she washed the travel stains away and dressed, Brianna brushed her hair and, with Molly's help, coiled it in a loose chignon. Sitting in front of the elaborate gilt mirror, she wondered just when she should present her husband with the wicked birthday gift she had planned.

The timing needed to be just right.

She intended for him to remember it for the rest of his life.

The frail-looking woman with the rug over her lap and quizzing glass to her eye was, as always, wearing a well-executed disguise. "Nice of you to finally find time for your family," she said gruffly.

There was nothing weak about his grandmother's spirit, no matter her age, Colton thought fondly. He did his best to not sound defensive. "I believe I am dutifully here, aren't I?"

The Dowager Duchess snorted derisively. "Only because that pretty young wife of yours forced you into it."

Brianna merely smiled. "Colton is very busy. I am so pleased he agreed to come."

Damien leaned back, one brow raised in his enigmatic way. Robert looked amused. There they were, Colton pondered as he sought something diplomatic to say, three large males, yet he felt outnumbered by one old woman and one young, very distracting beauty. He cleared his throat. "I am looking forward to this."

His grandmother narrowed her shrewd blue eyes and lowered the glass. "I am not sure I quite believe that, but I won't argue. You are here, Damien is finally home for at least a short time, and Robbie has forgone the pleasures of London to rusticate in the country. That hasn't happened since . . ."

She trailed off and Colton saw her suddenly rearrange her cane next to her chair as if it was the most important thing in the world it be at just the right angle, her eyes suspiciously bright. Since his father—her son—had died suddenly of an unexpected fever, he finished for her silently. Colton had been twenty, Damien just barely at Cambridge, and Robbie still at Eton. For the funeral, they'd assembled as a family, and he was damned if she wasn't right. They'd determinedly gone their separate ways ever since, the three of them pursuing their particular passions. He had an inherited dukedom to learn to manage, Damien had always longed for travel and intrigue, and Robbie was the careless charmer.

Good God, that seemed like a lifetime ago, when they'd all stood by their father's grave and felt their world slip into another dimension. At least that was how he'd experienced the grief, and he'd sensed a change in Damien and Robert also. Reality had bashed them most unpleasantly over the head and they were forced to deal with the devastation in their own ways.

What was your childhood like? Did Brianna even realize what that simple question stirred up in terms of memories?

After his father's death, he'd been overwhelmed for a while, but determined to make sure he ran his estates and other financial interests with the same precision and expertise as all the Rolthven dukes before him. He was so absorbed he didn't even really pay attention when his mother reentered society after her mourning, and consequently was stunned when she announced her intention to remarry. Damien, too, was absent most of the time, and with his grandmother residing permanently in the countryside and his own obligations making London much more convenient, Colton didn't really realize how much he missed Rolthven and seeing his family. Robert was the only close relative he saw on a regular basis, and that was usually because they crossed paths in the normal course of society's entertainments and shared the same clubs.

Though he rarely displayed affection in front of other people, his grandmother was one of the few who could inspire him to do it. Colton reached over and touched her blue-veined hand. "It is time we were all together, Grandmama. You are correct when it comes to that point."

She gave him a fierce stare. "I am always correct, young man."

Relieved to see her tears had evaporated, he inclined his head. "Yes, madam, you are correct."

"Always."

He definitely saw her lips twitch. One of his brothers—he had a suspicion it was Robert—laughed. "Always."

"Now that that is settled, I shall allow you to escort me in to dinner."

He did so, offering his arm for support, feeling her slight weight lean on him as she rose and walked very slowly at his side, her fingers tight on his sleeve. Behind them, Colton heard Robert say something and Brianna answer with a musical laugh. Now that he considered the matter, he was ashamed of his initial reaction to his wife's idea. He wondered for the first time whether he kept himself constantly busy so he didn't have time to miss his family. Why hadn't he considered the situation before today?

The dining room could never be called cozy by any standards. The high ceilings boasted decorative frescoes by an Italian master who had been paid a fortune to adorn the house several centuries before, there was dark paneling on the walls below, polished to a rich sheen, and the vast table could seat close to thirty people at one time. Two separate doors on each side of the room allowed for the flow of servants with trays. Several massive chandeliers offered illumination, and fireplaces flanked each side of the room. Five places had been set at one end, comfortably close so they could all converse without shouting. Colton first seated his grandmother and, with a singular possessiveness he hadn't even realized he felt, turned to pull out a chair for his wife, waving off his younger brother.

By God, Brianna looked gorgeous this evening. Dressed in a simple gown of blue silk, her upswept golden hair gilded by the candlelight, her flawless pale skin glowing, she was femininity personified as she gave him a brilliant smile and sank down in a whisper of sweet, tantalizing perfume.

Later, he promised himself, he would take great pleasure in removing that gown and loosening her lustrous hair. Then he would take her to bed and hear her make those small, arousing sounds that signaled she liked every single thing he did to her and wanted more.

"Are you going to sit?"

Her question, asked so delicately, made him realize he was still standing there by her chair, gaping at his wife like a fool.

And fantasizing about making love to her in front of his entire family, including his grandmother, no less.

Brianna had that kind of unsettling effect on him.

"Sorry. I just remembered something I forgot to do before we left. No matter, my solicitor can deal with it," Colton lied and quickly took the chair at the head of the table, feeling like an idiot. The minute he sat down a footman moved forward to pour the wine and Colton picked up his glass gratefully, trying to ignore the slight smirk on Robert's face. Whether or not anyone else had noticed his moment of temporary absorption with his wife, his brother certainly had. In petty retaliation to Robert's irritating expression, Colton asked coolly, "So, do tell me, my dear, are any single young ladies invited to this soiree?"

Brianna smiled mischievously, a delightful dimple appearing in one cheek. "How could I not invite a few with two of the most eligible bachelors in England in attendance?"

Damien looked comically alarmed. Robert gave an audible groan. His grandmother cracked a laugh. The Dowager Duchess said with asperity, "Good for you, child. I'd like to see the lot of them married off before I leave this earth."

"I have always wanted you to live forever, Grandmama." Robert lifted his glass in a small toast. "That comment reinforces my sentiment."

"Amen," Damien muttered.

"I was only making a jest," Brianna told them, her lovely eyes full of amusement. "The guest list is fairly limited. Besides the Earl and Countess of Bonham, there are the Marstons, Lord Bishop and his daughter, Mrs. Newman, Lords Knightly and Emerson, and the Campbell sisters with their parents. That is the extent of it. My sister and her husband were unfortunately unable to attend."

"The extent of it? It includes five unmarried young ladies." Robert turned positively green.

"Five bachelors as well." Brianna sipped her wine with serene grace and furrowed her brow. "One cannot throw a party like this and not match the gentlemen to the ladies evenly. Your grandmother told me so, and I arranged the guest list accordingly. Besides, you are used to being present at entertainments with unmarried young women."

"Not five of them at once and not for five days of their constant company."

"Good God." Damien already had the look of a hunted man.

"Oh, don't make it sound so horrible. I promise you they are all perfectly agreeable or I would never have invited them."

Colton had the feeling his wife was laughing behind that composed façade as he watched her expression.

He found it quite fascinating, actually. How the devil had she persuaded him to agree to this, and more perplexing, how did she maneuver his stalwartly detached brothers into a similar situation?

"You'll enjoy yourselves immensely, I'm sure," he murmured. "We all will."

Robert, who was aware Colton hadn't wanted the party at all, shot him a sardonic look. Damien grimaced and gestured for more wine, as he'd just drained his glass. His grandmother watched them all with avid interest, and Brianna reached over and touched Colton's hand.

A touch. Just a brush of her fingertips. Yet his body tingled. Her blue eyes were misty. "I am so glad you just said that, darling. I have worried so over this idea."

Darling. Normally he would not have appreciated an endearment in public, even if it was only in front of his family. But her expression caught him somehow and rendered him helpless to even summon a frown. Irrationally, he found himself casting back to recall if she'd ever called him darling before. No, he thought not.

I have worried so. . . .

Had she? He'd been annoyed over the idea and she had fretted over it. Colton felt like an ass, especially when he caught his grandmother's glare.

Well, how the hell was he supposed to know how a married man should act? He'd had as little practice as Brianna, after all. "I don't know why you would worry."

His two younger brothers both exchanged glances and it irritated the devil out of him. Robert said, "Perhaps she thought you'd be reluctant to leave London and spend one moment of your time relaxing? I can't for the life of me imagine why she'd get the impression."

Colton leveled a chilly stare at his youngest sibling. "Sarcasm is unwelcome at the table, Robbie."

"Was I being sarcastic?" Feigned innocence gave Robert's features an angelic cast, though he was the farthest thing removed from an angel—unless it was a fallen one.

The arrival of the first course saved Colton from having to reply. He studiously turned his attention to his soup. To a certain measure he understood his brothers' objections to the atmosphere of the gathering, but then again, the young ladies invited were Brianna's friends, and if they wanted to avoid entanglements with eligible young misses, they could simply be polite for five days and be done with it. In his opinion, it wasn't much to ask. He was the head of the family. He could demand more.

Hell, maybe even one of them would find a wife, he thought as he watched Brianna dip her spoon into the creamy soup and take a delicate taste.

God help them.

Chapter Eight

The primary conflict between males and females doesn't result from the games we play with each other so much as the different rules. We have one set, they have another.

From the chapter titled: "The Whys and Wherefores"

It wasn't until Brianna pounced on him that Robbie realized she was anxious. He'd no more than stepped into the central hall before he found himself amidst a bevy of footmen carrying massive vases of flowers in from the conservatory and a slim hand clamped with surprising strength around his forearm.

"I need help." His sister-in-law practically dragged him toward an Italian marble fireplace near a grouping of velvet chairs. "The guests are starting to arrive and tea will be served in less than an hour. What do you think of the roses right here?"

A brilliant spray of bloodred blooms set a dramatic note against the white stone, so he said reasonably, "I think they look lovely."

Imploring blue eyes looked into his and there was an actual smudge of something yellow on her porcelain cheek. "You're sure?"

He removed his handkerchief from his pocket and wiped the substance, which looked suspiciously like pollen, away. "I'm quite sure."

The flush in her cheeks and the nervous clutch of her hand reminded him she was barely twenty years old, and though she usually looked remarkably self-possessed, not at all used to her new position as the Duchess of Rolthven. Her level of experience with this sort of thing was limited. "Mrs. Finnegan, the housekeeper," he said as tactfully as possible, "has been in our family's service for thirty years, and she would know exactly where to place the roses for the best effect. She's managed house parties often enough before. My mother would have shamelessly stolen her away to Italy if she could have persuaded her to go. I think Finnie would be delighted if you gave over some of these decisions to her."

Brianna said with endearing earnestness, "I do so want this to be perfect. I rather thrust this affair upon Colton, and if it is a social disaster, I will not only have wasted his time but caused him embarrassment."

For one brief moment, as Robert looked into her lovely face and saw the sincerity in her eyes, he envied his brother his wife. Not Brianna specifically, though she was beautiful in every way a woman could be and he admired her spirit and wit, but the idea that she had gone to the trouble of planning this party. Not that his older brother would even notice the roses, much less where they were placed, but above all she obviously wished to make Colton happy.

What a notion. Robert was more than well acquainted with ladies who wished for *him* to make *them* happy. They craved the pleasure he could bring them in bed, the prestige of dallying with the younger brother of a duke, the expected jewelry and other expensive gifts.

Did they ever think about *him*? Not the Lord Robert Northfield with his generous inheritance and exalted connections. Not whether or not they found him handsome and a skillful lover. But about his life and his thoughts and aspirations?

Never, he had a feeling, did it occur to any of the women he bedded to ponder over his state of happiness. It was his fault, too, he realized as he stood there staring at Brianna, breathing in the scent of hothouse flowers that filled the air. He deliberately chose companions who desired nothing but casual sexual liaisons without emotional involvement. He seduced a specific kind of woman and they enjoyed his attentions immensely.

But was it enough? No woman ever looked at him the way Brianna looked at his brother.

Colton too, in unguarded moments when he wasn't locked away, shutting out the world in favor of shipping contracts and letters to estate managers, looked at his wife with a singular softness in his eyes Robert suspected his older brother didn't even know was there.

It was astonishing that at the age of twenty-six, with his level of experience with women, Robert had never contemplated the possibility of falling in love with anything but derision.

"You are nothing but a credit to him in every way, and I don't just mean his title." Robert patted the hand still holding his sleeve, listening to the hoarseness in his voice with disbelief. He wasn't sentimental . . . at least, he didn't think he was. "Now, let me go find Mrs. Finnegan for you, shall I? Then I suppose I need to go change. I've been out riding most of the day."

"Thank you." Brianna released his sleeve with a rueful smile. "I would actually be grateful for her help."

"My pleasure, Madame de la Duchesse." He bowed with exaggerated courtesy, which made her laugh, and then went in search of the ever efficient Finnie (as he'd called her since he was old enough to talk), explained that Colton's bride could use some guidance, and went upstairs to change.

All the time cognizant that he'd experienced some kind of a profound moment.

As he adjusted his cravat in the mirror, a grim-faced image looked back at him, very unlike his usual devil-may-care expression.

A knock on the door made him turn. He said curtly, "Yes?"

Damien opened the door to his bedchamber and

strolled in. "I thought we might go down to tea together to present a united bachelor front."

Robert forced a grin, trying to shake off this unprecedented contemplative mood. "Have you been plotting how to survive this?"

"I'm a military advisor." His brother shrugged. "It seems like a clever strategy to me, though I admit I'm more accustomed to gauging the movement of French forces than eager young ladies and their motivations."

"Perhaps we are flattering ourselves," Robert said dryly. "It's possible none of the young women Brianna invited are interested in either one of us."

Damien's expression was resigned. "I haven't been about in society for a while, but I think you are being optimistic. We're Northfields, Robbie—we could be the most boorish men in all of England and we would still be considered eligible bachelors."

Robert thought so too. "You're probably right," he admitted. "At least Miss Marston is charming." Though it was ill-advised, he added because he was thinking about her specifically, "And beautiful."

And where the devil had *that* comment come from? It was disconcerting to think seeing the young lady again was in the back of his mind.

His brother's brows lifted. "Miss Marston? As in the daughter of Sir Benedict Marston?"

"Yes." The reply was clipped. Robert hadn't told Damien about his disagreement with the man in question.

"We've had some communication." Damien's face took on the neutral expression it always did when discussing his profession. "He has the ear of the War Minister and of Liverpool. Odd, when Brianna mentioned it last night, I didn't make the connection immediately."

"She's quite good friends with Rebecca."

"Rebecca, is it? You are familiar enough with the lady to use her first name?"

Robert thought of a moonlit garden and the brush of his mouth against the corner of soft, tempting, rose-colored lips. "No. It's a liberty I wouldn't take in her presence. We barely know each other."

Except he remembered the pliant fullness of her breasts against his chest and the delicate, haunting essence of her scent. . . .

"Well, I might suffer her presence for a chance to speak with her father. Wellington can use all the help he can get with Horse Guards, and Marston has influence. I'm glad to hear she's at least passably pretty so my interest seems sincere."

Passably? A flicker of irritation ran up Robert's spine for some unfathomable reason. It was unfathomable because Damien, always reasonable and even tempered, rarely irritated anyone. He answered in a cool voice, "She's very striking, actually, and rumor has it her father has turned down many offers for her hand. Once you meet her, you'll understand why. She isn't one of those milk-faced misses who simpers and takes pride in the fact there is nothing but fluff in her head."

Damien's demeanor took on a certain cheer. "That's welcome news. This party might not be as tedious as I thought."

"You'd pretend to take an interest in her to gain audience with her father?"

"Nothing so nefarious." His brother looked perplexed at his annoyed tone. "I merely meant that I assume she'll be in the company of her parents most of the time and in courting Marston's attention, I am sure I will be required to also court hers."

It made sense. Why Robert even cared was a mystery.

One brief exchange of casual conversation and a quick dash into the bushes to help her escape a boring oaf like Watts hardly constituted anything but a passing acquaintance.

"Go ahead and court her." He lifted his shoulders in a deliberate nonchalant gesture.

"I didn't say I was going to—"

"Damien, do as you damn well please."

Had he really just interrupted his older brother with such vehemence? Bloody hell, that moment downstairs with Brianna had him off balance.

He moved toward the door. "Sorry. I hate affairs of this sort. They make me edgy. Let's go have a stiff brandy before it all begins, shall we?"

If the past hour was any indication, Rebecca would be lucky to make it through the next five days with her sanity intact.

She sat perched on the edge of an embroidered settee, her teacup in her unsteady hand. If she lifted the delicate porcelain to her mouth she was sure she'd dribble tea all over her lap, so instead she pretended she wasn't thirsty.

In short, she faked having tea, which wasn't something a respectable Englishwoman should ever do, but she was rather tired of the rules of respectability. Those selfsame rules had her stuck listening as Damien Northfield—who was almost as handsome as his rakish younger brother but completely lacking the dashing air and wicked smile—and her father grew engrossed in a conversation about the war on the Peninsula. On the opposite side of the room, Robert conversed with Loretta Newman, a widow who was both attractive and still quite young.

Of course, Rebecca thought crossly, the woman had to be fashionably blond and petite and all the other things a gentleman might like. As she watched, Robert leaned forward just a fraction too far for propriety and whispered something in his companion's ear. Mrs. Newman laughed and fluttered her lashes in a teasing way that made Rebecca want to grind her teeth. What they were talking about she couldn't tell, but they'd been standing there in a cozy corner for the last fifteen minutes and—

"Miss Marston?"

She tore her gaze away, chagrined. Damien Northfield looked at her with perfect equanimity from a nearby chair. She stammered, "I—I'm sorry. Did you say something?"

Dear God in heaven, do not let him catch me staring at his brother. There was a keenness in his eyes that spoke of a superior intelligence.

"I wondered," he said with particular courtly seriousness, "how you were enjoying London this year?"

At least it wasn't a difficult question. "About as much as last year," she said honestly. He had nice eyes, she noted, but they were dark rather than an arresting azure blue. His clean-cut Northfield features didn't show Robert's slightly sinful charm or Colton's reserve, but were something his entirely, something watchful and quiet.

A quixotic smile quirked Lord Damien's lips. "I see."

Her father frowned at the ambiguous nature of her response. She refused to look apologetic but instead focused on Robert's older brother. Surely she could do better. "I meant it is quite a whirl."

Apparently she couldn't do *much* better.

Lord Damien didn't seem to mind. He said in a mild tone, "I find it such myself. Even without the war, I fear I am a bit too solitary to spend a great deal of time in London. Robert is quite the opposite." He glanced in the direction where his brother still stood flirting with the desirable Mrs. Newman.

"He does seem to go about in society." It was a banal comment and Rebecca wished violently she could drink her tea to give her hands something to do, but really she was afraid of embarrassing herself.

"He mentioned the two of you were acquainted."

That comment got her full attention. How *much* had he mentioned? Their collision in the doorway? The flight through the gardens? That almost kiss she couldn't stop thinking about? She hoped Robert hadn't detailed the whole story to his brother, and she prayed that if he had, Damien wouldn't choose to repeat it now in front of her father. Surely, as an attaché to Wellington, he had more tact than that.

Everything would have been fine except she blushed. To her horror she felt the rush of blood upward and the warmth invade her face. "We've been introduced," she said just a little too quickly, not daring to look over at her father.

"Yes, well, I imagine so. You are a good friend of my sister-in-law, I understand." Lord Damien's expression was bland.

Tact indeed. He made it sound very natural that she would be acquainted with a rake of the highest caliber, even one her father despised. She nodded, grateful for his explanation. "Brianna and I have been friends most of our lives. Our families have estates quite close by each other, and we met as children."

"Our acquaintance is still brief but she seems like a lovely person."

"She is." At least Rebecca could say that with conviction.

To her relief, he turned back to her father and asked a question about the upcoming Parliamentary session, and she was once again abandoned to her now tepid but still full cup of tea. It was torture not to look, but she didn't dare so much as a glance over to where Robert and the pretty widow stood, at least not for a few moments.

To her dismay, when she did sneak a quick look, they were gone. Both of them.

A sick feeling curled in the pit of her stomach.

It was one thing to have a hopeless passion for a known rake, and quite another to be witness to his indiscretions. Oh, she'd seen him dance and chat and smile in crowded ballrooms before, but there were always a great deal of people milling about, and she'd never seen him *leave* with any of his fawning admirers. When a man and a woman disappeared at a house party together . . . well, she read the gossip columns and was worldly enough to know what happened.

Had they gone upstairs to where the bedrooms were located?

It was possible.

It stung, though she had no right to feel upset or betrayed. She just . . . did.

With only a small rattle of her cup in its saucer, she

managed to set aside her tea. If she didn't escape this room she might scream. When she stood, naturally her father and Lord Damien rose politely also. Rebecca murmured, "Excuse me. It is so lovely out, and the estate's gardens beckon. Brianna has complimented them so many times. I must see for myself."

Damien's brows elevated a fraction, and to her horror he offered his arm. "Please allow me to escort you."

No! He looks so much like him ... that thick chestnut hair, and his profile. . . .

What she truly desired was to be alone and to compose herself. But if she refused Damien's proffered escort, her father would be immensely irritated and she would seem churlish. So she set her fingers on his sleeve and dredged up a smile. "That would be lovely."

They left the room together through a set of French doors open to the late afternoon. Damien led her around the sweep of the huge terrace toward the back of the house where the formal gardens were laid out, at least fifteen acres of them, he informed her in his diffident way, their walk more of a stroll. Had she really been interested in the flowers and sculpted bushes, she would have been glad of his company, but not now, considering her mother's aspirations for her to look at Lord Damien as a possible candidate for a husband.

This was most uncomfortable.

He selected a path and she walked next to him, hoping she looked composed. Lest he think she was a complete idiot without a gracious bone in her body, she murmured politely, "Are you enjoying your leave from your duties in Spain, my lord?"

He looked reflective, a faint smile teasing his lips. "I would be a fool to say I wasn't, wouldn't I? Who would wish to trade this wonderful place, a chance to see my family and friends, and time to relax for the hardships of war?"

Rebecca wasn't sure how to respond. If she wasn't mistaken, there was a slight edge in his tone, but she didn't know him well enough to judge.

"I am," he said succinctly, "occasionally foolish."

She blinked. "I take it that means you would rather be back in Spain?"

"I enjoy my duties," he admitted. "It is a pleasure to align myself against Bonaparte and his venal ambitions. The visit home is nice, but though it might sound odd, I am anxious to get back to the war."

"It's admirable." In secret, she devoured the newspaper accounts of the quest to wrest free the Emperor's inexorable hold over Europe. "Everyone, from the Duke of Wellington himself to the lowliest soldier, risks much for England and the world."

"I relish the challenge."

He spoke the truth—she could tell. Rebecca smiled up at him. It was the first genuine smile she'd been able to give since she arrived at Rolthven. "I think you do."

"I love my family too—don't mistake me—but I am not Colton, with his estates and responsibilities. Nor am I Robbie, with his *joie de vivre* attitude toward life. Not that my youngest brother is shallow in any way. I am not sure if it is common knowledge, but he has a canny knack for numbers of any kind, from financial investments to card games. Never pit yourself against him in whist, Miss Marston, for I promise you, you will lose."

Why were they talking about Robert again?

Or was she just sensitive to the subject? It was natural enough for him to mention his younger brother.

Rebecca murmured, "I shall take your warning to heart, lest I be lured into a contest of that sort."

"He's a brilliant cellist too. Did you know?"

Why would he think she knew anything at all about a rogue like his younger brother? "Of course not," she said too brusquely. "We are no more than passing acquaintances."

"I just wondered," Damien said in his quiet, amused way, "if Brianna might have mentioned it. Robbie doesn't advertise it, naturally, for music isn't such a manly pastime, but he has a true talent for it. Once again, I think it is the mathematician in him. He can easily glance at a piece of music and understand the meter and measure without even having to think about it like the rest of us might."

Rebecca felt as if her heart had stopped beating. Robert was a musician? Briefly, she shut her eyes. It was nothing, just a small flutter, but it happened against her will.

The lover of her dreams was a kindred soul. She pictured his long, graceful fingers holding a bow—and *then* she envisioned them sliding over her skin.

So she could now add a new daydream to her repertoire. Wonderful. This would be her undoing.

"How clever of him." The inadequate mumble was decidedly *not* clever, so she deflected the conversation away from the possibility of any more disconcerting revelations about Robert Northfield. "What about you, my lord? What are your talents?"

His face took on an enigmatic expression. "I do not know if it is a talent, but I can think like the enemy. I am sure genteel young ladies do not need to concern themselves with such matters, but it does aid our effort to thwart the French now and again."

Long shadows had lengthened over the path and the crunch of their passage along the gravel mingled with the twitter of the birds in the ornamental trees and beyond, in the huge elms in the grassy park. Rebecca took in a breath and let it out gently. "I feel confident it is a talent England needs. Make no mistake, some genteel young ladies also worry about the war, my lord."

"Do they?" He glanced down and she thought she saw a glimmer of amusement in his eyes over the firmness of her tone. "I take it you are one of them. Forgive me, then, for my underestimation of your interest in our struggle against Bonaparte."

"There's nothing to forgive." She made a small face. "My mother finds my interest in politics unladylike." An understatement. Talking about the war was placed into the same category as admitting one composed music.

"You are feminine in every way, my lady," he said gallantly.

"Thank you."

He motioned up ahead to where a small folly sat near a gleaming pond. In the late afternoon sun it looked charming and peaceful. "Shall we go this way? It is a pleasant place to sit that does not involve tea trolleys and the buzz of a dozen other conversations."

"If you wish." Rebecca inclined her head, not really sure if she did want to sit but helpless to refuse without seeming rude. The shallow steps led to an exquisite jewel of a summerhouse, she discovered, the interior holding small couches with plush pillows in brilliant colors, little tables scattered everywhere, and even a drinks cabinet in one corner complete with crystal glasses and assorted decanters lined up in an artistic fashion. Rebecca chose a chair that faced one of the open vistas to the pond and settled into it, self-consciously smoothing her skirts. Damien Northfield leaned a shoulder against one of the Grecian pillars and leveled a very disconcerting gaze her direction.

Then, to her complete and utter surprise, he said, "Is this better? You looked rather miserable earlier."

There went her hope he hadn't noticed.

She opened her mouth to deny it, but he forestalled her with another insightful comment.

"I am not trying to pry, I assure you. If you choose to not say a word, consider the subject dropped."

It was tempting to lie, to take him up on the offer, but at the moment she felt rather defeated. Between her parents, Robert's well-known aversion to eligible young ladies, and now the flirtatious Mrs. Newman, she was definitely outmaneuvered. The lovely widow wasn't something she had anticipated. Maybe she did need Lady Rothburg's book. On her own she didn't have any idea how to proceed. Or should she even try? Her father's unconcealed dislike of Robert was a real obstacle. Rebecca just shook her head. "I hoped no one would notice I wasn't paying attention to the conversation. Please excuse my distraction."

"Being observant is second nature to me now, after a

few years in Spain." Damien tilted his head just a fraction, as if studying her face. "Robert mentioned you earlier."

Well, *that* was straight to the point.

So he'd caught her watching his brother. Maybe she could still bluff this through. She hoped the enemies' minds were the only ones he could read. Betraying warmth washed into her face for the second time. Some vestige of pride made her feign confusion despite her blush. "Are you referring to Lord Robert?"

"Indeed." His response was dry. "The one who told me you were beautiful and charming. The one you were covertly observing during the entire course of high tea while not consuming one drop from your cup or a single morsel of food."

Robert Northfield thought she was beautiful? And charming? She wasn't sure which pleased her more, but with males, she thought the former might hold the most weight. She could think of absolutely nothing to say.

Damien went on in a conversational tone. "I suppose it really is none of my business, but I do get the impression that the two of you are acquainted but want to give the appearance of *not* being acquainted. I admit it piqued my interest."

It was true that when Rebecca entered the drawing room, flanked by her father and mother, Brianna had breezily introduced her brother-in-law and Rebecca had mumbled something utterly unnecessary about how she thought they'd maybe met once before. If anyone had been paying attention, it was hardly a convincing performance. Robert had certainly been amused. She could see it in those azure eyes before he briefly bent over her hand.

"I don't think acquainted is the right word. We were introduced last season briefly and then ran into each other recently. That is the extent of it."

"I would consent to believe you if you didn't blush every time his name cropped up in the conversation."

There was refuge in outrage, even if he was infuriatingly correct. Her color was high at the moment, she was sure. Rebecca straightened her spine. "You, sir, are very direct."

"At times," he conceded, faintly lifting his brows. "I'm devious also. Whatever the situation demands. You might keep it in mind."

"Whatever does *that* mean?" Rebecca gazed at him in utter confusion.

"It means my younger brother, whose reputation would make even a seasoned libertine blush, is finally showing interest in a marriageable young lady who seems to return it. I wouldn't be a worthy sibling if I didn't find it amusing. I would definitely not be a worthy brother if I didn't take delight in the idea of his possible downfall."

Men were just the oddest creatures, she thought with a twinge of irritation. "Maybe I am more obtuse than I thought, but I am afraid I am not following you very well, Lord Damien."

"What I mean is, you have an ally, Miss Marston, should you choose to engage your adversary."

"My adversary?"

"Haven't you heard," he said with open amusement, "that rakish young bachelors are quite resistant to the idea of matrimony? Robert, at a guess, will prove more resistant than most. He has money, so he has no need of your dowry. He has infinite freedom, and has shown a propensity to enjoy it. This will be a challenge."

"There is no 'this.'" Rebecca twined her hands tightly in her lap, giving up on denials since she had so obviously betrayed herself. "Whether or not you are correct over your brother's possible interest, an insurmountable problem exists in my father's dislike for Robert. I don't know what happened to cause it for he shows no aversion to the Duke or yourself. It is obviously personal."

"Robert and your father?" Damien straightened, his dark brows drawing together. "And you have no idea why?"

She helplessly shook her head. "Besides, Robert and Mrs. Newman . . ."

"That's nothing," he remarked as she trailed off. "And as for the other problem, I admit I find that rather interesting. Let me see if I can gather more information. It's the secret to any successful campaign."

Chapter Nine

What defines pleasure? A physical joy, a serene moment, an appreciation for something beautiful? A sexual encounter can be all three if orchestrated correctly.

From the chapter titled:
"After Is As Important As Before"

The evening had gone tolerably well, Brianna thought, pulling the pins from her hair and feeling exhausted but hopeful for the rest of the gathering. There was that one unfortunate moment when one of the footmen had dropped an entire tray of pickled fish on the expensive carpet. Oddly enough, the recollection made her smile as she gazed in her mirror and deposited the pins in a small crystal bowl.

The poor young man had been positively horrified to be so clumsy in front of his employer, but Colton merely gestured to one of the other servants to help the young man mop it all up as best as possible and resumed his conversation with Lord Emerson as if nothing had happened. It was likely the rug would have to be discarded, but it had been obvious Colton merely felt such things happen in the course of life, and he was willing to pay for a new one.

That was one of the things she loved so much about him. He took his responsibilities very seriously, and that included his staff. Though she doubted he realized it, the household regarded him with a mixture of awe and affection. He wasn't one of those haughty aristocrats who acted above everyone else, though he certainly could if he wished. He was unapproachable in some ways, but that was just his reserved nature, not a conscious effort to hold himself apart. He routinely thanked servants just as politely as he would his noble friends.

She flicked a glance at the clock on the mantel. It was late. The day had been filled with arriving guests, the formal afternoon tea, and an elaborate dinner, before which Lord Knightly had entertained the group with a rendering of several passages of *Hamlet*, all performed with appropriate theatrical pomp. To her surprise, it had actually been entertaining, and everyone had seemed to be enjoying themselves, even Colton.

Would he come to her?

He might be too tired. After all, he had risen early and spent hours in his study before the family gathered for lunch, and . . .

The door clicked open.

In a dark blue silk dressing gown, her husband entered the room. The few candles she had burning didn't provide much illumination for such a big space, so Brianna saw his glance first stray to the empty bed and then shift to where she sat in the semi-gloom. She turned and smiled, hoping he wouldn't notice the sudden shaking of the hairbrush in her hand.

His mere presence affected her *that* much. So much she trembled. "I was just speculating on whether I might see you yet this evening, Your Grace."

"See me?" His brows went up. "I suppose that is one way of putting it." He walked over and placed his hands on her shoulders. "I was rather hoping you'd wish to *see* me in your bedchamber, madam."

"Always," Brianna responded, with feeling.

One of those rare smiles lit his face. "To be so welcomed is flattering."

"I would never deny you." She could feel her return smile was tremulous.

There was a small silence while he simply looked at her, his expression hard to read in the flickering, dim light. Then he asked quietly, "Because you want me, or because you feel it is your duty to allow me my conjugal rights?"

That he really considered the question was another step forward. Duty was one of Colton's favorite words, and it was no secret he felt his obligations keenly. Brianna stood and pressed one of her hands to his chest, feeling the strong beat of his heart through the silk material of his robe under her palm. "Can you doubt I want you?" She arched a brow. "I believe I am the one who upon occasion dresses in a provocative way to catch your attention."

"I remember." His reply was more a growl than regular speech. "Unfortunately, so does any other male who saw you that evening at the opera. Mine was not the only attention you captured."

"Are you jealous?"

"I don't know. I find it rather hard to waste time trying to define my feelings when you are in close proximity. Reasonable thought and my beautiful wife don't seem to exist in the same sphere." Without warning, he swept her up off her feet. "Can we save the analytical discussion for some other time? Right now I'd like to pursue a more physical type of communication."

Brianna merely laughed as he stalked across the room and deposited her on the bed, his hands moving swiftly to the tie on his dressing gown. He was magnificently aroused, she saw as he shrugged the garment off, his erection high and swollen, the tip catching the light where a bead of sexual discharge glistened.

With deliberate intent, holding his gaze, she reached up and pulled free the ribbon on the bodice of her nightdress. Catching her lower lip with her teeth, she parted the material slowly to bare her breasts. They felt tight and needy, and that singular warmth she recognized as desire was already building between her legs. "I am very anxious to *communicate*," she whispered, her lids feeling heavy as she gazed up at her husband through the fringe of her lowered lashes.

"We are in accord then." Colton moved in one fluid motion to settle on top of her. His mouth brushed hers once and then he was teasing the hollow of her throat, making love to her neck, nipping, then ravishing as she arched beneath the pleasant imprisonment of his much larger body, her puckered nipples brushing his hard chest. His breath tickled the sensitive spot just below her ear and she moaned.

Yes, the dynamics were changing, she thought hazily as he stripped off her nightdress and his mouth followed the progress of his hands, feasting on her breasts, sucking her nipples deeply, then skimming the tense muscles of her abdomen before brushing her pubic hair. He was going to do that glorious thing with his mouth again, Brianna realized, his hands insistent as he pushed apart her thighs.

That scandalous, glorious thing.

Her hands bunched into fists in the bedclothes and she opened more than willingly, eager to embrace the tumultuous sensations, the wicked, wild experience. Long fingers parted her sex, making her feel vulnerable and yet excited. Somehow the sight of his head between her legs was the most erotic and exhilarating thing she had ever seen.

And the pleasure. Oh God, the exquisite rapture as his tongue began to tease and stimulate her in just the right spot . . .

It took a startlingly short amount of time before she gasped and began to tremble in unbridled ecstasy, her climax so vivid and intense she clenched her fingers in his hair and shook uncontrollably, needing somehow to push him away and pull him closer at the same time. To tell him to stop—if she could speak, which wasn't possible—and yet demand he continue the erotic torture.

It was utter heaven. And when Colton moved back upward and thrust into her still quaking body, it happened again. She wanted to protest the excess of sensation. It was too much, too soon, too overwhelming. He began to move in long, hard strokes and she managed somehow to recover enough to respond, though she clung to his strong shoulders like a drowning woman, which perhaps was an apt description.

Drowning in passion.

Drowning in the wash of sensation.

Drowning in love.

Why was it that each time he made love to his beautiful wife, Colton was convinced it was more tempestuous and pleasurable than the last?

This time was no exception.

His combustible release, in conjunction with her third climax, was so feral, so primitive, so earthshaking he might have stopped breathing, his neck arching back so every tendon stood out in relief, his body captive to the force of it. As her inner muscles gripped and held, his raging orgasm consumed his body. Maybe even his soul.

By damn, he thought when the first trickle of consciousness returned to his brain, Brianna must have some kind of mystical power. He was an experienced man. Women had been throwing themselves at him since he was old enough to understand how male/female interaction worked, and though he'd always been selective and discreet, he felt fairly well versed in sexual matters.

With Brianna it was different.

Very different.

Even on their wedding night, when she'd been shy and nervous, he'd been able to draw a response from her untutored body. Her unexpected sensuality was a boon to his marriage, and as a male with a healthy sexual appetite, he was grateful his wife enjoyed his attentions in bed.

There was more to it, also. It was difficult to do so, but he was starting to acknowledge it to himself. Sexual desire was a normal part of life. Most men would find someone like Brianna attractive....

And that unsettling thought made his brows shoot together in a scowl she thankfully couldn't see because his face was still buried in her outspread hair. He didn't give a damn what most men might want, she was *his*.

Only his.

"Uhmmm." Her slender fingers drifted down his spine.

Colton gave an inelegant grunt of assent at her unspoken sentiment and shifted so he wasn't crushing her, rolling to his side and cradling her in his arms. The scent of sex mingled with her delicate perfume, and he couldn't think of anything he liked more. Her damp, enticingly curved body rested languid against him, the silk of her long hair spilled across his chest.

"Today went well, I think," she murmured. "Did you enjoy yourself?"

He'd *just* enjoyed himself immensely, and though he wasn't fond of an overflowing houseful of guests, at the moment he felt quite charitable. "It was pleasant enough. At least the people you invited are all acceptable."

"High praise." Her voice was dry.

"Actually, it is," he countered. "I usually loathe these types of gatherings."

"I was afraid you'd feel that way when I planned this."

"You were correct." He brushed a gold curl off her shoulder, a singular warmth that had nothing to do with his recent climax building inside him. "You know me so well?"

"Biblically, Your Grace."

Colton laughed. It was drawn out of him before he could think about it. "You do realize," he murmured, kissing her jaw, "that you can be very impertinent for a respectable duchess."

"As long as my candid nature doesn't repel you, I will not argue with the assessment."

"You? Brianna Northfield? Not argue? I find it hard to believe."

"Colton," she said in laughing protest, but he loved

the light in her eyes, and relished the tender clasp of her arms.

"But," he continued, "despite your sometimes irreverent treatment of your august husband, nothing about you repels me." He nibbled on the corner of her mouth, astounded to realize he might become aroused again. After such an explosive release, it was a testament to her seductive beauty and appeal.

"I hope it always stays that way."

The slight wistful note in her voice made him pause. "Why wouldn't it?"

Her shrug was apparent since he held her so closely. "Men do tire of their wives. In fact, few desire them deeply in the first place."

He frowned, chagrined. She was absolutely correct. "I desire *you*. Perhaps you recall what just happened between us."

"It would be difficult to forget." She touched his cheek, just a feather brush of her fingers.

His wife had an innocent air combined with a courtesan's allure, he thought as he smoothed his hand over the supple curve of her hip. Golden hair and those long-lashed, midnight blue eyes, not to mention her mouth, so lush and soft. Several of the men in attendance had complimented her beauty during the course of the afternoon and evening. He hadn't thought too much about it because he agreed wholeheartedly, but now, since they seemed to be discussing fidelity, he had his own opinion on the matter.

"You belong to me." The words came out a shade too clipped.

Brianna's reaction was to tilt her head back and give him a puzzled look. "What?"

He hesitated, not sure what had prompted his arrogant declaration. Of course she belonged to him, she was his wife. He'd given her his name and his protection. The trouble was, to some of his class that didn't matter. It was common practice that once a wife had borne her husband an heir she could seek entertainment elsewhere if she wished as long as she was discreet.

Not Brianna. He wouldn't allow it. The idea of some other man touching her—well, he didn't care to analyze the primitive depth of his reaction to that image.

Colton chose to kiss her rather than explain himself. Or maybe the kiss *was* an explanation, for he hungrily devoured her mouth, his encircling arms holding her close, his rising cock hard against her hip. This time, when he rolled her onto her back and settled between her legs, he entered her slowly, with measured control instead of impetuous force, listening to the change in her breathing as he moved her closer and closer to the brink. The sleek, velvet warmth of her body enveloped him, and every sense was riveted on the woman below him: sight, sound, taste, touch, the fragrance of her arousal heady as any drink.

Afterwards, when they'd shuddered together, when their slick bodies ceased trembling and they were sprawled in a tangle where he didn't know when one of them ended and the other began, she touched his hair. "May I ask something of you?"

Generous did not even begin to describe his mood after a second such mind-shattering release. Colton smiled lazily, not remembering ever feeling so satisfied. "Of course. Let me guess, a diamond necklace?"

"I don't really like jewels, you know that. I rarely wear them unless I must."

Did he know that? Now that he thought about it, he realized with a small twinge of dismay, it was true. He very rarely saw her drape herself in expensive gems like so many of the ladies of the *ton*, for whom each expensive bauble was a trophy. Was he really that unobservant?

Yes, a scolding voice answered in his head. *You have a tendency to be absorbed in your own life. Now, as she has pointed out, you share it with someone else. You might wish to keep it in mind.*

"I was joking," he said, lounging back against the pillows. "Not that if you wished more jewelry I wouldn't purchase it for you, but the Northfield family vault is already filled to the brim with every form of it, and you know it is all at your disposal."

Next to him, the rumpled sheet pulled to her waist, her voluptuous breasts bare and her shining hair spilled across the bed, Brianna gave him a sleepy smile. "This is much simpler to give than diamonds and will cost you nothing."

He watched her lashes drift lower, an indulgent smile on his face. "What is it?"

"Stay."

"I beg your pardon?"

No answer. She was asleep. Not that it surprised him, for he felt pleasantly exhausted himself, and she'd risen early to prepare for the arrival of their guests. Even with the servants to help, his grandmother's advice, and the efficiency of Mrs. Finnegan, he knew Brianna had worked hard to make sure each detail was taken care of before the first carriage rolled up the drive.

Stay. What the devil did that mean?

Chapter Ten

*If his behavior changes, mark the date and ana-
lyze the cause. It could be you are making an
impression.*

From the chapter titled: "Cause and Effect"

Her parents were not the most subtle people who
ever graced God's earth, Rebecca decided, wanting
to crawl under the dinner table.

It was painfully obvious—and Rebecca had the uncomfortable feeling everyone attending knew—she was
being thrust underneath Damien Northfield's nose like
a prize cow being trotted out for an affluent farmer.

To make matters worse, it was equally apparent to
everyone that Mrs. Newman had set her sights on Robert. Whether it was a serious attempt to snare the most
resistant bachelor in England or merely the desire for
a pleasurable interlude, who knew? But if the woman
thought she was being sly about her intentions, she was
gravely mistaken.

After all, what was a house party without the appropriate seduction, Rebecca thought dismally, reaching for
her wine. At the moment, the lovely Loretta was bent
provocatively near her quarry, her décolletage exposed
to the best advantage by her position, the limp ruffle on
her bodice doing nothing to conceal the entire upper
curves of her breasts.

"You might want to adjust your expression."

The mild suggestion made Rebecca jerk, her wine sloshing dangerously close to the edge of her glass. Damien, seated—by her mother's machinations—next to her, leaned in close as if saying something intimate. "He's talking to her, but watching you. I haven't been so entertained in years."

Robert was watching her? If so, she couldn't tell, but then again, she was taking great pains *not* to watch him either. "My expression?" she asked in a strangled voice.

"You look like you want to cleave out her heart. That would be decidedly *de trop* at the dinner table."

"Your amusement is noted, my lord."

Damien laughed softly and turned his attention back to his fish course.

Damn him. She took pleasure in the silent profanity even as she stifled an inner groan over his perceptive observation. Across the table, her mother had seen their private exchange, and she beamed.

Good God, what a nightmare.

Rebecca tackled her baked cod in butter sauce with false enthusiasm, though her appetite was nonexistent. She managed to choke down a few bites, studiously intent on her plate—on anything but Robert and his infamous, infectious smile. The candlelight from the chandelier did some wicked things to the structure of his face, emphasizing his elegant cheekbones and the seductive line of his mouth.

Stop it, she instructed, *before you embarrass yourself and other people begin to notice.*

What would Lady Rothburg suggest in this situation? The same kind of eye batting, coquettish behavior as Mrs. Newman displayed across the table? Surely there was a better way; Rebecca just had no idea what it might be. Maybe she'd ask Brianna for the book this very evening. It was either pursue that drastic measure or give up and follow the mandates of her parents and choose a husband.

With grim determination Rebecca slogged through

the roast beef and creamed potatoes, though her stomach wasn't exactly settled. A wash of relief swept through her at the arrival of dessert. As soon as the plates were cleared, the men would be served their port and the ladies would gather for some after-dinner gossip. She, on the other hand, could plead a headache and escape to her room.

It was a perfect plan, since her temples truly throbbed.

Until it was neatly thwarted.

When she attempted to excuse herself, her mother's glare could have pulverized a mountain into rubble. "Maybe all you need is a little fresh air. Step out on the terrace, my dear. Perhaps Lord Damien will accompany you."

There was no way she could endure four more days of this overt pairing of the two of them. Rebecca cleared her throat. "I'm certain he is as anxious for his port as the other gentlemen. I am fine on my own."

"*I* am sure he'll insist."

Well, now he had no choice, she thought crossly. Damien inclined his head. "I'd be delighted, of course. But I did promise Mrs. Newman earlier I'd show her that rare map of Manchuria in the library this evening. Perhaps Robert could escort Miss Marston instead?"

A look of horror crossed her mother's face. Rebecca stifled an audible laugh. It was one thing, of course, to shove her out the door on the arm of the most eligible bachelor in attendance, and another entirely to send her blithely on a stroll with a known rakehell, even if they were brothers.

"I . . . I, well . . ."

"Naturally, it would be my pleasure." Robert stepped in smoothly, perhaps in an effort to help Damien escape the overt ploy, maybe because he found it amusing to tease her mother, or . . . she hesitated to believe it. Could Damien be right? Could Robert truly be interested? He murmured, "I fancy a bit of fresh air myself. Shall we?"

And that easily, Rebecca found herself on his arm, her heart beginning to pound at the proximity, though thankfully she didn't crash into him as they exited the dining room in a repeat performance of their last encounter.

A much better start than the last time they were alone together. There was no ravening Lord Watts hot on her heels either, she thought, not sure whether to be grateful to Damien or not. Clearly he found her infatuation with his younger brother diverting enough to interfere—or maybe he was just trying to spare himself her mother's matchmaking.

Had Robert really been watching her through dinner? Rebecca slanted a glance at the tall man next to her through her lashes. Like the last time, she found herself quite lost for words. If there was a chance he found her even half as attractive as she did him ... well, she needed to know if it was true.

She was *desperate* to know if it was true.

I need that dratted book....

"It's cool out. Would you like a wrap?"

His question made her jump for no reason at all. "Uhm, no ... no, thank you. It was rather warm in there. Cool sounds delightful."

"Your cheeks are a bit flushed."

Of course they were. As Damien had pointed out, she blushed on a consistent basis in Robert's presence. It was infuriating she couldn't control it, and now even *he* had noticed it. How mortifying. "I'm quite well, I assure you." It came out more tartly than she intended.

"Indeed." Robert followed her outside, looking very much the debonair rogue in his tailored evening clothes, a faint smile on his mouth. "So, do tell me, Miss Marston, are you enjoying the party so far? I notice my sister-in-law did you the favor of keeping the persistent Lord Watts off the guest list."

"That's because if she had invited him, Brianna knows I would have strangled her," she said with feeling. "My parents consider him to be extremely eligible. My opinion differs somewhat."

The cool air did carry an autumn chill, but it felt marvelous as it drifted across her bared shoulders. Clouds had gathered during the course of the day, the moon obscured by a haze. Nearby, a bird called in a low, mournful sound. Their footsteps echoed on the smooth stone, the huge terrace deserted except for their presence.

They were alone.

Well, for now. Her mother wouldn't be content with the situation for long. Rebecca didn't even want to think about what her father might do.

Robert cocked a brow in amusement. "And now they seem to favor Damien."

He'd noticed that, too. Well, maybe she shouldn't feel a rush of jubilation, a practical voice in her pointed out. It probably meant nothing. *All* the guests had no doubt noticed how her parents were thrusting her into the arms of his brother.

"Yes." Rebecca muttered. "Poor man."

Robert laughed.

The sound held a compelling note she wished she could capture in music. There was something special about his face, too, when he gave that flashing signature grin that made her knees feel weak. Both his brothers were equally handsome, she supposed, but Robert's charisma was what drew her. It was an energy, a vital force, and though she was hardly an expert on the subject of seduction, she'd guess if he owed his success with women to anything, it was that undeniable pull.

"He'll survive. One tends to forget that my older brother gives advice to one of the most important men of our times," Robert commented as they walked to the balustrade and he leaned a hip against it, turning to face her. "Damien doesn't look wily, but he is. How neatly done was that back there? A quick rescue with one small but inventive ploy."

Rebecca could not help but grimace. "I suppose by 'rescue' you mean him avoiding my mother's more than obvious technique."

"Actually, I was thinking more of myself and the determined Mrs. Newman. Do you really think she cares about a map of Manchuria? Myself, I doubt it. I wouldn't guess geography is one of her interests. She seems to be more absorbed in the latest style of hats than mountain ranges in distant countries."

"I rather thought you liked her." Rebecca probably shouldn't have said it, but it came out anyway. She hastily amended, "At least that was my impression."

"Was it?" His tone was dry and his gaze flickered out over the shrouded back gardens. "Like most things in life, appearances can be deceptive." He shrugged. "I don't mean to sound ungallant. She is a pleasant enough young woman."

Relief washed over her, for that hardly sounded like the observation of a lover. If they really had disappeared earlier for a romantic tryst, surely he wouldn't now be quite so detached. He might have a reputation for indulging in casual affairs, but she hadn't ever heard of him leaving behind a trail of broken hearts either. If he was that callous, he wouldn't be so universally well liked, so if the careless lift of his broad shoulders was any indication, the mild flirtation hadn't led to a seduction.

She had no right to feel relieved, she reminded herself.

She had no rights when it came to the man standing next to her at all.

"I see." That was hardly a brilliant comment, but she wasn't sure brilliant would ever describe her when in his company.

"Do you?" he asked in a soft voice, looking at her in a way that made her pulse flutter in her throat.

He could do that, she sharply reminded herself. Beguile with a look, a smile, a touch. It didn't mean Damien was correct.

But it gave her hope he might be.

"I think so. We shackle ourselves sometimes with all the rules of politesse," his companion murmured. "It might encourage someone to think there is an interest where, in truth, we are just being polite."

Robert barely heard what she said.

Sable. That was the color of her hair. He'd been trying to define it all evening. Rich, dark, shining. It contrasted with the purity of her fair skin, and those long-lashed aqua eyes completed the tantalizing picture. Robert gave an inner curse. Damien thought he was being helpful, he was sure, by diverting Mrs. Newman.

It was not helpful in the slightest, for it placed temptation right under his nose.

As damn foolish as it was, Robert had found himself all too aware of the lovely Rebecca ever since her arrival, parents firmly in tow, the day before. This unprecedented attraction to an unmarried young lady had him unnerved. And he *was* attracted. If it wasn't for Rebecca, he probably would have considered Mrs. Newman's unspoken offer and spent a very pleasant night in her bed.

Disconcertingly, his current fascination seemed to preclude a casual interest in another woman, and a moment like this didn't help. Rebecca stood there and gazed up at him, the filtered light sliding across her face, her soft mouth just slightly parted, and he had to consciously stop himself from leaning in to her sweet scent. Luckily for him, her mother's reaction hadn't been much of a secret, so he doubted their little stroll would last long before someone was sent to rescue the innocent fair maiden from his nefarious clutches.

"At least Brianna doesn't seem determined to fill our every waking moment with activities we are all too polite to decline." She favored him with a tentative smile.

It was a shy, sweet curve of her mouth that made him realize just how little he knew about naïve young women. In his life, he'd made it a point to *not* know. He didn't have a sister, he'd been not much more than a boy when he'd become involved with Elise, and it seemed from there his path had been set. Not necessarily in the wrong direction—or so he'd thought before—but now it came home to him that he'd slammed some doors behind him because of his choices. Respectability was a word he'd always viewed with amusement. Colton was respectable enough for all of them.

It was unfortunate that his entire attention was now on Rebecca's lips and her beguiling smile. It would have been better if he hadn't had that brief almost taste of her.

He'd be damned if he didn't want more. What would it be like to be the man to initiate the delectable Rebecca into the joys of sexual pleasure? Now *that* was a new fantasy. Virgins had never, ever interested him, not when there were so many experienced lovers eager enough for the casual type of liaison he preferred. But there was something about her, something besides her willowy body and admittedly spectacular breasts—an unconscious aura of sensuality perhaps, that told him she'd be a very satisfying bed partner if tutored properly.

Bed partner for someone else, he reminded himself sharply, wondering what the devil was wrong with him. For her *husband*.

Robert lifted a brow and endeavored to respond to her remark with nonchalance. "That is one of the beauties of being family. I would decline if Brianna tried to drag me into a game of charades or some similarly insipid pastime. As far as I know, other than a musical performance tomorrow evening, we aren't to suffer any of the usual horrible affronts to our sensibilities. I believe one of the Campbells is going to mutilate Haydn or the work of some other composer who should be glad he's dead and can't hear the sacrilege."

Something flickered in Rebecca's expression. Then she said quietly, "Actually, *I* am to play."

He felt immediately like a fool. Bloody hell, he was supposed to be charming to a fault, not a buffoon who insulted young women—in this case a rather intriguing and beautiful one. Brianna must not have told him which of the young ladies was going to play, because in his current state of what seemed to be an infatuation, if she had mentioned Rebecca, he would have remembered. Someone else must have said something about the Campbell sisters and gotten it wrong.

"My apologies." He ran his hand through his hair and sighed. "Forgive me if you can, please. I've sat through one performance too many where I left with my ears ringing and cursing the man who invented the pianoforte. Still, it is no excuse to insult you, though it wasn't intentional. I don't suppose I should have maligned one of the Misses Campbell, either, without hearing her play."

Instead of turning on her heel and walking away in affronted hauteur, Rebecca Marston laughed prettily, her tense manner easing. Her expression held a mischievous glint. "I don't know, my lord, whether you realize you just issued me quite a challenge. It seems I must change your mind about young ladies and their musical skills. May I challenge you back?"

The unexpected reaction set him off balance. And by damn if he wasn't looking at her tempting mouth again. "It seems to me you are the injured party, so how can I refuse?"

"Play with me."

He stared, startled at the soft statement. *Play with me? God yes,* some wayward voice in his brain whispered. *I'd love to. Play with those full, firm breasts I know exist under your demure gown, twine my fingers in all that silky hair, kiss you breathless, part your thighs and sink my hard cock deep, deep into paradise....*

A very different voice, this one cold and practical, reminded him playing with virgins was a very poor idea. Playing with a virgin who had a powerful and protective papa (who despised him, no less) was one of the worst notions a man might take into his head. Besides, he was sure what she was suggesting didn't follow at all along with his less than pure thoughts.

"Could you be a little more clear, Miss Marston?"

"Your brother tells me you are a talented cellist. I happen to have a piece of music for pianoforte and cello. How about a duet?"

The kind of duet he had in mind had nothing to do with keys or strings.

Had they been in London, he could have refused gracefully on the grounds that his instrument was not available. As it was, he did have his cello here at Rolthven, and if neither of his brothers knew that, his grandmother certainly did. He'd just insulted Rebecca, and as a gentleman he could hardly compound the sin with a lie. He wasn't much for playing in public, but this gathering was small enough. Besides, there was something in the ingenuous wideness of her eyes that made him want to please her.

He was going to have to analyze that later.

"I haven't played in a while, but I suppose I could oblige you."

"Excellent. I will make sure you are given the music tomorrow morning so you can practice it a time or two." A teasing dimple appeared in her cheek. "We wouldn't want you to insult the composer by committing musical sacrilege, now would we?"

His laugh was spontaneous. "I don't suppose I will easily live down that unfortunate remark, will I?"

He preferred women with a sense of humor. They made for more entertaining bedmates, for one thing, and had a tendency to not be as spoiled and haughty.

Damn all, his thoughts needed to stay *out* of the bedchamber when it came to Miss Marston.

"Not when it was said to someone who takes her music seriously," she told him. "I'm afraid I do."

Fascinating. He did also, though it wasn't something he shared with many people. For him it was private, the beauty of the cadence and sound a balm to his jaded soul. "Do you?"

"Yes, indeed." The conviction in her voice was unmistakable, and it seemed to him she wanted to say something else, but instead she fell silent.

The air smelled like fall, he decided, trying to force himself to focus on anything besides the young woman next to him. Like gently decomposing leaves and wet earth overlain with a hint of chimney smoke. The fragrance of autumn in the country. London was redolent of less appealing odors most of the time. When he was younger, he couldn't wait to leave Rolthven for the city, but he found the peaceful setting more appealing than he remembered. Maybe some of his youthful male restlessness was fading with age.

Could it be he was maturing into a less reckless, more settled man, even to the extent he had a legitimate interest in an unmarried young lady?

No. He instantly banished the thought, as visions of primrose paths and cathedrals full of wedding guests and smiling, plump babies danced before his eyes and gave him pause. Miss Marston brought all those things with her, and he wasn't *that* ready to give up his freestyle existence.

Besides, he clearly recalled the aghast look on Lady Marston's face when Damien had maneuvered a switch in escorts for her daughter. Maybe she knew of the rift between Robert and her husband, or maybe it was just his reputation in general, but whichever it was, Robert's suit—if he ever contemplated such insanity—would not be welcomed.

"So, how long before your mother invents an excuse to join us?" he asked in amused cynicism, a realist at heart, but still admiring Rebecca's pure profile.

"I'm surprised she isn't out here already." She shook her head. "We are in plain sight, though, and I suspect she is watching us."

He liked the honesty. Perhaps that was what drew him to her. Beauty coupled with a refreshing lack of duplicity. She was genuine. Not vain, not simpering, not superficial.

"Maybe we should allay her anxiety. I'll take you back inside before she falls into an apoplexy." He cast a glance at the vast stone expanse of the terrace, a smile twitching on his lips. "Though this really would not be a comfortable place to ravish you, I have the feeling she is worried I might try anyway."

Perhaps Lady Marston should be worried. . . .

Rebecca gave a choked laugh. "Surely a rake of your standing shouldn't find stone floors a deterrent."

It could be done, of course. He'd had quite a bit of experience in utilizing less than ideal locations, but he was hardly going to say so out loud.

"Do I have a standing?" he asked, fully aware he did, offering his arm.

"I don't listen to gossip much," she demurred, contradicting her previous statement.

Everyone listened to an extent, he reminded himself.

The sound of a deep voice with an unmistakable icy edge interrupted them. "Rebecca. I understand you aren't feeling well. Perhaps, after all, you should go upstairs."

Rebecca jumped. Not much, but Robert felt the sudden clutch of her fingers through the sleeve of his jacket.

He turned and sent her father a cool smile. "I was just about to escort her back inside."

"No need." Sir Benedict stood framed in the doorway, his face impassive. "I'll see her in myself."

Rebecca hesitated one moment, looking both uncomfortable and bewildered at the sudden—but very palpable—tension, and then she whispered, "Good night, Lord Robert."

"Good night." He watched her go in a graceful swirl of silken skirts, followed by her father's derisive last glance before he ushered his daughter inside.

He'd just been warned off.

"If you have some sort of absurd romantic inclination toward Robert Northfield, you may put it aside."

Each terse word was like a small lash. Rebecca fought both indignation over being treated so summarily like a child in front of someone else—much less Robert—and a sense of confusion. Being practically dragged up the stairs toward her room wasn't exactly dignified either. "It was merely a stroll on the terrace. Mother can tell you he didn't even ask me. His brother suggested it."

"Don't think," her father said in the same chill tone, "I haven't noticed your reaction to that young man."

That left her at a loss. If she could deny it, she would, but she couldn't, so she simply fought to not trip over her skirts as she tried to keep up with his long strides.

"He is entirely unsuitable."

The set of her father's face did not invite questions. Yet Rebecca ventured one anyway, since she felt entirely in the dark over what precisely was going on. "You dislike him. Why?"

"I dislike him," her father confirmed. "And I will *not* tell you why."

"You like the Duke. You accepted his hospitality. And obviously Lord Damien has your approval, for you are embarrassing me with your enthusiasm for me being in his company."

"Neither of them have anything to do with this. Robert Northfield is his own man, and this is none of your business."

"How not?" she asked incredulously. "Since you are issuing ultimatums after nothing but a simple conversation in plain sight of the whole party."

They had been given rooms in the left wing, the long, elegant hallway full of carved doors and lamps left burning on small, polished tables. His face like granite, her father fairly stalked to her door and opened it for her. "I will see you in the morning, my dear."

Chapter Eleven

As the chase begins, remember you are the prize to be won. If you relinquish the power, he will gladly take it back. If you choose to hold it, as I strongly recommend, do so in the most subtle and pleasurable of ways.

From the chapter titled: "Things Every Woman Should Know"

The whimsical hunt wasn't Colton's idea of a pleasant way to spend a morning, nor was it very dignified, but he agreed because Brianna had asked him in such a way it would have felt churlish to refuse. The other guests seemed to enter into the spirit of the event with enthusiasm, and truthfully, it was probably more entertaining than sitting in his study with his secretary.

Especially at moments like this one, he thought, strolling along behind his wife and catching a glimpse of her shapely ankles as she bent over and triumphantly scooped a prize from beneath an ornamental bush. Brianna straightened and turned around, extending her hand. "Look. I think this one is rather nice."

"It's a rock," he said mildly.

"A pretty one, though, don't you think?"

"I must admit I don't sit around thinking about their aesthetic properties very often."

Brianna gave him a mock glare. "Your Grace, do you

not wish to win this contest? I would think someone of your exalted rank would show a little more spirit of competition. We are supposed to find the most interesting rock. If this one doesn't impress you, let's carry on until we find one that does."

While he found the game absurd, he couldn't help but admire the way the sunshine lit her fair hair. This morning she looked wholesome and fresh, dressed in a simple cream muslin gown trimmed in pale green satin ribbon, the slightly puffed sleeves emphasizing her slender arms, a matching ribbon holding back her fair tresses. Youthful feminine beauty personified, Brianna fit the bucolic setting of garden and park, healthy, young, alive . . . and fertile?

He wondered. It was a little early to question her on the matter, but he was fairly sure her courses were late by at least a few weeks. Not that he kept a calendar, but he did notice when he couldn't share her bed. It had been awhile since she'd admitted it was an inconvenient time for him to make love to her. They hadn't been married long enough for him to know if this was unusual for her, but there was no question the sexual part of their relationship was most satisfactory and he exercised his rights often. It would not astound him if she was pregnant already.

A child.

He liked the idea—and not just because it was his blasted responsibility to get an heir, either. It surprised him, because he'd always viewed the concept of children as an abstract one. Yes, one got married and in the natural course of things, offspring were created. But Brianna ripe with his babe, *their* child: unexpectedly, the idea moved him.

"Is something wrong, Colton?" His wife cocked her head to the side, a faint frown between her fine brows. "You have the strangest look on your face. I know you aren't much for this kind of game, but—"

"Games in general are not my usual fare, but I don't mind." He smiled. "And I think that's a fine rock. Quartz, I believe."

"Is it?" She looked at her hand and brightened. "Rather lovely, if I say so."

"Dazzling," he agreed, looking at her, not the damned rock.

His pretty wife blushed, catching the inference and the direction of his gaze. "You are not going to participate in this hunt, are you?"

"I'll carry the rock, how is that?"

One dark gold brow inched upward in challenge. "What about the caterpillar?"

"I beg your pardon?"

"The list is in your pocket. I believe we are supposed to find one. I would prefer you pick it up."

"The list or the caterpillar?"

"Definitely the latter. Stop teasing me. What else do we need to find?"

Teasing her? Well, he supposed he was. Odd. He didn't tease. Bemused, Colton obligingly dug out the piece of vellum and studied it. "'A red flower. An admirable stick'—how the devil can a stick be admirable, anyway?"

"How should I know? Your grandmother made up the list and it is her wording." Brianna laughed. "I do know it is a glorious day, the sun is shining, and our guests are scrambling all over themselves to beat us in finding the selected items. Shall we continue now that we have settled the matter of the rock? It would hardly do for us to come in last."

The term "come" took on a whole new meaning when spoken by his luscious wife, but the sexual inference was hardly appropriate to the moment, and she clearly had no idea she'd brought an erotic image to mind. Colton took the piece of quartz, slipped it into his jacket pocket, and followed her across the lawn. They managed to collect the whole list, including an unhappy bright green caterpillar he had to cradle in his hand and prevent from crawling all over him. When they finally returned to the terrace, his grandmother sat there in all her glory, presiding over the hunt with more animation than Colton had seen on her face in years, and her cane actually set aside.

Robert, who had been paired with one of the Campbell sisters—Colton couldn't tell them apart—also held a wooly worm. The resigned look on his face suggested that he, too, thought the game ridiculous.

However, for their grandmother and her delighted expression, Colton would have collected a dozen such creatures and carted them around.

Damien joined them, muttering under his breath, "How rude would it be of us to retire to your study for a brandy, Colt?"

"It isn't even noon."

"So? Aren't you holding an insect? How often does that happen before noon—or ever, for that matter? I, for one, need a drink."

His brother had a point. Colton said austerely, "I don't think it can be actually classified as an insect. Aren't they required to have six legs? This definitely has a great many more."

"This isn't the time to debate over trifles." Damien's specimen was definitely the smallest and least attractive, covered in mottled spots and bristles.

In the end they did have their brandy, escaping into his haven. Colton dismissed Mills with a casual wave and a request to finish what they had discussed and report the next morning. His secretary seemed astonished at the idea that Colton was going to take the rest of the afternoon off work, he noted.

Maybe he did devote a bit too much time to business. Not all of it needed his individual attention. Inside him still existed the unsure young man who'd had a dukedom and the responsibility of his family thrust upon him, and he wasn't sure how to let go of the compulsive need to see to each and every detail. Maybe if his father had fallen ill and gradually wasted away he would have been more prepared. One day his parent had been there, hale and hearty—and then he was gone.

It had shattered Colton's world.

Taking a hearty gulp of brandy, Colton brought his attention back to the conversation at hand. Such deep introspection unsettled him.

"...had to have the best damned red flower." Robert was still grumbling about his partner for the scavenger hunt. "I swear she examined every rose on the estate. Then we lost to Lord Emerson and his partner anyway."

"Grandmama had a grand time picking the winners," Damien remarked. "Though I think her selection has a great deal more to do with matchmaking than color and scent as she claimed. Emerson and the oldest Campbell chit seem to have that particular starry-eyed glow when together that makes me want to run straight back to Spain."

"Rather difficult, that," the Earl of Bonham—who had joined them—drawled, a small smile spreading across his face, "the ocean being between here and there and all."

"To drown myself in the attempt, then," Damien countered, grinning, relaxed in a sprawl in his chair. He lifted his hand. "And no, I don't need any lectures on the virtue of getting leg-shackled for life to one woman and settling into marital bliss. The French are challenge enough."

"Bliss?" Bonham grinned. "Well, at times the term applies. The bedroom being the spot that comes to mind."

"One may have the same bliss without being tied to one woman for life," Robert pointed out.

His younger brother should know, Colton thought. If ever there was a young man who had sampled the bliss offered by England's noted beauties, it was Robert. "I think we all have noticed you subscribe to that philosophy, Robbie."

"Who knows though," Damien said, "if that might not all change? Maybe even soon."

Colton's interest sharpened. Was he missing something? When Damien spoke in that tone of voice—meaning no tone at all—it was prudent to take notice.

His younger brother rarely wasted words. What was more, a small flicker crossed Robert's face that could actually be construed as an expression of consternation.

"Do you know something I don't?" Colton asked bluntly, curious as hell, for it wasn't often his youngest brother became disconcerted over anything.

"No, he doesn't." Robert set down his glass and rose. "I think Damien is so used to playing spy he feels he must drop cryptic remarks just to stay in practice. Please excuse me, gentlemen. I have been forced into the musical performance this evening and need to make sure I haven't forgotten how to wield a bow."

"You agreed to play?" This little house party was becoming more interesting by the minute. Robert was notably reticent about his love of music.

"Your wife asked me, so how could I refuse? I believe she is doing her best to make this a resounding success." Robert elevated a brow. "I think we were just discussing how difficult I find it to refuse a beautiful lady."

After he left, Colton gazed at Damien. Bonham, too, looked curious. "What the devil is going on?"

His brother laughed in his quiet way. "Let's just say I have an interesting theory and leave it at that, shall we?"

Brianna disliked parties that structured every moment of the day, so she left the afternoons free for the guests, offering them the choices of long walks over the grounds, rides in the countryside, relaxation in the enormous library, or a trip into the villages nearby if they wished for a bit of shopping. She wouldn't even have suggested the scavenger hunt that morning, but Colton's grandmother had insisted, and now Brianna was glad she'd agreed. For one thing, everyone seemed to jump in with light-hearted enjoyment, and she got to spend some time with her husband during the day, which was a rarity.

She, Arabella, and Rebecca had chosen her sitting room as a retreat, the décor at least not full of flounces of lace, but more in the style of an elegant Louis Quatorze drawing room, with antique French furniture and

silk-covered walls. The color palate of lemon yellow
and cream was soothing and she'd already decided to
extend it to her bedroom, though she was sure Colton
would insist they return to London the minute everyone
departed. Mrs. Finnegan, she thought with a sigh, could
doubtless oversee the changes, though she would have
loved to do so herself.

"You really couldn't ask for nicer weather for this,
Bri." Arabella, pretty in a gown of sprigged muslin, held
her glass of sherry in a dainty hand. "Everyone has commented on it."

"It's lucky, I agree." She nodded. "How dismal it
would be for all of us to be trapped inside the whole
time."

"And Lord Emerson and Belinda Campbell have
definitely developed a penchant for each other. A grand
success for any hostess." Rebecca smiled, her words teasing, but there was a set to her shoulders that suggested a
strain of some kind.

Brianna could all too easily guess what it might be.
"I really did not dream your mother would decide you
and Damien would suit, Beck. Not that he isn't a good
catch, but the situation is obviously making you uncomfortable. I will do my best to see to it you are not paired
with him all the time."

"I like him—that isn't the problem." Rebecca made a
face. "It is just so mortifying to be shoved under his nose
on a constant basis."

"Besides," Arabella said, looking sympathetic, "isn't
he going back to Spain? It would be horrible if you were
to form an attachment and he returned to the war."

"I don't think my parents see past his fortune and
impending knighthood." Rebecca glanced away toward the window, a wistful look on her lovely face. "My
feelings are taken less and less into account as each day
goes by."

The confession Rebecca had made in the Marston's
music room back in London came to Brianna's mind.
. . . I'm in love . . . he isn't suitable . . .

Brianna said impulsively, "Can't Bella and I help in some way? You look so unbearably miserable at times. I think you should tell her what you told me. It isn't as though the three of us keep anything from each other. Maybe it will ease things to talk about it."

"Tell me what?" Arabella looked mystified, her brows drawing together.

Rebecca turned back and gave her a resigned smile. "I have an unfortunate affliction. It must be a disease, mustn't it, to fall in love with entirely the wrong man?"

"In love?" Arabella stared, repeating the words as if she'd never heard of the concept. "Oh dear. That's marvelous . . . or I suppose not. Why is he the wrong man?"

"She claims her parents wouldn't approve," Brianna chimed in.

"Why not? Unless he's some stable boy . . . oh, he isn't, is he?" Arabella seemed as much at a loss as Brianna had been when she first heard of the problem.

Rebecca shook her head. "The two of you are wonderful in every way, but I can't tell you."

Brianna and Arabella looked at each other. If Rebecca hadn't wiped a stray tear from the corner of her eye in a surreptitious motion, Brianna might have just let the matter drop. Instead she said firmly, "We always respect your privacy, Beck, you know we do. Trust us. Maybe it isn't as awful a situation as you think."

"Trust is not the problem. Far from it, but it's complicated." She sighed and lifted a slim hand to smooth a loosened lock of hair from her cheek. "Complicated and simple at the same time. My parents are adamant I marry this season, and who can blame them? To their credit, they have no idea what is truly going on. They just think I am being stubborn on the subject. I suppose I should have said yes to the Marquess last year. He would have been . . . acceptable."

Acceptable. Brianna thought of her feelings for Colton. Who wanted an *acceptable* husband, especially if one was wildly in love with someone else? "This mystery man, does he return your interest at all?"

"I think it is possible my interest is reciprocated, but good sense tells me that will be the extent of it. I am probably a passing fancy, if I am that at all."

"Maybe," she said, "as I suggested before, Lady Rothburg can help you."

Arabella let out an incredulous laugh. "Dear heaven, Bri, tell me you don't still have that scandalous book?"

"Of course I do." Brianna smiled, unrepentant. "I assure you it is fascinating. I've read it from cover to cover now."

"I assure *you* no respectable woman is supposed to even glance at it."

"It is somewhat fun to be *un*respectable now and again." She thought of how much more ardent her husband had become. His passion was no longer constrained, and the last time he had come to her bed she had done nothing to provoke him. Not only had he forgotten his ritual of dousing the lights, he had picked her up and nearly tossed her onto the bed as if he couldn't wait.

It was exactly what she wanted. That elevated sexual sense of her as a woman, and not merely a wife. As a woman who could, and would, please him.

And, she was beginning to discover, also enjoy herself. The enhanced experience was not Colton's alone. She shot a sideways look at Arabella, also newly married. "You know, you might benefit from the book also. It's quite enlightening. I wish I'd read it before, well, you know, *before*."

Arabella's cheeks took on a pink hue at the allusion to her wedding night. "Would it have helped? I mean, not that it was terrible or anything like that. Andrew was very understanding and gentle, but I was so horribly nervous. It's fine now."

"That's the point." Brianna had a feeling she was blushing a little also. "It can be much, much better than fine." She looked at Rebecca. "The book isn't strictly about intimate matters either, Beck. Lady R has an entire chapter dedicated to how to make a reluctant man come up to scratch. As a married woman, I didn't really need to read that one, but it is all so fascinating I couldn't help myself. Lady R has personal experience in capturing the attention of any gentleman she desires. She claims complete success in attaining her goal using certain techniques."

"Actually, I was hoping you would lend me the book after all." Rebecca's voice held a slight quiver. "Perhaps if I try.... My parents would be horrified, but I have come to the conclusion that if I don't do something soon, I will be forced to accept a proposal from a man of *their* choice, not mine."

"I think it is an excellent idea. As you both know, I am a great believer in Lady R's methods." Brianna rose. "The book is in my room. Let me fetch it."

She went into her bedchamber, recovered the tiny gold key from her dressing table, and dug out the ornate antique box that had once belonged to her grandmother—who would be scandalized beyond measure over the current contents—from the bottom of her armoire. The book sat against faded velvet like a precious jewel—at least, that was how Brianna viewed her forbidden possession. The cover was unassuming leather embossed with scarlet letters, and the pages well worn. Brianna had wondered more than once about the previous owner or owners. She felt a certainty that Lady Rothburg had helped many women before her, or surely the book would have been destroyed rather than finding its way into that dusty little bookshop.

Brianna returned and handed over the volume. "Do try the chapter titled, 'Never Forget You Know What He Wants More Than He Does.'"

Rebecca stared at the cover, straightening her spine. "I wish I did know what *he* wants. I definitely know what my father doesn't want, but I have thought it over. ... In truth, I've thought of little else lately." Her face took on a resolute expression. "I have come to the conclusion that what *I* want should count for something. After all, it is my life and my happiness at stake."

Brianna understood that sentiment all too well. It had made her purchase the book in the first place. She said firmly, "The advice might be unconventional, I warn you, but trust Lady R to help you, Beck."

Chapter Twelve

The more effort he puts into the seduction, the more you should contemplate his sincerity.

From the chapter titled: "If It Isn't Love, What Is It?"

The baroque drawing room was warm in the early evening. Or perhaps, Robert admitted to himself, he was nervous. Not terribly so, but nervous enough his cravat felt tight even though he had adjusted it twice. Playing for a crowd, even one as small as Brianna's party of guests, was not something he agreed to often. Occasionally he did so for his family, at his grandmother's request, and he'd played for his mother's small, discreet wedding to her Italian count. Lazzaro had wanted Vivaldi, naturally, and it had been Robert's pleasure, the Italian master being one of his favorites. And when his mother came to him afterwards with tears in her eyes and hugged him fiercely, looking so young and lovely in her wedding finery he felt a little misty himself, for he loved her and it was moving to see her happy again after the devastating loss of his father.

"Imagine London's premier rake, he who is purportedly addicted to lovely ladies and the turn of a card, a magnet for scandal, playing at a country house party in a duet with a virginal young miss just to please his sister-in-law."

Damien's caustic observation interrupted Robert's

thoughts. He glanced up at his brother, who had strolled up and stood next to him. "No one will believe it," Robert answered, "so I am quite safe in keeping my notoriety secure."

Damien's expression was bland, but that was hardly something new. "I find it rather hard to believe, myself. Tell me, is there something about an entrancing pair of aqua eyes that moves you to your present generosity with your talent? Brianna told me she was delighted Rebecca was able to persuade you to play. I distinctly heard you imply to Colton that Brianna had asked you to perform. In fact, you outright lied, which is not like you. Nor is playing before an audience. Since the delectable Miss Marston is a common denominator in both unusual occurrences, it has me wondering."

It was too close to the mark for comfort and Robert gave his brother a black look. "Doesn't pitting your wits against Bonaparte give you enough to worry about? Surely my personal life can't compare to that level of intrigue."

"Alas, Bonaparte is far away. You, however, are right here." Damien chuckled, just a small sound.

The trouble was, there *was* something about a pair of aqua eyes that made Robert do impulsive, irrational things like dash about in moonlit gardens, damn it all.

As guests began to take their seats, arranged in the corner of the huge room around the dais that held the pianoforte, he shook off his thoughts. He'd play the blasted set with Rebecca because he'd given his word, though he was glad she had suggested he practice it first. The piece was unfamiliar, but intriguing for all that.

The sheet music one of the footmen had brought him that morning was handwritten, transcribed no doubt, but the composer's name had been left off when it was copied. He would make it a point to ask her after their little concert was over. The almost haunting quality of the notes had surprised him, for it was soft yet powerful, lyrical and moving. There was no question but he had never heard it before, and he had a wide repertoire, so it was puzzling. The style was unique, precise—brilliant.

"She looks extraordinarily lovely tonight, doesn't she?" Damien's question was quiet, speculative.

"Yes." Robert hoped his voice sounded normal, but had a feeling it didn't.

Rebecca entered the room with her parents, naturally. Arrested by her appearance, he stood to the side, for a minute unable to move. Her gleaming dark hair was up-swept but only loosely, so a few strategic curls danced along the graceful line of her neck. Her gown was made of some silvery gauzy material, gathered fashionably under her full breasts. She walked demurely between her father and mother, and the latter said something to which she responded with a small nod. Then she walked up to the dais and sat down at the pianoforte and gazed expectantly around the room, finally spotting him stand-ing there with Damien.

It was a little hard to be inconspicuous when hold-ing a cello, even when hovering in a doorway. Robert inclined his head, not in acknowledgement of her arrival but in homage to her stunning beauty this evening.

She didn't need to know that, did she?

Her tentative smile in return made him want to curse out loud, surely not a polite thing to do in a room full of his sister-in-law's guests. But he had begun to admire her smile too much for his own good, like some sappy suitor who would pen volumes of odes and other dog-gerel to the luscious curve of those lips.

Time to get this over with.

He walked across the room and the individual con-versations fell silent, some out of polite attention, but most, he guessed, out of surprise at his intent to perform. He glanced around, making sure all of the ladies were already seated, and took the chair provided.

He was close enough, devil take it, to smell a hint of her perfume.

Quickly he placed the sheet music on the stand, checked his bow, and glanced at Rebecca to indicate his readiness. Her slender hands lifted and she took in a breath.

And began to play.

About two bars in, he realized the depth of his earlier insult. She played like an angel, her touch delicate, and the beautiful notes made the small audience fade completely into the background. He waited for his part to begin, bow lifted, and when the first long note came from the strings of his instrument, soft and mellow, he had to admit he was transported to a place where no one else listened, no one else breathed the same air, no one else existed except for the woman next to him and the music they shared.

He hadn't even realized the piece was near the end until the last quivering note died. Robert tore his gaze from the music in front of him and turned his head to see Rebecca still bent over the keyboard, very still, her face almost like someone in a dream. Then their audience burst into applause, flattering in its volume, and it was over.

He could now escape. It should fill him with joy.

It didn't. He'd rather sit and play again.

Still, they hadn't discussed more than one piece so he rose, graciously bent over her hand, and because he really couldn't think of anything to say, left the dais to take his place in the audience.

To his dismay, the open chair was next to the youngest Miss Campbell. When he sat down, she fluttered her hands, and beamed. "Well done, Lord Robert. I had no idea you played so well." She giggled. "I actually had no idea you played."

God save him from giggling females. Robert smiled, listening intently as Rebecca began another piece.

He didn't recognize that sonata either. Or the next. Near the end, she played some Mozart and Scarlatti, but most of her performance consisted of music he'd never heard. *All* of her performance was brilliant.

After it was over and she rose, becomingly flushed by the enthusiastic response, it was time for them all to move to the dining room. He was forced to offer to escort Miss Campbell, who stood and looked at him expectantly.

Then, to make matters much worse, he found himself seated next to Rebecca's mother at the long table. Lady Marston's disapproval of him was so thinly veiled he should have found it amusing, but somehow it irritated him intensely. She did grudgingly compliment him on his performance, the disbelief in her tone probably an echo of what he would hear once when he returned to London.

When he said something about Rebecca's extraordinary talent, she looked dismissive and waved a hand. "A pastime, of course. All proper young ladies should be able to play adequately."

"Adequately?" The word came out in a strangled protest before he could help it. Maybe it was the glass of wine he'd just downed in a single gulp. "Madam, she's remarkable as well as beautiful. The composer would weep with joy if he'd heard his work so eloquently executed."

He would have done well not to speak so vehemently, but the woman's detachment annoyed him. Rebecca's mother looked at him with sudden cool speculation in her eyes, as if suddenly seeing him not just as a young man with a dubious reputation, but maybe an active danger. He had to wonder what her husband had—and hadn't—told her.

She murmured, "Thank you, my lord. I'll convey your appreciation of her skills on the pianoforte to my daughter."

In other words, Robert must *not* tell Rebecca in person. What the devil did he expect, Robert asked himself. Even if he and Sir Benedict had a cordial acquaintance, half the eligible bachelors in London had asked for her hand and been turned away. Her parents were obviously selective, and so they should be. Rebecca Marston offered anything a man could want in a wife. Beauty, poise, accomplishment. Then there was that unconsciously seductive smile . . .

If a man wanted a wife.

It hardly mattered. He didn't. Not now, not at his age, not when his life was all his own.

He *didn't*.

Did he?

He'd been too sinfully handsome, too close in such limited company, too *him*. Rebecca could still hear the lilting strains of someone else playing her music for the first time, see the sensitive touch of his long fingers on the strings of his cello, the intense look of concentration on his face, the sweep of his bow.

Someone *else* playing her music. Not just someone else. Robert. However difficult the situation of her infatuation might be, at least she would always have the secret joy of hearing him play her notes, of him joining her in something so personal, so intimate; in a sense, she felt as if they were lovers.

For it was clear he loved music. It had been there in his face, in his mesmerizing blue eyes, in his posture and the beautiful way he'd played.

Had she sensed it in him from their first meeting? Maybe this soulful, unlikely communion is what had drawn her to the notorious Robert Northfield in the first place.

Before their performance she'd been infatuated. By his good looks, his intoxicating smile, the air of confident, sensual male.

But through her music . . . her second love . . . now she was truly lost.

The volume sat in her hands, still unopened. Rebecca perched on the edge of the bed in her nightdress and robe, a low lamp burning for reading light. She gingerly touched the thin leather cover of *Lady Rothburg's Advice* and lifted it, then randomly selected a passage from the middle of the book. If there was a chance at a possible true romance, this might be it.

. . . isn't so much ticklish as acutely sensitive. Cup the sacs of his ballocks gently in your palm and lightly touch the skin behind them with a stroking finger. I promise a most gratifying reaction to this caress. . . .

Rebecca snapped the book shut with a low gasp, the knock on her bedroom door making her jump. She glanced at the ornate clock on the mantel of the fireplace and wondered who might be wandering the halls at this hour as she hurriedly shoved the book under her pillow. Her maid had already been dismissed, and so she tightened the belt on her dressing gown and went to answer it.

Thank goodness, it was only Brianna, still clad in her elegant evening gown. "I rather hoped you'd still be awake."

"Yes, I was reading." Rebecca gave a self-conscious laugh and relaxed. She'd never thought before of touching a man's genitals—other than Greek statues, she hadn't even *seen* a nude male—and good heavens, was the rest of the book like that?

"I see." Brianna's mouth twitched in knowing amusement. "That accounts for your somewhat guilty look, I suppose. May I come in for a moment? I promise to not stay long."

"Of course you may." Rebecca stepped back in invitation, always glad of her friend's company. As girls, they had often stayed over at each other's homes, and, in the summer especially, were inseparable. At times they took their lessons from their governesses together, which was a great advantage for Rebecca, for it had been Brianna's governess who had a family background in music and had taught her not only to play, but also some music theory and the more technical aspects. After she had exceeded Miss Langford's store of knowledge, Rebecca had begged for a music teacher of her own. Her parents had been more than happy to find one and indulge her love of what they considered something every accomplished young lady should be able to do. It wasn't until she began devoting hours upon hours every day to not just playing but composing music that they became alarmed.

Young women should be able to play a pretty tune, but only men *composed* music. That was her parents' attitude. It was an intellectual task and hardly suitable for the upper echelon of society. Composers were like painters and sculptors. These might be artistic endeavors, but still for the working class.

Brianna came in and perched on the edge of the bed, looking very much like the mischievous girl Rebecca remembered from her youth, with that expression on her face that meant they had gotten away with something that might not have met with parental approval. "Well, how are you feeling? It was a triumph. Everyone adored your performance this evening. They talked about it all through dinner, and more than one person asked me to beg you to play for us again."

"Is this part where you say 'I told you so'? I suppose you are entitled. If it wasn't for you, you and Bella would remain my captive audience of two." Rebecca went over and gave her friend a quick, fierce hug. "Thank you."

"Don't thank me. How many hostesses can say the talented Rebecca Marston played for their country house party and was a smashing success?" Brianna smiled. "It is a true coup. I am the one who owes you. Besides, how on earth did you ever get Robert to agree to play too? That event will go down in the history books. I imagine the two of you will be besieged with requests once the word gets about London."

The two of you. Like they were a pair. It was an illusion, but Rebecca liked the sound of it.

She sank down next to Brianna and laughed. "I used an age-tested method. Guilt. He made the observation— one I secretly agree with—that some young ladies should never be allowed to desecrate music in public. When I explained to him *I* would be performing, he was appalled at his blunder. I shamelessly extracted his agreement to a duet as penance."

"Well, I thought it was spectacular." Brianna squeezed

her hand. "Perfect. Colton assures me Robert likes to keep his musical talent a secret, so I thank you for your little spot of blackmail."

"He's very good."

"Indeed. It isn't what one would expect from a man with his . . . well, let's just say his reputation centers more on his talents in other areas," Brianna said dryly. "There is more substance to him than meets the eye, as this evening proves. He is very good friends with his brothers, and you can tell he is fond of his grandmother. He teases her constantly, and she dotes on him in her own dignified way."

The last thing Rebecca needed was for someone to extol his virtues. She switched the subject back to her music. "I would be happy to play again, but I shall probably have to promise my parents to confine myself to Mozart and Bach. I am not sure if he realized how many of the pieces I'd written, but my father knew some of them were mine. I caught a hint of disapproval across the dinner table."

It was irksome that at nearly twenty-one years of age she had to answer to him for almost every choice she made in life, but that was how things were for all young ladies of her class. From father to husband, always at the bidding of some domineering male. Not even Brianna, with the prestige of being married to a very wealthy Peer of the Realm, had any real independence, though she'd confided that her husband had for no apparent reason told her recently he would no longer monitor her expenses and she could spend her allowance as she wished.

"I don't want to be the cause of any conflict, so play whatever you wish." Brianna rose and yawned. "Oh dear, I am so tired lately. It must be the country air. After the chat with you and Bella this afternoon, I took a nap. I was so surprised, for I thought to lie down for a minute and just rest a little. I never have been able to fall asleep during the day for some reason. Perhaps I'd better say good night."

"I imagine your husband would appreciate your company." Rebecca grinned.

"I hope so." Brianna smiled back, a shimmer of laughter in her eyes. "I am certainly working on keeping it that way."

"If the Duke should ever find out you bought that book—"

"He won't. Why should he? Besides, isn't it marvelous?"

Since she hadn't had a chance but to read that one wicked paragraph, Rebecca hedged. "I just don't think he'd approve."

"He can be a bit imperious now and then, but I refuse to worry about any consequences for purchasing the book." Brianna told her. "I will see you in the morning."

After she left, Rebecca quickly locked her door and retrieved the book. She settled back against the pillows and cautiously reopened the slender volume, turning straight to the chapter Brianna had suggested.

Never Forget You Know What He Wants More Than He Does

My dear reader, do you doubt the interest of the man whom you have decided to favor with your attention? If so, you will find this segment enlightening. There are a variety of ways to gauge the attraction of a specific man to your charms, if one is but aware of them. A glance caught from across the room, his perusal of your bosom, a certain heated light in his eyes. Those are the subtle nuances, of course, but a more practical test can be performed.

For this experiment you will need three essential elements. The first is your intellect. The second is your femininity. The third, and most obvious, is a moment of privacy with the object of your interest.

In short, you need to plan, to be as beguiling as possible, and to secure a clandestine spot to conduct your test of his possible affection for your person.

It is necessary also, to decide ahead of time your level of determination. What is it you want from this gentleman? Do you wish to become simply his lover? Do you wish for him to take you in as his mistress, shower you with gifts, and satisfy your desires? Or is your plan of a more permanent nature?

The latter, depending on the male involved, is the most difficult—but rarely impossible.

Heavens, Rebecca hoped the woman was right. She turned the page, even the sound of the rustling paper making her look around the room with guilty perusal. As much as Colton might disapprove of Brianna having purchased the book, Rebecca knew her parents would faint dead away if they found it in her possession. There would be no way to explain it. None at all. They would be outraged, and with good cause, considering the tidbit she'd read earlier. At least this chapter seemed less outrageous.

The circumstances of how you secure his undivided interest are up to you, but you must get him alone. Then the dynamics are in your favor. Should he choose to seize the moment and attempt a seduction, you've achieved your goal very easily. If he doesn't, you must be inventive and convince him that he wishes to seduce you. Do not be shy about using your charms to gain control of the situation. After all, when a man meets a woman, her appearance is the first thing he notices about her. This does not mean you must be beautiful to capture his attention, but honesty compels me to remind you that the basic fact he is a man and you are a woman is what drives you together. It is a matter of logic.

Men desire women. Oh yes, women also desire men, but we are much more understated in our approach. Where they pursue, we feint. Where they grasp, we touch. Where they need, we want.

What a beautiful dance of nature it is, and the civility of our age only adds to the intrigue of it. We mask our steps of seduction in politesse and meaningless protocol, but no one is truly fooled. It is basic, it is inevitable, and it is all to our advantage as women of our time. Honorable men cherish us, and it is up to us to decide to which level to elevate their regard. Once you know a gentleman is interested, do not wait for him. Take charge at once. After all, you know what he wants.

Women of our time?

Rebecca lowered the book, more than a little surprised. She'd always equated her position in life with having very little freedom, but perhaps the author was right. Robert knew full well he couldn't dally with her in a casual way. So she needed to somehow convince him that a dalliance of the permanent sort would be to the advantage of them both.

If she didn't do *something*, she would find herself wed to another man.

Here she'd been waiting for him to make the first gesture, but why must it be so?

Apparently she needed to get him alone and just see what might happen. The night in the garden he was just being helpful in her escape from Lord Watts, but on the terrace after dinner last night, she'd felt something different in him. A certain tension under his usual effortless charm, especially when they'd stood by the balustrade, talking.

. . . a certain heated light in his eyes . . .

It was possible she'd seen that very light.

Rebecca was beginning to allow herself to hope it was true. After their performance this evening, he'd avoided her. She'd fully expected him to find her afterwards and say something about the music or the duet. Everyone else had—but he hadn't. It was out of character in a man who was usually so smoothly polite.

A good sign, surely, if he didn't trust himself to talk to her in front of other people. What would happen if they were alone?

Lady R, as Brianna called her, might just be brilliant.

Chapter Thirteen

It is my belief that women love more deeply and men more fiercely. What is the difference? I am not sure how to define it.

From the chapter titled: "The Mystery of It All"

This was a poor time to be coming down with an illness, Brianna thought in dismay as she lay in bed, watching the sun pour in across the room. Even the smell of the fresh flowers in the vase by the side of the bed was cloying and overwhelming. Of course, the party was almost over and the guests would leave tomorrow, but today was Colton's actual birthday and tonight she planned to give him his surprise gift. Not a good evening to have a touchy stomach.

This queasy feeling wasn't conducive to romance.

"Just hot tea and some toast," she told her maid, sitting upright against the pillows piled behind her, her smile wan. "And I'd like to bathe."

"Of course, Your Grace." The girl bobbed a curtsy and hurried off.

It was a relief when an hour later she felt much better. The toast stayed down, but it was doubtful for a while until the tea seemed to settle her nausea. Though she had considered abandoning the idea of a morning ride near the river and the picnic she had so carefully planned, she donned her new riding habit after all. It was her husband's celebration, and if she'd planned all of this in his honor, she was determined to not only enjoy the day, but to make sure it all went as she intended.

Especially this evening.

If she dared.

Lady Rothburg had been a font of wisdom so far, so even though it sounded more than a little wicked to follow her suggestions, she was willing to give anything she thought Colton might enjoy.

Brianna adjusted her hat, gave her appearance a look of approval in the mirror—for the midnight blue of her riding habit suited her eyes—and went downstairs. To her surprise, Colton was at the stables, conversing with one of the lads, his sleek, huge horse saddled and ready.

He turned as she approached, his chestnut hair slightly ruffled by the breeze, his azure eyes assessing her. Approval? She wasn't sure. Her husband's formidably impassive expression was never easy to read.

Brianna always thought him attractive—but this morning he was strikingly so, dressed like a country gentleman for riding with no cravat, his white shirt just open at the throat, his coat a dark blue that nearly matched her habit, his chamois breeches fitted and tucked into boots that were well worn but still highly polished. Flustered for some reason, she said breathlessly, "Good morning."

"Good morning." He glanced over her attire. "You look lovely as always, my dear."

There it was again, the same look he'd given her a few times lately. She found it puzzling, almost as if he was deliberately making some judgment, and she wasn't sure what it could be. "Thank you," she murmured. "I admit I didn't expect you to join us."

His smile was merely a quirk of his lips. "Riding out on a beautiful morning such as this is far preferable to capturing errant and indignant caterpillars and collecting sticks. Besides, it is my birthday, and I had a feeling my wife might scold me if I stayed in my study all day."

Uncertain, because of the tone of indulgence in his

speech, Brianna bit her lower lip. Most of the guests
were already mounted and she turned to ask for her
mare, a little surprised when one of the stable lads led
out a sedate older horse. Colton said in a bland tone,
"You weren't feeling well this morning, I understand.
Hera is a little spirited. I requested a calmer mount."

She blinked, surprised he knew she had been indis-
posed. She hadn't even said anything to her personal
maid other than to order the blandest breakfast possible. How the devil would he know what she ate unless the cook or her maid ran off to tell him after every
meal—and that seemed absurd. Surely her husband
wasn't *that* controlling.

He extended his hand and looked at her expectantly.
"Brianna?"

"Yes." She put her gloved hand in his and let him draw
her forward and then lift her into the saddle. Gathering
the reins, she looked down at him, still a bit puzzled. The
solicitude wasn't precisely out of character, for he was
polite always, but his appearance for this ride and the
glimmer in his eyes set her aback.

"You are sure you feel well enough?"

"To ride a horse?" She smiled and shook her head.
"Of course. My goodness, Colton, what has you so
concerned?"

"I'm always concerned about you, my dear." He
swung himself gracefully into the saddle, reminding
her of the honed body under those well-fitting clothes.
"Shall we?"

He led them across the park and down several scenic
country lanes, naturally athletic and easy on his mount,
conversing with Lord Emerson but all the time aware
of her.

How did she know it? She wasn't sure. Brianna
could *feel* it. He watched her even as she rode next to
Arabella.

Because Brianna sensed he was paying more attention than usual, she kept her voice low. "Rebecca declined to come along because she wished to practice for

this evening. Or so she said. I think she's in the music room, but she's not playing. She's *reading*."

Arabella stifled a laugh behind a gloved hand. "You are a bad influence, Bri."

"Or a good one. You and I are lucky, for we married men of our choice."

"True." Her friend gave her a sidelong glance. "Both of whom look quite handsome this morning, if I may say so. Did you expect the Duke?"

"No," Brianna admitted. "I was sure after sacrificing his morning yesterday, he would be too busy. I didn't even mention the picnic to him."

"Yet he apparently invited himself." Arabella's eyes held a hint of mischief. "Simply because he wished to accompany us. I think he might be enjoying the festivities after all."

Brianna hoped so, but it was, as always, hard to tell with Colton.

There were only eight of them, most of the guests having chosen to sleep late or take a stroll in the unusually warm fall weather. Brianna walked her horse, not discontented with the sedate pace, but surprised. Colton was usually in a hurry to get back to his ever present duties. She was actually embarrassed she hadn't invited him personally to the picnic. There was no part of her that thought he'd accept, and pressuring him into the hunt yesterday had only worked because his grandmother was so pleased.

But he'd come on his own. That alone was enough to buoy her spirits, and when they all arrived at the designated grassy spot for lunch, her enigmatic husband lounged next to her on the provided blanket, relaxed and apparently content.

Colton? Content out of his study and in a group of people having a picnic at midday?

It really was unusual, but she was delighted.

Two footmen had been sent ahead with linens and the food. Under a spreading oak, they served sliced cold chicken, meat pasties, several different types of

cheeses, ripe pears, and crisp apples. Chilled white wine
and champagne lent a festive air to the informal meal,
and Brianna was grateful the clear weather, unusual in
England for so many days in a row, held. Besides herself and Colton, Lord Emerson and the oldest Campbell
sister had joined the party, also Damien, Mrs. Newman, Arabella, and her handsome husband, the Earl of
Bonham. Brianna found she was famished after having
eaten so little for breakfast, and when she asked for a
second meat pie, Colton's eyebrows went up a little but
he obligingly passed the plate over.

"They're delicious," she said defensively, but also
laughed. "You see? This proves I am quite recovered."

"Apparently so." He sipped his wine, watching as
she inelegantly licked crumbs from her fingers. A half
smile lifted the corner of his mouth and his azure eyes
were shaded by lashes too long to be wasted on a man.
It was warm enough that most of the men had removed
their coats, even him, and the casual look of a white, full-
sleeved linen shirt, breeches, and boots emphasized his
uncharacteristically relaxed state.

He looked happy, Brianna decided, watching the
dappled sunlight slide along the clean line of his nose
and jaw. No, perhaps that was going too far, but he
looked content certainly, and more at ease maybe
than she'd ever seen him except in the aftermath of
lovemaking. Brianna considered another apple, decided against it, and said, "That was unexpectedly delicious. Maybe it is all the fresh air that makes it taste
so good."

"Perhaps." Colton reached over and with one long
finger, brushed the corner of her mouth in an unexpectedly intimate gesture in front of other people. "A stray
crumb, my dear. We can't have everyone knowing about
your fondness for pork pasties."

"I ate too much as well," Belinda Campbell said. She
was a pretty young woman with sparkling dark eyes and
a curvaceous figure. "I think I'd better take a walk."

Lord Emerson could scarcely take his gaze off her

as he scrambled to his feet and extended his hand. "A capital suggestion. Shall we?"

Arabella poked her husband in the ribs, making him give a small grunt. "Let's walk over to the stream. Today is so glorious, and winter is approaching. I hate being inside for months, so I refuse to let this opportunity pass."

"Then by all means we should walk, lest you injure me in the meantime." Lord Bonham rubbed his torso theatrically.

Damien and Mrs. Newman decided they would ride back to the house, and in moments, Brianna and Colton were relatively alone. It was impossible to believe, but she realized she was sleepy again. Perhaps it was all the food; maybe it was the wine, though she hadn't drunk much at all.

"I think I must be staying up too late, or maybe it is just that the party is winding to a close and so I am not quite so anxious over every little thing," Brianna murmured. "I slept late this morning and I still swear I could nod off at any moment."

"By all means, if you wish a nap, take one. Here." Colton rose in one lithe movement and shifted position, so his back rested against the tree. "May I offer you a comfortable place to sleep, my lady? My shoulder is available as a pillow."

Brianna looked at his outstretched arms, not quite able to believe it. Her austere husband did not believe in public displays of affection, and while the middle of Rolthven Park was not precisely a busy street in central London, it wasn't the privacy of one of their bedrooms, either.

Still, how could she refuse the gallant gesture, even if he was acting oddly? She moved, scooting over so she could crawl onto his lap. His muscled shoulder actually made a very nice pillow as she nestled against him and his arms cradled her. He smelled wonderful, slightly spicy: a woodsy scent to match the surroundings of grass and trees. A breeze whispered overhead and she let her eyes close, wondering if she deserved such happiness.

A beautiful day, the clasp of her husband's strong arms, and that wisp of a cool fall breeze.

Heaven.

Colton was coming around, she thought drowsily.

And promptly fell fast asleep.

"I hope I am not keeping you from your regular schedule."

In answer to Colton's question, his grandmother gave what sounded like something close to an unladylike snort, though he would never dare to describe it in those terms. "Please, Colton, you are the one forever buried in estate affairs and political agendas and whatever else it is that requires your constant attention. I suspect this audience is keeping *you* from something, not the other way around."

It was. The morning ride and picnic had taken up hours of his day, but he really wasn't concerned at the moment. He chose the one chair in his grandmother's delicate sitting room that didn't look too fragile for his height and weight, the feminine surroundings all pastel colors. A Gainsborough portrait of his grandfather hung over the mantel, the stamp of the family features recognizable.

"Now then," his grandmother said, narrowing her pale blue eyes, "what brings you here?" She waved a thin hand, her cane resting against her knee. "Not that I object, mind you, but I am surprised."

Hell and blast, this was a little awkward, but he had no idea where else to turn. "I wish to talk to you."

"That I gathered." Her eyes were bright with speculation. "I am old, but not yet feeble in the brain."

No, she wasn't. She was one of the most intelligent people he knew. She was also a woman. *And* she'd had three children. He had two aunts, one in Sussex and one in Berkshire.

"It's about Brianna," he said, not sure how to begin this conversation—with his grandmother, no less.

"Lovely young woman," his grandmother said stoutly.

"At first I worried she would be one of those empty-headed, spoiled twits without a grain of sense, but she's quite the opposite. Her beauty doesn't exceed her intellect. Good choice."

Well, he thought so too, but an affirmation of his selection in a wife wasn't why he came. "Thank you. I agree. However . . ."

His grandmother gazed at him as he trailed off, her gently wrinkled face expressionless, her white hair up-swept, one blue-veined hand resting on her cane. "However?" she repeated.

How did a man do this? He cleared his throat. "However, I'm concerned over her health."

"Brianna? She looks wonderful."

He said carefully, "She's suddenly sleeping quite a lot, and this morning her stomach was upset. More than that, I have noticed a few other symptoms. I suppose I am here because I need an experienced opinion on whether or not my suspicion is correct."

"A child?" His grandmother's eyes grew suspiciously bright. "So soon? Well done."

Lord, why he should be uncomfortable talking about this was a mystery. He was a married man, and of course his grandmother knew he was intimate with his wife, but it still wasn't the easiest conversation to have. "She's late. Of that I'm certain. It's been a while since she . . . well . . ."

"Kept you from her bed?"

"Yes." He was relieved not to have to go into specifics. He might be a duke, might be twenty-nine years old this very day, but he wasn't sure he was sophisticated enough for *this* damned conversation. "All I want is to know whether you think I am right and she's indeed pregnant. I could call in a physician, but Brianna doesn't seem to think anything is amiss, and that seems presumptuous. It's my opinion she really isn't educated enough on the subject to realize the implications of the fatigue and nausea."

"The signs are certainly promising. Are her breasts larger, more sensitive?"

There were some things he was simply unwilling to discuss. He muttered, "I hardly keep charts on the matter."

"You could check. I feel certain it would not be a hardship on your part."

He glanced up sharply, noting the wicked twitch to his grandmother's mouth. He said dryly, "With all due respect, I do not appreciate your amusement over my discomfort with this conversation. I came for advice, not for your entertainment."

She chuckled, tapping her cane on the rug. "Forgive me, but it isn't often I see you disconcerted, Colton. You are always the model of composure. I could not resist that last comment, but concede it was not very sporting of me. By way of apology, let me say this: if Brianna is carrying your child—and it sounds likely she is—it's a perfectly normal event. We all got on this earth the same way. You love her, so you are understandably concerned, but don't fret. If it has happened, she will come to the conclusion soon enough on her own. Do not rob her of the joy of being able to tell you."

You love her.

He opened his mouth to deny it. To explain he married Brianna because he desired her, because she was gracious and intelligent and her family lineage impeccable.

It certainly wasn't because he'd fallen in love with her.

Was it?

Did he love her? A helpless feeling of ignorance settled over him. Of course he loved his mother, his brothers, his grandmother, but that was quite different from romantic love. There was no experience in his life to compare his feelings to, and why did a man have to constantly examine his emotions anyway?

He said nothing.

His grandmother was still speaking. ". . . you must understand there is something quite special about a woman being able to tell her husband she has conceived his child. I think you should simply wait until your wife realizes she's breeding and then act appropriately delighted when she breaks the news."

"I *am* delighted," he protested. "I hardly need to playact the part."

"Masking your concern wouldn't hurt. She'll be nervous enough without you hovering over her."

He'd never *hovered* in his life. Irritated, but mindful it was his grandmother he was speaking to, he said crisply, "I have no intention of treating her like an invalid."

Though he *had* enjoyed holding Brianna as she slept after their alfresco luncheon, her slight weight resting against his chest, her breath brushing his throat as she slumbered. When the others wandered back, he'd put a finger to his lips to make sure no one woke her and continued to hold her until she finally stirred, a good hour after everyone else had mounted their horses and ridden back to the house.

So maybe he'd hovered a little.

One white brow inching upward, his grandmother continued the lecture. "Don't. She's young and healthy, and the fatigue will pass, as will the sickness in the morning. Take my word on it. I went through it more than once."

"Should she ride? I deliberately went along today to keep an eye on her. Surely a fall would be bad in her condition." His ignorance on the subject of pregnant ladies had never bothered him before, but now it held him almost paralyzed. He didn't know how to act, and he disliked being at a loss. Used to making weighty decisions on everything from investments to politics, he was in the dark right now when it came to Brianna.

"Well, she shouldn't gallop across country and jump fences, but a nice leisurely ride won't hurt until she gets too ungainly to get on and off. She'll know when it is time to stop."

"How? I am certain she has no idea she could be carrying."

"My dear boy, how do you think any animal breeds? We may bury it under a veneer of civilized behavior, but

human beings still have instincts. Trust me, she'll know
how to take care of herself to ensure a healthy child,
and what you need to do is be there to lend your support. Make it clear if she needs anything from you, all
she needs to do is ask you, and all will be well."

All will be well. He hoped so. Naturally he wanted an
heir, but he hadn't expected this apprehension. Child-
birth was not without its dangers. A fear he'd never anticipated tempered his joy.

What if I lose her?

Shrewdly, his grandmother seemed to understand his
thoughts. "Celebrate the miracle, Colton. A little concern is natural, but most women do just fine. There are
some things even title and wealth cannot control. It is
a waste to ruin the happiness of this day by worrying
about the next one."

Damn all, she was right, of course.

He rose and went to bend over her hand. "Thank you.
Your advice is invaluable."

The thin fingers clasped in his felt like bird bones,
light and brittle, but there was nothing but fierceness in
her eyes. "I am so glad you have Brianna. Now all we
need to do is see Robert settled with his young lady and
we can work on Damien, though I doubt he'll be coop-
erative. Then I can go peacefully."

"I am uninterested in you going anywhere and what
the dev—" He caught himself just in time, he was so
startled. "I mean, what are you talking about? Robert's
young lady?"

"Miss Marston. He's quite taken."

Miss Marston? Miss Rebecca Marston, who came
complete with a militantly protective father and a pristine reputation? It was impossible. Not his rakish and independent younger brother. Colton said carefully, "You
must be mistaken."

"Did you not see them last evening?"

He frowned. "Yes, I did. They played well together,
but honestly—"

"I agree," she interrupted, smiling. "They were very

beautiful together indeed. How she got him to do it, I am not sure, but it proves Miss Marston has some influence over him, doesn't it?"

"Miss Marston persuaded him to play the cello?" Colton contemplated a moment. "He told me he played because Brianna asked him to do so."

His grandmother gave a gleeful chuckle. "He lied to you about it, then, because I asked your wife how she got him to cooperate and she told me directly that her pretty young friend was the one who convinced your brother to drag out his instrument before all and sundry."

Telling falsehoods wasn't at all like Robert, and now that Colton thought back on it, Damien had made some interesting insinuations.

A romance right under his nose, involving his youngest brother no less, and he hadn't noticed?

Apparently, he *did* need to spend more time out of his study.

Chapter Fourteen

*When you and your lover have become familiar
with each other's needs and wants, it is time for you
to surprise him, confound him, and make him realize he knows only part of his woman. Each time
you try something new, you may unearth his deepest hidden desire or fulfill a specific fantasy. For
men have them, even more so than women.*

*From the chapter titled:
"Using Secrets to Your Advantage"*

Fate must be having a lovely time mocking him, Robert thought grimly. He had made that cynical remark
about clumsy young ladies on the pianoforte and now
here he was, listening to one of the most sublime performances possible from a very beautiful, extremely talented young lady.

He couldn't take his eyes off of Rebecca as she bent
over the keys, her face serene. Because he was in the
audience, he had a perfectly good excuse to study the
graceful pose of her shapely body, the symmetry of her
nose in profile, and the luster of her dark, shining hair.

Damnation.

Remarkable was the word he'd used to her mother.
It was an understatement, he'd come to realize, listening to Rebecca play a second time. Hers was a rare gift,
a unique skill that so enthralled the listeners it almost

felt as if everyone in the room, even the most tone-deaf philistine among them, had stopped breathing. No one coughed, cleared his throat, or even shifted in her seat.

She was *that* good.

He reminded himself of the reality of the situation. She would be married off to some very fortunate man, and though she might play now and again for a small group like this if he chose to allow it, the world would never have the pleasure of hearing her genius.

A damn shame, in Robert's opinion, but then again, no one had asked for his thoughts on the matter.

This evening he had recognized all the pieces performed but the last two. She used no music for those, and her expression changed from tranquil to contemplative as those slender hands moved over the keyboard like she caressed a lover.

The image *that* comparison conjured up needed to be squelched immediately, he told himself savagely as he rose after the applause died away, turning blindly to offer his arm to the woman beside him.

It happened to be Mrs. Newman, who looked at him provocatively from under her lashes and set her hand on his sleeve. "That was rather pleasant, wasn't it?"

"Brilliant," he said truthfully.

"You did seem engrossed in her performance."

Even as she spoke Robert found himself watching Lord Knightly escort Rebecca, the blasted man saying something to make her laugh. He caught himself, registered what the woman clinging to his arm had just said, and forced what he hoped was a nonchalant smile as they entered the dining room. "I think we all were."

"Not with your level of attention." The words were softly said, but her eyes had narrowed a little. "Like a child looking in the window of a sweetshop."

He'd so rarely had to hide his interest—no, he hadn't *ever* had to hide his interest in a woman before—he apparently wasn't very good at it. "Miss Marston has an unusual beauty. I am sure every man in the room noticed it."

He was sure. And it annoyed him.

"Maybe so." She raised her brows just a little and regarded him as they reached the table. To his surprise, Loretta Newman said with more insight than he would have expected, "You are going to have to make a choice. I will be interested to see what it is."

Why bother to try and deny it? He pulled out her chair and muttered, "I'll be interested as well."

For dinner, the array of dishes was even more lavish than usual in celebration of Colton's birthday. The food was sophisticated without being fussy, and had Robert been in a mood to enjoy it, he would have appreciated it more. As it was he ate sparingly, drank more than his share of wine, and restively waited for the affair to be over. Once the ladies excused themselves and the port was served, he relaxed a fraction. The strain of having Rebecca seated across the table—directly across from him, to his dismay—had made the meal seem endless.

He barely listened to the conversation around him as he drank port with ill-advised speed. Maybe if he numbed himself properly, the evening would come to an end earlier. Yes, he might not feel his best in the morning but what the hell, he wasn't exactly all sunshine and smiles now.

When it came time to retire to the drawing room and rejoin the ladies, he declined. "I might go and read for a bit."

"Read?" Damien asked on an incredulous laugh. Even Colton looked dubious. Lord Bonham quirked a brow in surprise.

Robert muttered, "Bloody hell, from your expressions you'd think you'd never heard of the pastime. I'm tired and wish to retire with a good book. Is there some harm in that?"

"None at all." Damien grinned. "Perhaps there's a nice romance on the shelves. Something dark, melodramatic, and Gothic to match the gloomy expression on your face."

To his credit, Robert refrained from crashing his fist

into his brother's jaw. He swung on his heel instead and stalked from the dining room. Thankfully, Rebecca's father had already left the room and missed the exchange. Robert had the feeling that if both Damien and Loretta had noticed his absorption in Rebecca, her father might have as well. Since he and Sir Benedict had an unspoken agreement to avoid each other, nothing had been said, but the other night on the terrace Robert had received the clear message that Rebecca was off-limits.

Damien followed him, strolling into the library just a few moments after he did, his look pointed as he saw Robert had gone straight to the brandy decanter, not the bookshelves. "Getting drunk won't solve your dilemma."

"Do I have a dilemma?" Robert sloshed a generous amount into a crystal glass. "And if I did, would it be your business?"

His older brother shut the door behind him. "No, I suppose not." Damien walked over and examined one volume, running a finger along the dusty spine. "Maybe you should read one of the Greek tragedies. Or a Shakespearean play. God knows you're acting like some dramatic lovelorn character in one."

"I've read most of them already, thank you. I believe you went to Eton also. And I'm afraid I have no idea what you're talking about."

"Yes, they did drill the classics into our thick skulls, did they not?"

Robert let out a noncommittal grunt. He was just a little bit foxed, it was true. Two stiff brandies should push him the rest of the needed distance.

"Robbie, why don't you court her?" Damien turned, shaking his head and crossing his arms over his chest. "Surely you've heard of courtship? Flowers, afternoon calls, a ride in Hyde Park with a chaperone, maybe a carefully penned poem waxing eloquent on the exquisite color of her eyes—"

"Care to tell me who the devil you are referring to?"

Damien fixed him with what seemed to be a pitying

look. "Snapping at me won't solve anything and we both know who I'm talking about, damn it."

True. Robert raggedly exhaled and ran his free hand down his face, clutching the brandy glass in his other like a lifeline. He said heavily, "I don't *wish* to court anyone."

"History would bear that out, so I believe you." Damien chose one of the comfortable chairs next to the fireplace and sat, crossing his long legs at the ankle and canting a brow. "You don't wish it. Fine. At least you're willing to admit it has crossed your mind. That's a good start. Have a seat and let's talk about it."

"Is there some reason we should?" Robert nonetheless dropped into a chair, his moody gaze accusing. "In case it has escaped your notice, Rebecca's parents would swoon if I as much as showed a glimmer of interest. Her father in particular."

"Ah, you can say her name out loud and confess the fascination. That's progress."

If a glower could kill someone, Damien would be writhing in agony, but apparently the method was ineffectual. Robert said acerbically, "Who knew you could be just as annoying now as you were when I was ten?"

"I was eleven then, and I've improved my technique with age."

"There are some things that shouldn't be improved on."

Damien chuckled. "I'll concede that. So, tell me, what's the problem between you and Sir Benedict? After all, though you hardly have a pristine reputation, you are a Northfield, the younger brother of a duke, and you have your own fortune. She could certainly do worse. It would be a prestigious match."

"I don't want a match," Robert said peevishly, his jaw set.

"But you *do* want her. Therein lies the aforementioned dilemma." Damien lifted a hand, palm outward. "For argument's sake, let's put forth the idea you honestly wished to woo the fair Rebecca. That would naturally mean gaining her father's permission."

"He wouldn't give it, believe me." Robert moodily contemplated the tips of his boots and then sighed. Heavily. "Several years ago, I was at a less than respectable establishment, full of young bloods eager to drink and gamble. Sir Benedict's nephew was also there. He's young, was in his cups, and not the most prudent fellow even when sober. He lost a fortune that night, and I do mean literally. Several of us cautioned him to remove himself from the game because we could see he had foregone all good judgment, but he was a belligerent fool and refused. The deeper he got into the mire, the more determined he was to extricate himself. It didn't happen, I'm afraid. He ended the disastrous evening in the arms of a prostitute, who apparently gave him a case of the pox." Robert glanced up with a cynical twist to his mouth. "Sir Benedict, naturally, administers his nephew's inheritance, which was significantly decreased that evening. Young Bennie, named after his uncle, of course, couldn't remember which gentlemen were involved in the game, except myself and Herbert Haversham. We both received scathing letters accusing us of cheating and leading the young man into debauchery, and though I took the time to reply and explain the truth, the missive was returned unopened."

Damien murmured, "I see."

"To an extent, I do not blame Rebecca's father, for he was faced with either believing whatever tale Bennie came up with or facing the fact his nephew had made not only a fool of himself, but also squandered his portion and lied about it. How much easier to blame us. Neither Herbert nor I kept the money we won from him, but returned it before we left that evening with a caution that fell on deaf, drink-befuddled ears. Bennie just lost it promptly in another game. I've wondered if he remembered the two of us because we were the ones who returned the money."

"Could be. So . . . I think I see things clearly. Besides your rakish reputation, you are now considered a depraved influence, and dishonorable in the bargain. Is that correct?" Damien had one of his inscrutable expressions firmly in place.

"I would guess so. The man can hardly bring himself to grate out a polite greeting if we come face-to-face." Sir Benedict's thunderous expression when he saw Robert with his beautiful daughter came to mind. "To say he has no regard for me is an understatement, but though I have never claimed angelic status, in this matter, I am entirely blameless."

"I agree. So, what is your plan then?"

"What the hell are you talking about? I don't have a plan, Dame."

"To win the object of your desire." His brother cocked a brow irreverently. "I admit it isn't going to be easy. You are going to have to modify your behavior considerably. This is one young woman you can't simply lure into your bed. Actually, I get the impression you *could* lure her into your bed, but while you aren't perfect, I don't see you dishonoring her any more than you would cheat a drunken man of his money."

"Such high praise," Robert drawled sarcastically. "I feel my head beginning to swell."

His brother ignored him but kept talking as if musing over one of his damned tactical problems. "So you are for once going to have to rely on something other than your pretty face and a façade of superficial charm. Luckily, the two of you have one very important thing in common, besides a mutual physical attraction."

The problem was, Robert was afraid Damien was exactly right. He was experienced enough to know when a woman was interested, and Rebecca was too inexperienced to hide it. More than once he'd caught her watching him and seen the quick turn of her head coupled with the stain of a blush in her cheeks.

He should find it amusing, but he didn't, especially because the only reason he'd caught *her* watching him was because *he'd* been watching her.

"My own reservations aside, it's impossible and we both know it."

"Not at all." Damien smiled. "It's a challenge to be sure, but impossible? Nothing is impossible. If Badajoz could be taken, this is a mere skirmish. Though I do admit this black mark against you isn't ideal for an approved courtship."

If Robert even *wanted* to court anyone.

"We have nothing in common," he objected. "She's an innocent, marriageable young lady, and I can't even remember what the term innocent means."

"You and Rebecca have a deep mutual love of music." Damien rubbed his jaw. "Damned if I'm not jealous of that. Think of how many evenings you could pass discussing it and playing together—"

"We aren't passing any evenings," Robert snarled, against his will sounding like a surly child. Carefully, he calmed his tone and said more reasonably, "Look, this unfortunate interest will pass. It's like catching a chill. I don't want those either, but they run their course and you move on."

"Is this like any other *chill* you've caught?"

It wasn't, but then again, he'd never been interested in someone like Rebecca. All the other times he'd just been playing at passion—and played with, for that matter, though he'd never thought of it that way before. There were no promises, no expectations above the usual casual ones. Those liaisons were simple. This was not. He clipped out, "I don't see the point in discussing this further."

"I do." His brother rose. "Just wait here. I'll be right back."

Rebecca glanced up, startled. Damien Northfield's offer was most unexpected.

"Just a short walk," he said in his mild way. "Your mother can come with us if she'd like. I was unable to escort you the other evening and would like another opportunity, if I may."

Her mother smiled in delight and waved them on. "A short walk alone would be fine, of course."

Of course. Her mother would love to see them go off alone. The idea of a developing romance was firmly planted in her head, but the real question was why Damien would encourage it. So far he seemed nothing but amused by the matchmaking attempts, though perhaps he wouldn't think it so funny if he hadn't already guessed her infatuation with his brother and so felt safe enough.

In the end, Rebecca inclined her head in acquiescence, more out of curiosity than anything. She needed to ask him a favor anyway, so this would be a good time.

He had something in mind. She was beginning to realize he *always* had something in mind. The minute they stepped outside the door of the drawing room, she took in a breath to make the request she hoped he would agree to, but he turned and gently touched his fingertips to her lips. He said in a low voice, "No questions. Not yet. Just come along."

Puzzled, Rebecca let him lead her off the terrace and around the side of the house. "Lord Damien—" she began as they rounded the corner. It was dark, the house lit against the night, and the air smelled like rain for the first time since their arrival.

"Here." He stopped and turned. "The bush is inconvenient, but not an insurmountable obstacle. I'll lift you over it."

"What?" Rebecca stared, not sure what on earth he intended. The evening breeze brushed past and stirred her hair.

"I'll assist you."

What he indicated, she discerned, was a long window, open despite the cool evening, the draperies inside billowing in the moving air. "My lord, I'm not sure what you mean."

He glanced at her, the spilling light doing nice things to his chiseled features. "Miss Marston, let me boost you inside this window. Then I will stand outside and look nonchalant for a short while before I demand you rejoin me. That is about all I have to say on the matter until I deliver you safely back to the drawing room. What happens between now and then is entirely up to you."

"I'm—"

"You are wasting time. Talk to him."

He took her arm and urged her toward the open window, stepping through the bush himself and then turning to grasp her waist and lift her so she could sit on the sill. Since he seemed so determined, Rebecca obediently swung her legs over, modestly clutching her skirts to keep them in place before she slid into the room.

And saw *him*.

Robert, sitting in a careless sprawl in a chair by the fireplace, holding a glass of brandy and staring at her as if she was some kind of apparition. He muttered an imprecation she didn't quite catch as he set his glass on a small, polished table with a definite click. He surged to his feet. "Is this the type of thing Bonaparte has to deal with? I pity the little Corsican, I really do."

The room was shrouded in gloom. And empty except for the two of them. In short, they were alone, she realized, which was exactly what she had planned to ask Damien to help her with in the first place. Both elation and panic seized her at once. It was well and good for Lady Rothburg to tell her to use her wiles to tempt Robert, but something else entirely to be faced with the immediacy of the daunting task. He was scowling also, which could hardly be a good sign.

"We—we went for a walk," Rebecca stammered out, less than glib as usual in his presence. "Your brother then insisted on lifting me through the window."

"Well, I insist on lifting you back out." Robert came toward her, his handsome face taut and set. "Of all the interfering, meddling, intrusive ... well, words fail me. Damien is worse than some well-meaning, matronly aunt."

Damien was like a benevolent fairy godmother—in an utterly masculine way, of course—and Rebecca needed to gather her wits and make the most of his gift.

It was as if time stopped and the scene crystallized, everything coming clear at once.

This was it. Her chance. Their chance, actually.

You Know What He Wants. . . .

Robert wouldn't be angry if he wasn't taken off balance. If he had no feelings on the matter, she imagined he would simply be amused and puzzled as to why his older brother would shove a young woman through a library window. Besides, what he'd just said implied he understood why Damien was interfering, and that meant they'd discussed it.

Discussed *her*.

The surge of hope held her locked in place, her heart beating a sudden slow slam in her chest. "I missed you this evening," she said, her voice barely more than a whisper.

That halted him only a few feet away as effectively as if someone had struck him. An undecipherable emotion flickered across his face. After a moment, he said quietly, "Missed me?"

"I meant I wish you'd played with me again. You have a very skilled touch." Her voice was hushed.

He made a low sound, something between a groan and a cough.

Play the vixen. Even the most inexperienced woman can do it, for nothing entices a man like a woman who desires him in the same way he does her.

Lady Rothburg encouraged boldness, but it was easier said than done.

"Did you wish you were with me?" She couldn't help the note of shyness in her voice, but for the first time since she'd first seen him across that crowded ballroom over a year ago, she realized—no, she *knew*—that things were not as hopeless as she had assumed.

Well, that was true if she allowed herself to forget about her father for one brief, liberating moment.

"This is not a good idea, Rebecca." Robert shook his head, but he looked strained.

"This?"

The helpless gesture he made with his hand was not

the movement of a polished rake but of a frustrated young man. "You here. Us here. *This.*"

She took a step toward him. Her knees felt a bit odd, as if they might decide to stop working altogether. "Why not?"

"It would imply something significant, and you don't need that connection, not with me." He sighed and shoved his hand through his hair, ruffling the thick strands in a way she'd always secretly longed to do.

"What if I wished for the connection?" That was bold beyond belief. Lady Rothburg would definitely approve.

"Don't say that." The statement would have been more effective if he hadn't taken a physical step backwards, as if the distance would help emphasize his words. "My misguided brother seems to have come to the conclusion we have an interest in each other. We need not act on it."

Rebecca said nothing, just continued to look at him. He was struggling. Not arguing with her, but with himself.

"If things were a little different," he went on, his azure eyes glittering, "then I admit he could be right, at least as far as I am concerned. I think you're a very beautiful girl, and exquisitely talented."

"I am not a girl." She said the words carefully, not combative, but unwilling to let him see her as anything but a woman. "I am almost twenty-one. Old enough to know my own mind," she added softly.

Robert seemed lost for words. After a moment, he cleared his throat. "Of course. My apologies if I offended you."

"No offense. I just wanted to make my position clear. Did I succeed?"

"A little too well." His breath came out in an audible exhale that sounded like frustration. "Don't do this to me. I am trying to avoid temptation. Which, by the way, is a new exercise. What did Damien say to you?"

Rebecca smiled. It took some effort to look serene when she was shaking inside, but she did her best. "That I should talk to you. Tell me, how different do things need to be?"

"What?"

"You just said 'if things were different,' your brother would be right. What can I do?"

"Nothing." He stared at her, his mouth tight. "I can't offer you anything, so whether Damien is right or not, it doesn't matter. Your father has a mistaken perception of me." Speaking a little too forcefully, as if trying to convince himself of something unpleasant, he continued, "And that doesn't even really signify anyway. I don't really wish to marry. At twenty-six, I'm not ready. I like my life as it is."

So much for that fleeting sense of triumph. Her throat felt suddenly tight. "I see. You make your position very clear, sir."

His eyes glittered and his voice was hoarse. "Rebecca, you had to crawl through the window to be alone with me for a few minutes. How do you think your parents would react if I came calling, hat in hand? Besides, I don't call, not in the sense we are talking about. You aren't at all like . . ."

When he stopped, obviously at a loss, she supplied delicately, "All the other women?"

She could swear that even in the illumination of only one small lamp in the vast space of the Rolthven library, his face took on a dusky color. "I wouldn't have put it that way, but yes. I don't normally pursue eligible young ladies for the exact reasons I just gave you."

Maybe not, but he'd just spoken of marriage, even if he'd said he didn't wish it. And the way he looked at her was telling, especially since now she'd read the book. Desire was a powerful force, yes, but there was more than that between them. She didn't have the same turmoil he did. She knew what she wanted.

"My parents are not completely immune to my wishes, though they are becoming less and less sympathetic with

each passing day. They want me to be happy. Surely that
counts in our favor."

He stiffened. "The implication I have anything to do
with your happiness is ridiculous."

How little he knew. Since they were being honest,
maybe she should just tell him everything. What did she
have to lose? She said quietly, "The day Brianna met
Colton, I met you."

This time, he was the one who took a step closer
and stared down at her, his eyes narrowed. "That was
months ago. Last year, if I recall. We were introduced,
no more. Rebecca, don't tell me you've . . . I mean, all
this time—"

"I just did." Her voice trembled as she interrupted.
He was close enough she could smell the hint of his cologne and clean linen. "I haven't married . . . because of
my feelings for you."

There was a silence. Finally he rasped out, "I am going
to strangle my brother."

He was going to kiss her. *Then* Robert was going to
throttle his interfering brother.

But first, the kiss. The one he should have stolen that
night in the garden, the one he'd sell his soul to the devil
for right now.

She knew it, too. Women had unerring instincts when
it came to predatory men. Robert could tell by the way
her eyes widened and her breath quickened as he stepped
closer, his hand touching her waist. She tilted her head
back and her lashes drifted down that very meaningful
distance that indicated willingness and desire. It was a
signal he recognized easily, even if she didn't know she
gave it.

Or maybe she did know, though he'd wager his last
coin she hadn't been kissed often, if ever.

Desire. It whirled in his blood, and clogged his brain,
for surely something prompted him to such a rash action
as kissing Miss Rebecca Marston.

Robert lowered his head just as he had in the garden a

few weeks ago. This time he didn't merely brush against her, but brought his mouth to hers with light pressure. Soft, subtle, tentative.

Completely unlike any kiss he'd ever given or received. A virginal kiss for her—though he was the farthest thing from an innocent possible. As he'd imagined, she felt like heaven, tasted like purity, and was sublimely perfect in his arms.

Rebecca's hands settled on his shoulders, her touch as light and delicate as when she bent over the pianoforte, and he stifled a low groan, picturing that same dreamy look on her face. He could feel the rush of blood to his lower body, the urgency of arousal, then the inevitable swelling of his cock against the cloth of his breeches.

He shouldn't be doing this. Not coaxing her mouth open to delve his tongue deep, not nipping at her soft lips, not imagining her warm and naked in bed beneath him.

It went on. The subtle exchange of breath, the dance of tongue against tongue, the shift as their bodies moved closer and closer . . . his arm fully encircled her now, and surely she could feel his physical reaction, yet instead of being girlishly alarmed, she clung to him with unrestrained passion, twining her arms around his neck.

The rap on the glass of the window shook him out of his madness. Damien called out, "I think the walk Miss Marston and I have taken is over, don't you? If we are gone too long, her mother will expect me to arrive back and request an audience with Sir Benedict."

Robert wrenched his mouth away, looked into the eyes of the woman still pressed against him, and wondered if he was downright stupid or just gripped in the fist of lust.

Though his body screamed in protest, he managed to let her go. He bowed. "Your swain awaits."

She stood there, her mouth damp from his attentions, her chest rising and falling quickly. "We leave tomorrow."

"I know." The devil take it, he was hard and hot,

his bodily discomfort echoed by his inner turmoil. He wanted this party to end immediately and ease his confusion. If he could only get away from her distracting presence, he would be fine.

He was sure of it.

Almost.

Bloody hell.

"What happens next?" she whispered, the innocent longing in her expression like a knife neatly carving up his soul. "Maybe we can meet later tonight. Once everyone is asleep."

It was an insane suggestion in an already extremely unreasonable situation. "No," he bit out too sharply, her suggestion sparking visions of her with her hair unbound, creeping into his bedchamber. "It's out of the question."

"Why?"

"For one thing, should your father catch us—and I am going to guess if Damien has noticed our . . ."

"Our?" she prompted when he groped for the right word, looking somehow innocent and alluring at the same time, and exuding a feminine triumph unmistakable in the depths of her beautiful eyes.

He didn't cooperate by supplying the definition of what he wasn't sure he could define anyway, but snapped out instead, "If Damien has noticed, your father may have also. I have no desire to meet him on the field at dawn. It would tarnish your reputation and cause you distress. There is no way I would want to injure your father, and the alternative isn't all that appealing either." He added abruptly, "I may leave for London early tomorrow."

God, yes, he needed to get away from her.

She looked at him and said nothing. Then she said without inflection, "I suppose Damien is right and I should go. My mother will be selecting my wedding dress in another five minutes."

Wedding dress.

If she could have picked better words to bring him

back to stark reality, he wasn't sure what they would be. Robert inclined his head. "Who could blame her? After all, my brother is," he said in full irony, "an excellent catch. In your father's eyes, I assure you, I'm not at all in the same category."

"My father told me to stay away from you," she admitted. "I don't understand—"

He made a helpless gesture with his hand that said more than he really intended. "It was something that happened several years ago. I won't go into the details, but suffice it to say he has the wrong impression and has disdained me ever since. Should I wish to formally court you, I couldn't."

"Robert," she whispered, her lips trembling.

Her tentative use of his first name was the last thing he needed. As calmly as possible, he said, "Rebecca. Go."

To his relief, she turned and left him.

Chapter Fifteen

I know it is a cliché, but reformed rakes do make admirable husbands. Why? First of all, their wild oats are thoroughly sown. The second reason? They know how to please a woman between the sheets. Think about it. After all, that is what made them rakes in the first place.

From the chapter titled: "When You Know, You Know"

If her courage held, it would be a miracle. Brianna adjusted her negligee, custom-made for the occasion, and tried to conquer the bevy of butterflies holding court in her stomach.

The nightdress, she reminded herself, was *supposed* to be provocative. He was her husband; he was allowed to see her in any attire, and he had seen her wearing much less in the past.

But it was beyond daring, and obviously meant for seduction.

The neckline plunged down between her breasts, making the gown she'd worn to the opera seem demure. Her arms were bare, there was a slit up both sides of the skirt, and the back dipped so low she was sure if she turned her bottom would peek out.

A good start to what she hoped would be a memorable evening.

Practically nude, Lady Rothburg advised, could be

more alluring than the real thing. Veil yourself in sheer cloth, give him a glimpse of paradise, and then tantalize him into losing his control.

Think like a courtesan.

Maybe she could, but not without a little help from the infamous seductress. It would never have occurred to Brianna to think about keeping Colton intrigued by trying something new, not when he seemed to so enjoy their lovemaking as it was—vastly improved from their less than auspicious beginning. As she looked back on her wedding night, she realized just how little her mother had actually explained about the act of love. A wry smile touched her mouth as she recalled their woman-to-woman "talk."

Colton had done his very best to relax her, including dousing the lights before he undressed. Which made matters worse because then she really couldn't see him—and when she felt the hot, erect length of his arousal against her, she'd all but panicked. But the truth was, she was very much in love with her husband and she'd wanted to please him, and once the stinging pain of his first entry had passed, she found she liked the feel of him over her and in her.

She looked forward to it *now*.

No longer a timid young bride, she was going to make this celebration wickedly different from anything else they'd done.

Tonight she was going to seduce him in the most sinful way possible, beguile him, and if Lady Rothburg's book was correct, satisfy a hidden male fantasy most men declined to acknowledge. Brianna intended this to be their most memorable evening yet.

There had been women before her, she knew that. When she first met Colton, enjoyed the first fateful waltz and fell headlong into the warm glow of love, she hadn't really given his past a thought. Now, a little older and definitely more sophisticated, she understood he'd been hardly innocent when they married. He wasn't Robert, but he wasn't a saint, either.

Good. She didn't want a saint. She wanted a man crazy with lust for her.

With love, if she was honest with herself, but Colton wasn't one to talk about his feelings, so she would settle for demonstration until he was ready to acknowledge deeper emotion in a verbal way.

Maybe he would never say it. That disheartening possibility existed, but if she knew he *felt* it, maybe that would be enough.

Brianna ran her brush through her long, loose hair one more time, smoothed the sheer silk at her hips, and turned to survey the room. Candles were lit, a hint of perfume in the air, a bottle of champagne and two glasses by the bedside, the bed turned down invitingly to show cream silk sheets. It was perfect.

All she needed was her husband.

Walking to the door separating their bedrooms, she listened to see if his valet had left for the evening, and upon not hearing voices, opened it a fraction. To make sure she wouldn't embarrass herself if she was mistaken, she peered through the cracked door.

And caught her breath. Colton was clad only in his breeches, his torso bare. His back was turned to her, and she saw the ripple of hard muscles as he bent to pick up his dressing gown, neatly laid out on the bed.

The timing was perfect. He was undressing and she wanted him undressed. Brianna slipped into the room and walked toward him. "Preparing to retire, darling?"

He swung around and his brows shot up as he took in her attire. He stood frozen in place.

Brianna smiled, hoping her nervousness wasn't evident. "May I suggest my room?"

For a moment he appeared lost for words, and then he flicked another glance over her very scandalously clad body and said, "Not that I object to what I see, but what if my valet had still been here, Brianna?"

"I listened." She pointed at the door. Leave it to Colton to scold her even as he stared at her with that promising hungry look in his eyes.

Still holding his robe, he asked with just a slight rasp in his voice, "Did you?"

"I've been waiting for you." She indicated her gown—if one could call a froth of lace that covered nothing a gown—with a small wave of her hand. "It's your birthday."

"So it is," he murmured. "Are the two things connected? My birthday and your 'waiting'? If that siren's costume is part of my gift, I gladly accept it."

"I want to make love to you."

As she had expected, he misunderstood her meaning, covering the distance between them in three long strides. "It will be my pleasure to oblige you."

Her palm flattened against his chest as he reached for her. "No, Colton, I wish to oblige *you*. This is my birthday gift. You need do nothing but lie back and enjoy. *I* am going to make love to *you*, not the other way around."

"Brianna—"

"It is rude," she interrupted archly, "Your Grace, to churlishly refuse a gift."

"As if I would decline this one," he said, holding her gaze. "Fine, then. Since we seem to be playing by your rules, what is it you would have me do?"

She pointed to the door. "Go in there, remove your breeches, and lie down on the bed. You may leave your dressing gown here, as you will not need it."

"I won't, will I?" A trace of the pompous duke lingered in his voice. He was used to giving orders, not taking them.

"No," Brianna responded, holding his heated gaze.

As long as the man in question has a modicum of intelligence and self-confidence, he is intrigued when a woman takes charge in the bedroom. Oh, he will not want it to be this way all the time, for the male of our species feels the need to dominate, especially when sexual intercourse is involved—but trust me, he will find the reversal of your roles exciting now and again.

He walked to the door, glanced back with an unfathomable look on his face, and went into her bedchamber.

Brianna took a deep breath and followed.

She watched as he deliberately unfastened his breeches and shoved them down his lean hips, releasing his erection. Then he lay down on the bed on his back and looked at her, one chestnut brown eyebrow raised in unmistakable challenge, his cock at full attention.

I really can do this, Brianna assured herself, looking at his blatant arousal. Indeed, she was already halfway there—for he'd cooperated—at least as much as she ever expected him to cooperate.

But what would he do when she tied him up?

She continually surprised him, and that wasn't always a bad thing. The nightdress, for one—or whatever that concoction of froth that did nothing but showcase her delectable breasts and emphasize the length of her legs could be called. It was something a harlot would wear, yet with her tumbled golden hair and pale, perfect skin, she managed to make it look angelic.

Pure.

As in purely intoxicating.

He wasn't Robert, downing wine this evening like he had a financial interest in the vineyards of France, but he did feel off balance enough to wonder if he was dreaming. Brianna's recent fatigue made him leery of taxing her strength by keeping her up late, and he'd promised himself to not approach her this evening.

Instead, she'd approached *him*.

"Close your eyes."

The sultry suggestion made him laugh, a sound torn from deep in his chest as she walked across the room toward him, her hips moving in a seductive sway.

"If you wished me to close my eyes, madam, you shouldn't have chosen that particular attire," he said, admiring the gentle shift of her breasts with each step.

"Can you humor me?" There was a breathless quality to her voice, and her midnight blue eyes held his with a curious luminescence.

I would give you the world.

He didn't say it out loud, and even the thought was startling. Brianna had taken on a new persona in his eyes. She wasn't just a very beautiful young woman who aroused his lust and graced his bed. Over the past five days he'd watched her interact with his grandmother, charm his brothers, act the gracious hostess to their guests, laugh with her friends, and most of all be his *wife*.

Not just the Duchess of Rolthven. No, not just that.

But his *wife*. He had the oddest feeling that if he lived in a fish shack off the shore of Wales and relied on the sea for his living, he would still be happy with her at his side.

The most confounding thing of all was that he realized he'd never even considered the *idea* of happiness before. That emotion was just something he'd always assumed was his. He was privileged. Titled. Wealthy. Powerful. Hence . . . happy.

Upon reflection, no, not so. He knew too many of his class who led meaningless lives. They spent their fortunes, drank to excess, exchanged mean-hearted gossip, and avoided one of the fundamentals that made existence on this planet worthwhile.

Love.

It was the first time he'd contemplated the matter, and with his wife so close—and so naked—he couldn't exactly concentrate. "Humor you?"

"Close your eyes," she repeated. "And put your arms over your head."

He'd walk across glowing coals for her at this point. "I see little sense in your request, but I'll comply."

Colton let his lashes drift down and lifted his arms above his head so they rested on the ornate headboard. His cock, hard against the plane of his stomach, pulsed in time with the beat of his heart.

Brianna joined him on the bed. He could feel the give of the mattress and the wash of her evocative scent made his muscles tighten. When she bent over him and her silky hair brushed his bare chest, he groaned. "Don't move," she ordered.

It took some effort to not simply trap her in his arms and roll her onto her back so he could take possession of her luscious body, but he was curious. He felt the slide of fabric a moment later, encircling his wrist and he realized incredulously she had bound his arm to the bed. His eyes flews open. "Brianna, what the devil are you doing?"

"Rendering you helpless to resist me." She knelt next to him, finishing tying the knot. Slender fingers grasped his other wrist, urging it back into position. "Though I imagine you could get free if you truly wished to, so it is more symbolic than anything else."

It was insane—that's what it was. He'd never had a woman try to tie him to a bed. "I am almost afraid to ask this, but symbolic of what?" Colton muttered.

"Trust." She looped the silk twice just above his hand, and then tied it to the post of the headboard, her brow knitted in concentration. "Are you comfortable enough?"

His shoulders were propped against the pillows and other than feeling a bit a foolish over being trussed, naked and fully aroused, to a set of bedposts, he was fine, so he gave a grudging nod. "Can you please tell me why the issue of trust has arisen?"

Her fine brows rose as she sank back and surveyed her handiwork. "*I* trust *you*. It goes without saying. You are much larger and stronger and if you wished, you could do whatever you pleased and I would be helpless to stop you."

"I would never force you to do anything against your will," he protested, testing the bonds. There was enough slack he could move his arms a little, but he hardly wanted to tighten the knots into impossible tangles, so he tried to relax.

"I know." Brianna looked down at him with a glimmering smile. "I trust you to want to give me pleasure, and not just take yours. That is what this is about. I wish to give *you* pleasure."

"You always give me pleasure."

That purely female smile deepened to something else, a small dimple appearing in her cheek. "Yes, but this time I will do all the work. Does that sound appealing?"

It did. A man would have to cease breathing to deny it. She sat next to him on the bed, close enough he could feel the warmth from her body, her wicked gown revealing more of her beautiful form than it concealed, rosy nipples peeking from beneath a veil of lace, the downy thatch of golden hair between her slim thighs enticing him with each movement she made. Her hair, so pale and shimmering, fell over her bared shoulders to nearly her waist and he ached to touch it, to bury his fingers in the satiny strands, to see it spilled over the bed as he took her.

"Does it?" Her fingers went to the tie at her bodice and she looked at him under the fringe of her lush lashes. "Colton?"

He'd forgotten the question. He was pretty sure he'd forgotten to breathe, his gaze riveted on her hand poised to reveal paradise. "Yes," he said, his voice just a rasp of sheer need. "Do whatever you want."

"I rather hoped you'd say that." His wife pulled the ribbon free and the filmy garment slid down, over the full, pale globes of her breasts, past her thighs, and she shifted to remove it completely. Gloriously nude, Brianna rose on her knees, her hand lifting to trail down his bare chest, past the tense muscles in his stomach to his stiff cock. He gasped and closed his eyes as she gently circled him and began to stroke.

Up and down, base to crest, squeezing gently at the top. He felt the fluid of his own discharge from the distended tip begin to aid her efforts, the slick motion of her hand increasing its erotic rhythm. His hips lifted spasmodically, his spine arching as he broke out in a sweat. Between his teeth, Colton said, "You should probably stop or this will be a very short evening."

"You like this?" Her fingers tightened, just a fraction. Almost a fraction too much, for he was ready to explode.

"I like it," he confirmed.

"Then why should I stop?"

He didn't have a definitive answer since the glide of her hand held him spellbound.

"Do you ever do this yourself?"

The extremely personal question made him open his eyes. It didn't help matters. The sight of her caressing him to climax almost made him lose control. Ejaculation was about two heartbeats away. "What?" he growled.

She looked thoughtful, continuing her erotic torture, the motion of her hand the focus of his world. "I have never touched myself, but I know women do."

How the hell does she know that?

It was too much. The image flashed into his brain of Brianna, naked and flushed, bringing herself to climax, and he went over the edge. Any control he had vanished and he felt the hot rush of ejaculation over his chest, his cock flexing as he spilled, her hand still working him until he went lax in the prison of his bonds.

She released him, and when he was able to have a coherent thought, he realized his lovely wife had an odd expression on her face. She reached out a finger and traced a path through the pool of hot seed on his skin. "I am not sure I realized that was exactly how it works. I mean I've felt you do that inside me but it's quite a bit more than I supposed."

How the hell could she be so innocent and at the same time exhibit more sensuality than any woman he'd ever known? "I'd rather do it inside you," he said. "And I intend to if you'll give me a minute or two."

"You forget, darling." Her voice was a low sensual purr. "I happen to know you can, well, do *this* more than once in a short amount of time. Here, let me clean you off and then see what I can do to help."

She used her peignoir to swab the stickiness from his torso and then she stretched out on top of his supine body and kissed him. Slow, soft kisses with delicate little swipes of her tongue against his lips, wiggling just enough against him in a manner so effective he felt the returning swell of his erection in record time. The sorcery continued, her supple body moving, arousing, her arms clasped around his neck as they lay skin to skin in a position so sexual, so *intimate*, he felt moved, and it was more than just the returning hardness of his cock. Brianna kissed his neck, his jaw, the shell of his ear, her breath warm and moist, her breasts cushioned against his chest. Her nipples were jeweled peaks and he longed to taste them, to suck them deep until she made that special little sound he loved.

True to her promise, she made love to him.

When he was ready, she straddled his hips and lowered herself onto his throbbing shaft, her silky heat slowly taking him deep. Colton found himself for the first time in his life fascinated by the look on a woman's face as he was inside her, not just by the sensation the act itself evoked. Brianna moved and wooed exquisite feeling as she rode his hips, her hands braced on his shoulders, the faint furrow of concentration on her brow as arousing as the symmetrical sway of her breasts with the motion of their bodies.

Still bound with his arms above his head, he could do nothing for her, but he needn't have worried. She climaxed first, her mouth parting, her lithe form going tense as her inner muscles clenched and she made a sound somewhere between a scream and a gasp.

It undid him, and his powerless body responded, his hips surging upward so he could deposit his seed against her womb. When she collapsed against his chest, he managed to say, "Untie me."

"When I can move, I will," she mumbled against his damp skin. "That could be in about a century or so."

There was no help for it; he chuckled. "I have a vision of your maid coming in tomorrow and finding us like this. I am not sure how I would explain it."

"I'll try to revive enough to release you." Brianna lifted her head and gave him a heart-stopping, teasing smile. "Though I am tempted to keep you my prisoner."

He was already too much her captive. "That sounds pleasant enough," he said in a husky tone.

She reached up and slid loose the knot confining his right wrist. "I warn you, I am not done with your birthday gift yet."

Colton gave a theatrical groan. "I am not eighteen any longer. Have mercy."

"It will require no more stamina, I promise." She loosened his other wrist, wrestling with the tie.

Something in the tone of her voice and the averted angle of her profile gave him pause. "Is that so?" he asked slowly. "You can only imagine my anticipation. So far this has been an evening of pleasant surprises."

"I rather hope you will find this pleasant, Your Grace."

The use of his title was usually an indication he was in trouble of some kind. Colton peered at his wife, trying to read her expression.

"I love you."

He went entirely still. Paralyzed. Immobile.

She whispered again. "I love you. I've wanted to say it before but there never seems to be the right time. I thought perhaps I should finally tell you."

I love you.

"I've known," she went on, when he didn't speak or move, "since the second we met. And I really believe that is true. Actually, it might have been before we were formally introduced. I looked across the room and saw you and just *knew.*"

Good God.

"Could you possibly say something?" Brianna looked at him with those beautiful dark blue eyes, her mouth trembling just a little.

No, he couldn't. He literally could not speak. Instead, he caught her to him, taking her lips in a crushing, soul-shattering kiss.

Chapter Sixteen

Instead of attempting to move around the obstacles in your way, occasionally it is necessary to bump into them. It is the same with love.

From the chapter titled: "The Philosophy of Romance"

"I understand Lord Robert left quite early."

Rebecca looked up sharply, not sure how to interpret Loretta Newman's remark. Or if there even was an interpretation. Maybe the woman was just making conversation.

"Did he?" Rebecca picked up a piece of toast and took a small bite.

"At dawn's light. It's a nasty day for travel, isn't it?" Mrs. Newman glanced at the window, which showed streaks of moisture. The morning was dismal and gray, but at least it coincided with the end of the party, not the beginning. When Rebecca had risen and gone down to breakfast in the vast dining room, she'd discovered Robert had been as good as his word and departed for London hours before, despite the drizzle falling steadily from sooty skies.

"At least we had lots of lovely sunshine during our stay." It was a banal remark. She hoped the pretty widow was just making casual conversation, but her subject selection made Rebecca wary. They sat in relative privacy at the end of the long table, two of the last guests to come down for the morning meal. Rebecca was fairly sure she'd slept not more than an hour, not certain if that glorious kiss was something to celebrate or simply destined to become a bittersweet memory.

Loretta reached for the marmalade. "Well, yes, the weather was generous. The company also delightful. The Duchess did an admirable job for one so young and new to her consequence. It is quite an illustrious family to marry into, after all. I'm sure you'd agree, since you aspire to marry into it yourself."

Whatever she'd expected, it wasn't such a frank comment. Rebecca took a spoonful of shirred eggs to excuse her immediate lack of response. Then she dabbed at her lips with her napkin and murmured, "Lord Damien would make a fine husband."

"No." Mrs. Newman shook her head, a sly smile on her mouth. "He would make a fine husband in your *parents'* estimation. Let's be frank with each other. Robert is the one who draws you."

So she had a list of people who had noticed her interest in the youngest Northfield son. Her father. Damien. Now Mrs. Newman. How many others? Brianna hadn't said anything, but then again, she was preoccupied with seducing her duke.

"I am sure," Rebecca said with as much equanimity as possible, since she was flustered and irritated with Loretta's presumption at beginning such a discussion, "you understand why, since he also draws you."

"I see we are now conversing woman to woman."

"Apparently so."

There was a pause while Loretta sipped her tea. Then she set it deliberately aside. "You aren't as unassuming as I first thought. And since we are being so open with one another, I do wish you luck. Admittedly, when we first arrived I thought Lord Robert might be a most pleasant ... distraction, but I began to see his interest lay elsewhere. For what it is worth, from the way he's acting, I believe there is hope you might succeed and bring him up to scratch. Now, if you will excuse me, I think my carriage should be ready for my departure."

More than slightly astounded, Rebecca watched her go.

She simply had to talk to Damien. Hurriedly she rose and left the dining room, leaving the rest of her breakfast uneaten.

Lord Damien, she was informed by the very formal butler, was with the Duke in his study.

Her heart sank. It defied the imagination to picture rapping on the door of the Duke of Rolthven's study and blithely asking to speak to his brother. Rebecca was fairly certain that even Brianna didn't interrupt her husband when he was sequestered away and working. It was also perfectly possible Robert had said nothing of the kiss, anyway. Maybe he'd just expressed annoyance over Damien's subversive matchmaking attempt and let it go.

So what did she do now?

. . . you aren't like . . .

No, she wasn't. She was nothing like the experienced beauties the notorious Robert Northfield normally pursued. Yet he was attracted to her anyway. Enough he'd kissed her in a way that would have fulfilled any young woman's fantasies. She would remember the touch of his mouth, warm and tender on hers, until she took her last breath. It hadn't been fiery or passionate, nothing designed to sweep her away and overwhelm her—instead it had been *perfect*. Unless she was a complete besotted fool—and she wasn't sure the description didn't fit—she thought it had been different for him also. There was a certain reverence in the light touch of his hand at her waist, and she could swear the emotion in his face had been genuine.

In short, she thought maybe he was as confused as she was—and for an experienced rogue, that was saying something.

Rebecca squared her shoulders. "Would it be possible for me to see the Duchess?"

The Rolthven butler, stately and white haired, inclined his head. "I believe she is in the foyer, bidding farewell to some of the guests, my lady."

She was indeed, Rebecca found a few minutes later, the ticking of the clock echoing in her soul. When Lord Emerson bowed and left the room, she waited until the footman closed the door after the departing gentleman before she said in the same informal rush she'd used when they were younger, "I need a favor, Bri."

Brianna caught the urgency in her tone. "Of course," she said simply. "Anything. What is it?"

This was truly taking a chance, but Rebecca was past caring. "Would you mind intruding on your husband and Damien in the Duke's study for me? I don't quite have the nerve to knock on the door and ask myself, but I really must speak with him."

Her friend's mouth parted in surprise. "Certainly, I will, if you wish. Which one do you need to speak with?"

Rebecca stifled a nervous laugh. "I'm sorry, I probably am not making much sense, but my parents will be down directly so we can get on our way, and, well, I *need* to see Lord Damien if possible for a moment."

There was a slight hesitation when it was obvious Brianna wanted to ask her why, but she proved to be the best kind of friend. She merely nodded. "The morning room will be deserted right now. Colton's grandmother only uses it to answer her correspondence. Would that suit?"

"Perfectly, thank you." Grateful did not describe Rebecca's feelings because she had never really been this rattled before in her life.

All that introspection during the night had brought home some very startling convictions.

The most compelling of all was that she wanted only to marry for love.

And the conclusion if that incident was the only time in her life Robert kissed her, she would be forever bereft.

Following the footman Brianna instructed to escort her, Rebecca found herself in a small, charming space with a delicate veneered desk nestled by a window, the dreary outside scene of rain-streaked glass and wet gardens lightened by pale yellow walls. She paced over and stared out, wondering just what she was going to ask.

When Damien came in a few moments later, she stood there still, looking out over drooping, overblown rose bushes and dripping hedges. There was cool, understated amusement in his voice. "You do realize if your mother hears that you wanted to see me privately before you left, she will start planning our wedding."

Rebecca turned, a rueful smile curving her mouth. "I was actually just standing here wondering what on earth I even wanted to say."

He moved into the room, that slight signature smile on his good-looking face. "Ah, that's the beauty of dealing with a spymaster. We know what you are thinking even before you do."

Rebecca lifted her brows. "*Are* you a spymaster? I thought you were a tactical advisor or something like it."

"I wear many hats." He indicated a chair. "Now then, sit, and we'll discuss what to do about my stubborn brother."

She sat down, her legs feeling rubbery anyway. Damien settled on a settee embroidered with butterflies, his blatant masculinity at odds with the feminine décor, and he elevated one brow in a mannerism she'd seen before. "Now then," he drawled, "I take it from Robert's surly mood that things went quite well last evening."

"Define 'well.'" Rebecca plucked at her skirt. "He isn't interested in marriage. He made that much very clear."

"My dear Miss Marston, I hate to tell you that few men wake up one morning and decide what they want most in life is to be tied forever to one woman. I will even go on to explain that men like Robert—who don't need an heir in particular, who have a fortune already, and whom most women find quite irresistible—are particularly immune. At this point in his life, he does what he pleases and he believes he's happy."

It was all true. She knew it, and it was pretty much what Robert had bluntly told her.

"*Is* he happy?" she asked, trying to hide the waver in her voice.

"If I thought so, would I have found myself in the ridiculous position of boosting a young lady through a library window?"

He had a point. A laugh bubbled forth, half despair, half real mirth at the dry tone of his voice. "I suppose not," she conceded. "Even Mrs. Newman told me this morning she thought he might be sincerely interested."

"Did she now? I suppose I am not surprised, for anyone truly paying attention would notice. Perhaps, then, since his sincere interest has been established, we should develop a plan."

"A plan?" Her stomach tightened.

"Or whatever it is you wish to call it if we want to make him set aside his misgivings and see what is staring him in the face. I'd hate to have a stubborn fool for a brother. It reflects poorly on my family bloodlines."

It was a backhanded compliment if there ever was one, and though she'd been showered with enough flowery words from other gentlemen to last a lifetime, Rebecca had never felt so moved. "Thank you," she whispered.

He waved a hand in a deceptively languid movement, but those dark eyes held a reflective gleam. "Don't thank me yet. My strategy is not in place. I will have to think on this. Defeating the French is a challenge, but bringing a determined bachelor to his knees might be a greater chore. Here I feared my leave would bore me to death. At last, something of a feat to accomplish."

There was no help for it; her mouth twitched. "Robert said he pitied Bonaparte if you were against him."

Damien looked bland. "So he should. Just imagine my brother's peril. I can taste victory already."

The kiss had been a bloody mistake, but he wouldn't exchange the error for anything.

And that was about as stupid a sentiment as any man could express. Robert touched his heel to his horse. The damp weather soaked his coat, his hair, and filled the air with the smell of fecund vegetation. Autumn, held at bay by the sunshine and balmy breezes of the past days, was finally announcing its presence.

When he arrived in London hours later he was soaked to the skin, in a foul mood, and more unsettled than he could remember being since his father died. He wanted nothing more than to bathe away the fall chill and forget the entire episode.

Well, except for Rebecca's moving performances on the pianoforte. No one who could consider himself a true musician would banish those from his mind.

Nor could he forget *her*. She'd pointed out she was no longer a girl, but neither was she yet a woman. Not until she gave her herself in marriage to some lucky bastard who would touch that delectable body, taste her sweet mouth, and experience passion in her arms. . . .

If there wasn't such a bitter misunderstanding between himself and her father, would he consider being that fortunate man?

Maybe.

That realization was frightening enough to send him right to his club once he was dressed in dry clothes, the memory of her soft lips parting in innocent invitation unnerving. Since when did untutored young ladies exude such irresistible allure?

He walked into his club at just a little after nine, intent on a drink and a hot meal. But it soon became apparent that he was too restive for conversation, so he excused himself after eating only half his dinner, right in the middle of a discussion of the fall race meets, leaving several friends with startled expressions on their faces.

He'd explain his erratic behavior some other time. Or maybe he wouldn't. He sure as hell was not going to mention Rebecca Marston's name.

Too restless to go home and get some much-needed sleep, he found himself on Curzon Street. Since it was early yet, he decided to call on an old friend. Knocking on the door, he discovered Sir John was indeed home, and Robert handed over his engraved card before being shown into an informal parlor crammed with all sorts of oddities, including a carved totem from one of the American Indian tribes, brought back after one of John Traverston's trips to the colonies. In a bizarre way it fit with the Italian marble fireplace, the antique tapestry depicting St. George and his legendary dragon, and all the other sundry items one would never find in a typical London townhouse.

"Young Robert!" At not quite sixty, his face showing rugged lines from the time he had spent outdoors in the course of his travels, Sir John rose from a battered chair where he'd been reading. His thick hair, blending from gray to white, was untidy as usual, and he wasn't yet dressed for the evening, wearing instead wrinkled trousers and a plain white shirt. The tang of tobacco hung in the air and a smoldering pipe sat in a tray on a small table. "This is a nice surprise. I haven't seen you in months. Come in and sit down. Drink?"

Robert still had a slight headache from the previous evening and he'd made the mistake of tasting Sir John's imported liquor before. "Yes, but please, not that revolting concoction made by deranged monks you served me the last time."

John chuckled. "Actually, it's from a monastery tucked into a remote part of Portugal and considered a rare find. I take it you weren't impressed? Ah, well, then, how about a dull glass of ordinary claret?"

"That would be fine, thank you."

"For a young lad who is adventurous in some ways, you have an ordinary palate—but very well." His host moved to select a glass from a mismatched collection on a nearby bamboo table, some of them probably irreplaceable pieces from only God knew where. Sir John, his father's lifelong friend, loved to roam the earth and returned from each adventure with a new collection of peculiar treasures, the vile beverage among them.

Robert accepted the glass and sat down. He wasn't sure what had brought him to seek out Sir John.

No, not true. He needed to talk to someone. Someone older and definitely wiser. Colton was the head of the family now, and Robert loved and respected his brother in every way, but the three-year age difference hardly made him a father figure, duke or not. For as long as Robert could remember, John Traverston had been a part of his life, like an eccentric uncle. Now he represented what Robert had lost that fateful night of his father's death. John had thankfully been in England at the time, and had lent his gentle support to a shocked widow and her young, bewildered sons.

If ever Robert needed sound, unbiased advice, this was the time.

"How was Colton's birthday?" John picked up a bottle of opaque green glass and poured a brown substance into his glass. "I was sorry not to make it, but quite frankly, house parties are for the young. It is the privilege of getting older that one can refuse to attend certain events. Can you picture me doing charades after dinner?"

It was a perfect segue, but still Robert hesitated. He wasn't even sure he'd come to talk about the tempting Rebecca. "It was pleasant enough," he said in an offhand voice, which, it turned out, was not very effective.

"Oh?" John's white brows lifted. He drank some of the liquid in his glass with obvious relish and Robert stifled a grimace. He remembered how he'd nearly choked and inelegantly spit it on the rug when he'd been served the nasty stuff.

"Brianna did a wonderful job in her first real foray as hostess. Grandmama helped, and, I believe, enjoyed herself immensely. She pretended to be stern, but I could see the sparkle in her eyes the entire time."

"Your grandmother has always been a perfect matriarch in every way: regal, and yet warm. I remember when your father and I were boys she had the ability to terrify us with a single look, but if we got into mischief, she was the first to defend us. Even your grandfather deferred to her. They had a good marriage, which is refreshing in a society that all too often places more emphasis on bloodlines and wealth than affection."

Marriage.

That word seemed to haunt him. Robert nodded and stared at his glass. "Yes, I know."

"Your parents also were lucky in that regard. It was an arranged match that blossomed, but I don't need to tell you that."

Robert shifted in his chair. "I remember. Now Colton and his bride seem to share the same . . ."

He couldn't think of how to finish the sentence. Not that there wasn't still some misunderstanding between his older brother and his beautiful wife, but when they were together, there was an unmistakable bond.

Therein lay the problem. Robert wasn't sure he wanted that sort of a commitment. It entailed a great deal of responsibility.

"The 'same'?" A gentle prompt.

Silence. Damn all.

"Whenever you care to tell me why you are really here, feel free. I have no plans that can't be changed." John sipped his vile drink and simply sat there, a benign look on his weathered face.

Oh well, hell, Robert told himself in mocking reproof, he might as well blurt it all out. "There is someone. A young woman."

"My dear, Robbie, I am not surprised. With you, there is always a woman."

"No," Robert said tightly. "Not like her."

"That I gathered, so forgive the facetious remark. Go on. What about this young lady?"

"She's unmarried."

"I see." John merely looked vaguely amused. "Some of them are."

This was foolish. Why was he even thinking about it, about Rebecca Marston, whose father would toss him out on his ear *after* her mother fainted if he arrived on their doorstep? "Very unmarried," he expostulated, rubbing his jaw.

"I was unaware there were degrees, but do continue. So there is a *very* unmarried young lady out there. Why does she bring you to my sitting room on this dreary night?"

"I don't know why I'm here."

"I see. Can I venture a guess, then?"

Robert laughed out a choked sound of assent and John furrowed his brow. "I am going to say this young lady has captivated your interest and you—despite your determination to ignore it—can't quite get her out of your mind. So, with casual seduction not an option—if it were, we wouldn't be having this discussion—you are forced for the first time in your life to ask yourself if permanence is as frightening as you have always considered it to be."

His mouth tightened, and Robert said more curtly than he intended, "Frightening? Excuse me if I resent the word choice. I do not think I am a coward."

"Robbie, my boy, one's fears do not evaporate when one becomes a man." John contemplated the worn tip of his unpolished boot. "We are challenged by our emotions our whole lives. I think very few people who know you well are unaware of your wariness of emotional commitment. You were young when your father left this world so unexpectedly. All focus shifted to Colton because of the pomp and responsibility of the title. He felt the need to suddenly become a pillar of respectable behavior, maybe to a degree not necessary in a man of only twenty. Damien, also, became a direct ducal heir. He dealt with it by absorbing himself in the intrigue of the war at the first opportunity. You, on the other hand, decided to handle your life by indulging in as much pleasure as possible, be it women, wine, or a throw of the dice. You've followed your chosen paths a little too well, all three of you."

The assessment was not necessarily flattering, but it was insightful. Robert nearly choked on his mouthful of wine. "Is that so?"

"You did come here for my opinion, correct?" Amusement glinted in John's eyes, but it was benevolent. "Why don't you tell me who this young woman is who has finally tugged at your formerly inviolate heart?"

Good God, he was reluctant. But Robert had the growing fear that for the rest of his life he would remember the touch of her lips parted beneath his and the telltale catch in the soft exhale of her breath.

. . . I did not marry because of you. . . .

More than anything he wished she had never told him. Maybe, if she hadn't, he could have just walked away.

But it was too late for that. He knew, and moreover, she *knew* he knew.

"Rebecca Marston," he confessed heavily. "Sir Benedict Marston's daughter."

His father's old friend leaned back, his drink suspended in his hand. After a moment, he said heavily, "I believe I now understand your dilemma. I know him fairly well. Benedict is not a very flexible man, and I know he thinks ill of you."

"Don't think I don't realize that." Robert said with a hint of bitterness. "There is virtually nothing to stand in my favor. Correct or not, he despises me as a cheat, my reputation as you know is far from pristine, and though my finances are solid, his well-dowered daughter could have anyone. He doesn't need my money, I bear nothing but a courtesy title, and even the Northfield name isn't enough to ease this situation."

"Are you sure? You've spoken with Sir Benedict?"

"No. The lesson in futility doesn't appeal to me. Take my word, he'd never let me approach his virginal daughter."

"Perhaps. Perhaps not. Colton wields considerable influence, and Sir Benedict is an ambitious man."

"Given my reputation, I'm not sure that fine breeding makes a difference." Robert rubbed his temple. "Damn all, if I could really blame the man, John. If the story he thinks is true *were* true, I wouldn't be fit to touch her hand. I don't know that I am anyway. Before now, I hadn't considered the ramifications of carrying around a certain brand of notoriety."

"Our pasts do have an uncomfortable habit of dragging along behind us. Wait until you get to be my age." John regarded him with slightly uplifted brows. "Tell me, what does she think?"

"Rebecca doesn't know the whole story, but she is aware of her father's disapproval of me."

"Ah, you've spoken with the young lady, then."

A pair of aqua eyes, hair silken as a moonlit midnight, intoxicating lips, soft, warm, and willing . . .

"We've talked," Robert bit out, unwilling to discuss the kiss. "She claims she didn't marry last season because of her . . . her absurd infatuation with me."

He'd just stammered. Robert Northfield did not stammer.

"Is it absurd?" John twitched up a bushy brow. "If it is mutual, I mean."

Robert gave him a moody look. "It could just be lust. She's quite lovely."

"But you understand *lust* quite well, Robert. If this young lady has such a grip on you, perhaps this is different."

"One does not change one's entire life on a perhaps." Robert really could not stay seated one more moment, so he shoved himself to his feet. He walked over to the totem and stared into one of the grinning faces. "What if it isn't in me to stay faithful? I would hurt her and—"

"And you couldn't bear to do so," John finished for him when he hesitated. "That says quite a lot right there. Your sentiment is in the proper alignment, at least. Does he suspect this romance?"

"He" being Sir Benedict. Robert thought about Loretta Newman's comment and Damien's interference. That black look he'd received the night he'd strolled with her on the terrace, also, was hardly subtle. "Others have guessed, and Sir Benedict is an observant man. I would guess he does. Though I am not even sure *I* suspect a romance."

"Forgive me," John said gravely, but there was a hint of laughter in his voice, "but I think you do. And I, for one, have been waiting for this moment for quite some time."

Chapter Seventeen

Deception can take many forms. On occasion, concealing the truth is a prudent course of action. But it can also be a death knell to a tentative bond of trust. If you are deceiving your lover, tread carefully.

From the chapter titled: "What He Needs to Know"

Lea waved a hand. "We'll ring if we need anything else, Mrs. Judson."

"Very well, madam. Your Grace." The elderly woman inclined her head formally and left the room.

"Normally," her sister informed Brianna with a laugh, "she bustles around and orders everyone about like *she* is the mistress of this household. Not that I mind, for she is beautifully efficient and the children adore her. Only when you come to call does she suddenly recall I am the sister of a duchess."

Brianna managed an absent smile. "How lucky you are to have her. Tell me, how are the children?"

It was a question that always sparked a litany of descriptions of their various exploits, but Brianna adored her nieces and nephew, so usually she was both entertained and eager to hear—but this particular morning, she had to admit she was distracted.

"... found it under the bed, of all places ... Bri, are you even listening?"

"Of course," she said automatically, but under the

power of Lea's skeptical gaze, she added with a sigh, "maybe not as closely as I should. Forgive me."

They sat in her sister's "formal" parlor, but, warmly decorated with chintz-covered chairs and embroidered pillows, the room could only be described as cozy. Hung on the walls were several watercolors her sister had painted recently. Lea set aside her teacup. "Is something wrong? You said the house party at Rolthven was a success. From the comments in the newspaper, everyone seems to agree. I wish Henry and I could have been there."

"It was fine. I do believe the guests enjoyed themselves. Even Colton seemed to relax." Brianna moodily contemplated the bottom of her cup. "At least that was the impression I received. Now he's acting quite different."

It was true. Ever since their return, he'd been more preoccupied than ever. In retrospect, revealing her true feelings had been a mistake. She should never have told him she loved him. With those simple words, everything had changed, though she could have sworn that at the time, he'd been moved. Certainly the passionate kiss they'd shared afterwards had been long and hard, and his lovemaking both tender and urgent, but maybe she'd misinterpreted physical desire as an emotional response.

"Define different." Lea frowned in concern. "I can tell this is deeply bothering you."

"It's hard to describe. He's . . . distant."

"More than usual?"

That brought a wry smile. Yes, the formal façade Colton presented to the world did give the impression of ducal privilege, not easygoing warmth, but she knew firsthand he was capable of both. "Yes. Definitely more than usual. It could be he is just busier than ever after those days in the country I imposed on him, but he hasn't . . ."

She stopped, not certain how to proceed. Unexpected tears welled in her eyes, and she looked away, at the rain-streaked window.

"Hasn't?"

The sob locked in her throat made her choke out the words. "Come to my bed."

"I . . . see." Lea looked nonplussed. "I take it that is not at all the usual way of things."

"Not at all." Brianna blinked several times, cursed inwardly at her reaction, which was probably over nothing, and steadied herself. "If Henry were acting this way, what would you do?"

"Ask him flat out, of course. But my Henry is not your duke, darling. I doubt Rolthven is very used to people questioning his actions, even his wife." Lea rubbed a finger along the arm of her chair, her face thoughtful. "This might mean nothing except you are being too sensitive. Men do have their moods, and marriages experience seasons, just like in nature."

"Or," Brianna pointed out, voicing one of her worst fears, "he could have a mistress. I've done everything I can to prevent it, but—"

When she ended on a small sob, Lea gazed at her with open curiosity. "Done what?"

"Never mind." Brianna rose and set aside her own cup, the rattle of china loud. She was never like this, never so weepy, so unreasonably emotional. Lady Rothburg's advice had been working—she could have sworn it. "I should probably finish my errands."

The return to his routine should have been just what he needed, yet Colton found he had to consciously loosen the set of his jaw as the carriage rattled along the wet street. Orderly his life suddenly was *not*.

He and Brianna had been back from the country for a week now, and though the birthday celebration was considered a resounding success by all, including him, things in his marriage had taken a definite downward spiral since the erotic evening of his birthday.

His beautiful wife was hiding something from him. In retrospect, he'd had a sense of it for some time.

She *wouldn't*, he assured himself, sinking lower in a

moody sprawl on the seat of the moving vehicle. Brianna wasn't deceitful, or at least he didn't think so. Quite the contrary, she was warm, intelligent, engaging, and very, very beautiful.

The latter detail caused him some concern.

He was hardly the only male to notice. She garnered attention wherever she went, and though she'd never been remotely flirtatious with another man in his presence, there was something inherently sensual about his young wife that was hard to miss.

It was a damnable thing to realize that when a man married a woman as attractive as Brianna, he might be doomed to endure the very repugnant emotion of acute jealousy. Colton hadn't considered it in that light until recently, simply because it hadn't occurred to him he might have reason to worry.

The carriage rocked to a halt. He alighted, noting the neighborhood was neither fashionable nor run-down, but full of respectable houses and businesses. The small sign of the establishment he sought was both discreet and neatly painted. It gave no indication of the nature of the service it offered, and that was exactly how he wanted it.

He entered Hudson and Sons and immediately a young man behind a desk sprang to his feet and bowed. "Your Grace. My father is expecting you. Right this way."

"Thank you," he said grimly.

Moments later he sat in a cluttered office across from a dark-haired man with flinty eyes and a small goatee. Colton cleared his throat, wondering if any human being could possibly be more miserable than him at that moment, but Mr. Hudson forestalled him by saying with surprising empathy, "Your note was fairly to the point, Your Grace. No need to go over it all again. You wish to engage us to follow your wife, correct?"

"I don't *wish* to engage you for anything, but yes, essentially you are right."

"You can be assured we are very competent in these

matters and your confidence will never be compromised."

"It had better not be." Colton rarely used his rank to intimidate, but this was important to him. "Madame de la Duchesse is never to know. If there is an issue, I will deal with it privately."

"I understand." Hudson inclined his head. "Please realize we are experienced in these sorts of things."

"I'm not experienced in them at all," Colton said, abstractly glancing over at where a detailed map of London hung on the wall. "I abhor hiring you, to be frank."

"Very few people wish to walk through our door, Your Grace."

"I would guess that to be true. How often will I get reports?"

"As often as you wish. I suggest once a week unless we see something out of the ordinary. Very often, if an affair is being conducted, we discover it quickly."

"I do not think for a moment my wife is actually having an affair."

Hudson lifted his brows as if to say, "Then why are you here?"

His dignity be damned. Colton said quietly, "I pray she isn't. My secretary will send you a bank draft for your fees."

"I need a description and some details about her daily routine. How does she spend her time?"

"I am not sure of the Duchess's exact schedule. The usual things a lady might do, I suspect." It was true. He didn't keep track of his wife's movements throughout the day; quite the opposite. Since the livelihood of not just his family but a great many other people depended on him doing it well, Colton put most of his attention into his work. Brianna was often out shopping or visiting friends, and she also conducted charity work at several orphanages, for which he gave her extra funds. Her day was her own, and the only time they had together was in the evenings. Even then, he spent the night at his club often enough. It was a perfectly normal arrangement for a couple of their station.

No wonder so many men and women found the opportunity to have casual liaisons.

"I see. It would be helpful, but isn't a necessity. My man will quickly ascertain Her Grace's habits." Hudson scribbled on a piece of paper, his face professionally bland.

"I am not even certain she has habits." Colton defended his wife, even though technically speaking he was her accuser. "Not of the sort you refer to. There has just been a moment here or there when I have been surprised by some of her actions, that is all."

"Surprised? In what way?"

Yes, surprised. He needed to face the irrefutable facts. Methodical by nature, he'd even sat down and penned a list of reasons why he had begun to feel concerned.

It all started with that fiendishly provocative gown she'd worn to the opera. That, he noted, was the beginning of her change in her behavior. She'd grown in confidence in the bedroom at an astonishing pace, doing things he couldn't imagine any proper young lady would think up on her own. Hell, she'd lashed him to the bed and brought him to completion with her hand, and then straddled him and rode his hips as if she knew exactly what to do.

He'd certainly never made love to her in that position before. Or suggested she use her mouth on his cock, either. The suggestive undergarments, also, seemed out of character for a formerly innocent young woman with a sheltered upbringing, and he was damned if it wasn't torture to be out with her in public, knowing she wore those sheer, tantalizing bits of cloth under her gowns.

The first few months of their marriage she'd been exactly as he expected. Shy in bed, uncertain, almost always a little embarrassed the next day.

Something had changed since that time. He needed to face it. His wife now made love like a courtesan, and she certainly hadn't been instructed by him.

Men noticed her, wanted her. She was beautiful and possessed a certain vitality that did not go unremarked.

Was this why she refused to tell him she was pregnant? She had yet to even mention the possibility.

Perhaps the child wasn't his.

Dear God, how the thought tore him apart. It had nothing to do with his family lineage, his bloody money, or the damned title. The idea of her in another man's arms. . . . He couldn't take it. Could she so sweetly claim to love him and yet be betraying him at the same time?

No, he didn't really believe it, but at the same time, he had to *know*.

Yet he was hardly going to tell all that to Mr. Hudson, of Hudson and Sons Inquiries, not just for the sake of his own pride, but because he would never willingly embarrass Brianna. "It's private," he said briefly, his gaze steady.

If Mr. Hudson felt Colton was hindering his own cause, he was too diplomatic to say so. "Quite. A physical description would be helpful, though, since your household is no doubt large and there are many coming and going."

The physical description was easy, for he knew every single inch of her delectable form from the top of her shining head to her toes.

"Does this help?" He handed over a small miniature, painted recently. Just by relinquishing the locket case he felt a sense of loss.

"Very much. My compliments. The Duchess is lovely. Tell me, is there anyone you are suspicious of specifically, Your Grace?" Hudson fingered the miniature portrait of Brianna with thoughtful contemplation. "A friend, colleague, relative? Very rarely is it a stranger who betrays you."

For a moment Colton was so sick at heart he contemplated getting up and abandoning the quest. Then he shook it off. If his wife was blameless, all would be well. If she wasn't . . . well, then he wasn't sure what he would do except be shattered. Into one thousand fragments.

"No." He stood, ending the painful interview—and he had never been so grateful to depart an appointment in his life.

Soon he would know, he thought morosely as he clambered back into the carriage.

He just hoped the revelation wouldn't send him straight to hell.

"You refuse to tell me?" Brianna looked at her brother-in-law in open accusation. She'd finally cornered him in the hallway that ran through the suite of family apartments in the huge family mansion in Mayfair, and it had taken some doing. She knew now why he was so invaluable to Lord Wellington. Damien was *crafty*. It was almost as if he had sensed she wanted to talk to him and cleverly avoided her.

"My dear Brianna, I would refuse you nothing." He smiled in that enigmatic way he had, and if she hadn't had him trapped and literally unable to exit his rooms without pushing her aside, she had a feeling he would have walked away on that unsatisfying note.

"Damien," she said with careful intonation, "I like you very much, but I might be moved to violence if you don't tell me what is going on in this house. Robert was so short and distracted the other night at dinner I thought he would choke on his food if he was required to participate in polite conversation. Colton, also, is acting strange. I am the only family female who lives here and I have the oddest feeling something is going on that all you men are deliberately keeping from me."

Then it happened again. There was almost no warning except for the tightening in her stomach. The rush of nausea was so acute, she gasped and clapped her hand over her mouth, afraid she might be sick over her brother-in-law's boots and disgrace herself completely. To her chagrin, he whipped out his handkerchief and handed it over, saying urgently, "Here, use this and let me run for the basin."

Moments later she found herself half reclining on the

sofa in his sitting room, and Damien offering a cool, wet cloth for her forehead. The only redeeming part of the whole embarrassing incident was she hadn't actually lost her breakfast. When she could talk once more, she whispered, "My apologies. It happened so fast."

Crouched next to her, Damien smiled. "Not surprising, or so I hear. Though I am no physician, one cannot be in the army and not gain some experience in these matters. Where there are soldiers, there are camp followers and therefore the inevitable results. My felicitations."

She stared at him in confusion. "What on earth are you talking about?"

His brow furrowed. He said nothing for a moment and then asked gently, "How often does this occur?"

Too often lately, though she rarely actually vomited. Just now and again she felt queasy, and she'd been avoiding rich sauces and heavy desserts for the past few weeks. "Now and again," she told him, sitting up and swallowing hard. "It passes. Please do not worry Colton by telling him. I am sure I am fine."

"I think you are perfectly fine," Damien agreed and smiled. "But you might want to think about a few things. If Colton is acting strangely, maybe he has already discerned the cause of your ailment."

"The cause?" Brianna wished violently for a cup of tepid tea, which always seemed to help, and tried to swallow the dry feeling in her mouth.

"Well, you are a married lady."

She blinked, not sure how to respond. Of course she was married.

Damien swore softly. "The tendency of the English aristocracy to not enlighten our young women on practical subjects always astonishes me. I've been living too long in a place where death is more common than the celebration of life, so I'll be blunt. Brianna, are you by any chance breeding?"

Was she *what*?

A small inadvertent gasp escaped her lips. Did he mean . . .

Her brother-in-law rocked back a little on his heels and looked amused. "That hadn't occurred to you?"

It took a moment, but then she shook her head and licked parched lips. "Until now, no," she confessed. "It makes you sick?"

"In some women, at first. They sleep more, also, I believe, for growing another human being takes some energy, and of course, the most significant sign of all is missing your monthly courses."

He said it so matter-of-factly, but she still blushed. A very vivid color, if his reaction was any indication. Her face was on fire.

She felt like an idiot. This was worse than her mother telling her to endure her wedding night without complaint. That a young unmarried man like Damien knew more than she did about this subject was mortifying, and his implication that Colton might have guessed was somehow even worse.

Why hadn't her husband said anything to her? She managed a wobbly nod. "I suppose it's possible."

"I would suspect that to be the case." Damien's mouth twitched. "My older brother is a little reserved, but he is still a man. May I beg you to give birth to a boy and rid me of the shackles of being the heir to a dukedom? In Spain it isn't such a concern, but the war won't last forever. I hate to imagine I might be forced to postpone my return to England just to avoid the pointed pursuit of ambitious young ladies."

"You wouldn't ever be amiss in your duties to the Crown." Brianna sat up a little, grateful to feel the nausea subsiding. "And as far as an heir goes, I will do my best."

Damien stood. "Colton will be delighted."

"I suppose most men are." It still bothered her. If her husband thought she might be pregnant, surely he would have mentioned it. Now that it had been brought to her attention, she realized her menses were late by at least a few weeks. She remembered how he'd known she felt unwell when they were at Rolthven, and his attentiveness took on a new significance.

It was rather like he was spying on her.

Damien insisted on escorting her back to the ducal apartments, and when he left, Brianna rang for her maid. When Molly appeared, Brianna asked without inflection, "Has the Duke inquired about me lately?"

Soft-spoken and deferential, the young woman looked suddenly uncomfortable. "What do you mean, Your Grace?"

"Rest assured I am not angry, just curious. Has he asked you any questions about my state of health?" Brianna sat on the edge of the bed, trying to not clasp her hands together too tightly.

Molly pursed her mouth and nodded hesitantly. "When you slept rather late whilst we were in Essex, he inquired if you seemed more tired than usual, Your Grace. It's perfectly natural in your condition. We are all very happy for you both. 'Tis a blessing."

We? How wonderful. Everyone in the household was attuned to her state of conception except her. Brianna was overwhelmed, speechless, until she managed to say, "Thank you."

"Would you like some weak tea to settle you, perhaps?"

She managed a nod.

After Molly left, Brianna still sat with her hands folded in her lap, her mind whirling in tune with the unsettled somersaults in her stomach.

Was she really going to have Colton's baby? A lump lodged in her throat. She was happy. Why would she cry?

He hadn't come to her bed once since their return from Rolthven. Was this why? She'd been feeling so lonely and confused by his behavior lately, which was part of the reason she'd tried to talk to Damien.

That hadn't really been successful either, she realized. Damien had very neatly sidestepped every single one of her questions in a smooth, effortless way only he could manage. She'd ended up being the one answering personal questions.

Brianna sat forlornly on the edge of the big bed. She still didn't know what was going on with Robert, and though Colton's abstraction might be due to his anticipation she was going to have their child, she had a feeling that wasn't a satisfactory excuse for his recent distance.

It was wrenching to admit she had absolutely no idea how to handle this development.

What would Lady Rothburg do, Brianna wondered, squaring her shoulders and shaking off her melancholy with determination, casting back over the book.

As infuriating as the average male can be, usually he has a good reason for his actions. Not one we would necessarily agree with, but to him it is valid and motivates his behavior. Using discretion is necessary, for no man appreciates a woman prying into his life, but it is only to your advantage to know what compels him to act a certain way.

It is not a cliché to say knowledge is power; it is the simple truth.

It made sense. First things first: she needed to find out if she truly was carrying a child before she confronted Colton about his sudden distance.

Chapter Eighteen

When things go wrong in matters of love, as they do all too often, simply trust your instincts. You will know what to do.

From the chapter titled:
"The Sun Cannot Always Shine"

"Do you mind telling me what the hell we're doing here?" Robert turned to his brother, his face set as he recognized the street outside the carriage windows, the fashionable address only blocks from their family home.

"I might have intimated to Lady Marston I'd call this afternoon." Damien looked unrepentant at his blatant ploy. "Besides, I need to talk to Sir Benedict. My new orders are in. Just a quick stop, so don't look so alarmed."

"This is a very unoriginal tactic," Robert pointed out sardonically. "I should have been more wary when you asked if I wanted to go with you to Tattersalls. I occasionally forget the little fact that *nothing* you do is straightforward. I'll wait here in the carriage."

"In this weather?" Damien squinted out the window. "Deuced uncomfortable, if you ask me."

Outside, it was cold, wet, and about as cheerful as an ancient dungeon, with rain falling in steady, thin sheets. Robert crossed his arms over his chest and gave Damien an irritated look. "I'll live. Don't be long or I'll have the driver take me on without you."

"How do you think Rebecca will feel to know you'd rather shiver in the damp than see her?"

"Encouraging her is the last thing I want to do. Let it go."

His brother gifted him with one of his infamous assessing looks. "You do realize that her emotions should count, too. Not just your selfish need to be self-indulgent and pursue your hedonistic interests without censure. A bright, beautiful young woman from a good family has a romantic interest in you. I am going to have to stop defending your intelligence should you let this opportunity pass by."

There was so much to find offensive about the statement, Robert wasn't sure which caustic point to address first. He opened his mouth to defend himself, then snapped it shut.

"I sent flowers earlier. I just signed the card NORTHFIELD. Her mother will think they are from me. Rebecca will hope they are from you."

"Are you completely mad?" Robert demanded explosively. "Stay out of this."

"Robert, since we've returned from Rolthven you've been so out of sorts I hardly recognize you. Your temper is as foul as a Parisian gutter." Damien leaned back in his seat. "Deny it. Everyone has noticed. Brianna hunted me down the other day to ask about it. Look, brother, you don't want the change in your life, fine, but I put it to you that your life has *already* changed. Where is the charming, roguish Robert Northfield who flits through life with devil-may-care panache and has a different woman in his bed every night?"

"I. Do. Not. Flit." Robert ground out the words with singular emphasis.

"Not any longer, true. I am going to guess lately you haven't even entertained any of those oh-so-willing beauties usually vying for your attention."

"Who I bed or do not bed is not your concern," Robert shot back.

The trouble was, Damien had made a shrewd deduction, blast him. Robert hadn't pursued any sexual contact with a woman since before that damned house party.

He hadn't been in the mood, which was an anomaly in his licentious life.

"You are my brother. Your happiness is my concern whether you give me permission or not." Damien adjusted a glove and glanced back out at the house. "Consider this. We both arrive for an afternoon call. Rebecca's mother favors me as a suitor, so our visit is welcome. It allows both her and Sir Benedict to adjust to *your* presence in their drawing room. A proverbial foot in the door, if you will."

"You have heard the story." Robert said it through his teeth. "Good God, man, if I walk through the door, the chances are he'll have me bodily removed. I don't want to subject myself—or more important, Rebecca—to such a scene."

"I doubt that will happen." Damien went on with the same casualness. "I also suggest you waltz with Miss Marston at least once tomorrow night at Phillips's ball. Just take it slow and don't get the gossips twittering. When the Marstons get the sense your intentions are honorable, I believe they will be more accepting than you think. After all, they could have forced her to marry before this and didn't. That suggests to me that they care about her choice in the matter."

Robert was still pondering Damien's initial assertion. "What makes you think Sir Benedict won't throw me out on my ear?" Robert gazed suspiciously at his sibling, wondering just what Damien might have been up to in the past week.

"Trust me."

"It isn't that I don't trust—"

"Robbie, the Duke of Wellington takes my word when the lives of thousands of soldiers hang in the balance. Do you not think I can be given some confidence from my own brother?"

There didn't seem to be any possible answer to the question except for a brief nod, so Robert just sat there and barely tipped his head.

"If"—Damien raised a finger—"you prove to be a model of decorous behavior in order to court their daughter, and Rebecca accepts your suit, I think their objections will fade."

"A model of decorous behavior," Robert repeated, amusement warring with outrage. He wanted either to laugh or to hit something. "Oh, that sounds appealing. Besides, I am not sure I know how. I am not sure I want to even *try*."

"But you aren't sure you *don't* want to either, which says quite a lot." Damien looked just a shade smug and indicated the door. "Shall we?"

With an oath, Robert exited the carriage and moments later found himself ensconced in the Marstons' formal drawing room, only half listening to his hostess make brittle small talk. He tried to come up with appropriate responses, but his attention was all on Rebecca.

Robert, who could blithely walk away from any woman, couldn't even *look* away. What the devil was wrong with him?

She looked delectable in a pale pink silk gown that showed off her dark, glossy hair and those captivating aqua eyes. She sat in a graceful—but obviously self-conscious—pose on the very edge of her chair, and when Damien excused himself after a brief interval to go speak with her father, her eyes widened slightly.

Sardonically, Robert realized that while he had a reputation as a rakish libertine who could lure a woman into a compromising situation with ease, making polite conversation with a proper matron and her innocent daughter was completely out of the realm of his capabilities. The only good news was they appeared to feel as awkward as he did.

He managed some commonplace responses to a few

questions before he asked one of his own. He turned to Rebecca. "I have been meaning to inquire as to where you acquired the music you played so well when we were at Rolthven. I recognized some of the pieces, of course, but not all of them. I believe my favorites were the ones I hadn't heard before."

For whatever reason, Rebecca grew pink. Confound it. And here, he finally thought he'd introduced a subject he knew she found interesting.

"Do tell, Lord Robert," Lady Marston asked in an icy voice before her daughter could answer, "speaking of that evening, where did you learn to play the cello so divinely? I had no idea you had such talent."

The words were polite. Her tone of undisguised disdain was not.

"My brothers and I all had music masters," he said with deliberate vagueness, his gaze still fixed on the young woman sitting so nervously across the room.

"The cello is one of my favorite instruments." Rebecca adjusted her skirt fussily.

He murmured in a noncommittal tone, "Mine too. I can play the violin and am passable with the flute, but it remains my first choice."

"Your sister-in-law, the Duchess, is a charming young woman, isn't she? We had a lovely time."

Another pointed switch in subject.

Very well.

"Brianna is most certainly both gracious and beautiful. My brother is a lucky man." He smiled at Rebecca. "I understand you have been friends since childhood."

"They were inseparable as little girls," Lady Marston informed him, cutting off her daughter's reply. "A bit on the mischievous side, the both of them, but that has all changed. Like most well-bred young ladies, they outgrew any tendencies to impropriety. Look how well Brianna married. Your brother is the soul of respectability. A true gentleman, not just in name, but in deed. Lord Damien also has an impeccable reputation."

Under other circumstances he would be amused to

be so obviously left off the list of his family's respectable males. But he wasn't amused at all.

The implication was clear enough. Any association with him would be the height of impropriety for a well-bred young woman. That it was true didn't help matters. He couldn't defend himself, and what was worse, Lady Marston seemed to know it.

In the end, he didn't try. "Both my brothers are fine men, though I might be biased on the subject." He hoped he looked bland.

"They hold you in the same high regard," Rebecca said after sending her mother a quelling glance.

"I hope so." He smiled at her leap to his defense.

"Yes, well, family members do tend to be blind to the faults of other members, don't they?" Lady Marston looked at him pointedly, the remark so direct that Rebecca made a small sound, like a low gasp of dismay.

He hadn't held any illusions about the nature of his probable reception here, but he had expected maybe a little less bluntness.

"Yes, but then again, they do tend to know each other better than anyone else. All too often public perception and the truth about someone's character are quite different," Robert remarked evenly.

"That's true," Rebecca agreed quickly. Too quickly.

"Perhaps in some cases." Lady Marston didn't look particularly swayed by his comment. "But every rumor has some basis in fact."

Robert fought the urge to look at the doorway. Where the devil was Damien?

This close, all he could think about was the soft curve of Rebecca's mouth and how it had felt under his, the gentle clasp of her hands, the scent of her hair, and bloody hell if the way she looked at him didn't tell him she remembered it also.

And quite obviously her mother hadn't missed it.

Rebecca's lack of sophistication was disconcerting and yet endearing at the same time. Some of the ladies he usually associated with could carry on a flirtation under the noses of their husbands. Hell, he'd flirted back under the very same noses. Others were experienced widows, or kept women—like that infamous Lady Rothburg who had written an instructional manual on how to lure your husband back or some such nonsense. Robert didn't frequent brothels, nor did he pay to have a mistress on hand, but he never lacked for female company if he wanted it.

Seduction was an art. He'd studied it, perfected his technique, and all of that did him no good when sitting in the stilted atmosphere of the drawing room of an ingenuous young lady who deserved every courtesy, every flowery word and romantic gesture of a proper courtship.

Damien was right, he probably could seduce Rebecca—the offer of a clandestine meeting at Rolthven came to mind—except he'd passed that chance by and would probably never get her alone again. Besides, he was opposed to the idea. Giving in to a visit to her parent's drawing room was one thing, but compromising Sir Benedict Marston's daughter meant a trip to the cathedral, all the trimmings . . . and why the devil he was even having this recitation in his head he didn't know.

To his infinite relief Damien finally returned, and they hastily made their excuses and left. Once they were settled in the carriage again, Robert said dryly, "I hate to criticize your legendary craftiness, but that was a complete disaster."

"How so?" Damien lounged on the seat across from him, looking unimpressed by the declaration. "Losing your touch, are you? Is the fair Rebecca no longer interested? I could swear after that tender kiss—"

"You watched us?" Robert interrupted, not sure why it made him so irritated.

"Not on purpose, you surly fool. I was standing outside in the dark and you were in a lighted room. Even through the curtains it was obvious what happened. Not to mention her face afterwards when she rejoined me and I escorted her back inside. That dreamy glow is unmistakable."

"You are doing your best to make me feel guilty about this." Robert shifted, indicative of his unrest. "It won't work."

"It's working already. Heavens, Robert, why are you being so thickheaded? Everyone else just falls into your arms at the crook of your little finger, and you have to work for what you desire just this once. I do not see how that is so terrible. The fair lady is already won. All you have to do is convince her parents your intentions are honorable."

"Oh, is that all?" Robert's voice was wry. "Lady Marston's very thinly veiled remarks on my lack of character pose somewhat of a problem. Had she said out loud she thought I was a scoundrel unfit to court her daughter she couldn't have been clearer."

"So? It will take some effort. Is the lovely Rebecca not worth it?"

"How easy it is for you to spout advice when you are not in my place." Robert hesitated, torn between resentment and something else. Something he was afraid to examine too closely. Finally, he said, "Look, Damien, what she thinks she wants and what I am may not be the same thing. You have a point. So women like the rakish Robert Northfield. But they aren't interested in the real me. I love music. I enjoy quiet evenings at home. I adore my grandmother and visit my father's friends simply because I *like* them. There is every chance that Rebecca sees only the side presented to society. I am not so sure I am proud of that Robert Northfield, but women *do* like him."

"So you worry she is infatuated with the rogue, not the real man?"

He wasn't sure how he felt about the situation. He'd never had to examine his feelings before with the idea of permanence hanging in the balance. "I don't know."

"Oh please, give her credit for more perception than that. She can separate the man who plays the cello like a poet creating verse from the rakehell who only now and then shows a glimmer of sensitivity."

That declaration made it all sound so simple, when it was anything but. Robert lifted a brow in a cynical movement. "A glimmer?"

"I said occasionally 'shows a glimmer,'" Damien expounded, unruffled at Robert's terse tone. "Quite frankly, of the three of us, you are actually the sensitive one. Colton seeks his solace in his work, I find it in war and intrigue, and you sought it in the arms of beautiful women. I do not pretend to be a philosopher, but at least you favored pleasure and human contact. Come now, brother: please explain to me why it isn't possible for you to fall deeply in love with an equally sensitive young woman and find contentment in her arms only. Obviously moving from one bed to another hasn't satisfied you."

"What makes you think I am not content?" Robert realized he'd raised his voice and lowered it. "I have no interest in changing my life."

"What about children? It has always been my opinion you will make a remarkably wonderful father. You have that sort of personality children love. You are very physical also, just the kind to cavort with your sons on the lawn or twirl your daughters in your arms. With your sentimental nature—"

"Good God, Damien, would you stop?" Robert said it thickly, suddenly picturing himself holding a laughing little girl with sable curls and eyes the color of a tropical sea. Nothing of the sort had ever crossed his mind before, and the surge of panic and emotion that gripped him at the thought was paralyzing.

"I will be quiet if you will honestly answer me one question."

Anything to shut him up. Anything. Robert nodded once in brief, unwilling agreement.

Damien sat back against the squabs, his eyes steady. "Can you bear to hurt her? Because, trust me, if you walk away after that kiss, you will."

Frustration rose in Robert's chest and he choked out, "I have no intention of hurting anyone."

His brother said softly, "Good, then don't."

* * *

The silence was weighty. Rebecca studied the Grecian urn on the table in front of her with forced concentration as she felt her palms begin to dampen. Her mother's gaze could only be described as both steely and speculative.

Lady Marston finally broke the strained quiet, speaking in clipped tones, "May I inquire as to what that was all about?"

Rebecca transferred her gaze to her mother's set face. "What do you mean?"

"I cannot believe it myself, but I think Robert Northfield just called on you. For all I know, he sent you those gorgeous tulips, which must cost a fortune, because where on earth would one get tulips this time of year?"

Actually, Rebecca had the suspicion Damien was really the one who had the flowers delivered. It was just the kind of gesture she pictured the enigmatic Northfield brother making. Her assumption wasn't based on the lovely blooms themselves, rather on the cryptic card signed with a generic surname. That seemed to be a much more Damien sort of thing to do. Robert would have put his own name. "I very much doubt it," she was able to say with sincerity.

"He came to see you."

"He came with Lord Damien. They stopped off merely on their way to another destination, remember?"

"Rebecca, I am your *mother*."

She certainly didn't need to be reminded of that fact. "I didn't realize it was in dispute," she said unwisely, as resorting to sarcasm was rarely a good idea.

Upright, her hands crossed in her lap, her mother stared at her across the room. "I sat here and saw the way he looked at you. Moreover, I saw the way *you* looked at *him*."

Well, maybe it was best Rebecca could finally tell the truth. "I've been," she said quietly, "looking at him that way for quite some time."

It wasn't often her mother was rendered completely speechless.

Rebecca went on in a matter-of-fact tone. "Not, mind you, that he noticed me until lately. I might have been invisible, really. Whatever you've heard about him, I am sure you will agree he avoids young women like me who carry the dreaded label of *marriageable*. He isn't interested in permanence."

But his arrival this afternoon perhaps meant he was reconsidering. Her hands were definitely damp, and she felt flushed. Robert Northfield had come and sat in their drawing room and had been unable to hold onto his usual debonair nonchalance. Surely that was progress?

"Whenever would you have had such a personal conversation?" Her mother's fingers fluttered theatrically to her throat. "I knew I should never have allowed you to walk outside with him, even for such a short time."

Rebecca wasn't going to explain. "Tell me," she said, "why Lord Damien is perfectly acceptable as a husband and Robert isn't? They are both younger brothers to the Duke, both have respectable inheritances, both are handsome and well-educated, both—"

"Are not womanizing rascals," her mother interrupted in a choked voice. "Are you seriously telling me you wish for us to allow *Robert Northfield* to court you?"

"You do not have to say his name as if it were some kind of a curse," Rebecca murmured, stifling a hysterical urge to laugh at her mother's incredulous expression. "And since you pose the question, though I doubt it will actually happen, I would like for you to not only allow it, but encourage it."

"Encourage it? He's ..."

Rebecca lifted her brows and waited politely as her mother obviously sought the right words.

"He's ... well ... *promiscuous* is the only way to describe it."

"He has been, or so rumor has it," Rebecca conceded, feeling a twinge of jealousy. "But then again, many supposed gentlemen of the *ton* are, Mother. I am not that naïve. In marrying any man of our class, I run the risk he will keep a mistress or have an affair." She thought of Brianna's determination about that matter, and Lady Rothburg's book. "I think every woman carries that concern when she chooses a husband, no matter how respectable he might seem. For whatever reason, I believe Robert would be quite the opposite if he should settle on one woman and decide to wed. There is something about him that tells me he would be loyal."

"You hardly know him well enough to judge." Her mother's voice held a wobble.

"Don't I? I've been in love with him for over a year. If you think I haven't watched him, even if it was from afar, milked every possible detail from Brianna, read the gossip columns, and generally listened to anything said when his name came up in conversation, you would be wrong, Mother."

"Rebecca!"

"It's the truth," she said simply.

It was an immense relief to say it out loud. Keeping this from her parents had been a strain, and refusing the offers of marriage had required explanations that weren't entirely straightforward. Having everything out in the open was for the best.

Another silence descended, this one not so tense, but more contemplative.

Her mother examined her as if she'd never laid eyes on her before, the outraged expression fading from her face as the clock ticked on the mantel in a solemn rhythm. Eventually, she said, "I believe you mean this."

Rebecca stifled a choked laugh over the echo of horrified realization in that statement. "I do."

"I wondered once or twice when we were at Rolthven Manor, if you want the truth. When the two of you played together that evening . . ."

"Yes?" she prompted, curious as to what her mother had sensed.

"One cannot develop a penchant for a man just because he can play the cello beautifully," was the prim rejoinder. "You *would* be particularly susceptible to that talent."

"I didn't know that about him," Rebecca reminded her. "And I just told you I've been in love with him for over a year."

"So you did." Her mother massaged her temples. "I'm still assimilating the implications of this—this—"

"Catastrophe?" Rebecca supplied ironically.

"I wasn't going to say that, but well, yes. I suppose it fits. You really do think you love that rash, handsome young man?"

"How many times must I say it?"

"Your father has something against him."

"I know." Rebecca looked briefly at her clasped hands. "But I have been informed I am not going to be told the details. Robert, on the other hand, says he is innocent of whatever accusation is leveled his direction. But he didn't tell me what the source of the contention might be."

"Not for our ears, apparently. Men have an annoying habit of excluding us from their personal disputes."

Rebecca hadn't been expecting sympathy, so the observation made her blink in surprise.

"He isn't the Marquess of Highton," her mother murmured reflectively, looking pensive.

"No, he isn't. But if Robert had proposed like the Marquess, I would have married him."

"Would you now? I suppose that's promising. And though he isn't a marquess, he is the younger brother of a duke. An excellent match by any standards."

It was Rebecca's turn to be stunned into silence.

Her mother straightened in her chair. "What did you think? That I would discount your feelings? I love you. You are my daughter and my only child. I want you to marry well, but marrying for love is a special thing. Now, had I not seen Lord Robert here today, I believe I would be more upset about this. But, quite frankly, he wasn't really the roguish charmer I expected. He looked more like a man on unfamiliar ground."

It was an apt description.

"And he *really* could not stop looking at you." Her

mother adjusted her skirt with a languid hand, her expression thoughtful. "You know, bringing him to the altar would be the social coup of the decade, in a way."

Making a social splash was the last thing on Rebecca's mind, but if it made her mother more inclined to accept the situation, Rebecca was hardly going to argue. "I don't have any idea if it is possible. Damien seems to think so, but I don't know. Robert doesn't *wish* to be married."

"How do you know?"

"Like I said, he told me."

"Robert Northfield discussed his feelings on marriage with you?"

Right *before* he kissed her. Rebecca decided not to mention that lapse in decorum. She looked at the floor, studying the roses on the beige background of the rug. "He doesn't want to change his life."

"Men rarely do." Her mother lifted her brows in a delicate, ladylike mannerism. "But we usually know what they want better than they realize themselves. They often need to be guided in the right direction."

It sounded so close to the title of Lady Rothburg's helpful chapter that Rebecca turned her face away to conceal her expression. Her mother would collapse in a horrified heap if she knew she shared the sentiments of an infamous courtesan.

Yet the advice was the same.

How interesting.

"Your father is the true obstacle."

Rebecca didn't need to be told that piece of information. Her shoulders drooped. "I know."

A peculiar smile crossed her mother's face. It wasn't exactly sly, but hinted in that direction. "Let's make a pact, darling. If you manage to bring the roguish Lord Robert to heel, I will take care of your father. Keep in mind that women have a more understated approach to matters of the heart, but it usually works beautifully."

The second almost word-for-word quote from *Lady Rothburg's Advice* rendered Rebecca at a complete loss for speech. The book had been banned after it was released ten years ago, but it had sold in record numbers before Parliament declared it too risqué to be sold publicly. Surely her mother never would have purchased a copy?

Impossible.

Chapter Nineteen

Duplicity always has a price.

From the chapter titled:
"What Your Husbands Keep from You"

Colton felt like a liar.
A cheat.

If he was wrong, he was insulting her in the worst way possible. Unfaithful? Brianna?

God, please let him be wrong.

He took a drink of wine and studied his wife across the table. She looked beautiful, as usual. But there was something about her manner that spoke of unease. For one thing she was quieter, preoccupied. He was rarely the one to start conversations, but this evening he'd had to make the effort to fill the silences between them.

Was it because she felt guilty?

He was the one who felt guilty, damn it, for hiring a man to dog her every footstep.

Colton murmured, "This is very pleasant, isn't it? Just the two of us for a change."

"I think having a quiet evening at home is a very lovely idea." Brianna sipped her wine, her blond hair gleaming in the candlelight. "We don't do it often enough."

What they'd done infrequently lately was make love. It was his fault—because he couldn't get past his doubts—but he wanted her. Hell and blast, he wanted her. The self-denial had been a lesson in pure torture.

The first report had been delivered to him that afternoon. Though the words stuck in his throat, he said, "Tell me, what did you do today, my dear?"

Please, do not lie to me. Please.

"Errands mostly. The milliner, that sort of thing." She lifted her shoulders in a dainty shrug. "I called on Arabella on my way back home."

"Oh?" He waited.

"Yes."

Nothing more. He knew about her visit, of course. He knew in intimate detail her every move. For instance, he'd been informed an unescorted gentleman had arrived at Arabella Smythe's town house twenty minutes after Brianna had entered the building. He knew that the curtains in the front parlor had been drawn. And he knew that the gentleman remained for over an hour, after which time he and Brianna had exited the house in quick succession. Hudson did not yet know the identity of this mysterious gentleman, but he was investigating. The description was a little vague because Hudson's man had been watching from across the street, but the report stated the stranger moved well, like a young man.

Arabella had been Brianna's friend for years. Was it possible Arabella would provide a discreet meeting place for his wife to meet with her lover? Colton wondered about the incident with an inner agony he hoped didn't show in his face.

It was all he could do to spear another piece of the roast lamb on his plate and chew and swallow it. It was perfectly cooked, but it tasted like sawdust. He managed to wash it down with a mouthful of wine. "I see," he murmured. "How is the countess?"

"Fine."

Another one-word answer? He waited for her to elaborate, but instead she merely took a forkful of potato. If he inquired whether Arabella had company when she arrived, he would sound too suspicious. How could he know such a thing if someone hadn't told him? He said nothing, but the silence was torture.

When the devil was she going to tell him she carried a child?

He set aside his fork, no longer able to even make a pretense of wanting to eat.

Perhaps he should just ask her. Maybe he should also inquire why she was also patently uncomfortable around him all of a sudden.

"I want to go visit my mother and father. I think I'll leave tomorrow." His wife spoke so quietly he almost didn't catch the words. In the candlelight, her long lashes lent shadows to her perfect cheekbones.

"No." His autocratic refusal came out before he could help it.

Obviously startled, Brianna stared at him. "I—I beg your pardon?"

He needed to keep her near him, just in case he was right. What if her lover was someone she'd known since before her marriage, and now that her innocence had been given to her husband so the deception couldn't be detected, they could freely indulge themselves in a torrid affair? What if he was a family friend, a neighbor perhaps, and she wished to tell *him* about the child first?

He'd tormented himself with a dozen theories. A ruthless, practical voice inside his head reminded him that *someone* was teaching her how to drive him wild in bed. Colton wasn't her instructor, so who was?

When forced to look at the situation with the light of cold logic, he couldn't come up with any explanation besides another lover. There was little doubt Brianna knew exactly what she was doing.

Well, he'd already said it, so he might as well make his position clear. "No, I do not give you permission to go."

"Per—permission?" she sputtered, her linen napkin dropping from her hand and drifting to the floor.

"You must have it. I don't give it." He enunciated each word clearly.

He was being both petty and tyrannical but he didn't

care. A lack of sleep and restive doubts weren't conducive to civility.

"Colton," she whispered in shocked reproof. "Why wouldn't you wish for me to see my parents?"

"I'll escort you myself when I get the time."

"Time? You? God in heaven, when would that be? They live in Devon, which is several days' journey in either direction. I had to use coercion just to get you to Rolthven, which is convenient to London."

"Do not blaspheme in my presence, madam." Now he was being truly overbearing, but he'd been dwelling on nothing but thoughts of his wife's possible infidelity for weeks and it was eating him inside. She was entirely right, but he was not in the mood to admit it.

Two red splotches appeared on her smooth cheeks. "Colton, what on earth is wrong with you?"

"There is nothing wrong with me."

"Yes, there is." Brianna tilted her chin, defiance in her dark blue eyes. "Or do I need *permission* to disagree with you?"

She shouldn't have goaded him, not in his current state of mind. He leaned forward, holding her gaze. "You might keep in mind you need my permission for just about anything you do. The day we wed you gave a vow to be faithful and to obey me. I expect both. You are my wife and under my rule."

"Rule?" She gave what sounded like a hysterical laugh but it could have been a sob.

It hadn't been the right word to choose probably, but he wasn't at his best.

The arrival of a footman to clear their plates, with another right behind him with the dessert course, put an end to any further conversation, which was probably just as well for the moment. The minute the servants exited the room, his wife rose. "Please excuse me."

"Sit down. I have no wish to have the household staff put it about that you walked out on me in the middle of a meal." That was true anyway. His troubles with his wife were a private matter. It had been humiliating enough to express his doubts to Hudson when he hired the man to follow her.

Brianna sat back down, her soft mouth set in a mutinous line. She eyed the frothy chocolate concoction on her plate as if someone had set an asp in front her. "My stomach has been unsettled lately. Does it meet with your royal approval if I decline to eat any more or must I choke it down and deal with the consequences if it doesn't agree with me?"

Her acerbic question reminded him of her pregnancy. His or not, she nurtured a child in her body and he wasn't an ogre, though he might be acting like one. Colton inclined his head. "If you wish to skip dessert, that is fine with me. But you will stay here while I eat mine."

He didn't have the stomach for it either, but some perverse part of him was insisting he make a point.

She looked at him as if he'd sprouted a second head and made a helpless gesture with her hand. "I truly do not understand your mood this evening. And it isn't unique to this meal either. It is as if I've done something wrong but I don't know what it is."

Colton couldn't help it. He said in a silky voice, "You've done nothing wrong, my dear. Have you?"

"*Have I?* What kind of question is that?" Brianna gazed at her husband in unconcealed consternation.

He was a stranger, the cold-eyed man across the table, calmly sipping wine from his glass but looking at her as if she'd committed some heinous crime. True, Colton was rarely warm and open, but tonight he looked positively *shuttered*.

Was he happy about her possible pregnancy? Damien had assured her that his older brother would be overjoyed at the news, and she assumed he'd be delighted since he needed an heir, but he hadn't said a word to her about the subject. Not one blasted word. That he would ask her maid about it and not say a word to her was disturbing. He wanted children, didn't he?

Maybe he didn't, she thought with a sinking heart.

Maybe he considered her condition indelicate and inconvenient. After all, before long she'd be fat, ungainly, and unable to go about in public without everyone knowing she was enceinte. Some aristocrats never interacted with their offspring, relying on nannies and governesses to raise them, relegating them to nurseries and schoolrooms until such a time as they could either be sent away to school or married to some male who would take them off their parents' hands.

She just hadn't imagined Colton would react that way. Especially now that her suspicions were confirmed and she knew the pregnancy was real, the notion he wouldn't share her joy was unsettling in the extreme. And because of his uncertain mood, she hesitated to tell him. It was precisely because of the way he'd acted lately that she'd asked Arabella to arrange to have a physician make a discreet call at her town house rather than summoning their own doctor. If she wasn't pregnant, why cause more tension between them? But the physician had confirmed her condition and she was going to have to tell her husband soon.

He regarded her with no visible emotion. "I didn't say you'd done anything wrong. Those are your words, not mine."

Bewildered, she just looked at him.

Maybe it sounded childish, but Brianna wanted her mother. She may not have done an admirable job in instructing Brianna on the details of what would happen on her wedding night, but her mother adored children and was going to be delighted when she heard the news. Brianna needed that, needed to talk to someone about what things were going to be like until she gave birth, someone who would be equally happy over her condition, someone who would both coddle and counsel her. Both Rebecca and Arabella were wonderful, but they hadn't had children, and they couldn't help. Lea had sent her a hurried note to say that one of the children was ill and she expected the whole household would come down with the malady. Lea would send word when the sickness ran its course, but right now Brianna couldn't even talk to her sister. Devon sounded like heaven, at least until this cloud over her marriage passed by.

Colton had just refused to let her go. Moreover, he'd meant it, too. She wasn't sure she'd ever heard him use that particular arrogant tone.

It wasn't like him at all. He was solicitous and generous, and at all times a gentleman. But there he sat, handsome and urbane in his formal evening wear even for a dinner at home, his thick chestnut hair gilded by the flickering light, his long fingers ceaselessly toying with the stem of his wineglass, looking every inch the dictatorial husband.

She was more confounded than ever.

The convulsive, edgy movement of his elegant fingers told her something. The restless motion wasn't his normal behavior. Impulsively, she blurted out, "Damien told me I might be going to have a baby. It's true."

Her husband's brows shot up and his eyes grew even colder. Glacial would be appropriate. "What? How the hell would *Damien* know?"

This was all wrong, she thought with an inner grimace. Since Colton had just sworn in front of her for the first time ever, he probably agreed. Brianna calmed herself and sought a more reasonable tone. "He guessed after I almost vomited on his shoes the other morning. Please don't tell me this comes as a complete surprise. I know you've questioned my maid."

Another of what felt like several hundred awkward silences of the evening ensued. *Well done*, she told herself caustically. Saying the word *vomit* at the dinner table surely had to be a blunder of the worst sort.

Not at all how she'd pictured telling him.

"I have wondered if you might be pregnant." Colton's face resembled a granite statue. "So I asked a few questions, yes."

"Why didn't you say something?" Her humiliating ignorance rankled, and she would much rather her husband had asked her about the possibility of a pregnancy than her brother-in-law.

"I was waiting for *you* to tell *me*."

Something inside her crumbled at his acid tone. Brianna fought the bite of tears. "You aren't happy about this."

"Don't be absurd. Of course, I'm happy."

He was? A wash of relief went through her, but she still didn't really believe him. He looked like someone going under the executioner's axe. "Then what's wrong?"

"I'm not sure."

Could two people have a more vague conversation and yet have it be so loaded with emotion?

She felt like the affronted party, but had the impression he did also.

"Colton, I've seen a physician. We are going to have a child. Shouldn't we celebrate rather than argue?" Her voice was soft and held a betraying tremor she wished she could hide.

For a moment, his face changed and she saw a vulnerable cast to it that wasn't at all haughty aristocrat, or privileged lord. He was just a man, and an uncertain one at that, and she realized that as unsure as breeding this new life within her made her feel, maybe the weight of this new responsibility was affecting him in the same way. He always seemed so strong, as if he didn't need guidance, so she assumed he was in control of his emotions at all times.

His fingers stilled on his wineglass and when he spoke his voice was weary. "I think I must apologize to you. My behavior this evening has been boorish."

Azure eyes looked into hers, making her heart skip a beat. She didn't think he'd ever, ever looked at her with such poignant entreaty.

He had, actually, been unbearably boorish, and she was still in the dark as to why.

But it didn't matter. She loved him. She was going to be the mother of his child. "I have missed you so much," she said softly. "More than you can imagine. I am still not sure why we are arguing, but I do know I cannot bear another lonely night."

"I quite agree." His voice was hoarse and he stood, tossing his napkin aside. He held out his hand, the gesture not imperious, but a token of compromise. "Let's go upstairs."

He needed her so desperately it frightened him.

His hand at the small of her graceful back, Colton hoped Brianna couldn't sense his intense hunger as they climbed the stairs, feel the slight tremor of his fingers, hear the increased cadence of his respiration.

"My bedchamber," he said tersely. It was a possessive decision sparked by his volatile emotions. His bed, his room, his body claiming hers . . .

His beautiful wife, *his* child. It must be.

Brianna merely nodded, her fragrance tantalizing, a promise of warm, smooth skin and silken, perfumed hair. Colton opened the door for her, followed her inside, and had barely shut the door behind them before he caught her in his arms. He swallowed her gasp of surprise as his mouth claimed hers with almost violent possession. There was something primeval in the force of the emotion that gripped him, something beyond his control, and the realization that if he battled it he might just lose was unique in his life. If there was one thing he could do and do well, it was command his emotions.

Not so when he was with Brianna. He was bewitched, beguiled, and utterly baffled by his lovely wife. Just when he thought he understood her, he found he was wrong yet again. This evening was a perfect example. Just moments before he'd been inexcusably autocratic, and yet here she was kissing him back with a fervor that matched his wild need, trembling against him. She should be furious with him. He deserved it.

If she was innocent.

His hands fumbled with her gown, undoing buttons, parting cloth to find bare flesh. Their lips still clung and her hands moved under his jacket to flatten against his chest. One small palm was positioned over his heart and he was sure she could feel the riotous pounding there as he slipped her dress off her shoulders.

"I've missed you so," Brianna murmured against his mouth.

He certainly had missed her, and his rigid cock agreed. The recent self-imposed abstinence had been a tactic to help him work out his doubts—something he didn't think he could do with impartiality when sharing her bed.

The trouble was, he hadn't worked out anything except a terrifying conviction that he couldn't live without her.

Colton stripped off her chemise and knelt to remove her slippers and stockings, making short work of the task, running his fingers lightly up over her calves, the inside of her knee, and skimming her thighs and hips. She looked the same, he thought, wondering when he would notice the swell of the new life that he would claim and give his name. Anything else was out of the question, and there was no doubt that whatever else might be going on, there was a good chance this child was his. He kissed the still-flat plane of her stomach, a gentle, soft pressure of his mouth.

"Oh, Colton," she whispered, lightly touching his hair.

"Get into bed," he ordered as he rose swiftly, the sight of her nude body, a becoming pink in the flickering light, making his arousal surge. He added as an afterthought, "Don't cover yourself. I want to look while I undress."

She complied, climbing onto the big bed and reclining there, her delectable breasts visibly tight, the nipples pink and erect. They *were* larger, he realized as he examined them with heated deliberate perusal and untied his cravat. The mounded flesh was fuller—though they'd been lusciously shaped before—the thin veining of blue under her translucent skin more prominent. The evidence of change made the pregnancy more real, more immediate.

To regain some semblance of calm, Colton took his time, removing each article of his clothing with deliberation, forcing his mind away from anything except the shimmer of desire in his wife's eyes and the eager clasp of her arms as he joined her on the big bed.

It was time to tamp down the complex roil of his thoughts and concentrate on purely carnal sensations. She was there with him, she was willing and soft, and so damned beautiful. . . .

"Kiss me," she said on a breathy exhale. "Make love to me."

It halted him even as he lowered his head to take her mouth and adjusted his hips between her open thighs.

If he did this, he would be truly making love, Colton realized with a shock. It was no longer about desire, or conjugal relations, or any of the other reasons men and women came together in the oldest of ways.

I love her.

If he didn't, he might be angry over a possible betrayal, he might be affronted at the slight to his pride, he might even wish retribution, but none of that was particularly significant. Revenge was the last thing on his mind, his pride be damned, and as for anger, it wasn't the right word to explain how he felt.

He was afraid. Of losing her. Oh, not in a literal sense. He could keep her no matter what—she was his wife, he was a duke and wielded power and influence—but he needed more.

All of her.

She was wet, ready, her body primed for the culmination of their joining. He could feel the slick heat as he positioned his cock, the willing give of her body as he tested his welcome, the grip of her hands on his buttocks as she urged him without words to take her.

The night of his birthday, she'd made sweet, sultry love to him. Soft kisses, subtle movements, suggestive caresses. Colton was determined to do the same, entering her body with exquisite slowness, kissing her temple, the side of her jaw, the tempting arch of her throat. When they were one, he rocked forward, making her give a low cry of pleasure, her pelvis tilting up so he could effectively put pressure in just the right spot.

And she shuddered in response.

He selflessly continued the erotic, measured rhythm, her pleasure his goal. A faint film of sweat sprung out on his brow as he held himself back until Brianna arched frantically beneath him in fevered ecstasy and her cry of release echoed through the bedchamber. He followed, intense, riveted on the rapture, his explosion leaving him both replete and exhausted.

Later Colton lay in the dark, cradling his wife in his arms. Brianna slept warm and lax against him, her naked body all feminine curves, her breath a light drift against his throat.

He loved her, and not just with his body.

By God, he *loved* her.

Whatever he had expected of marriage, it wasn't *this*.

How could she respond to him with such sweet enthusiasm, their bodies in such perfect harmony, he marveled, if she had betrayed him? How could she gaze at him with such innocence in her eyes if she was in truth a Jezebel? How could she cling to him and kiss him with open abandon if she yearned for someone else?

He didn't think he was so besotted he'd be fooled by a façade, but he'd never been in such a situation before. It was true, at dinner she had looked astonished over his behavior, not guilty. Hurt, not wary.

If they hadn't had the argument, would she have told him she was pregnant? That was the question that hung at the back of his mind. To solve their differences, she'd gladly taken him to her bed. His physical hunger for her was a weakness—had she exploited it to divert his attention?

God, how he hated this inner war.

Brianna stirred and then subsided back into peaceful slumber. Colton toyed with a golden curl, testing the silk of it between his fingers.

Though he was tired as hell, he had a feeling sleep

was going to be elusive yet again. At least he had the pleasure of holding her, he thought, shifting her closer. It was a simple thing, but now that he recognized the depths of his feelings, an important one.

He just hoped falling in love with his wife wasn't the worst mistake of his life.

Chapter Twenty

*When it comes to social intrigue, do not underesti-
mate men. They may remark on how females take
too close an interest in the lives of others, but men
can be just as observant, just as interested—and just
as capable of meddling. Trust me on this point.*

> *From the chapter titled: "Rumor, Gossip,
> and Innuendo, and How They Work for You"*

Robert hadn't followed Damien's advice and waltzed with Rebecca. Touching her, even in such a socially accepted manner, was a dangerous idea.

So he'd completely lost his mind and waltzed with her mother instead.

"I do so love this new tune, don't you, my lord?" Lady Marston smiled at him pleasantly, as if unaware that the sight of the notorious Robert Northfield dancing with a middle-aged, married woman had more than one tongue wagging. Not that Robert didn't dutifully ask one of the dowagers upon occasion, but most often they were relatives of some kind, or the hostess of the event. Lady Marston was neither.

It had taken some fortitude to make the request, for he had to brave the ranks of the matrons, usually ensconced together in a formidable mass so they could gossip and chat while keeping a keen eye on their daughters, nieces, or wards. His approach stilled more than one conversation, and when he bowed over Lady Marston's hand and asked her for a dance, mouths literally hung open.

It was clearly a deranged moment. Yet here he was.

"It's pleasant, I suppose, but not at all as impressive as the music we heard at Rolthven." He swung her into a graceful swirl.

"Yes." The reply was neutral. "You've mentioned several times you enjoyed Rebecca's performance."

"She is as talented as she is beautiful, which is high praise indeed."

Lady Marston looked up at him, her mouth pursed. "I am aware of my daughter's interest in you, and I am sure, with your level of experience and sophistication, you are aware of it also."

Though he tried not to analyze his motives in dancing with Lady Marston, he supposed he wished to test the results of his visit the other day. He was still not sure whether Damien's diabolical interference had been helpful or the worst idea possible, but he'd done nothing but think about it. In his current state of disquiet, he couldn't sleep or concentrate on even mundane tasks.

What if I could court her?

"I'm both flattered and at a loss," he said with rueful sincerity. "And I am sure *you* are sophisticated enough, my lady, to understand why."

"With my daughter, you don't have your usual options." She added in a dry tone, "That is both an observation and a warning, my lord."

"Do I have *any* options?" he asked bluntly. "I've wondered."

"It depends on your level of determination, I suppose. When you arrived the other day and I realized it was not just the random social call your brother intimated it to be, I admit I was taken aback."

Her low level of enthusiasm had been duly noted at the time, though he was too polite to mention it.

At that moment the music came to a halt. Robert had little choice but to release her hand and bow. In return, she gave him a gracious inclination of her head and a level look. "I think what happens next is up to you. Weigh the strength of your interest, and if it is sincere enough, for my daughter's sake, I will help you with Benedict."

She turned and walked away, leaving him standing with what was probably a very surprised look on his face. Aware of the avid stares around him, he composed his expression and strode off the dance floor.

Weigh the level of your interest.

He went into one of the card rooms and sat in on several games, but his inattention was obvious, and when he won the last hand, the gentleman next to him had to give him a nudge to collect his winnings. Bloody hell, he might as well face it, he thought as he rose from the table and made his farewells; he couldn't concentrate on anything else. It was hard to believe, but he'd even pictured what it would be like to walk down the hallway of his home and hear the sound of a pianoforte being played skillfully in the background.

The result of all the moody introspection seemed inescapable.

He might not want to court anyone, he might not wish marriage, but he simply couldn't quite put Rebecca Marston out of his mind. He wanted her—wanted to taste her lips again, wanted to feel her warm and willing in his arms, but it wasn't *all* he wanted.

Making his excuses, he left abruptly, and headed toward some place that wouldn't remind him of the woman who had him so distracted.

Fifteen minutes later Robert alighted from his carriage, noted the lights blazing in the house in front of him, and grinned at one of the other arrivals. "Palmer. How are you?"

Lord Palmer swayed a little, obviously foxed as he came up the walk. "Doing deuced well, Northfield. Thanks. Sounds like a capital party, eh? I hear Betty is sending some of her best girls for this one."

Robert tried to look noncommittal. Now that he was there, he really wasn't interested in a troupe of Cyprians, to his dismay. "Sounds diverting."

A diversion was what he desperately needed.

"Well, there's nothing like gambling and women to entertain a man, is there?" Palmer clumsily elbowed Robert in the ribs as they went up the steps. "I know you agree."

Perhaps he *used* to agree. The only reason he'd chosen to leave the ball and attend this particular event was that it was the one place he could think of where he couldn't possibly run into Rebecca. If he went home and spent the rest of the evening alone with his thoughts, he would drive himself insane. A mindless evening of debauchery sounded like just the ticket. He'd attended bachelor affairs like this many times before, and they always involved a great deal of flowing champagne, the purchased warmth of willing women, and bawdy entertainment.

"Yes," he murmured and preceded Lord Palmer through the door held open by a liveried footman.

The next hour passed with excruciating tedium as he attempted to make merry when he wasn't merry at all.

It was a damnable exercise. He didn't want to sit at home and brood. He couldn't attend any of his usual entertainments lest he see Rebecca. He obviously didn't want to be here either.

A drunken voice called out that the girls had arrived, and a buzz of anticipation filled the room.

It was probably best, Robert decided, given his restive state of mind, if he left now. He really wasn't in the mood to watch half-naked women drape themselves over a bunch of drunken fools. Whatever had made him think in the past that this passed for entertainment? He asked a footman for his greatcoat, quelling the need to tap his foot as he waited.

Sure enough, the door opened and a mass of giggling young ladies entered the townhouse. Betty Benson ran the most upscale brothel in London and her employees were always clean, disease-free, and at the least pretty, but usually gorgeous. This group was no exception. Blondes, brunettes, at least two striking redheads strolled in the door and were immediately offered champagne. The din of the party rose to new heights as the men began to single out their partners for the evening. Robert watched the proceedings with a jaundiced eye as he waited for his coat. All of the men in attendance were unmarried with only a few exceptions, the girls would be treated and paid well, and when in the hell had he acquired the morals of a bishop anyway?

Suddenly, he froze in the act of accepting the garment from a servant, not quite certain he could believe his eyes. The last girl to trail in the door was not dressed at all in a suggestive manner, her gown modestly covered by a dark blue cloak, her sable hair upswept in a ladylike style than made him want to yank the pins from it and feel the warmth as it tumbled over his fingers.

What in the devil was *Rebecca* doing here?

And why had she arrived with a bevy of prostitutes?

He stood there, aghast. What on earth was she playing at?

Once his muscles unlocked, he grabbed his coat, dashed across the foyer, and took hold of her arm with more force than intended. "You can explain later. In the meantime, I am going to get you out of here. I swear if you argue, I'll sling you over my shoulder and carry you out like a sack of potatoes."

Rebecca stifled a gasp. Robert's hand clamped on her arm so tightly it almost hurt as he more dragged than escorted her down the front steps into the cool night.

The expression he wore when he spotted her arrival was something she would remember the rest of her life.

He'd been horrified. It had been stamped on his handsome face, a caricature of surprise and dismay, unmistakable—and not very flattering, considering the trouble she'd gone through to get there.

Why?

Because she'd arrived alone? Well, not precisely alone—a carriage had pulled up just before the hack she hired had rolled to a halt in front of the brilliantly lit townhouse, and quite a few young women had alighted. She'd wondered how to enter without an invitation anyway, and following them inside had been easy.

"My lord—" she began to say.

He cut her off ruthlessly. "I have no idea why you are here, but until we are safely away, don't say another word and for God's sake pull up your hood."

She'd risked censure and her parent's displeasure to slip out of the ball and come to find him in the first place. If she hadn't felt the desperate need to talk to him, she wouldn't have done it.

He practically tossed her into his carriage, rapped on the roof sharply after he clambered in, and they rocked away. He stared at her from across the small space, his brows drawn into a taut line. "Do you mind telling me," he said through his teeth, "just what you were doing showing up at Houseman's gathering? I know for a fact you were not invited. Weren't you safely with your parents at the Tallers'?"

Rebecca opened her mouth to reply but he cut her off.

"I watched you all evening." His blue eyes glittered. "You must have danced with every gentleman in attendance."

"You didn't ask me." Her voice was quiet.

"Of course not."

Of course not. Those three words stung and she lifted her chin.

But he had danced with her mother. Surely it meant something. That single act had given her the courage to follow him.

Robert went on, forestalling anything she could have said, though she wasn't sure she even knew how to reply. "As for your arrival a few moments ago, in case you didn't notice, the other ladies in attendance are from a slightly different walk of life than you are. Let's just pray no one saw you."

It was true, she hadn't recognized any of them, but they'd been dressed in sumptuous gowns and. . . .

Oh. *No.*

Comprehension dawned.

"Yes." He correctly interpreted her appalled expression and inadvertent gasp. "That is exactly what I mean. They make their living a certain way and were hired as, well, I don't need to say anything more. Rebecca, why were *you* there?"

She crushed her fingers together in her lap so tightly the bones actually hurt. "I overheard several gentlemen discussing this party. They mentioned your name as one of the invited guests and that it was your probable destination when you left so abruptly. I didn't realize. . . ." She faltered.

His jaw set like a marble statue's.

"I very much want to talk to you," she added, the excuse feeble even to her own ears.

"So much you may have damaged your reputation beyond repair?" he asked in an acidic tone. He shook his head and turned away, for a moment staring at nothing but the side of the carriage. "This," he said with measured emphasis, "is a disaster."

She was very much afraid he might be right, but she straightened her spine. "All I knew was that it was a party to which my parents had no intention of going. I thought I might get a chance to at least speak with you if I managed to sneak in. I really had no idea—"

"Where do they think you are?" He cut her off with borderline discourtesy. Rebecca was beginning to get a true sense of what her reckless idea might have just cost her and she felt a little faint.

"I pretended I was going with Arabella and her husband to another event."

"In other words, you tricked your parents."

Well, she had, though at the time, she'd excused it more as a necessary falsehood. She nodded.

He said a word she'd never heard before under his breath, but not quietly enough she didn't wonder what it meant, though this didn't seem like the time to ask.

"I don't think anyone saw me slip away and flag down the hack," she defended herself. "Arabella knows, of course, but no one else."

He transferred his gaze back to her face. "What if someone *did* see you?"

She really couldn't think of a single thing to say.

"They will blame me." He ran his hand down his face. "Your parents will blame *me*. And God knows the world will believe them."

"How was I supposed to know it was a . . . a . . ." She couldn't think of a proper word to describe the party she'd almost attended.

Robert slouched a little lower in his seat and his smile was an ironic twist of his lips. "A depraved, self-indulgent male gathering? My dear, did you not wonder why you and your parents were not invited? You all are on the list of every fashionable hostess in London. Besides, when a reprobate like Gerald Houseman throws a party, it is just an excuse for men to get together and behave far less politely than we usually do when there are ladies in attendance."

"Is that why you were there?" she asked. "So you could behave impolitely?"

"I think that was the original idea." He paused, then added curtly, "But as you saw, I was leaving."

"Why is that?" she asked softly.

His hand tightened convulsively where it rested on his knee. "I found I wasn't in the mood, after all."

"Damien said you've been spending a great deal of time at home."

"Is there something amiss with that? Contrary to the popular opinion I spend every night gadding about London, I actually stay home on a regular basis. Anyway, my activities don't really matter, for I do not have a reputation in peril, but you do. We are going to have to figure out a way to safely and discreetly return you home."

Considering all the trouble she'd gone to, and the possible disaster looming ahead, she wasn't willing to let him simply return her without at least saying what she'd risked so much to say. "Since the damage is done and a small difference in time is moot at this point, could you not ask your driver to drive around a bit so we can discuss this?"

A muscle in his jaw twitched. "In my experience, too much conversation with a woman is never a good idea. And though I hate to ask, can you define *this*?"

She hesitated, knowing her next words could make all the difference in her future. Rebecca took in a deep breath. "Us."

Robert muttered that unfamiliar word again, shifting his tall body on the opposite seat. "Rebecca—"

"Can't we negotiate?"

"Negotiate?" He stared at her and narrowed his eyes. "How so?"

She swallowed down a lump of nervousness and went on with what she hoped was credible calm, though her heart pounded. "Please understand, I am quite the opposite of you."

For the first time since he'd spied her walking into that foyer, a glimmer of his usual reckless charm surfaced. "Unfortunately, I've noticed, Miss Marston."

Her laugh was a combination of tension and some well-needed relief at his levity. "I mean I understand you have no wish to relinquish your freedom. Fine. As someone who has no freedom to speak of, I believe I can see why you value the commodity. Perhaps we can work things out to our mutual satisfaction. Make a bargain, if you will. All I ask is for you to give me a chance."

He didn't move.

Was she really going to do this? To say this outrageous thing based on a book written by a fallen woman? Stake her happiness on the advice of a harlot?

Yes, she was. Because while Damien was doing his best to help her, he would soon leave for Spain, and besides, this was a woman's problem and it needed a woman's touch.

Even her own mother had said it. *We know what they want better than they do.*

She'd read that wicked book in its entirety, and *enlightened* didn't even begin to describe the revelation. Oh yes, she'd been quite shocked by the frank descriptions, but also fascinated, and by her reaction, maybe she really *was* just the woman for Robert Northfield.

What she really wanted was to do all of those forbidden things with *him*.

So she went on. Impossibly so. She couldn't believe it, but she did it.

"Will you marry me?"

His lips parted in undisguised surprise. The stunned expression on his face would have been comical except she was dreadfully nervous and had a feeling this was the most important moment of her life.

"If we are wed," Rebecca explained, hearing the quaver in her voice, "and I do not satisfy you in every way possible, feel free to live your life as you did before. If you grow restless because I can't hold you, there will be no objection on my part over your lack of interest." Rebecca paused and gave him a calculated smile before she added in a hushed tone, "However, in the spirit of being sporting about this whole thing, I must warn you that I have every intention of being all you need."

Robert had the feeling his face reflected his incredulity. Not since he was seventeen had he been so bluntly propositioned. Elise had been twelve years older, an actress, and her intentions strictly lascivious. One sultry summer evening she'd sought him out—after a performance he'd attended with his family, no less—and whispered in his ear just what she wanted to do with him. She adored beautiful young men, she'd explained in her signature husky voice with an unapologetic, overtly sensual smile.

At the time, he was both sexually curious and flattered. Naturally, he managed to find a way to the lady's lodgings. That first affair had marked the beginning of his notoriety, and he'd been offered sexual favors in many different ways—and from many different women—in the years that had passed.

This was something else completely.

Maybe he was hallucinating. Maybe a very innocent young woman hadn't just told him in plain terms she wanted to capture his sexual interest and had the confidence somehow—considering her inexperience—she could keep it.

If he married her.

Robert closed his mouth, and fought to find something remotely intelligent to use as a response.

Nothing came to mind.

God help him, he was more intrigued than ever. She probably really didn't even realize what she promised, but the idea of teaching her was tantalizing in the extreme.

He was fairly sure he couldn't tear his gaze from her face even on pain of death. Had she really just *proposed* to him?

Her luminous blue-green eyes regarded him from across the small space as they rolled along the street. He'd been so rattled when he saw her walk in the door at the party he hadn't given his driver any instructions, so her request for more time was already granted, whether she realized it or not. George would wait until told to take them to any certain address. He'd undoubtedly seen the young lady enter the carriage with him.

That was another point. Cloak or no, she still could have been recognized. Robert had told the perfect truth earlier. If word got out she'd been seen at such an event as Houseman's party, there would be an enormous scandal.

Perhaps he *had* to marry her.

Maybe I wish to marry her.

Did he? As Damien would no doubt point out, Robert wasn't sure he *didn't* want to marry her, and he was dead certain he didn't want her marrying anyone else.

"Your father won't agree." The words came out hoarsely.

If I don't satisfy you in every way possible . . .

"He just might. My mother likes you. She isn't precisely in favor of a match between us, but she isn't opposed, either. I think the intrigue of the situation appeals to her." Rebecca arched a brow. "It was really a stroke of genius to dance with her."

"I wasn't trying to be a genius," he muttered. "I was just . . ."

She waited, looking interested in his response.

He had no idea what he even meant to say. Why *had* he danced with Lady Marston? He finally settled on rasping out, "Rebecca, you needn't be so selfless. You are beautiful, gifted, an heiress. We both know every eligible man in London is at your feet."

"Good, then that must include you. My parents are pressuring me to choose a husband soon. I choose you. Can I assume you accept my offer?"

"It is hardly that simple."

"Tell me why. You *are* eligible, aren't you?" Her smile was slow and enticing. "Unless there is a secret wife none of us know about."

Damn her, she knew she was winning. No, worse, she knew she'd *won*.

It was time for him to take charge of the situation again.

At least he had the satisfaction of eliciting a surprised gasp as he suddenly reached across the small distance between them and caught her by the waist, hauling her onto his lap. Robert grazed his mouth against her temple. "Why do you do this to me?"

"I've asked that same question about your effect on *me* many times." Her laugh held a breathless note. "I'm afraid there isn't an easy explanation."

His lips traveled across the satin curve of her cheek, much like that first night in the garden. He nibbled at the corner of her mouth in a reenactment of the moment when he held her against the hedge as she dodged Lord Watts. "Fine, I agree to your terms, as long as you agree to mine."

Her arms slid around his neck. "I doubt I will object to anything you say."

His smile was deliberately wicked. "If I don't satisfy you in every way, feel free to seek solace elsewhere, but be warned, I intend to hold your interest."

She quivered against him.

Then he kissed her. Not with the same restraint as the first time, but a lover's kiss, hot and hard and long. It was a promise and a silent vow. He ravished, but he also gave back, letting her feel his hunger, but also his restraint.

In fact, when he finally resurfaced and lifted his mouth a fraction, he had no idea where in London the carriage might have taken them, but he did know a wonderful inner peace he hadn't even suspected could exist after such a monumental decision. Robert murmured against her lips, "We'll need to marry soon."

"To save my reputation in case anyone saw me to-night?" Rebecca laughed in a sweet exhale, lush and warm in his arms.

"Because I can't wait long. Perhaps you can tell." He shifted so she could feel his erection against the curve of her hip.

"Oh."

He laughed at the underlying uncertainty in the ex-clamation, happy to have the upper hand again. "I do have a certain reputation, you know."

Then she turned the tables. Her hand slipped from his shoulder downward, across his jacket to rest on his upper thigh, and then she touched him. It was through his breeches, but still he sucked in a breath in an audible rasp as she pressed her palm against the length of his hard cock. "Why wait at all?" she said in what could only be described as a sultry whisper. "We're betrothed and just agreed to an expedient wedding."

It shocked the hell out of him. The suggestion, but also the boldness of the pressure of her hand. It was a rather adventurous act from an innocent maiden.

"Good God, don't say that." Robert shifted, but she leaned into him, so he could feel the luscious pressure of her breasts, and spiking desire shot through him. "Trust me, I don't need the temptation."

"Your house is close to here." Her lush lashes lowered. "Take me there. My parents don't expect me home for hours."

Take me....

He shouldn't. Just a moment before he'd agreed to join the ranks of respectable married men who honored their wives with proper vows. "Rebecca ... no. I can wait."

"What if *I* can't?" She sounded breathless. "Don't forget I've been dreaming of this for over a year, ever since I first saw you. I want you." One slim hand tugged at his cravat, loosening it. "I intimated I might stay with Arabella. I've done it before. We have all night. If I do not return home, my parents will not be alarmed."

She had no idea what she was saying, what she offered. Robert caught her wrist. "Your father could still very well refuse. If I behave dishonorably—"

"Do you plan on telling him? I don't." She freed her hand and kissed him again, untutored but inquisitive, the tentative brush of her tongue into his mouth making him stifle a groan. All the time her hands were busy, discarding his cravat and fumbling with the top fastenings of his shirt. One small palm crept inside and pressed his bare chest, cool against his heated skin.

Bemused, aroused, and undecided, Robert broke the heated kiss with effort, trying to hold on to his honor. "I need to take you back to your parents' home."

"Don't worry about my father. I'll marry you anyway, with or without his permission. He probably would refuse to pay the marriage settlement—"

"I don't care a fig for his money," Robert interrupted curtly. "I don't even want it if he gives us his blessing. I want *you*."

It was prudent to settle Rebecca back on the seat across from him and he deposited her back that short distance, but it did nothing to help him. She looked just a little disheveled—delectably so—with her mouth rosy and a flush on her cheeks. The aquamarine of her eyes shimmered. "Please."

His resolve wavered at that one small word. Her allure was so powerful he had to close his hands into fists to keep from reaching for her again. With an inner curse, Robert tapped sharply on the ceiling to signal his driver.

Chapter Twenty-one

Society has a set of rules to govern the behavior of gentlemen and ladies. But in the bedroom, we are simply men and women. Instead of the rules, I recommend you follow your instincts.

> *From the chapter titled: "Is It Scandalous, and If So, Should You Care?"*

Lady R was nothing short of a genius. Rebecca felt her fiancé's hands linger at her waist as he lifted her from the carriage, and the smoldering hunger in his eyes made her stomach tighten. Without a word he guided her up the steps of his town house.

Her fiancé.

Robert Northfield, no less.

"I keep only a modest staff." He unlocked the door himself. "And they are discreet."

So they would have to be, she thought in unwilling amusement, to serve a disreputable rake of his stature. To her surprise, she didn't resent the notion any longer, for she would remember as long as she breathed the moment when he reached across his carriage and snatched her into his arms.

He'd looked *unguarded*.

"They're used to you bringing women here." She clasped his extended hand.

Robert shook his head, his azure eyes direct. "No one like you. Ever."

That was true enough, she would guess. No eager virgins who had shamelessly half undressed him in his carriage after they brazenly proposed marriage along with a scandalous promise of a lifetime of sexual fulfillment. Rebecca would be more embarrassed over her actions if they hadn't produced the desired result. Had she couched her proposal in terms of romantic love, told him how much she wanted to cradle his child in her arms, how she'd dreamed just as often of his smile across the breakfast table as she had heated passion in his bed, what would have been his reaction? She wasn't sure, but she could guess.

To men, love represents vulnerability. When a man becomes emotionally attached to a woman, she wields a great deal of influence in his life. You must understand that this frightens most of them, whether they admit it or not. Of course, their fear varies in degrees from one male to another. They embrace passion, but they tread around love most carefully. It is a glorious gift when a man gives you both.

His bedroom was on the second floor and she got a brief glimpse of a huge bed hung with dark silk, an armoire in the corner, a pair of boots by a carved chair, before he caught her shoulders and stared into her eyes. "You're sure? You've had no time to prepare, to talk to your mother or whatever brides do. Rebecca, I can't say with honesty I am reluctant to take you to bed, but I can say I have no desire to ruin you."

One of the servants had left a lamp lit for his return and the light gilded his golden brown hair. She reached up and touched his jaw, feeling the faint hint of a beard under the clean-shaven surface, her fingers both questing and gentle. "I'm prepared, and I have no need to talk to my mother."

Arched brows lifted but his hands slid down her arms in a light, practiced caress. "Is that so? I am curious as to how."

"Show me," Rebecca whispered evasively, as she pushed his coat off his shoulders so she could finish un-buttoning his shirt. "I want you to show me every wick-edly wonderful aspect of what happens between a man and a woman. I want to see you, to *feel* you."

When she tugged his shirt out of his breeches, he helped, slipping it off his shoulders. His chest was hard, the musculature well defined, his shoulders dauntingly wide. "I doubt we have time for every wicked bit of edu-cation in the next hour or so," he murmured, clad only in boots and breeches, a noticeable bulge in the front of the latter. "But I will do my best. Now, if you don't mind, I'd prefer to not be the only one undressed. Turn around, my sweet, and let's see if my fantasies do you justice."

It wasn't that Robert had never been seduced, but he certainly had never been seduced by an innocent ingé-nue. First she'd proposed—and he'd accepted—and now in a somewhat clumsy but entirely arousing way, Re-becca had managed to divest him of most of his clothing with an enthusiasm that resembled nothing of what he'd pictured in his imagination of fearful virgins.

It appeared he needed to adjust his thinking, at least when it came to his future wife.

Wife.

That was something he'd have to digest later. Right now the throbbing between his legs precluded rational thought.

He unfastened her gown with practiced ease, pushed it off her creamy shoulders, and sent a fall of lemon fab-ric to the floor in a gentle swoosh of muslin over smooth, warm skin. Under the demure lace of her chemise, her full breasts were outlined in a way that sent the blood rushing through his veins, and he plucked out the pins confining her hair with impatient fingers, carelessly toss-ing them aside without care.

Sable silk tumbled downward, covering the graceful line of her spine. Robert leaned forward and inhaled her delicate fragrance. His hands cupped her elbows, and standing behind her still, he urged her backward against him. "From what I see so far," he whispered in a voice suggestive with erotic need as he admired the upper swell of her breasts, "you are more than I imagined. But I need to see it all."

"I would not be here if I didn't want everything." Rebecca leaned willingly into his chest, her bottom nestled with provocative softness against his thighs. "I trust you."

His fingers drifting through her soft hair, he stopped, arrested, not sure if anyone had ever said that to him before. *I trust you.* Certainly she must, to put her future in his hands. It was humbling, and the idea of marriage crystallized into something else for him at that definitive moment, something apart from his previous selfish reservations over his freedom being curtailed and his life changing in an irrevocable way.

"You *can* trust me," he assured her in a voice that reflected unexpected sincerity. "Anything you wish to give me is safe."

"Somehow, I have known that from the beginning."

She must be telling the truth, or she wouldn't be there now, in his arms, half naked. If she gave her virginity, there was no taking it back.

No going back for either of them.

Holding her in the circle of his arms, he reached around and slowly pulled free the ribbon on her bodice. Cloth parted, the shadow between her breasts deepened, and the garment slid downward, exposing pale opulent flesh, taut and firm, her nipples a delicate coral. His gaze strayed lower, to the dainty patch of pubic hair between her slim thighs, those dark curls beckoning his fingers.

And mouth, though maybe it was better to not be *too* wicked for her first time, no matter what she said. He'd be gentle, he promised himself, the fierce strain of his cock against the confinement of his breeches making him grit his teeth, use every bit of finesse he possessed and not rush things. . . .

"Hurry," Rebecca said, her head falling back against

his shoulder, "touch me. Do something. I'm—I don't know."

The request inundated his already heated blood and briefly he wondered if her eagerness was a result of this unmistakable chemistry between them or an innate sensuality. If he was lucky, it was both, he decided, and lifted her into his arms.

"Don't worry. I'm going to touch you." His voice was far from the practiced insouciance of his normal bedroom tones. Usually he teased, tempted, played at dalliance and desire. This was different. "I'm going to touch you so deeply you will never forget it, never forget this night." He laid her on the bed, his gaze admiring every detail of long legs, the sensuous curve of womanly hips, the fullness of those lavish breasts. Rich, glossy hair spilled everywhere, the contrast of dark against the white linens evocative of the superlative paintings of the old masters, when female beauty was an object to be revered and studied.

And her eyes—so long lashed, and that unusual luminous color, reminiscent of the sea under a summer sun—watched as he sat down to remove his boots and then stood to unfasten his breeches. Rebecca made no secret of studying his erection, her soft lips parting in ... surprise? Admiration? Trepidation?

"You're huge." Her gaze was riveted.

Robert let out a smothered laugh and joined her on the bed. His hand smoothed her bare hip. "But then again, darling, you have nothing to compare me to, do you?"

"No, but—"

He kissed her, trying to tamp down this first flicker of virginal misgiving, drawing her close enough his erect cock brushed her hip but no more, to get her used to his arousal and intentions. With reverent exploration he traced the graceful line of her spine, the dip of her waist, the arc of her rib cage, until he cupped one of her perfect breasts. The warm, supple weight filled his hand to overflowing. At the intimate caress, she quivered.

"Perfect," Robert told her, his lips grazing her cheek to her ear. He whispered, "You're perfect. Designed just for me. How many men have thought about being here like this, with you?"

The speculation was so out of character he was stunned by the question he'd just asked. To his surprise, he was jealous of those unknown fantasies, just as he'd stood in brooding disquiet watching her waltz in the arms of would-be suitors earlier in the evening.

"I can't think about anyone else, not now. There are only the two of us in the whole world." Rebecca turned her head and kissed his shoulder as he fondled one luscious breast.

She was right. The men who had wanted her in the past were banished. They'd lost and he'd won. He said softly, "No. There's no one but you and me."

In that one short quiet sentence, so loaded with meaning, all the lovers from his dissolute past were also set aside forever.

"I'm ready," she whispered, "whenever you are."

He was more than ready, and her naïve declaration brought a smile to his face, for he doubted she was there quite yet, and despite her willing acquiescence and responsiveness so far, he had every intention of making this moment not so much a denouement as a beginning.

"You will be," he murmured with a sinful grin as he bent his head, "soon."

When he took one taut erect nipple into his mouth, her shuddering sigh was an ample reward. "Robert." His name was a single exhale, poignant with meaning.

He applied himself to seduction, to the exquisite pleasure he intended to give her, to the magic of this unique moment for both of them. Normally he could be detached except on a physical level with his paramours, but the woman in his arms wasn't in that category.

He moved. She moved in heated response. His mouth sought out the erect tips of her breasts as his fingers found the moist tightness between her legs. With every suckle, every stroke, Rebecca shifted restlessly, her lissome body temptation incarnate, the brush of her skin against his almost more than he could take, his supposed sophistication be damned.

Carefully he tasted and teased her lush breasts while at the same time he rotated his hand in slow, tantalizing circles against the parted folds of her damp cleft. She clutched his shoulders and moaned, far less shy than he would have expected, her legs parted to allow him access. The delicate fragrance drifting from her skin and the more earthy scent of female arousal inflamed his senses—and he was already on fire. "Tell me how good it feels," he urged, exerting just the right amount of pressure, feeling wetness with deep satisfaction, the nub beneath his fingertips swelling.

Rebecca arched, her erect nipples brushing his chest. "It feels . . . oh . . . I . . ."

The incoherent answer was exactly what he was looking for, and he knew she was close to climax, both from the deepening color in her lovely face and the frantic clutch of her hands. He deliberately licked her lower lip in a sensuous glide. "Just wait. I think you are almost to the breaking point, my sweet."

When it came, a cry of surprise and pleasure tore from her throat and perceptible shudders rocked her slender body. Robert watched with heavy-lidded eyes, not sure he wasn't going to spend himself then and there just from the joy of being the one to give her the first taste of orgasmic bliss.

And he had only just begun.

She wanted a wicked tutorial. This was going to be a match made in heaven, for he certainly qualified as an instructor. He slid upwards, between her still spread legs and positioned himself with his cock just touching her small opening, his smile leisurely though his body was tense as a bowstring, waiting for her to recover enough to open her eyes. Braced on his elbows above her quivering body, he saw her eyelids flutter upward.

"Now," he said succinctly, "you're ready."

"That was . . ." She stopped, and then gave a choked laugh. "I haven't completed a sentence since we disrobed, have I?"

"A good sign." Robert moved enough to test the give of her passage, beginning his penetration into her body with slow pressure. "The most pleasurable way on earth to render a woman speechless."

She realized what he was doing, her eyes widening.

"Like this." He reached down and lifted her leg so it was bent at the knee, setting her foot down on the bed. "The more open you are, the easier this will be."

With encouraging alacrity, Rebecca moved to do the same with her other leg, her thighs spread open for his entrance, her gaze holding his with poignant emotion, her smile winsome and remarkably lacking in fear.

I trust you.

Never had he been so careful, so restrained, so consumed with lust he thought he'd combust. When he breached the barrier of her maidenhead and saw the flinch of pain, Robert kissed her then, her forehead, the tip of her nose, her lips in slow soft sips to reassure and comfort. "It will get better," he whispered, "I vow it. Much, much better."

"I'm not a delicate flower," Rebecca responded with surprising humor, her grip on his biceps easing. "And just because I love you, it doesn't mean I don't expect you to live up to your reputation, Lord Robert. If your virtuosity is so legendary, show me why."

I love you.

"You say it so easily," Robert murmured in response, his needy cock urging him to move but emotion holding him still. His voice was raw. "Rebecca, I . . ."

Maybe it was a woman's intuition, but she knew exactly the right thing to say. "Just show me." The entreaty was whisper soft.

And when he did, when he moved in her with slow sure strokes until she began to gasp, then moan, and finally cry out, his own pleasure was made more acute by her uninhibited enjoyment until, when the first telling ripple tightened around his thrusting cock, the burst of rapture shook his whole body as he drove deep and lost himself.

In her encircling arms, in her luscious body, in her soul.

Chapter Twenty-two

Misunderstandings are inevitable. They will rise to the surface when you least expect them and confound you both. How you handle the outcome of each one is a measure of your affection for each other.

From the chapter titled: "The Art of the Argument"

There he was again. It seemed incredible, but she was being followed.

Sure enough, the figure skulked in the doorway of the tobacco shop across the street. Narrowing her eyes, Brianna felt a surge of irritation and unease, wondering if she should report this to the authorities. After all, her husband was a rich man, and if someone wanted to kidnap her, she should be on the alert.

This was the third day in a row she had spotted him, and she was becoming more and more convinced the odd little man in the brown checked cap was trailing her. She'd first seen him when she'd forgotten her reticule in the carriage and had to go back outside in a hurry, almost bumping into him in her haste. It had meant nothing at the time, but then she'd glimpsed him again the next day.

Though he was dressed differently, he'd been there the day after that also. By the third sighting, her curiosity had turned to alarm.

Brianna went back into the shop, asked the wife of the milliner, a stout woman who ran the front part of the establishment, if there was a back exit she could use. Though obviously surprised, the woman directed her to a door at the rear, and accepted some coin to send her clerk outside in an hour or so to instruct Brianna's driver to take the carriage home. Something about the woman's expression told Brianna that the vagaries of the rich and titled were to be met with resignation, and Brianna slipped into the alley behind the shop with a feeling of liberation.

She wasn't sure if her ploy was necessary, but she nurtured a child inside her and that precious life, growing more real as time passed, meant the world. It was prudent to be careful.

It was a pleasant day, if a bit cool, and the sky of cerulean blue above held just the slightest dusting of clouds. When she had gone a good ways down the alley, skirting some very dubious piles of rubbish, Brianna let herself in the back entrance of a tobacco shop, apologized to the startled proprietor, and regained the street.

Arabella lived not too far away, and since the weather was agreeable, it wasn't a hardship to walk to the Bonham's townhouse, just off St. James. When she arrived, she was told to her relief Lady Bonham was home. Moments later, she was ushered into an informal sitting room upstairs and her friend rose to greet her. "Bri, how nice of you to call."

Brianna forced a smile. "I am sorry to just drop in, but it seemed expedient."

"Expedient?" Arabella motioned her to a chair and frowned. "That's a curious thing to say."

Brianna sat down. Though the queasiness was something she'd learned to deal with, she still had an attack now and again. "Could I have perhaps have a very weak cup of tea?"

"Of course." Arabella reached for the bellpull. "Is it the baby? Good heavens, you're pale suddenly. Do you need to lie down?"

"A little tea will do the trick," Brianna assured her. When the beverage arrived, she sipped gratefully, then waited for the nausea to subside. "I'm just a little upset," she said with a watery smile. "Thank you for being home."

During her walk, a very unpleasant suspicion had occurred to her, and she needed to talk to *someone*.

Arabella looked concerned. "Whatever is the matter? You don't look at all like yourself."

"I am not even sure where to start. Or if I *should* start."

That made her friend blink. "Please pick a point. You are talking in circles."

"I don't mean to, but that rather seems to be my life lately." Brianna took another drink from her cup and felt fortified enough to set it aside. "I've told Colton he and I are going to have a child."

Arabella nodded in approval. "I can only imagine your husband's delight."

"One would think he *would* be delighted."

The Countess of Bonham frowned. "What does that mean? He's happy, isn't he?"

"So he claims." Brianna turned to look out one of the mullioned windows and fought tears. "He says he is. But I am not so sure. He treats me differently. And now *this*."

"Whatever do you mean? What *this*?" Arabella asked after a moment.

"I am being followed around. At least I think so. By some horrid little man in a brown hat. I've seen him now and then, and really, while in the course of going through life you do encounter coincidences, this does not seem like one at all."

"I don't understand."

Brianna shook her head. "I don't understand either, but I can tell you it would not surprise me—considering how moody he's been lately—if Colton has something to do with it. He has asked me the most bizarre questions, and he acts as if he's glad about the baby, yet *not* glad at the same time. Oh, I am not describing it well, but suffice to say, it has me at a loss as to what to do. Why would my husband have me followed?"

Arabella opened her mouth to respond but just let it hang open for a moment before she snapped it shut. Then she flushed and looked away, squaring her shoulders.

Brianna watched the process with interest, her inner turmoil making her stomach still churn. "What?" she asked flatly with the familiarity of long acquaintance. "If you know something, please tell me."

"I don't *know* anything, and I suppose I am not surprised this hasn't occurred to you because it didn't to me, but maybe I can venture a guess." Arabella turned back, looking resolute. "Rebecca gave me the book after she finished it, you know."

Brianna nodded. There was no need to expound on what *the book* meant. *Lady Rothburg's Advice.*

The book.

"I still can't believe we all read it. Our mothers would faint dead away. But—I—oh dear, there's no delicate way to say it, I—"

"Bella, I adore you, but please just tell me before I scream."

"I did that thing in chapter ten."

Chapter ten. Brianna cast back, recalled what her friend meant, and only barely managed to hold in a gasp. She hadn't even dared chapter ten, so she fully understood the blush. "I see."

Arabella rushed on, "It wasn't nearly as unpleasant as it sounded and—"

"If you do not tell me how you think this pertains to my situation at once, I may lose my mind." Brianna felt her teeth grind together, her uncertain stomach not helping at all.

"Andrew demanded to know where that idea came from. He was pleased, but not pleased, if you know what I mean." Arabella sat back, looking resolute despite her pink cheeks.

"No, I don't, I'm afraid."

"Don't worry. Your name was left entirely out of it but I finally had to confess I'd read the book because my husband wouldn't let the subject go. He was so relieved he wasn't even angry."

"Relieved?" Brianna wasn't following the logic. "Why?"

"His first reaction was to think another man might have given me the idea."

Brianna was rendered completely speechless.

Arabella looked back with sympathy. "I believe my expression was close to what yours is now. I couldn't fathom how he could jump to such a conclusion. I mean, how *could* Andrew think that? His answer was he couldn't for a moment imagine how I would dream of doing such an outrageous thing on my own. The trouble is, he was right. I wouldn't. I didn't even know women did things like that. Without the book, it wouldn't ever have occurred to me. Perhaps, if you are being followed and Colton is behind it, he has drawn the same conclusion Andrew did."

God in heaven, Colton couldn't really think she was conducting an affair, could he? Brianna sat statue still, her mind whirling, casting back over the past weeks.

He *had* asked after she tried the advice in chapter two where she got such a notion, but she'd evaded the question. Unlike Andrew, Colton wasn't one to pursue a subject, and he'd let the matter drop.

Then . . . oh dear God, she'd tied him to the bed on his birthday and it was after that, now she thought about it, that everything changed.

You haven't done anything wrong, my dear. Have you?

The vulnerability in his eyes had struck her—and had there been accusation as well?

Her hand, when she lifted it to brush a tendril of loose hair off her cheek, shook like a leaf in a stiff wind. She dropped it back in her lap and said in an unrecognizable voice, "Upon contemplation, you could be right. Oh, Bella, are all men completely mad?"

"I think so on a regular basis," her friend said dryly. "Whatever are you going to do?"

"I suppose," Brianna muttered, "murder is still a crime in England?"

"Unfortunately, yes," Arabella said with a hint of laughter in her voice. "Sending an august duke to his just reward would carry a particularly stiff penalty, no matter how thickheaded he might be."

"It is still tempting."

"I imagine. I was as outraged as you are now. Well, maybe a little less. Andrew didn't go so far as to have me followed around."

Her husband had had her followed. It was inconceivable.

Brianna looked at her friend, straightening in her chair. "I think Colton is about to discover that, unlike him, I am not unwilling to discuss subjects that might be uncomfortable. If you still have the book, I'd like it back, please."

"It's hidden in my room. Let me get it." Arabella rose gracefully and left the room, coming back in a few moments with the leather-bound volume. She handed it over, her dark eyes glimmering. "What *are* you going to do?"

Brianna stood, more furious than ever before in her life. "Teach my infuriating husband a lesson in the merits of honesty."

The door to his study flew open with such force it actually hit the paneling on the opposite wall. No knock, no request for permission to enter. Unprepared for such an invasion, Colton glanced up, startled. His secretary, built like a lanky scarecrow, jumped up so fast he toppled over his chair. Rising politely to his feet a little more slowly, Colton registered the angry flush on his wife's smooth cheeks as she came into the room with an expression that promised imminent disaster. He said as smoothly as possible, "Good afternoon, my dear."

"Here." Marching straight to his desk, she dumped

a book on top of the pile of correspondence he'd been going over.

What the devil is going on now?

Brianna wore a light peach-colored gown, the fashionable style demure but still clinging suggestively to her enticing curves, and her beautiful eyes fairly flashed vivid anger. Realizing whatever the trouble might be he was not particularly in favor at the moment, Colton cleared his throat and said abruptly, "Mills, you may go now. And please, if you will, close the door behind you."

The young man complied with almost comical haste, and when the door clicked shut, Colton said in a cool tone, "It is quite apparent you are angry with me over something, but you know I dislike displays of emotion in front of the servants, Brianna."

"You dislike displays of emotion at any time, *Your Grace*," his pretty wife informed him with open sarcasm, "but I thought I could reform you. I suppose that was my mistake, for all I received in return for my considerable efforts was your distrust."

Distrust. The light dawned and he cursed silently at Hudson and Sons for not keeping up their part of the bargain and staying invisible.

This *was* somewhat of a disaster.

"Reform me?" He stared, taken aback by the shimmer of tears in her eyes.

She put her hands on the top of his desk, and Brianna leaned forward slightly, her fury evident. "Did you hire someone to follow me, Colton? Did you actually think I might be having an affair with another man?"

Relief flooded through him, for it was obvious her outrage was very real. The notion she was gaining sexual knowledge by leaps and bounds in someone else's bed was driving him more insane with jealousy each day. It was his turn to flush slightly, his cravat feeling suddenly tight. "Perhaps we should sit down and discuss this calmly."

"No." Her soft mouth set in a stubborn line, Brianna shook her head. "I do not feel calm at all and refuse to pretend otherwise. Unlike you, I am perfectly willing to let others see I have emotions."

"I have always been reserved, Brianna," he said stiffly, the implied criticism in her tone stinging more than a little. "You knew that before you accepted my proposal of marriage. I am sorry it disappoints you."

"You are more than reserved, sir, you are *stuffy*."

"Stuffy?" Colton slowly lifted a brow. The accusation was said with such scathing inflection, he felt as if she'd slapped him. "I see."

What was worse, he deserved it. A part of him almost wished she would take the satisfaction and go ahead and hit him.

"Yes, but you were improving, thanks to this." She pointed at the book lying amidst his scattered papers.

What the hell was she talking about?

For the first time, he glanced down and registered the title, etched in scarlet letters on the leather cover. "Good God," he muttered, "where on earth did you get this?"

"Does it matter where I found it? What matters is that it has been very informative."

He managed to stop himself from pointing out to his gorgeous bride that no lady of breeding should read the work of a loose woman who at one time made a living of selling her sexual favors and then had the audacity to publish details about her exploits. Instead he registered Brianna's statement with discomforting insight. "Why"—he managed to keep his tone conciliatory only with the utmost control—"did you think you needed to be so informed?"

"Because I have no intention of ending up like Lord Farrington's wife and forced to meet you at the opera with your mistress on your arm."

With a touch of relieved exasperation, he declared, "Brianna, I do not have a mistress."

"That is nice to know." Her lower lip quivered slightly and she took a deep breath. "But what about the future? You have pointed out to me often enough the lack of fidelity in aristocratic marriages, and I have ears and hear the gossip. I do not ever want you to seek another woman's bed because you find mine boring."

She looked so adorably sincere Colton had to stifle the urge to haul her promptly into his arms and assure her in the most physical way possible she was in no danger of his desiring anyone else. However, he had a feeling his attentions wouldn't be met with unbridled enthusiasm at the moment. First he needed to repair the damage.

He cleared his throat. "I can appreciate that sentiment about infidelity for I have been driving myself insane, wondering where on earth you were learning such adventurous techniques. Forgive me for even harboring a doubt, but it was logical to assume someone was tutoring you, and it wasn't me."

Her lashes lowered as she narrowed her eyes. "No, not you. Of course not you. You did not so much as remove my nightdress when we made love for the first few months, Colton."

It was true, a fact that held a certain level of mortification for him, especially coming from a young woman who had taken it upon herself to improve their sexual relationship.

Damn all, she was his *wife*. He was only attempting to be polite and protect her sensibilities.

"I was *trying* to be a gentleman." He felt defensive—for what he'd done, and what he had wanted to do were two entirely different things, and his self-denial had been for her benefit.

"Lady Rothburg says there are no ladies or gentlemen in bed."

"Is that so?" Moving to lean one hip on the surface next to him, he crossed his arms over his chest and stared at his wayward wife, recalling the outrageously pleasurable interludes he'd recently enjoyed as she followed the advice in the notorious book. "I take it, since you sought to change matters, I was the one you found boring."

Silence. No denial. Now *that* was flattering.

Color spread up her graceful throat to stain her cheeks. Still standing on the other side of the desk, she admitted, "Not boring, for I enjoy it every time you touch me, but something was missing. What happened between us in bed was pleasurable, but not exciting."

He felt like a fool. She was perfectly right. "You wish excitement, I take it?"

"Only with you, Colton, for I love you. But, yes, I suppose I find it more exciting when you lose some of that formidable control and show how much you desire me." Her gaze was utterly sincere, and he couldn't help but feel humbled.

Ashamed of himself in many ways, but humbled. Still, how was he to know she had a copy of that outrageous book?

"Brianna—"

"I am not," she announced as if she truly meant it, "currently speaking to you."

Then she turned and left as impetuously as she'd entered, but not before he saw the wet trail of a tear making its way down her cheek and the furious telltale brush of her hand to dash it away.

If there was one thing worse than being an ass, it was being an insensitive one, he reflected morosely.

He needed to make amends and really had no idea how to go about it, and though he was thoroughly annoyed with himself for hurting his wife with his suspicions, another part of him sang with joy.

Brianna was his exclusively. The child nurtured in her womb was a symbol of their love for each other, and while he'd made a grave error in judgment, he'd never been so elated to be proven wrong in his entire life.

Curious, he picked up the nefarious book and studied the gilt lettering on the cover. Maybe it merited at least a perusal, for if Brianna had used it to seduce him—and she had done so very effectively—maybe Lady Rothburg could teach him something as well.

Chapter Twenty-three

Life is full of surprises—and love is the most perplexing mystery of all.

From the chapter titled: "Keeping What You Have"

It was the only possible course of action. Robert had already made a leap into an abyss of insanity by accepting Rebecca's proposal before making wild—and very satisfying—love to her. The very least Colton could do was accompany him and lend some respectability and support when Robert approached her father. She'd declared she would marry him anyway—and now she must—but in truth, they both wanted her father's approval.

"If you don't mind," he said for the second time, since Colton had yet to respond. "If I have any chance at all of convincing Sir Benedict to let me wed his daughter, it is through you."

Reclined in his chair behind a desk littered with correspondence, Colton was silent.

"Do you mind saying something, damn you?" Robert muttered.

"I think I might be rendered mute until eternity," his brother answered, staring at him incredulously. "Did you really ask me to accompany you to petition for a young woman's hand in marriage?"

"I did," Robert confirmed. Though it took effort, he added, "Please."

"You wish to marry."

"No, of course I don't." Robert couldn't help the biting tone of his voice and stood, once again wanting to pace. "Don't be a dolt."

Colton lifted a brow. "I try not to be one, but my wife will tell you I don't succeed all the time."

Robert couldn't help it; he laughed. It had been a long time since he'd seen his older brother exhibit a sense of humor.

"If you don't wish it, why are you considering marrying Miss Marston?"

"I simply meant I haven't been sitting around thinking I want to get married. In fact, I've been fighting this like hell. She won and to my surprise the defeat is not quite as painful as I imagined."

The defeat, if one could use that term for those tender hours in her arms, had been a triumph.

Robert added quietly, "I wouldn't ask this favor, Colt, but this is important."

"If I may be forgiven for being simplistic over something that isn't simple at all, marriage usually *is* important." Colton steepled his fingers together. "Of course I will go with you. Was it ever in question?"

"We want a special license."

Colton's brows shot up. "Do you need one?"

This was the problem. If they married in haste, people would think he'd seduced Rebecca. The fact that the seduction had been the other way around was a moot point. It was no one's business but their own, but Robert hated the idea of having his wife the subject of backhanded gossip.

Still, she could carry his child.

He said testily, "Did I say we needed one? We *want* one. It is her idea as much as mine." Several days had passed and not one whisper had surfaced about her arrival at the party with a flock of fallen women, which was a great relief. But even without a possible scandal, he didn't wish to delay making her his wife.

It was a curious thing, but once he'd accepted the

idea, it took hold over his life. He wanted Rebecca in his bed, in his home—but most of all, in his life.

"Let's get Sir Benedict's permission first, shall we, before we mention a special license?" Colton said wryly. "I love you, and *I* assumed the worst. No need to make him suspicious from the start."

Had Colton—standoffish, preoccupied Colton—just said casually he loved him? Robert stilled in astonishment, gazing at his brother across the desk. After a moment, he managed to say with equal aplomb, "I agree."

"We'll go this afternoon. I'll have Mills send someone to make sure he expects us. In the meantime, sit back down. I need your advice."

Robert sat. He needed to sit, actually.

Colton didn't seem to notice Robert's dumbstruck expression. He stared at the piles of paper on his desk and then looked up. "I do not want a lecture, understand?"

"Very few people do," he managed to say. "I've yet to meet the person who begged for one. But why the devil would I lecture you?"

"I *especially* don't want one."

That was clear enough. Robert stifled a laugh. "Point taken."

"Brianna is furious with me."

Ah, so this was about his brother's lovely wife. No surprise. She was the center of his life, whether he admitted it or not. Robert cocked a brow. "Since you seek my counsel, am I allowed to ask why?"

"I hired someone to follow her and she somehow became aware of it."

Rarely had Robert seen Colton look so uncomfortable. It took a moment to assimilate the information. Robert was mystified. "Why?"

"Because the inept bastard slipped up, obviously."

"No, I meant why would you ever hire someone to follow Brianna?"

"Because I thought . . . no, I wondered if perhaps . . . oh hell." Colton shoved his fingers into his hair and said heavily, "I worried she might be unfaithful. I was wrong, as it turns out, but she isn't in a frame of mind to forgive me. We've barely exchanged a word in two days."

"Unfaithful?" Robert stared, not sure how to react. "Brianna? Why the devil would you think that?"

"I obviously had some compelling evidence or I wouldn't have taken things so far," Colton muttered. "It turned out just to be a misunderstanding of gigantic proportions, but I still say it isn't surprising I came to the conclusions I did. That aside, I need to find a way to reconcile with her. I requested an audience so I could formally apologize, but she refused. I am, quite frankly, surprised she hasn't left me and gone without permission to Devon and her parents."

The note of despair in his brother's tone did not escape Robert, though he was stunned that Colton, who usually thought everything through with a thoroughness that bordered on obsession, had made such a grave mistake. When deep emotion was involved, it was clear Colton wasn't quite as keen-minded.

Brianna would never even consider infidelity. Robert knew it as certainly as he knew the tide would come in on a predictable timetable. She was deeply in love with his brother—probably almost as much, Robert realized, as Colton was in love with her.

"She hasn't left," Robert ventured to guess, "because even though you've hurt her and insulted her integrity—then even worse, demonstrated an ignorance of the depth of her feelings—she loves you enough to stay. I am going to wager that as much as you wish to endeavor to make this right between you, she wants it even more. That is to your advantage."

A flicker of relief washed over Colton's face. "Do you think so?"

"It doesn't mean you won't have to grovel, Colt, and as far as I can tell, being an exalted duke does not train you in the art of groveling."

His brother gave a small grunt. It was hard to tell if it was assent or the opposite. "I think I am willing to do whatever it takes. I do not want her unhappy with me, but I especially do not want her *unhappy*. I have no idea how to rectify the situation."

"I may have a few thoughts." Robert felt a slight smile curve his lips. Soothing ruffled females was something he'd done before, and actually, he thought he was rather good at it.

"Excellent," Colton said. "Help me and I'll do my best to make sure Sir Benedict doesn't wring your neck when you impart to him your wish to marry his daughter with all due speed."

They were upstairs in her father's study.

Robert, her father, and the Duke of Rolthven.

Rebecca sat in the music room, idly toying with the keys of the pianoforte. At least she'd stopped pacing. That had become exhausting, and she could swear she'd worn through part of the rug.

She couldn't believe it was finally happening. It was like a dream. Robert Northfield had come to formally ask for her hand in marriage. *Robert.*

A wicked rake, a scandalous rogue, a libertine of the first order—or was he? When she suggested the other night—when she'd snuck away from the ball and almost encountered catastrophe with her inopportune arrival at an event where apparently proper young ladies were not welcome—she was willing to consider a stop at his townhouse before he returned her home, he had refused, insisting he could wait.

Not very rakish. She loved him all the more for it. And even more for allowing himself to be persuaded otherwise.

It was just as she'd told her mother. Robert had an overall gloss of easy charm and careless behavior, but underneath she'd known the substance of the man. He'd been gentle, ardent, and though she'd demanded wickedness in his arms, what he'd given her was instead exquisite pleasure and tenderness. He would make the perfect husband; she knew it.

Now, as long as her father felt it also, she might end up being the happiest woman in England.

But it was hardly a given. She'd turned down far more eligible gentleman with bigger fortunes, and even more elite places in society. Nor did any of them have his less than pristine reputation.

Unable to take it any longer and needing to soothe her soul, Rebecca picked up the first piece of music she could find and began to play. It was an unfinished piece she'd been working on weeks ago, before she'd slammed into the man of her dreams while trying to escape Lord Watts. She hadn't made progress since that definitive moment.

Her hands stilled when the door opened.

Not until Robert leaned an elbow on the instrument did she realize she was holding her breath. "Very nice. Yours?" he murmured.

She registered the faint smile on his well-shaped lips and elation soared through her. "Mine? Care to clarify?"

She meant a great deal more than the unfinished quartet.

He nodded slowly, looking impossibly handsome with his golden brown hair and intense blue eyes. "Yours."

Had her father really agreed?

"I suspected as much from the very beginning." He smiled in the way only he could, a tantalizing lift of one corner of his mouth. "I've wondered if perhaps you'd composed the music you played for us at Rolthven."

"It's an unladylike occupation to compose music, I realize." Her heart had started a hammer staccato in her chest.

"I like.it when you are unladylike." Robert's voice held a sultry note. "The other night comes to mind. I actually believe you promised me you would be unlady-like on a regular basis. I'm going to hold you to that vow, you know, as well as the others we will make to each other."

Thinking of the book and its outrageous suggestions,

Rebecca blushed. She said in a hushed voice, "I take it, since you are still here, my father was . . ."

"Agreeable?" He looked amused as she trailed off. "Not at first, I admit. But between your mother—who was true to her word and intervened—and my father's friend Sir John, who is also a friend of *your* father, I at least have had some aid in repairing my reputation. There are other mitigating factors like the fact your cousin, who got me into trouble with your father in the first place, hasn't shown much Christian rectitude in that he's now bound for the colonies rather than face his recurring gambling debts. Your father has reluctantly decided I might not be such a blackguard after all."

Robert had finally told her, in the aftermath of their lovemaking, why her father held such a dislike for him. She had been furious on his behalf at her weak cousin for assigning blame to someone who had done nothing but try to help him. "I'm glad he knows the truth."

"Colton, also, has an amazing presence when necessary." Robert grinned. "He was the one who pointed out the merits of a hasty marriage, lest I lure you to more reckless behavior. He didn't say so, but my older brother essentially implied that unless they lock you away, given my reputation, how could your father be sure a scandal didn't linger in the future? Why not a marriage instead, to forestall any catastrophe?"

"You haven't lured me into anything," Rebecca protested. "I told my mother the truth. Quite the opposite. I was the one who asked *you*."

Robert just lifted a brow. "I don't care if your father knows whether or not his worries have substance. Colton's method of subtle persuasion worked." He smiled. "No one understands better than my respectable brother what strikes terror into the hearts of other respectable people."

He came around the pianoforte and sat down next to her on the bench. One long finger reached out and struck middle C. The note quivered in the room. Rebecca could acutely feel the press of his muscled thigh against hers. He turned, so close she could see the blue of his eyes with vivid clarity. "You are sure," he asked softly, "you want this?"

She could, she realized, quite possibly stare into those mesmerizing eyes forever. "Yes." No hesitation.

"I have no practice." He grimaced. "Well, I have no practice being a husband, something you might wish to note."

"Usually one doesn't," she said with all due practicality, "when one marries for the first time."

He smelled marvelous. She was learning that enticing, spicy masculine scent. Who would think a member of the male species, which favored horses and rooms full of tobacco smoke, could smell so wonderful?

As if they were in sync in some mystical way, he leaned forward just enough and said, "I like your perfume. That first night, in the garden, I think it was what I couldn't forget about you afterwards. That, and the unique color of your eyes."

He was going to kiss her. She desperately wanted him to kiss her. And then to lean her down on the bench and take her again as he'd taken her the other night. "I shall endeavor to wear that particular perfume all the time."

"And your hair." He lowered his head just a little. "I analyzed the color in my mind. I'd never done that before. That alone should have told me something. A grown man sitting around philosophizing about the hue of a woman's hair has some sort of affliction."

"It isn't a disease."

He touched her chin. "Isn't it?"

She was no match for him, but she really didn't want to resist him in any way, so what did it matter? Rebecca licked her lips. "What color is it?"

"What?" He seemed focused on her mouth.

"My hair."

Robert brushed his lips against hers, apparently mindful of the open door to the music room. "Oh. I'm still not sure. I may have to study it for the next fifty years or so."

"That sounds lovely," she whispered. "Is this really happening?"

He laughed, a low, heated sound. "I keep asking myself the same thing."

Chapter Twenty-four

The true test of a man's affections is his ability to apologize when he is mistaken. If he does so, if he is sincere, you will be able to tell from the look in his eyes. I can't describe it, but trust me, you will know. Love has a luminescence all its own.

From the chapter titled: *"Does He or Doesn't He?"*

Brianna paused in the door of her bedroom. It was occupied, which she had expected, but she *hadn't* expected her husband to be the occupant. An evening gown was laid out on her bed, and Colton sat in one of the chairs by the fireplace, his gaze fixed on her as she stood in the doorway. He looked relaxed, his hand cupping a snifter of brandy, but there was a set to his shoulders that told her the nonchalance was feigned.

"Are you going to come in?" he asked as she still stood there.

"I don't know," she admitted. How long was she permitted her affront? His suspicions had been unforgivable. Absolutely so.

Except she worried she already had forgiven him. She *missed* him. To a certain extent, once her outrage had faded to misery, she understood his doubts maybe a little. It didn't excuse him, but Brianna did suppose her inexperience had been part of the problem also. All she'd wanted was to please her husband. It had sounded simple at the time.

It wasn't at all simple now.

"It's your bedroom. You'll have to visit it eventually," he said in a mild tone. "Aren't you going to change to go out? You must come in here to do so."

That had been her intention, since even if her personal life was a shambles, it would make matters worse to have everyone in society know it, and she'd accepted an invitation already. "Where's my maid?"

"I dismissed her for the evening."

His presumption made her blow out a short breath. "I suppose I can do my own hair."

"Or not do it at all."

"Colton—"

"When my father died, I was lost." The words fell quietly into the room. "I don't expect that tragedy to absolve me, but I do request, as your husband, a chance to explain my recent actions. Can't you grant me that much?"

He never spoke of his father. And the word *request* held a humility that spoke volumes. Brianna moved into the room, shut the door, and without speaking sat down at her dressing table, facing him.

Whatever came next, she needed it. *They* needed it.

"I was only twenty." He smiled faintly. "Your age, I suppose, so maybe you can imagine it. I feel vastly older sometimes. Suddenly all these people depended on me. He was strong. Vigorous. There was no reason to think my father would come down with a cough and be gone within literally a few days. I didn't believe it had happened until my mother turned to me, weeping, and asked me what we were going to do. Everyone was looking at me, *to* me, for direction. That was when I realized I really didn't know."

Brianna watched her husband struggle to reveal his feelings and knew—*knew*—that if he wished to apologize, this was the best way possible. For if he mouthed platitudes and tried to explain his actions, she might think it was an excuse to put the unfortunate incident behind them.

But this, no. This *cost* him.

Colton glanced away, and she could swear she saw a slight sheen to his eyes. "I didn't know what to do. I'd known I would probably be the Duke one day, but neither my father nor I ever imagined it would happen as it did. Oh yes, I'd been tutored and taught and advised, but never once did anyone tell me the transition would hurt so damned much. Being an heir is an abstract concept. Inheriting is something else altogether."

"Darling," she said in a husky voice, her anger evaporated by his raw expression.

"No, let me finish. You deserve this." He swallowed, the muscles in his throat rippling. "I think that day I felt betrayed to an extent. By him. By his dying. Ridiculous, isn't it? I was young, but already a man. It just wasn't supposed to happen so soon. He should be alive *now*. I had to set aside my grief; there was no time for it. So I threw myself into the role of duke in the best way I knew how, and I think maybe I forgot about some other important things in life. Lucky for me, you are doing your best to remind me."

She was frozen. Colton, the one she knew, didn't do this. He did not open up his soul.

"So, may I perhaps beg of you a little forgiveness for my stupidity? I tend to try and make sense out of everything. Your actions, no matter how captivating and enjoyable I found them, confused me." Her husband looked at her, his lean body tense in the chair. "I really can't excuse myself for thinking the worst, but I feel vulnerable with you in a way I haven't experienced for a long time. Nine years, in fact. Add in this coming child and the sense I had you were keeping something from me, and I had that same feeling of being overwhelmed. So I did my best to take control of the situation in the only way I knew how. I am an idiot, but at least I am an idiot who loves his wife to distraction."

She'd been paralyzed before, but now she couldn't move if she wished it.

"I must," he said, the words an obvious struggle, "or I would not be able to act in such an irrational manner."

Brianna adored him all the more for his typical logic surfacing even as he attempted what was turning out to be a very effective apology.

Then he devastated her with the most compelling statement of all. "I didn't realize this had happened to me. To *us*."

She sat poised on the bench before her dressing table, her hands folded calmly as she looked at him. But there was nothing calm about the flutter of her heart. "Didn't know you loved me?"

He was handsome, powerful, wealthy ... everything a man could hope to be. Still, he seemed at a loss. Then he rubbed his jaw and said raggedly, "I didn't realize it. And yes, Brianna. God, yes. I love you."

It got easier.

Saying the words to Brianna hadn't ever really been the problem. It was admitting he loved her to himself that had been the barricade between them. They loved *each other*. That was even more of a revelation.

Earlier, he hadn't ever intended to declare to Robert how he felt about him, brother to brother. It just came out. This time, Colton intended to tell Brianna he loved her, but he hadn't counted on the hoarse tone of his voice or the poignancy of the moment.

And that babe that grew inside her—he couldn't begin to express the depth of how it moved him that they were going to share a child.

There were tears in his wife's eyes and he was at fault again, but at least this time it wasn't because he'd hurt her. The tremulous smile on her lips filled him with relief. She stood and came across the room and courtesy dictated that he should rise also, but he just sat there and waited, locked in place by the expression on her lovely face.

She took his brandy glass from his limp fingers and set it aside on the mantel. Then she settled on his lap and touched his cheek very lightly with one hand. "We are very blessed, aren't we?"

Emotion held him mute as he looked into her eyes.

"I'd really already forgiven you, you know. As infuriatingly dense as you can be at times, I cannot stay angry with you."

Her soft mouth was a temptingly short distance away. "I won't argue with the accusation or your generosity," he said in a hoarse voice.

"I suppose I am not blameless." Her fingers traced the line of his jaw and brushed along his lips. "Though my intentions were good, perhaps I shouldn't have bought Lady Rothburg's book. It was an improper thing to do."

"Very," he agreed, but added, "But I think the woman is positively brilliant. I can't say I agree with every observation she makes about men, but on the whole, she seems to have it right. Very insightful."

His wife's hand stilled and her eyes widened. "You read it?"

"Indeed. Every word. After all, you left it there on my desk."

"What a very unstuffy thing to do, Colton." Brianna's lashes lowered a teasing fraction.

He fought a wince at the reminder of her scathing observation when she'd confronted him in his study. "I shall contrive to be more open-minded in the future."

Brianna leaned forward and licked his lower lip. It was just a slow, delicate slide of the very tip of her tongue, but it sent a jolt through his entire body. She murmured, "Tell me, what part of her advice did you like the best? As a woman, I am curious."

"You are definitely a woman," he muttered, grasping her hips and adjusting her position on his lap. His growing erection strained the front of his breeches uncomfortably. "What was the question again?"

"The." She kissed him. "Best." Kissed him again. "Part."

"You," he answered. "No matter what we do, the best part is you, Brianna."

"Are you saying I may tie you to the bed again some-day if I wish?" Her smile was playful and provocative.

He gave a small groan as her soft bottom moved against his aching groin. *That* pleasurable interlude he could recall in all too vivid detail. "I am, at all times, your servant, madam."

"That sounds promising. So I may keep the book?"

"I'll have it enshrined in a glass case." He pulled the pins from her hair and nibbled on her earlobe.

A breathless laugh brushed his cheek. "I am sure Lady R would be flattered, but you needn't go that far. However, there is one favor I would like to ask."

He'd moved his mouth to the side of her graceful neck, and made an incoherent sound of assent.

"From now on I'd like it if we could share a bed."

"We are about to, believe me," he vowed, his arousal not in question.

"No. Well, yes, but that isn't what I mean. I want to lie not just with you, but next to you. My room or yours, it doesn't matter, but when we make love and you leave me, I feel . . ."

She'd tensed in his arms. Colton drew back enough so he could see her face. If there was one thing he'd learned from the past few days, it was that one of his biggest failings was in following through with the task of trying to understand how other people felt.

This mattered to his wife and she was his world, so it mattered to him.

"Go on, please," he said quietly.

"Apart from you. Not just physically." Brianna's lips quivered, just barely, but enough. "Perhaps it sounds ri-diculous to you because you are so practical at all times, but I want to wake to hear you breathe in the dark, to feel your warmth next to me, to share more than just our passion."

He understood what it meant to feel *apart*. To be dis-tanced from others by his rank, by his responsibility—but mostly by the inner walls he'd constructed to protect himself from emotional attachment and commitment.

He followed the curve of one of her perfect brows with a forefinger and smiled. "I would be delighted to have you sleep next to me each night. There, you see? Done. What else can I give you? Ask and it is yours."

She shook her head. "I can't think of what else a woman could want except to be with the man she loves and his child growing inside her."

She was a duchess married to one of the wealthiest men in England, with all of society at her feet, possessed incredible beauty and a life of privilege, but she wanted only the simplest of gifts. One of the things he loved about her—and had sensed about her from the beginning—was she had never looked at her existence, or their marriage, in a calculating way. Had he been a shepherd, she would still have loved him in equal measure.

She could ask for anything and know he had the means to provide it.

Instead, she wanted to sleep next to him.

How had he found such a treasure?

He didn't deserve her, probably, but he could try. Colton stood, lifting her in his arms. "Shall we stay in tonight? We can dine en suite and just enjoy each other's company."

Brianna's smile was all languorous seduction. "It sounds marvelous. You do remember Lady Rothburg had a whole chapter about how women can become more amorous when they are breeding? I think she might be right."

Dear Lord, he hoped so. He'd seen that heavy light in his wife's eyes before, and his body was more than primed and ready just from holding her. "The woman is a scholar of the highest order," he muttered as he carried his wife into his bedroom, shouldering the door open and heading toward the huge bed. "A brilliant expert who has generously shared her knowledge with the world. A paragon."

His wife gasped with sudden laughter. "Did you just call a courtesan—a scarlet woman—a paragon? You, the

Duke of Rolthven, who wouldn't commit a breach in etiquette for anything?"

Colton deposited her on the bed and leaned over, looking into Brianna's eyes. "Indeed, I did."

Then he began to undress her, punctuated by long hot kisses and whispered, wicked words.

And her uninhibited response proved his point.

Lady Rothburg was an exceptionally wise woman.

Epilogue

Damien Northfield leaned back in his chair, his legs comfortably crossed at the ankle, a bottle of whiskey just within reach. His departure to Spain had been delayed on various administrative levels, which was frustrating, but other matters had turned out in a satisfactory manner.

His younger brother had married. And married well. Rebecca was even scheduled to have some of her music debut in a public recital soon. Robert had never been one to stick to convention, and flaunting his wife's extraordinary talent was typical of his audacity.

Colton, also, was more content, more open than he had been since Damien could remember. Impending fatherhood sat well with his older brother, and Brianna fairly glowed with happiness even as she increased. She looked more beautiful than ever, which was really saying something.

He smiled lazily at his two brothers, not bothering to hide his amusement. "So they both read it?"

"And God alone knows to whom else my errant wife might loan the book." Colton lifted a brow. "I have stopped even trying to control what she does."

"What you mean," Robert said in open amusement, "is you indulge her in every way."

"Perhaps." Colton looked both unrepentant and relaxed.

Relaxed.

Colton.

That *was* something.

"I'm rather an admirer of the book," Robert said and took a sip from his glass. "Damien, when you marry, you might want to see if Brianna won't lend it out to your bride. I promise you no regrets if you give it to your beloved. Let's just say there are certain things a gentleman won't address with his wife that Lady Rothburg has no trouble discussing in detail."

If his younger brother's sinful grin was any indication, it was true.

"I'm headed back to Spain tomorrow." Damien pointed out. "So I doubt romance of any kind is in my future, but I'll keep it in mind."

"One never knows." Colton commented. "Had anyone said it was in mine, I would have protested vehemently."

How true. How could anyone have guessed his upright older brother would marry such a lovely but impulsive young lady and manage to become a different man than the upright, unapproachable Duke of Rolthven?

On the same note, how could anyone imagine Robbie would marry a respectable young woman and be persuaded to play his cello in public, no less?

His secrets were far more volatile and private.

Damien picked up his glass and raised it. "Shall we toast her then? Here's to the wise but nefarious Lady Rothburg."

Epilogue to Lady Rothburg's Advice

In closing, my dearest reader, I wish to say I hope you have found my advice valuable, even if in only a small way. There is, naturally, no perfect formula for romantic love, as the subjects involved are human beings and therefore fallible, but if I were limited to only one piece of advice instead of an entire book, I believe I would remind both men and women that a successful partnership, sexually and emotionally, takes effort on the part of both parties. What happens in bed—or if you read chapter eight, in various other wickedly inventive places—is important, yes, for sexual desire is what draws us to each other in the first place. But as pleasurable as that may be, the most important part of any romance is the bond you grow as you share a life.

Finding the right partner is essential, and keeping him a joyous task.

Best regards,
Lady Rothburg, written in her retirement after
her marriage, this 19th day of April, 1802

Read on for a preview of Emma Wildes's
enthralling historical romance

My Lord Scandal

First in the Notorious Bachelors Series
Available from Signet Eclipse.

The ally below was filthy and smelled rank, and if he fell off the ledge, Lord Alexander St. James was fairly certain he would land on a good-sized rat. Since squashing scurrying rodents was not on his list of favorite pastimes, he tightened his grip and gauged the distance to the next roof. It looked to be roughly about the distance between London and Edinburgh, but in reality was probably only a few feet.

"What the devil is the matter with you?" a voice hissed out of the darkness. "Hop on over. After all, this was your idea."

"I do not *hop*," he shot back, unwilling to confess that heights bothered him. They had, ever since that fateful night when he'd leapt between the towering wall of the citadel at Badajoz with the Forlorn Hope. He still remembered the pounding rain, the ladders swarming with men, and that great black drop below....

"I know perfectly well this was my idea," he muttered.

"Then I'm sure, unless you have an inclination for a personal tour of Newgate Prison—which, by the by, I do not—you'll agree we need to proceed because it gets closer to dawn by the minute."

Newgate Prison. Since Alex didn't like confined spaces either, that notion held very little appeal. The story his grandmother had told him just a few days ago made him wish his imagination was a little less vivid. Incarceration in a squalid cell was the last thing he wanted, but for the ones you love, he thought philosophically as he eyed the gap—and he had to admit he adored his grandmother—risks had to be taken.

That thought proved enough inspiration for him to leap the distance, landing with a dull thud and thankfully keeping his balance on the sooty shingles. His companion beckoned with a wave of his hand and, in a crouched position, began to make a slow pilgrimage toward the next house.

The moon was a wafer obscured by clouds, which was good for stealth, but not quite so wonderful for visibility. Two more alleys and harrowing jumps and they were there, easing down onto a balcony that looked over a small walled garden.

Michael Hepburn, Marquess of Longhaven, dropped down first, light on his feet, balanced like a dancer, which made Alex wonder not for the first time just what his friend did for the War Office. He landed next to him, and said, "What did your operative tell you about the layout of the town house?"

Michael peered through the glass of the French doors into the darkened room. "I could be at our club at this very moment, enjoying a stiff brandy."

"Stop grumbling," Alex muttered. "You live for this kind of intrigue. Lucky for us, the lock is simple. I'll have this open in no time."

True to his word, a moment later one of the doors creaked open, the sound loud to Alex's ears. He led the way, slipping into the darkened bedroom, taking in the shrouded forms of a large canopied bed and armoire with a quick glance. Something white was laid out on the bed, and on closer inspection he saw it was a nightdress edged with delicate lace, and that the coverlet was already turned back. The virginal gown made him feel very much an interloper—which, bloody hell, he was. But all in a good cause, he told himself firmly.

Michael spoke succinctly. "This is Lord Hathaway's daughter's bedroom. We'll need to search his study and his suite across the hall. Since His Lordship's rooms face the street, and his study is downstairs, this is a much more discreet method of entry. It is likely enough they'll be gone for several more hours, giving us time to search for your precious item. At this hour, the servants should all be abed."

"I'll take the study. It's more likely to be there."

"Alex, you do realize you are going to have to finally tell me just what we are looking for if I am going to ransack His Lordship's bedroom on your behalf."

"I hope you plan on being more subtle than that."

"He'll never know I was there," Michael said with convincing conviction. "But what the devil am I looking for?"

"A key. Ornate, made of silver so it'll be tarnished to black, I suspect. About so long." Alex spread his hand open, indicating the tip of his smallest finger to his thumb. "It'll be in a small case, also silver."

"A key to *what* dare I ask, since I am risking my neck to find it?"

Alex paused, reluctant to reveal more. But Michael had a point, and moreover, could keep a secret better than anyone of Alex's acquaintance. "A tomb," he admitted, quietly.

Michael's hazel eyes gleamed with interest even in the dim light, but he responded with unerring logic. "A locked tomb? Very few people wish to break into graves, but I concede it happens. Why is this crypt so attractive?"

"It's . . . complicated."

"Things with you usually are."

"I'm not at liberty to explain to anyone my reasons for being here, even you. Therefore, my request for your assistance. In the past you have proven to not only think fast on your feet if need be and stay cool under fire, you also have the unique ability to keep your mouth firmly shut, which is a very valuable trait in a friend. In short, I trust you."

Michael gave a noncommittal grunt. "All right, fine."

"If it makes you feel better, I'm not going to steal anything," Alex informed him in a whisper, as he cracked the bedroom door open and peered down the hall. "What I want doesn't belong to Lord Hathaway if he has it. Where's his study?"

"Second hallway past the bottom of the stairs. Third door on the right."

The house smelled vaguely of beeswax and smoke from the fires that kept the place warm in the late-spring weather. Alex crept—there was no other word for it—down the hall, sending a silent prayer upward to enlist heavenly aid for their little adventure to be both successful and undetected. Though he wasn't sure, with his somewhat dissolute past—or Michael's, for that matter—if he was at all in a position to ask for benevolence.

Luckily, the hallway was deserted, but also damned dark. Michael clearly knew the exact location of Hathaway's personal set of rooms, for he went unerringly to one door to the left and cracked it open to disappear inside.

Alex stood at a vantage point where he could see the top of the staircase rising up from the main floor, feeling an amused disbelief he was a deliberate intruder in someone else's house, and had enlisted Michael's aid to help him with the infiltration. Friendship however was friendship. He'd known Michael since Eton, and when it came down to it, no one was more reliable or loyal. He'd go with him to hell and back, and quite frankly, they *had* accompanied each other to hell in Spain.

They'd survived the fires of Hades, but had not come back to England unscathed.

Time passed in silence, and Alex relaxed a little as he made his way down the stairs into the darkened hallway, only barking his shin once on a piece of furniture that seemed to materialize out of nowhere. He stifled a very colorful curse and moved on, making a mental note not to take up burglary as a profession.

The study was redolent of old tobacco and the ghost of a thousand glasses of brandy. Alex moved slowly, pulling the borrowed set of picklocks again from his pocket, rummaging though the drawers he could open first, and then setting to work on the two locked ones.

Nothing. No silver case. No blasted key.

Damn.

The first sound of trouble was a low, sharp excited bark. Then he heard a female voice speaking in modulated tones—audible in the silent house—and alarm flooded through him. The voice sounded close, but that might be a trick of the acoustics of the town house. At least it hadn't sounded like a *big* dog, he told himself, feeling in a drawer for a false back, before replacing the contents and quietly sliding it shut.

A servant? Perhaps, but it was unlikely, for it was truly the dead of night, well past midnight with dawn a few good hours away. As early as most of the staff rose, he doubted one of them would be up and about unless summoned by their employer.

The voice spoke again, a low murmur, and the lack of a reply probably meant she was talking to the dog. He eased to the hallway to peer out and saw that at the foot of the stairs a woman was bent over, scratching the ears of what appeared to be a small bundle of active fur, just a puppy, hence the lack of alarm over their presence in the house.

She was blond, slender, clad in a fashionable gown of a light color. . . .

Several more hours, his arse. One of Lord Hathaway's family had returned early.

It was a stroke of luck when she set down her lamp and lifted the squirming bundle of fur in her arms, and instead of heading upstairs, carried her delighted burden through a door on the opposite side of the main hall, probably back toward the kitchen.

Alex stole across the room, and went quickly up the stairs to where Michael had disappeared, trying to be as light-footed as possible. He opened the door a crack and whispered, "Someone just came home. A young woman, though I couldn't see her clearly."

"Damnation." Michael could move quietly as a cat and he was there instantly. "I'm only half done. We might need to leave and come back a second time."

Alex pictured launching himself again across more questionable, stinking yawning crevasses of London's rooftop landscape. "I'd rather we finished it now."

"If Lady Amelia has returned alone, it should be fine," Michael murmured. "She's unlikely to come into her father's bedroom and I just need a few more minutes. I'd ask you to help me but you don't know where I've already searched, and the two of us whispering to each other and moving about is more of a risk. Go out the way we came in. Wait for her to go to bed, and keep an eye on her. If she looks to leave her room because she might have heard something, you're going to have to come up with a distraction. Otherwise, I'll take my chances going out this way and meet you on the roof."

With that, he was gone again and the door closed softly.

Alex uttered a stifled curse. He'd fought battles, crawled through ditches, endured soaking rains and freezing nights, marched for miles on end with his battalion, but he wasn't a damned spy. But a moment of indecision could be disastrous with Miss Patton no doubt heading for her bedroom. And what if she also woke her maid?

As a soldier, he'd learned to make swift judgments and in this case, he trusted Michael knew what the hell he was doing and quickly slipped back into the lady's bedroom and headed for the balcony. They'd chosen that entry into the house for the discreet venue of the quiet, private garden, and the assurance no one on the street would see them and possibly recognize them in this fashionable neighborhood.

No more had Alex managed to close the French doors behind him than the door to the bedroom opened. He froze, hoping the shadows hid his presence, worried movement might attract the attention of the young woman who had entered the room. If she raised an alarm, Michael could be in a bad spot, even if Alex got away. Luckily, she carried the small lamp, which she set on the polished table by the bed, so he assumed his presence on the balcony would be harder to detect.

It was at that moment he realized how very beautiful she was.

Lord Hathaway's daughter. Had he met her? No, he hadn't, but when he thought about it, he'd heard her name mentioned quite often lately. Now he knew why.

Hair a shimmering gold caught the light as she reached up and loosened the pins, dropping them one by one by the lamp and letting the cascade of curls tumble down her back. In profile her face was defined and feminine, with a dainty nose, delicate chin, and though he couldn't see the color of her eyes, they were framed by lashes long enough he could see the slight shadows across her elegant cheekbones as she bent over to lift her skirts, kicked off her slippers, and began to unfasten her garters. He caught the pale gleam of slender calves and smooth thighs, and the graceful curve of her bottom.

There was something innately sensual about watching a woman undress, though usually when it was done in his presence it was as a prelude to one of his favorite pastimes. Slim fingers worked the fastenings of her gown and in a whisper of silk it slid off her pale shoulders. She stepped free of the pooled fabric wearing only a thin lacy chemise, all gold and ivory in the flickering illumination.

As a gentleman, he reminded himself, he should politely look away.

The ball had been more nightmare than entertainment, and Lady Amelia Patton had ducked out as soon as possible, using her usual—and not deceptive—excuse. She picked up her silk gown, shook it out, and draped it over a carved chair by the fireplace. When her carriage had dropped her home, she'd declined to wake her maid, instead enjoying a few rare moments of privacy before bed. No one would think it amiss, as she had done the same before.

It was a crime, was it not, to kill one's father?

Not that she *really* wanted to strangle him in any way but a metaphorical one, but this evening, when he had thrust her almost literally into the arms of the Earl of Westhope, she had nearly done the unthinkable and refused to dance with His Lordship in public, thereby humiliating the man and defying her father in front of all of society.

Instead, she had gritted her teeth and waltzed with the most handsome, rich, incredibly *boring* eligible bachelor of the *haut ton*.

It had encouraged him, and that was the last thing she wanted to happen.

The earl had even had the nerve—or maybe it was just stupidity—to misquote Rabelais when he brought her a glass of champagne, saying with a flourish as he handed over the flute, "Thirst comes with eating . . . but the appetite goes away with drinking."

It had really been all she could do not to correct him since he'd got it completely backward. She had a sinking feeling that he didn't mean to be boorish—he just wasn't very bright. Still, there was nothing on earth that could have prevented her from asking him in her most proper voice if that meant he was bringing her champagne because he felt, perhaps, she was too plump. Her response had so flustered him that he'd excused himself hurriedly—so perhaps the entire evening hadn't been a loss after all.

Clad only in her chemise, she went to the balcony doors and opened them, glad of the fresh air, even if it was a bit cool. Loosening the ribbon on her shift, she let the material drift partway down her shoulders, her nipples tightening against the chill. The ballroom had been unbearably close and she'd had some problems breathing, an affliction that had plagued her since childhood. Being able to fill her lungs felt like heaven and

she stood there, letting her eyes close. The light wheez-
ing had stopped, and the anxiety that came with it had
lessened as well, but she was still a little dizzy. Her father
was insistent that she kept this particular flaw a secret.
He seemed convinced no man would wish to marry a
female who might now and again become inexplicably
out of breath.

Slowly she inhaled, let it out. Yes, it was passing. . . .

It wasn't a movement or noise that sent a flicker of
unease through her, but a sudden, instinctive sense of
being watched. Then a strong, masculine hand cupped
her elbow. "Are you quite all right?"

Her eyes flew open and she saw a tall figure looming over her. With a gasp she jerked her chemise back
up to cover her partially bared breasts. To her surprise,
the shadowy figure spoke again in a cultured, modulated
voice. "I'm sorry to startle you, my lady. I beg a thousand
pardons, but I thought you might faint."

Amelia stared upward, as taken aback by his polite
speech and appearance as she was by finding a man lurk-
ing on her balcony. The stranger had ebony hair, glossy
in the inadequate moonlight, and his face was shadowed into hollows and fine planes, eyes dark as midnight staring down at her. "I . . . I . . ." she stammered.
You should scream, an inner voice suggested, but she
was so paralyzed by alarm and surprise, she wasn't sure
she was capable of it.

"You swayed," her mysterious visitor pointed out as
if that explained everything, a small frown drawing dark
arched brows together. "Are you ill?"

Finally, she found her voice, albeit not at all her regular one, but a high thin whisper. "No, just a bit dizzy. Sir,
what are you doing here?"

"Maybe you should lie down."

To her utter shock, he lifted her into his arms as easily
as if she were a child, and actually carried her inside to
deposit her carefully on the bed.

Perhaps this is a bizarre dream . . .

"What are you doing here? Who are you?" she demanded. It wasn't very effective since she still couldn't manage more than a half mumble, though fright was being replaced rapidly by outraged curiosity. Even in the insubstantial light she could tell he was well dressed and she caught the subtle drift of expensive cologne before he straightened. Though he wore no cravat, his dark coat was fashionably cut, and his fitted breeches and Hessians not something an ordinary footpad would wear. His face was classically handsome with a nice straight nose and lean jaw, and she'd never seen eyes so dark.

Was he really that tall or did he just seem so because she was sprawled on the bed and he was standing?

"I mean you no harm. Do not worry."

Easy for him to say. For heaven's sake, he was in her bedroom, no less. "You are trespassing."

"Indeed," he agreed, inclining his head.

Was he a thief? He didn't look like one. Confused, Amelia sat up, feeling very vulnerable lying there in dishabille with her tumbled hair. "My father keeps very little money in his strongbox here in the house."

"A wise man. I follow that same rule myself. If it puts your mind at ease, I do not need his money." The stranger's teeth flashed white in a quick smile.

She knew him, she realized suddenly, the situation taking on an even greater sense of the surreal. Not a close acquaintance, no. Not one of the many gentlemen she'd danced with since the beginning of her season, but she'd seen him, nevertheless.

And he certainly had seen *her*. She was sitting there gawping at him in only her thin lacy chemise with the bodice held together in her trembling hand. The flush of embarrassment swept upward, making her neck and cheeks hot. She could feel the rush of blood warm her knuckles when they pressed against her chest. "I . . . I'm undressed," she said, unnecessarily.

"Most delightfully so," he responded with an unmistakable note of sophisticated amusement in his soft tone. "But I am not here to ravish you any more than to rob you. Though," he added with a truly wicked smile, "perhaps, in the spirit of being an effective burglar I should steal *something*. A kiss comes to mind, for at least then I would not leave empty-handed."

A kiss? Was the man insane?

"You . . . wouldn't," she managed to object in disbelief. He still stood by the side of the bed, so close if she reached out a hand she could touch him.

"I might." His dark brows lifted a fraction, and his gaze flickered over her inadequately clad body before returning to her face. He added softly, "I have a weakness for lovely, half-dressed ladies, I'm afraid."

And no doubt they had the same weakness for him, for he exuded a flagrant masculinity and confidence that was even more compelling than his good looks.

Her breath fluttered in her throat and it had nothing to do with her affliction. She might be an ingénue, but she understood in an instant the power of that devastating, entirely masculine husky tone. Like a bird stunned by smoke, she didn't move, even when he leaned down and his long fingers caught her chin, tipping her face up just a fraction. He lowered his head, brushed his mouth against hers for a moment, a mere tantalizing touch of his lips. Then instead of kissing her, his hand slid into her hair and he gently licked the hollow of her throat. Through her dazed astonishment at his audacity, the feel of his warm lips and the teasing caress caused an odd sensation in the pit of her stomach.

This was where she should imperiously order him to stop, or at least push him away.

But she didn't. She'd never been kissed, and though admittedly her girlish fantasies about this moment in her life hadn't included a mysterious stranger stealing uninvited into her bedroom, she *was* curious.

The trail of his breath made her quiver, moving upward along her jaw, the curve of her cheek, until he finally claimed her mouth, shocking her to her very core as he brushed his tongue against hers in small sinful strokes.

She trembled, and though it wasn't a conscious act, somehow one of her hands settled on his shoulder.

It was intimate.

It was beguiling.

Then it was over.

God help her, to her *disappointment*, it was over.

He straightened and looked more amused than ever at whatever expression had appeared on her face. "A virgin kiss. A coup, indeed."

He obviously knew that had been her first. It wasn't so surprising, for like most unmarried young ladies, she was constantly chaperoned. She summoned some affront, though strangely, she really wasn't affronted. "You, sir, are no gentleman."

"Oh I am, if a somewhat jaded one. If I wasn't, I wouldn't be taking my leave lest your reputation be tarnished by our meeting, because it would be, believe me. My advice is to keep my presence here this evening to yourself."

True to his word, in a moment he was through the balcony doors, climbing up on the balustrade, bracing himself for balance on the side of the house. Then he caught the edge of the roof, swung up in one graceful athletic motion, and was gone into the darkness.

Also Available

FROM

Emma Wildes

An Indecent Proposition

It's the talk of the town. London's two most notorious rakes have placed a very public wager on which of them is the greatest lover. But what woman of beauty, intelligence, and discernment would consent to judge such a contest? Lady Carolyn Wynn is the last woman anyone would expect to step forward. But if the men keep her identity a secret, she'll decide who has the most finesse between the sheets.

To everyone's surprise, however, what begins as an immoral proposition turns into a shocking lesson in everlasting love…

"A spectacular and skillfully handled story that stands head and shoulders above the average historical romance."
—*Publishers Weekly* (starred review)

Available wherever books are sold
or at penguin.com